Aliens Abound

Lauryne Wright

BookLocker
Saint Petersburg, Florida

Print ISBN: 978-1-64719-216-7
Epub ISBN: 978-1-64719-217-4
Mobi ISBN: 978-1-64719-218-1

Published by BookLocker.com, Inc., St. Petersburg, Florida.

Printed on acid-free paper.

BookLocker.com, Inc.
2021

First Edition

For Mom and Dad,
whose love made me possible.

To my mathematical brain, the numbers alone make thinking about aliens perfectly rational. The real challenge is to work out what aliens might actually be like.

- Stephen Hawking

Chapter 1

"Do you have someplace where we can jitterbug?" Mom asked O.W., also known as Octavius Wynne and proprietor of Planet Wynne, the Las Vegas casino hotel where my family dined Christmas Eve.

My name is Rowan Layne, writer and associate of aliens, which is what Red Orbiters like Mr. Wynne are. Not to be confused with otherworldly, or OW—what I and pretty much everyone on our planet was due to hybrid alien-human DNA. I promote progressive planetary politics, so those who reject their partial alien identities, like the soon-to-be-ex-president, don't like me much.

Most might not realize Mom was as old as she was, or that she and Dad met when she was dancing with a now-famous journalist in college in Texas. She inquired about Dad and expressed interest in dating him. A good thing or my sister Gwynne, who I call G, and I would not exist.

G was currently in consult with her husband, Phil, about a town car to transport my folks and me back to my North Las Vegas neighborhood. I was fifty-seven years old, and G was sixty-one, and we weren't up to dancing the night away until Christmas morning on the Las Vegas Strip.

"In my next life, I want showgirl legs," I muttered as we made our way through hordes of people to reach the front of the casino hotel with Mom, fortified by champagne, greeting every employee in sight.

"I'm more *matooer* than I look," she said, grasping their hands and pronouncing *mature* like *manure*, "but I have to stay with it, especially here in Vegas!"

Mom spoke those words one last time to a parking valet before she and I were snatched by armed henchman and shoved into an unmarked van that peeled away from the curb with a piercingly loud screech. We were flanked in the back seat by two male thugs, not speaking but doing some heavy mouth-breathing.

Plenty of additional screeching came from Mom and me, but I could still hear Raucous Wilde's voice directly in my ear, because hearing Red Orbiters from a distance is my special power, and many of them can hear me.

"Damn it, Copper! You should have let me fly everyone in my orb and this would not have happened!"

I was gasping for breath but managed to reply, "You know Mom would insist you take her to Italy for shoe shopping if we ever let her in your orb, and what the hell do we do now?"

"Roger should be in the air soon. Just keep talking and we'll track you."

Mom was already on it, addressing the two ham-handed Neanderthals decked out in military camouflage with no identifying symbols as the van careened through downtown Las Vegas. "Those are the tackiest outfits I've ever seen! You have no manners or sense of style! And had you been in my kindergarten class, you would have learned bullying is bad! And my Doodles and I have arboretum friends who will teach you a lesson!"

Mom meant *Orbiters*, not a botanical garden devoted to trees, but she was correct about what would happen, as Red Orbiters were particularly devoted to me. In fact the two slated to rescue us, Rauc and Roger, were also intimate acquaintances, and I was supposed to write a book about them and what they do for our planet. Oh and Roger is sort of Superman, as he was the alien impetus for the comic book character. He even has an *S* shield tattoo on his chest.

As for *Doodles*, that's my childhood nickname, which Mom persisted in using publicly with embarrassing regularity.

I weighed in, twisting around to thump one of the paramilitary buffoons on the shoulder. "You realize you just nabbed an octogenarian—which means she's in her eighties, because I'm pretty sure you're an idiot—who has a weak bladder? What's next for you fascist lackwits? Babies and puppies? Oh wait, you've done that too!"

My octave was hurting my own ears, so it was nice to have the helmeted henchman wince. I reached around Mom to poke the other guy right about where a nameplate or information should be, other than the generic word *POLICE*.

"*Fourth Amendment!* Say it with me, fellas. As in the government shall not engage in *unreasonable* seizure. You're the pathetic equivalent of the *outgoing* president's personal G.I. Joe! Except he is not a dictator and you are not identifiable as any particular police and are therefore *unconstitutional* criminals engaging in assault, battery, kidnapping, and absolute, irrevocable stupidity!"

Rauc spoke, out of the ether but nonetheless right into my ear, "Keep at it, Copper. I'm explaining to your dad what happened, assuring him Roger will be there soon and we'll bring you back safely. We think you're headed to the air base out in Indian Springs."

"What the hell is taking so long?" I muttered.

"Roger was not in Vegas, as you might recall," replied Rauc. "If you want, I can hop in my orb and start dive-bombing the van, but we're concerned about heavy traffic on the freeway. I don't want to cause an accident." I could tell he was keeping his ire in check so as not to worry my family.

Mom was yelling, "You better not try to hurt my grandanimals!"

I felt a momentary pang of panic for my dog, Bodie, and cat, Morris, but realized they were surely safe in my home with a protective Red Orbiter magnetic force put in place months ago.

"You punks are more like Ken dolls playing at being big bad warrior wannabes. Please! I'm surprised the word *police* is even spelled correctly, but it is after all the only word on this desert camouflage meant for battle, not urban thuggery of innocent American citizens!" I yelled. "And on *Christmas Eve*! Have you no modicum of shame, no human decency?"

I kept at it for what seemed like a half hour, and finally I elbowed the still-silent guy next to me as hard as I could, and Mom, bless her heart, followed suit and did the same to the thug next to her.

"And what's with all the tattoos? Did you get those in prison? Because that's where you belong! Are they spelled correctly?" I sniped. "I know it might be hard to ink *fathead* on arms so scrawny they need big scary automatic weapons to perpetrate your terrorist tactics. Because that's what you are, *domestic terrorists*, and as a lawyer, I took an oath to defend against all enemies, foreign and *domestic—*"

The van came to a screeching halt and was immediately slammed by something on the outside, making it rock back and forth.

"What is it, Doodles?" Mom clutched my thigh, fingernails digging in. I winced but managed to whisper, "It's okay. They're here to help," just as clouds seemed to fill my cerebral cortex with the words, "Don't. Worry. Rowan," and the henchmen were inevitably idiotic enough to slide open the door and haul us to the curb.

Whereupon we were once again snatched with alarming alacrity and lifted in the air by Greens, otherwise known as little green men. Because I have lots of protective friends these days, don't you know?

As we ascended into the chilly night sky and entered an actual flying saucer, Mom looked at the entities rescuing us and, wide-eyed, over at me.

"They're not wearing shoes," she said in a stage whisper.

That's what she noticed about the small green creatures who had no mouths or other clothing of any kind?

Chapter 2

I barely had time to thank my rescuing pals before their flying saucer touched down on the second level of Planet Wynne. This level of the casino hotel was designed to look, uncannily, like a flying saucer but was also a Red Orbiter flight deck.

"Your. Mom. Funny," said one of the Greens, holding my hand.

The words were inside my head in a softly robotic voice that felt like wispy clouds floating through my brain.

I chuckled and took hold of Mom's elbow to disembark.

"Thank you for saving us from those awful men," gushed Mom. "I'm Audrey. You must come visit us in Rowan's new home!" She turned to one Green, now gray in artificial light, and grasped a three-fingered hand. The Green nodded to me.

My head filled with the words, "She. Won't. Know."

Rauc took Mom from me as we walked down a ramp, carrying her to join Dad, G, Phil, Octavius Wynne, and Rauc's crazy brother, Rowdy.

"This government harassment of my patrons has got to stop!" O.W. said to Rauc and me, wringing bejeweled hands. "I'm calling my niece!" He stalked—more like swished—off.

O.W.'s niece was Senator Cassandra Rojas-Ortiz of Las Vegas, who was already well aware of havoc being wreaked by a president less than a month away from indictment, once our newly elected leader was sworn into office along with an otherworldly vice president, who happened to be my congressman. He had light-green eyes and a whole lot of Venus—actually called Lacerta—DNA.

Dad took my arm and spoke quietly. "Doodles, I'm glad you're okay. I heard your friends sending messages that you were in danger!" Dad also hears entities, in this case Greens, communicating from afar, though he hears them in electronic form reminiscent of his Navy days, as in Morse code.

Rowdy stepped forward in all his hottie red-headed glory to embrace Mom. "Remember me? Rowdy Wilde? We danced at my sister, Ophelia's, wedding. And aren't you stylish in that stunning black outfit!"

"Why, yes, Rowdy. We could jitterbug here if we had some music. I like Jimmy Buffett. Do you think we could get someone to play 'Margaritaville'?" said Mom, taking hold of his arm.

"Maybe another night, Audrey," said my brother-in-law, Phil. "Rowdy's here to help Rauc get you back to Rowan's house."

"Yes, let's get you in the orb," Rauc said, turning to G and Phil. "I'll make sure they're home safe and can bring you to them tomorrow." My sister and her hubby were staying at Planet Wynne, as I only had a two-bedroom rental house and G's allergic to my cat.

She whispered to me, "How are we going to keep Mom from telling everyone she was abducted by little green men? She's already whipped out her phone, ready to text, no doubt with lots of green alien head and flying saucer emoji!"

"Not to worry," I whispered. "The Greens did their thing. She won't even remember the Neanderthals snatching us from the curb. Unfortunately, I will, and I agree with Octavius Wynne. I've had it with these anti-alien Gestapo tactics. It's gotten worse every day since the election, and now they're clearly using military bases for nefarious purposes, since that's where they took us."

"What are you girls whispering about?" asked Mom.

"Come on, Audrey," said Dad, taking her arm. "We get to ride in an orb!"

"Is that better than a town car?" she asked as Rauc guided them up a ramp.

"It's definitely faster," I said as we entered a control room complete with lots of lights, buttons, and a big screen that Rauc pointed to.

"Gene," he said to Dad, "you'll be able to view our path using this, and I'll make it so you can see the night sky." After Rauc hit a button, the roof of the orb became transparent and looked like a planetarium, with twinkling stars following us home.

Mom looked up and asked, "Are we going into outer space?"

"No, Audrey," said Rauc. "We can't travel that far in an orb, but I can take you around the area so you can see Las Vegas from above if you like."

Dad said, "That's why you needed the new spacecraft that George worked on?"

"Yes," said Rauc. "Orbs aren't equipped for long-distance travel, and the new iridescent craft is also harder to detect in daylight."

"Can you take me to Florence to shop for shoes in one of these new *eerie decent* airplanes?" asked Mom.

I rolled my eyes at Rauc and mouthed, "I told you so," sitting next to him in the copilot's seat. Then I asked quietly, "What happened to Roger?"

"Once he knew you were rescued by Greens, he stayed put, which is good because he's at a very important ceremony honoring his parents."

"I knew he was visiting them, but he didn't say where," It dawned that I had never asked Roger where his family was from. He and his twin sister, Maggie, may have grown up in El Paso and been on Earth more than a century, but they came from another world.

"He's on his planet of origin, which is why he wasn't able to get here at a moment's notice," said Rauc.

"Hey, bro," Rowdy said to Rauc. "You better make sure we don't run into Santa Claus!"

For once I was grateful for his snark, as it made Mom forget about shoes and stare, wide-eyed, at the big screen. It occurred to me that Rudolph's "nose so bright" was…a red orb. Could there be a correlation?

Chapter 3

"I did not have Mom dancing to Willie Nelson in a UFO with an alien spy on my bingo card," I said to G on the phone after they got home to Portland the day after Christmas.

"Rowdy's a hoot," she said. "I'm so glad Rauc could fly us home. We didn't have to go through airport hell again. The idiot president has lost his mind, thinking he's going to stop aliens from air travel by asking endless questions about planetary origins. Like they need our cramped, stinky airplanes."

"Any which way he can think of to violate the Constitution is his motto these days. He and his enablers. It's not safe out there. Rauc doesn't want me out alone until after the inauguration, but I don't want to spend weeks cooped up in this house, and I have to walk Bodie every day. At least Greens are keeping an eye out."

"I still can't shake the image of you and Mom carried through the air by those tiny creatures. Phil keeps joking about it, saying what good is it when your mother-in-law is abducted by aliens if they bring her right back?"

"Hey, at least you didn't have to experience disembarking from an orb with her. It's not like Rauc could land on my street, so Rowdy created cumulous clouds for camouflage while we hovered. Then he carried Mom to the door while Rauc brought me and Dad down. I kid you not, Mom sang 'Fly Me to the Moon,' and I was afraid she'd rouse the neighbors."

Rauc's delectable voice slipped into my ear. "Got a minute, Copper?" He persisted in calling me that due to my hair, but most of my red now came from a bottle. He was really the one with burnished-copper-colored hair, like my favorite red-rock formations.

"G," I said, "the handsomest, sweetest alien in the galaxy wants to chat, so I've got to run, seeing as how he's now the Red Orbiter boss in these parts."

"Tell Rauc hi," she said before disconnecting.

"Sorry to interrupt," he said. "But we're putting together an impromptu meeting at headquarters, and I need to know if you can be ready to go if Roger picks you up in a half hour."

"Roger's back? And hey, I have a question!"

"Of course you do."

"You said he was on his planet of origin, but I thought Red Orbiters came from Jupiter, or Cumulus in your world. Except you told me no one has lived there for a very long time."

"No one has, but it is where our species originates from. That doesn't mean it's any individual's planet of origin. That's of course different for each of us. Rowdy and Ophelia and I all originated in different locales, depending on where our folks were."

"Do you deliberately keep information from me, or do I somehow not ask the right questions?"

"Let's not go down that rabbit hole again, please. I started this life on a distant star not known to humans, so it doesn't matter anyway. Not all of us obsess about our birthplace as Americans do. I didn't live there long, and you need to get moving if you're going to attend this meeting."

"I'll get in the shower," I grumped.

I was shoving my feet into red boots when the doorbell rang, startling me because I expected Roger to simply pop in my ear to let me know he'd arrived.

Bodie yipped with joy as I opened my door, tilting my neck to look way up at Roger Rogers, aka Superman with the given name Domitian, of all things. Like most Red Orbiters, his hair was red but was also bleached white blond in the Las Vegas sun.

He pulled me into hugely muscled arms and kissed me, making my knees buckle, and we ended up kneeling down to Bodie's level, much to the dog's delight.

As Roger pet my panting pooch, he handed me a small round box. "I've missed you, beautiful. This is a belated Christmas present."

"It's only been—what—a week since we've seen each other? And you didn't have to get me a gift."

"I wanted to bring you something from my planet of origin."

"And where is that, exactly?" I said, flipping open the red box to reveal a delicate necklace of white metal links with a small pendant, a round clear stone set in metal.

"It's a mineral that derives from Proxima Centauri b."

My mouth fell open. "You realize that's—"

"Where 9 percent of your DNA is from? Yes, beautiful, I'm aware."

Roger helped me slip the necklace on. His fingers gliding across the back of my neck had me poised for the most intense pleasure I'd ever felt so effortlessly. But he didn't stroke over *that* spot—a Red Orbiter talent making unsuspecting females spontaneously orgasm.

"It doesn't contain some sort of spy tracking device, does it? So you'll know where I am at all times?" I squinted up at him as he stood to his full intimidating height of six foot seven.

"No." He smiled. "But our native stone is believed to have protective powers."

I grinned. "I've got Superman protecting me, so why do I need this necklace?"

Roger's eyes glowed bright green, indicating he liked what he saw. "I can't always be with you at a moment's notice—like on Christmas Eve. And you, my dear, have proved to be unpredictable."

I laughed, thanking him for the gift as we walked to his red Ferrari at the curb, which instilled a little thrill despite knowing he'd drive like a bat out of hell to reach Valley of Fire, oldest state park in Nevada and site of Red Orbiter North American headquarters.

"So do I get to know what this sacred ceremony was involving your parents? Or is that a Red Orbiter secret too?" I asked as we exited the freeway to the winding, two-lane, crumbled road leading to the park. I'd spent the first twenty miles babbling about my family's visit.

Roger looked at me, and I could tell he was contemplating pulling the car over. The last time he did that was the first time he ever kissed me. Sweltering and swoon-worthy.

This time I was also swooning—or more like nauseated from the loops and curves in the road he'd navigated practically on two wheels.

"Whatever I tell you will lead to more questions I likely can't answer." Roger's eyes reverted to amber gold as he gazed at me, one hand on the wheel. He looked somber, and Roger somber was daunting indeed.

"Did your parents die?" I said in a rush.

"Not in the human sense," he said. "They moved on, together, into another realm. So my sister and I will not see them again in this life. Which, I suppose, is kind of like human death, in that there is a profound sense of loss for those left behind."

"I'm sorry," I said.

"Don't be," I heard, but the words were not spoken aloud. They were inside my head.

"You're doing it again, that mind-meld thing that wigs me out. It's bad enough I've had to adjust to Greens communicating telepathically with me."

Roger smiled and shrugged. "Sorry. Most human hybrids don't hear me. But I don't want you to be concerned. This is a part of our existence, like death is a part of yours. And I've had many years with my parents. More than most get."

"More than most probably want!" I teased, given that Roger, though stalled at his chosen age of thirty-three as Red Orbiters can do, was actually 125 years old, his parents nearing 150.

He pulled up to the gate and handed over the ten-dollar park-entry fee.

"I can't believe you pay that every time. Your headquarters was here long before the park."

"We like to support land conservation," Roger smiled.

"One more question before we get to the meeting," I said.

"No such thing as only one more question with you."

"You said you won't see your folks again *in this life*. Does that mean you go on to other lives, even though you can stay in this one seemingly as long as you want?"

Chapter 4

Roger managed to both not answer my question and maintain a respectable speed once we were inside the park. We took White Domes Road north toward the towering red-rock range in the distance, where Red Orbiter headquarters was hidden and inaccessible to motoring tourists.

We parked in the White Domes area lot among huge, grayish limestone looming over us like ghostly figures. Red sandstone felt more alive to me, and somehow less foreboding. Roger took my hand and directed me behind one of the creepy pale domes, lifting me in his arms and swooping upward, flying into the cloudless sky.

The rocks became a blur until we touched down seconds later in front of an entrance to a network of buildings burrowed into a mountain.

"Don't we need to be worried about tourists seeing us zipping about like Superman and Lois Lane?" I asked.

"We moved too fast for too short a distance. And let's face it, the unassisted human eye isn't all that observant." Roger sounded more cynical than usual. Maybe his many years of dealing with Earth dwellers were getting to him.

Rauc walked out to greet us and hug me, keeping me snugly under his arm as we went inside, where I presumed the third in my trio of suitors would also be in attendance.

Oswald Winslow, aka Win, former CIA, though still very much a spy and matching my 83 percent alien DNA, waited until I sat at a large conference table before he approached me, his hands resting on my shoulders as he drawled close to my ear. "Merry Christmas, sweet pea. I brought you an OUTWARD coffee mug for your collection and a bottle of Oregon Pinot Noir. We're breaking ground on the new acoustics facility here in Vegas next week. Soon, I can assist you in interpreting alien languages."

I may hear aliens, but Win spoke nine languages, not all of them human. He also had a bullet imbedded in his bicep from past espionage exploits.

OUTWARD was the company in Washington State started by my physicist friend George, a Marine named Owen, and Red Orbiter Dr. Bruce Robertson, now married to Rauc and Rowdy's sister Ophelia, also a PhD, of marine science. The acronym stood for Other Universal Transport, Weather, Acoustics, and Research & Development.

"Everybody take a seat and let's get started, because Tim Rider is here despite being on vacation. We don't need to take up too much of his leisure time," said Rauc, the new leader of Red Orbiters for North America.

I was surprised to see Tim, my former-nemesis-now-friend who still toiled as an agent of Homeland Security. I offered a little wave to the thirty-year-old, enlightened beyond his years and far beyond the scope of his employment. He grinned and winked at me.

"Thanks, Rauc," said Tim. "And congratulations on your new appointment. I appreciate your agreeing to meet on such short notice. I'm here to tell you we've determined the henchmen who grabbed Rowan and her mom on Christmas Eve were not from Homeland, despite reports to the contrary."

"We know the president's ultimately behind this, so who is he using to carry out his pathetic temper tantrums and cowardly attacks on women?" said Roger. Aggression and testosterone emanated from him in waves. More than a little intimidating, as he was seated next to me.

Tim said, "Win and I think it's something cooked up from within Space Force. That's why they were able to use Creech Air Force Base out in Indian Springs."

I snorted. "It figures. Why is that base even necessary, given how close it is to Nellis, which already gobbles up a huge chunk of Nevada?"

"It's not like we needed a Space Force either, but the Air Force had to maintain relevancy," snarked Win, ever the agency man.

"I did research, because the thug van was stopped by Greens just shy of the entrance," I said. "Turns out it hasn't been an actual base all that long. Before 2005, the year I quit working for the Air Force, it was an auxiliary air field that sprang up as a training site after the 1941 attack on Pearl Harbor. Unfortunately, it now specializes in unmanned aerial vehicles, a fancy name for exceedingly invasive drones used in Iraq and Afghanistan by the Air Force and the CIA." I looked pointedly at Win, who didn't flinch. He never did.

"Shall we tell her?" Win spoke, steely-blue eyes boring into mine from across the table.

"Tell me what? Is this about those vile drones?"

Rauc said, "They're using them to monitor citizens on US soil, particularly those active in alien rights like you."

"Those drones have five-hundred-pound bombs attached!" I yelped.

"Could be why they're named the MQ-9 Reaper," drawled Win.

I realized the reason for rage emanating from Roger as he spoke through a clenched jaw. "Does anyone else have a problem with a president employing a remotely piloted, heavily loaded aircraft system to track whereabouts of Rowan Layne so secret police can snatch her and her mother right off—not the streets of Baghdad or Kabul—but the Las Vegas Strip?"

"Don't worry." I patted his hand, trying to placate. "I know you can stop missiles and bullets and such."

Roger turned to me, intense green-gold eyes flashing ire, his hand gripping mine. *Ouch.* "That's just it. I can't be available to protect you twenty-four seven right now. The senator is also at risk, and it's my job to protect her while she's here, until she returns to Washington."

"Pretty much any outspoken female is a target of this president, but right now things are entirely and insanely out of control," said Rauc. "Which is why it's important for us to get you somewhere safe and out of reach for the next few weeks." Rauc was looking at me from the head of the table, and his amazing voice had a touch of something I'd never heard from him. Fear.

"Where would you have me go?" I tried to stay calm. "I'm not leaving my critters for a month!"

Rauc stood and came over to me at the table, leaning down and imploring me with those teal eyes of his. "We want to send you to the moonship, Copper."

Chapter 5

It felt like the air had been sucked from the room, and it was way too quiet.

"I can't go to the moon," I whispered. "I get motion sickness, and Morris and Bodie need me, and what about my family? How would I communicate with them? Is the Space *Farce* still blocking satellite communications? It's too far away. You won't be able to hear me, or I you." I looked at Rauc, tears filling my eyes.

"Great, guys, it only took you five minutes to make her cry," said Rowdy Wilde, walking into the room. "Rowan, you know my brother can't take it when you get all teary. Buck up, will you, gorgeous? I brought allies."

My longtime friend George also entered, blond dreadlocks swaying as he beamed at me with his see-the-world-through-rose-colored-glasses vibe.

"And I'm here for girl-power reinforcement," said Genie Robertson, sashaying in with her Jessica Rabbit curves and stunning Red Orbiter looks, just like her brother, Bruce. "These silly men don't realize the first thing they should've told you is that Bodie and Morris can come. That, and Rowdy and I and George are going with you."

"Did you ever dream, Rowan, all those years ago when we met back in Monterey, that we'd be headed to the moon together someday?" said George as I stood to hug him and Genie. "How can you say no to an adventure of a lifetime?"

We crowded around the table, with George seated to my left, Roger still on my right. I looked at him, feeling his penetrating eyes on me as words filled my head. "Please do this, beautiful. Help us keep you safe."

I thought I might start crying again, realizing Roger was using this special gift, the ability to communicate telepathically, in a crowded room so that others might not hear. A private moment between us, and powerful.

Looking across the table at Win, I caught his unguarded expression of concern. "You'll learn so much there, Rowan, and I wish I could go with you to see you experience it for the first time, but I have to be here for the new OUTWARD facility plans. Though there's no need to worry about sat comms. You'll be able to reach me, and your family. We're setting it all up through OUTWARD. Your brother-in-law will make sure you get all of your mom's texts." He flashed me that sexually charged grin, and I couldn't help but smile back.

"And I promise Homeland won't think your mom's use of emoji are secret messages," teased Tim Rider. "I guess that's a good segue for the other reason I'm here today. I'm going with you to the moon, and I won't be returning to work for the government. I have a lot of use-it-or-lose-it leave time saved up, and I'm using it before I hightail it out the door."

"Well this is interesting," I said. "Are you OUTWARD's newest recruit? And is Maggie coming too?" Maggie was Roger's sister and a Red Orbiter pilot—as well as Tim's girlfriend, thanks to my matchmaking.

"She's going to fly us there, so we can have girls' nights in the moon!" said Genie.

"Terrific. Do try not to get yourselves kicked off the moonship," said Roger.

"Buzz off, Superman," said Genie. "You're just jealous because you can't come and boss us around in space."

"I can be there very quickly if I need to be," replied Roger, but he was looking at me when he said it, and I'd be lying if I said it didn't make me squirm.

"But Maggie needs a copilot, so you can't escape ole Oz!" said Oz Walden, gangly and still sporting that silver flat-top buzzcut, walking into the room like a swashbuckling pirate despite his advanced age.

"Well, I guess I can't say no if there's a former Marine and NASA astronaut flying me to the moon," I attempted bravado as I looked at Oz, but surging adrenaline left me light-headed. "At least it will get me and the critters away from the neighbors. They've been setting off firecrackers most nights since before the election—trying to intimidate because it's a diverse neighborhood—and they're still doing it in rage over their false prophet losing the election." I frowned. "It agitates Morris and terrifies poor Bodie, who hides in my closet. But I suppose you can't get away from ignorant and mean no matter where you go." I looked up at everyone. "Are we flying in the sparkly new pistachio-shaped spacecraft?"

"Yes, but a larger version than what you've been in. And why didn't you tell us about this neighbor issue before?" said Rauc.

"Everyone's been pretty busy, and I kept thinking they'd run out of money to waste on firecrackers," I sighed. "How long will it take to get to the moon, and will CBD capsules be available? Because I don't want my critters to feel my agitation."

"I can make that happen," said George. "Whatever you need, Rowan."

"And it will take you roughly six hours to get there in the new craft," said Rauc.

I turned to Roger. "No wonder you couldn't get to me in a split second the other night."

"Proxima Centauri, though the nearest star to this sun, is more than four light-years away, and there are six trillion miles in a light-year," grinned Roger. "I'm good, but that distance does take time. The moonship is only a little more than two hundred thousand miles from Earth."

I shook my head. "Will I ever understand any of this? Physics is nuts. I thought it was impossible for anything with mass, such as people or spacecrafts, to travel at light speed."

"That's true," said George. "To travel to, say, Proxima Centauri b using current human technology would take more than six thousand years. But we're not using our technology anymore, Rowan. We're living in a totally different world, whether people embrace it or not."

"Boy howdy," I said. "So where do we depart from? Monterey Bay?" I was hopeful, as it's a fav spot on Earth other than Valley of Fire, plus it's a deep-water, intergalactic port.

"The Grand Canyon, at the North Rim. It's the closest launch port to Las Vegas."

"Okay." I took a deep breath. "When do we leave?"

"The day after tomorrow," said Rowdy. "So you better get packing your prettiest wardrobe. Rowan Layne's debut into space!"

Chapter 6

Before we left the meeting, Rauc pulled me aside.

"I'm sorry, we won't be able to spend New Year's Eve together because I have to focus on my role here as head of this Red Orbiter gig. I know it was important to you." He gathered me in his arms, and I quivered from the feel of his body and the dreamy timbre of his voice.

"It's just that I haven't really had a fun or romantic New Year's in a really long time." I sighed. "I guess they probably don't celebrate it in the moonship."

"No, it's an Earth thing. But we can have our own private celebration before you go. And I'll be at your place tonight, with pizza."

"Great. I bet they don't have pizza in the moon either," I grumped.

"Not like you're used to, but the culinary school there will be glad to whip you up whatever you like. A new gastronomic world awaits!"

"Are you sure I should do this, Rauc?"

"You've got this, Copper." He touched my chin, pulling my eyes to his. "I'm available until you leave, to help you prepare."

I went from Rauc's arms to lifted into Roger's when he flew me back to his car. The usual conflicted confusion it caused had me thinking it wouldn't be bad to get a break from this romantic triad of men I'd amassed and emotionally wrangled with. It didn't help when Win said he would drop off a special communications device for me tomorrow. Not to mention Roger wasn't being his usual evocative self.

"You know, you being so gloomy doesn't make this any easier," I said as I fastened my seatbelt, knowing it would lock up on me once Roger hit the open road.

"Well, I could take you back to Mouse's Tank Trail for some fun, but it's daylight and we'd probably startle the tourists." He smiled, and it was blinding on several levels.

I caught my breath, remembering a wondrous night entwined with Roger—mind, body, and spirit—in my favorite spot in the park.

"I love it when your skin flushes like that, and I wish I had time to properly see to your needs. But make no mistake, beautiful—we will be together again. Naked."

"Yikes. I'm sorry I said anything." I shifted in my seat. "I guess that's what I get for not being sensitive to what you must be going through, what with the recent ceremony for your parents and having to keep Senator Rojas-Ortiz safe from gun-mongering psychopaths."

"Being a bodyguard is my job, which includes guarding your body, so remember that. I really can be at the moonship in a flash."

"That sounds a bit like a threat. What is it with you being so domineering?"

"You love it." He grinned again and accelerated to what had to be a hundred miles an hour after we exited the park.

Roger, like Rowdy, was also a Red Orbiter spy who knew way too much about me, and I'd do well to remember it.

"Okay, Mr. Snoop, in all your digging into my background, there's one thing I know you didn't learn! When I was a kid, I used to lay in bed and talk to the moon shining outside my window, telling it my hopes and dreams and troubles."

"So that's why you have all those lunar photos and other moon-themed items in your bathroom."

"How'd you know about that?" I swatted his arm and wished I hadn't. *Ouch.*

He cut intense green eyes at me, one hand on the wheel, the other reaching for the back of my neck. "I fixed your shower drip for you a couple of months ago, remember?" I imploded into a careening and highly satisfying orgasm at high speeds in his flashy red Ferrari.

"Now you're all relaxed and ready to begin preparing for your journey," said Roger as he walked me to my front door. "I'll be at the Grand Canyon to see you off. Please keep wearing this." He touched the necklace at my throat, and I swear I felt the clear stone grow warm, but it was probably a hot flash. Roger tended to instill those in women.

I called my sister once I'd greeted Morris and Bodie. "I'm going to the moonship."

"With whom? Superman, Smooth Operator CIA, or the nicest, handsomest alien in the galaxy?" G snarked.

"None of the above. And you have to tell Mom because I don't think I can."

"Whoa. I need details. And maybe vodka."

"You and me both."

Within thirty minutes after the phone call with my sister, I had a text from Mom.

"Doodles, we don't have time to get you outfits for your trip!!! What's the weather like where you're going??? Do you need new shoes or sandals??? Weather cloudy here, likely rain or snow. Ugh. (frowny face, shoe, cloud emoji)"

Before I could finish texting my answer, I had another ping of an incoming text.

"Doodles, Phil is bringing over a special phone for us to text with while you're on your trip!!! Shall I call you to try it out beforehand??? And I forgot to tell you I have your annual horoscope for the coming year!!! No time to mail it!!! Are my grandanimals going to be okay??? Who will take care of them??? (dog, cat, worried face, heart, six moon emoji)"

I called Mom, realizing she might be a tad discombobulated by my news.

"It's okay, Bodie and Morris are coming with me! They get to ride in the spaceship too! And I don't think weather will be a problem because it's all indoors. Do you want to read me my horoscope over the phone?"

"Okay, Doodles. But you make sure you write it down. It could be important!"

I grabbed a nearby pad and pen. "I'm ready. Fire away!"

"Be present in your life! Open yourself to your inner voice to assess choices you make. Reconnect to avoid feeling overwhelmed by the intricate maze of your life, to understand the very purpose of your existence. Advance toward the center of your own life, rather than hovering like a moon around a planet."

I scribbled quickly, realizing the word *life* was cropping up a lot. And "hovering like a moon around a planet"? Seriously?

"Got it!" I put down my pen. "Thanks, Mom."

"But there's also your lucky numbers!"

I picked up my pen. "Ready."

"Two, thirty-eight, eight, and fifty-five."

"Only four this year? Last year there were six lucky numbers."

I heard the rattling of the scrap of paper, torn from a magazine. "That's all it says. And '55 is the year your father and I married!"

"Yes, that's true! I've got it down and will take it with me. As for the special phone, wait to see what Phil's instructions are. He and G can help you use it. I'll be getting mine tomorrow. Tell Dad I'll email him with details."

Dad was hard of hearing in both ears despite being able to detect high-frequency electronic communications, so he didn't much like talking on the phone these days.

Immediately after I disconnected with Mom, Roger popped into my ear. "Interesting horoscope and numbers."

"Don't you have better things to do than invade my privacy again? Maybe this moon trip is a good idea after all, because you can't snoop on me there!"

"You sure about that, beautiful?"

Chapter 7

The next day as I packed, I kept telling myself it was just like going to a foreign country and at least I wouldn't be cramped on a commercial flight for endless hours. But I hadn't traveled extensively overseas, only to Europe with mostly no language barrier.

Except once—in a village in Scotland, there was a little old man who chatted it up with me, though I couldn't understand much of what he said. He had an equally aged Jack Russell terrier trotting around with a pipe in its mouth. So maybe he was a Gaelic alien.

It was giving me fits, trying to figure out what to pack for the moonship.

"Genie!" I said aloud. "Are you available for fashion consultation? I have no idea what to take on our grand adventure."

"I'm here, Rowan," she said in my ear. "Bring what you're comfortable in. Plan for a temperature of sixty-five to seventy-five degrees, and you'll be able to keep your suite how you like it. Also, there are places to buy clothes and pretty much everything else. You'll have an account. It's on Rauc and Rowdy," said Genie.

"I'm your sugar daddy," said Rowdy, invading my ear.

"Rowdy, what the hell?" I said.

"Sorry, I heard my name," he said, not sounding sorry.

"Genie said Rauc's name too, but you don't hear him popping in my ear without an invite. Are you going to be like this on the moonship? You're as bad as Roger!"

"Watch it, beautiful. I can be on your doorstep in seconds. Do you require assistance packing?" drawled Roger, also in my ear.

I said, "Genie, Roger has now interloped on our conversation too."

She said, "Boys, butt out!" making me giggle. Red Orbiter spy Genie was in her thirties in human years, but she could sound like a teenager. "Don't forget your favorite happy hour togs, Rowan, or we can shop and spend Rowdy's latest gambling windfall."

Silence. Although I swore I could feel Rowdy chomping at the bit to retort.

"While I've got you, I wanted to give you a heads-up that there'll be breaking news later today that involves me. Rowdy and I did the spy thing recently," she trilled.

"I can only imagine," I said. Genie was the femme fatale I'd once fantasized being, but I'd never had her Victoria's Secret body. Though we did have the same curly red hair.

My doorbell wrang, and Bodie started yipping and leaping.

"Gotta go. My space phone's arrived," I said. "See you tomorrow!"

I opened my door to Win, telling myself no way would I end up entwined in sheets with this man—this time. He may not have been alien, but his special power was making my hormones rage like I was seventeen, despite his being the same age as my sister. Oswald Winslow may have looked like an average guy, but his skills were deliciously daunting.

"Hey, sweet pea." He drew me in for a kiss. "I missed those luscious lips of yours."

"But not the words coming out of them, I'll wager?"

"And what would you wager?" he asked, bending down to Bodie and Morris, who vied for his attention.

"Don't befuddle a beleaguered woman. I'm already nervous enough."

Win pulled me back into his arms for another kiss.

"That's not helping," I panted.

"Maybe not, but I like it just fine. Let's sit and I'll explain your phone for keeping in touch with your family—and me."

"What, no more burner phones?"

Win let Morris the kitty settle into his lap while he showed me a device that worked pretty much the same as my cell phone, except it was the size of a tablet so I could easily and securely text and email.

"This is great, and thank goodness you made emoji available for Mom." I sighed. "I can't believe I'm doing this."

"You're doing the right thing. It keeps you out of reach and prevents you from being a pawn in the president's attacks on aliens,

Red Orbiters in particular. Now, I know you must have questions." He grinned, and I felt the inner tug that always gets me in trouble.

"Do I need to worry about language barriers? I mean, how many different types of aliens will I encounter, and will they hate me because I'm from the US whose idiot president tried to launch a missile at them?"

"You know our pal Owen Marsden has been up there, working that issue. He can fill you in on all things Martian, or Labyrinthian, which is the name you'll want to use. They make up the majority of residents on the moonship while Mars is being rejuvenated. Their language sounds a bit like Italian, or Portuguese, but those you encounter will speak English for you. Kind of like traveling to Europe." He chuckled. "You'll hear other languages for sure. There's about sixty thousand residents in the moonship at any given time."

"But no Greens, right?"

"No, because they're Earthlings. They don't tend to leave here, other than to fly around above us."

"About that, there's something bugging me. I thought Greens flew in cylindrical crafts, but they rescued Mom and me the other night using a flying saucer. And then I remembered it was a saucer that flew you and others into Monterey Bay last year when the world learned there were folks traveling from the moon."

"And from Mars, remember? That's where we flew from that day. Flying saucers are a spacecraft mostly associated with those originally from Mars. But Red Orbiters have also used them for space travel. And Greens fly them occasionally, mostly for diversion. You know how prickly they are about anyone being able to track them."

"Boy howdy! But how did I not keep this straight? I guess I was so focused on the moon because of news breaking about it being an actual spaceship, I forgot you flew from Mars."

"Well, we'd also been to the moonship, and that's where we stayed while in space, but we wanted the world to focus on Project Mars."

"So everything Owen the Marine said that day on TV was true, and not just a theory? Mars is like a phoenix, rising from the ashes after burning up, so that's why its inhabitants moved to the moonship?" Owen had been a Marine officer instructor at the Naval Postgraduate School where my friend George was also a professor at the time. He later revealed he was both a Martian, with less than 1 percent human DNA, as well as gay, when he left the Corps and launched OUTWARD with Bruce Robertson and George.

"Pretty much. Owen can fill you in on details. But what's got you looking so concerned, sweet pea?"

"I don't know." I looked away from Win's prying eyes. "But I really hope I don't have to visit Mars too."

"Rowan, you don't need to worry. You're not going to Mars."

"But can't those on Mars visit the moonship?"

"Yes, but that twisted piece of work you lived with in Yearntown won't be visiting. There've been problems with those private startups from Earth traveling to Mars to horn in on the mining industry there. Anyone working for them is currently banned from the moonship."

"Wow," I said. "I guess it wouldn't surprise me if Lucas was the one who caused the trouble. But I'm glad I don't have to worry about running into him. Ever again."

Chapter 8

Soon after Win left, Rauc arrived to spend the night, and the first thing he noticed was the necklace Roger had given me. He touched the stone, and I felt its heat again.

"I approve," he said before I could offer an explanation.

"How so?" I asked, feeling painfully awkward.

"It's a protective stone. But if you're concerned about me being jealous of you wearing another guy's jewelry, you can always take your shooting-star earrings to remind you of me." His lips twitched, but he also swatted my behind. "And to remember you're *my* shooting star."

"Are you going to get all Romulus on me tonight?" I teased as I skipped out of his way to head to the kitchen and pop open the champagne he brought. Romulus was Rauc's Red Orbiter given name, Raucous Wilde being his selected Earth name. And Romulus may have been the first king of Rome, but Romans got the name from aliens, who they mistook for gods that came down from the heavens. "You know you're a powerful god to me."

"Keep sweet-talking, Copper, and I'll haul you away to my Red Orbiter cave and never let you go to the moon. Not that I didn't think about it, having you stay at headquarters with me."

"Why am I not doing that? I always said I wished I could live in Valley of Fire. And we could finally work on getting the Red Orbiter book started." I sighed.

"You know by now that book won't really be the tell-all about Red Orbiters that people expect. It's more about what we've observed about humans on Earth over centuries. And the decision to ask you to go to the moon wasn't ultimately up to me."

"What do you mean?"

"The universe has more in store for Rowan Layne. After your performance at the Omni convention, you're going places with people in high places."

"Okay, but did it have to be to the moon?"

"Is it so preposterous that your writing skills might be desired in the moonship as well?"

"Absolutely. I find it hard to believe I'm that desirable." I looked at Rauc and he at me, and I knew it was time. I'd waited too long. "There's something I recently realized I haven't told you. I was in an awful relationship that ended not long before we met," I said in a rush, turning to pull champagne flutes from a cabinet and avoid Rauc's eyes.

"I know, Rowan." He pulled me to him, lifting my chin. "Rowdy finally told me about the intel he and Roger gathered. But don't be mad at him for sharing. They were concerned about you, and what you'd been through."

"That experience left me questioning my ability to judge human nature." I frowned.

"Well at least with me you're not dealing with a human." Rauc grinned. "But seriously, Copper, I thought you were the bravest human hybrid I'd ever met, and now I know for sure my instincts were spot on. What you went through doesn't have to define you, but you need time to realize it. Time to trust again."

"You've been so patient with me, so nice. I shouldn't be so conflicted."

"Isn't *nice* supposed to be the kiss of death for human men?" Rauc teased, swatting my butt again. "Copper, I've told you I want to spend the rest of my life with you, enough to stop stalling at this age of nearly fifty and grow older. But you're not there yet. You haven't made your mind up."

"But—"

"No *but*s, except this sassy butt of yours." He swatted me again, and heat flushed through me. "I'm okay with it. You've got experiences to have, new people to meet, and ideas to explore. I'm not going to hold you back from opportunity, or force you to choose to be mine alone. Now cheer up and pop open that champagne. Have you seen the latest breaking news? That might get you grinning again."

While sipping bubbly, I scrolled headlines on my phone:

"CONSERVATIVE CHRISTMAS PARTY SCANDAL EMBROILS VP, AG"

"HOLIDAY HO HO HOEDOWN: NAUGHTY AND NOT SO NICE"

"ALL THE RIGHT WING WANT FOR CHRISTMAS IS AN ILLICIT TRYST"

"What did Genie do?" I gasped.

"And Rowdy," said Rauc. "Shall I provide sordid details?"

"I'm all ears."

"Rowdy and Genie did some dramatic playacting for this particular covert project, becoming the Fitzgeralds of Boston, wealthy Irish Catholic donors to the cause of the Conservative Society of ultra-right-wing religiousness, which had their annual Christmas party a week ago," began Rauc.

"Because so-called conservatives wouldn't dare be politically correct and call it a holiday party!" Champagne sloshed from my glass, barely missing Bodie, underfoot as usual in the kitchen. "Not the folks who claim liberals are trying to cancel Christmas by keeping *their* god out of public school!"

"It's only about free exercise of their so-called religion—which is actually greed, in case you didn't know—so they have a decided interest in blurring the lines of church and state."

"How fashionably fascist. All to continue subjugating women by stacking the Supreme Court with misogynist bigots and religious zealots." I moved Morris from the countertop so he couldn't knock over the champagne bottle.

"Have some more champagne," Rauc grinned. "The attorney general certainly did. So much so, he grew bold and attempted to seduce Genie as Mrs. Scarlet Fitzgerald, who told him she was no cheap call girl. Whereupon he immediately offered to pay whatever she desired, and she desired the exact amount her devoted husband, Mr. Rodney Fitzgerald, had donated to the conservative cause, half a million bucks. It was actually some of Rowdy's latest gambling winnings."

"No way!" I waited for bubbles to subside in my glass before taking a sip.

"Yes way. The attorney general was tipsy enough to accompany her to her hotel room, where she requested prepayment once he had his pants off, and he got thuggish and claimed he didn't have to pay because he was the president's lawyer and could do as he pleased and take whatever he wanted, including her 'slut services.'"

"Rowdy taped it, didn't he?" I stopped pacing.

"That's not all he did. The soon-to-be-ex-attorney general then attempted to choke Genie-slash-Scarlet in his frustration when she told him no nookie for him then, whereupon Rowdy stopped taping and entered from the adjoining room as Genie put him in a headlock and they made him transfer half a million dollars back to them. Rowdy-slash-Rodney was very persuasive."

"So they have the AG on tape, attacking Genie, and have his electronic transfer of exorbitant sums for sexual services."

"Yes, and it was all leaked to the British tabloids with his pants down, so Mrs. Scarlet Fitzgerald went on TV today to tell her side of the story, claiming her husband likes to watch, so he taped her with the attorney general and that's how he came to her rescue. She had no idea how the tape got leaked, but it could be a friend of her husband's from Great Britain who was jealous because he also wanted to have sex with her, but he didn't want to pay either, but no way was she doing anything with fat, ugly men for free."

"So what did the soon-to-be-ex-vice president have to do with all this? I can't imagine he tried to seduce Genie too."

"No, he solicited Rowdy as Mr. Rodney Fitzgerald. For sexual favors. In the hotel bathroom."

"Oh the unnatural horror! But wasn't the Secret Service there with him?" I removed Morris from the counter, again. He protested loudly.

"Sort of."

"Sort of?" I racked my brain. "Roger! Roger was there too, as a Secret Service agent!"

Rauc nodded. "Roger was the *agent*"—he made air quotes with his fingers—"who supposedly cleared the bathroom for the VP but conveniently overlooked Mr. Rodney Fitzgerald, who recorded the encounter."

"And it was also somehow leaked to the media?" I gave Bodie a dog cookie.

"Rowdy-slash-Rodney approached Fox News' Ian Cassidy—who I know you like to call Calamity—also in attendance at the illustrious and lusty Christmas party, providing him with the tape of the VP."

"No way did Calamity or anyone at Fox air that footage."

"No, but every other cable news outlet will tonight, along with footage of Cassidy being given the tape and accepting a hundred bucks to air it."

"So we know who the *real* cheap floozy is in all of this. Ho! Ho! Ho!"

Chapter 9

I got excited thinking of the route to the North Rim of the Grand Canyon that passed through the narrow northern tip of Arizona (a total speed trap) and the scenic Virgin River Gorge. But Rauc said we'd only be driving my car to Planet Wynne, leaving it under the protective canopy of the flight deck. From there we'd fly in his orb to rendezvous with the new sparkly spacecraft.

As I crammed things into one of two small suitcases to accompany my large one, Rauc raised a brow. "Notepads and pens?"

"Do they have lined-paper pads and colored-ink pens in the moonship? Because that's how I draft questions and ideas. And if you want me to work on the Red Orbiter book while I'm there, I have to do it my way," I said, hands on hips.

"Okay, Luna Moth Woman, have at it." Rauc held up his hands in defense. "But come here so I can give you a very important item." He was holding something in each hand that looked like shiny copper.

"More jewelry?" I huffed, trying to zip the last suitcase closed. "You already gave me a new special phone to reach you with so no one else can hear us talking. Which is a good thing because Rowdy does not have your manners."

"No, Copper, this is not jewelry. It's something to help ground you in space, and it will eradicate any motion sickness." He entwined very soft metal bands to each of my wrists, kissing the insides of my elbows and turning me to mush. "Don't look at me like that or we'll end up being late for your space launch."

I looked down at the wristbands. "So what are these things made of?"

"Mixed alloys, mostly not of Earth, but yes, there is copper in there. And you need to wear them at all times. But don't worry, you soon won't feel them because they'll meld to your skin. But here's the thing, they'll still be visible to you and anyone else aboard the moonship."

"Is that bad? Bands identifying me as a human hybrid with gravity challenges? You said no one would hold it against me that I'm from Earth!"

"You'll be identifiable as being from the US the minute you open your mouth." Rauc grinned. "What I'm getting at is these bands might draw attention. And don't be surprised if Labyrinthians are drawn to you, and you to them."

"Well, Mars is the planet that rules my astrological sign, and 4 percent of my DNA is from there. Is that why?"

"It's primarily due to your auditory abilities."

"Can they also hear from afar?"

"No, not like Red Orbiter observers. But they have their own abilities, stemming from the inner ear, also called the labyrinth of the ear."

"Different from the cochlea?"

"The cochlea is part of the inner ear, but the labyrinth contains organs for hearing and equilibrium."

"Well, no wonder. I'm not great at the equilibrium part. My hairless cochlea doesn't help at all with balance. So what's their special ability?"

"You'll have to learn that from Labyrinthians. It's their story to tell."

"Why do you always say that? You're a Red Orbiter broken record." I grunted as I lifted a box of kitty litter to haul to my car.

"At least I know you're listening to me, or maybe not, because I distinctly remember telling you cat litter is not needed on the moonship." Rauc took the heavy box from my grasp.

"But what about on the pistachio craft? Won't Morris need his litter box for the ride?"

"The new spacecraft has a built-in system like the moonship. We had OUTWARD engineers include all potential needs for domesticated dogs and cats."

"Because of my Morris and Bodie?"

"Yes." Rauc's lips twitched. "Now let's get going, Copper."

We loaded Morris in his crate into the front seat of the car, and I took Bodie on his leash and sat with him in the back while Rauc drove us to Planet Wynne.

My critters were quite familiar with Rauc's orb after spending time in it during the Omni Party convention. So that part of the trip went smoothly.

Because the North Rim of the Grand Canyon was closed to visitors in winter, flying into it in an orb was not a concern in terms of concealment. The rocky cliffs dusted in snow were starkly beautiful, the air cold and clear in bright late-afternoon sunshine.

I'd always wondered what it would be like to descend into the canyon, but I imagined it as a mule ride, not swooshing downward via an alien spacecraft, flying through treetops versus ambling among them. Rabbits ran for cover like we were some menacing bird of prey.

The spacecraft awaiting us was huge and shimmering pinkish green, perhaps three times the size of one I'd ridden in during the Iridescent Insect War escapades. But it opened the same at a split in the middle, and a large magenta tongue-like ramp slipped out, where Genie and Rowdy strolled down to greet us.

"Well if it isn't Scarlet and Rodney Fitzgerald of Boston fame! Are you now fugitives fleeing the planet?" I snarked.

"Ha!" said Genie. "Rowdy never showed his goofy mug on camera despite his bushy mustache disguise, and I wore a long blonde wig and blue contact lenses to blend in with the Stepford wives. But that queen Octavius made me give back the ginormous diamond ring and necklace we borrowed for me to flash around. You should have seen me! I looked like a Christmas tree in a green dress with red shoes and gems."

"My mom might call that tacky," I said.

"Oh, it was." Genie laughed. "But I had some competition."

"*Goofy mug?*" said Rowdy to Genie. "I'll have you know, Rowan, the vice president was quite taken with me, and my mustache."

"Of course! You're such a roguish devil, how could he resist that Red Orbiter charm?"

"Let's get this show going," said Rauc. "Copper, your precious pooch just took a dump in a national park. Give me one of those plastic bags you brought that I mistakenly said you wouldn't need."

"He's nervous," I said, realizing I was too. "But now I know for sure you're not a human male because you just admitted to being wrong."

"Don't kid yourself, Rowan," said Genie. "Plenty of Red Orbiter males have issues with that. And speak of the devil…"

Roger chose that moment to play Superman and swoop down, landing in front of me, pulling me into a hug and communicating without speaking aloud. "You and the critters will be fine, beautiful. I'm only a shout away." His words filled my head as my tears sprang forth.

"Absolutely no waterworks!" said Rowdy.

Rauc pulled me into his arms next. "There's no crying in baseball, Copper. Or in space," he teased. "Besides, I'm the one that should be crying because I'm getting left behind this time. So climb aboard. Your friend George is waiting, and Tim and Maggie and Uncle Oz. And remember, you'll always be my queen of hearts."

Chapter 10

As we walked into a vestibule of the spaceship, George was there, holding up a huge container of CBD. "I've got you covered, Rowan!" He beamed.

"Looks like you've also been banded by metal. Do you think we should feel like we've been handcuffed or microchipped?" I asked.

"They're to help us ground to a different type of magnetized gravity on the moonship. Otherwise we'd be floating around like astronauts of yesteryear."

"Did I hear my name?" said Oz Walden, retired NASA astronaut. "Come on to the control room, rookies. You won't want to miss our launch out of the canyon!"

"What should I do with my critters?" I asked.

"Bring 'em with. Rowdy can take your stuff to your room."

"Oh fine. I'm your huckleberry ship steward, at your service!" huffed Rowdy, hauling my suitcases off as Genie called after him, "And don't scratch that luggage or you won't get a tip!"

The control room wasn't far, and it was roughly the size of the same on an aircraft carrier, with several huge screens that would ordinarily give me vertigo. Maggie was in full pilot-readiness mode, but she grinned and said, "Welcome aboard!"

She was my ideal Luna Moth Woman—strong, competent, and fierce, though some might be fooled by her sleek red ponytail. Plus, she was a former Marine pilot and Roger's twin sister.

I took Bodie off his leash so he could sniff around. Morris yowled, but I hesitated letting him out of his carrier. There were lots of easily accessible buttons and gizmos.

Tim Rider walked in with Rowdy. "Let Morris out, Rowan, and see what he does. I brought my cat too. They've got this—believe me!"

Out came my kitty. We all watched as Morris leapt up and planted himself next to Maggie's elbow, staring at a screen like he was some sort of copilot.

"He recognizes the vibrations of the engine," said Maggie, using one hand to stroke my cat as his extra-long tail swished. "He knows we're getting ready to take off."

"Space travel is in his DNA," said Oz. "Rowan, dear, you can see the Grand Canyon below us from this screen." He directed me across the room from Maggie as I felt a lifting sensation and Morris began to scramble in circles.

I stared, mesmerized, at a breathtaking, unique view of one of America's iconic landscapes until Morris made agitated noises and Maggie said, "We're on, Roger. Incoming."

She wasn't saying "Roger that," in typical pilot-speak for "Message received." She was apparently speaking to Roger himself, because I heard him respond, "On it."

"On what?" I squeaked. "What's incoming?"

I was immediately surrounded by Rowdy, Genie, Tim, and George, blocking my view of all screens but the one on which the Grand Canyon slowly grew farther away.

I shoved at Rowdy and shouted, "Tell me what's going on!"

"I've got this, beautiful," said Roger in my ear, but I was rushing for the screen in front of Maggie and Oz.

My heart thumped ominously in my ears when I saw what appeared to be a blur of Roger, flying across the sky to intercept a large cylindrical object.

"Fly ball caught," said Roger. "Operation Three Strikes commenced. Headed for home base. Over and out."

"Roger that," said Rauc in my ear. "Time to play ball."

"What the hell?" I screeched. "This is insane! I am *not* this important."

"You certainly are," said Oz. "But the bomb wasn't intended for you. They're after me. And Tim. The president's holding a wicked grudge over the Iridescent Insect War. Sociopaths are so thin-skinned."

"Rauc!" I shouted, "Please tell me what's going on!"

"Remember those drones, the remotely piloted aircrafts called Reapers from the nearby Air Force base?" said Rauc's soothing tone in my ear.

"With the five-hundred-pound bombs?" My voice cracked. "They dropped a bomb into the *Grand Canyon*?"

"What can you expect from a president who launched a missile at his own planet's moon?" Rowdy smirked, and I realized he was holding me up as my knees crumpled.

"Sit here," Oz said, giving me his copilot's seat next to Maggie.

Bodie's head landed in my lap as I sat. All my screeching had scared the poor pooch, and he was making distressed noises. I stroked his head, promising I'd keep him safe.

"I have control of the Reaper," said Maggie.

"Blow that fucking drone right out of the sky," I said, jaw clenched.

"Love to," said Maggie. "But unlike the president, Red Orbiters care about natural and cultural resources and won't engage in senseless habitat destruction."

"Understood. I might have overreacted." I squeaked. "Where is Roger taking that bomb?"

"The White House," said Rowdy.

"*What?*" I dug my hands into Bodie's fur.

Genie said, "Rowdy, you are not helping. It's okay, Rowan. Roger is simply dropping it off, placing it gently intact on the White House doorstep. Along with a message."

"What message?" I yelped. "It's a little late to say, 'Don't be stupid!'"

"That's why I lasered, 'You were stupid. Three strikes, you're out,' on the lawn," drawled Roger in my ear.

"I know this baseball metaphor was your idea, Rauc!" I said, hearing him laugh, and it was a calming sound. Rauc once dreamed of playing professionally, and baseball originated on Jupiter, along with Red Orbiter DNA. We both loved Jackie Robinson—and the movie *Bull Durham*.

"Well, the president already accused Red Orbiters of stealing baseball from Americans," Rauc said.

"Rowan." George crouched down next to me, concern evident behind his wire-rimmed glasses. "Do you want to take one?" He held out a CBD capsule and a flask of water.

“Sure.” I gulped.

Maggie said, “Sending footage to media. Reaper en route to BMG Range.”

“BMG Range?” I exclaimed. “You’re sending that drone to the Air Force’s Barry M. Goldwater bombing range in Arizona?”

“Hey!” said Maggie, cutting her eyes at me and winking. “It’s a Marine Corps range too, so it’s not like I haven’t dropped a few practice bombs there, back in the day. At least this aircraft doesn’t have its payload attached to crash and burn along with it.”

Chapter 11

I watched the screen long enough to see us fly through and above clouds, higher and higher until Oz said, "We are officially in outer space, folks. Which NASA defines as fifty miles above the Earth's surface."

Roger's voice slid into my ear. "Beautiful, why don't you get yourself settled? There's a lounge area with couches the critters will love, and you can get debriefed on what went down. I'm sure you have questions."

"Ya think?" I snorted. "And good grief, you're even bossing me around in outer space! Are you still at the White House, Superman?"

"No, Lois, I don't tend to hover in restricted airspace after I've dropped off a bomb."

"Roger's in your ear, isn't he?" said Genie. "Come on, let's clear out so Maggie can work. We'll have a cocktail."

"Sorry I can't join you," said Maggie, eyes locked on a different screen to her left. "Let me know if you like the décor!"

I picked up Morris, who made his usual disgruntled sound. Bodie whimpered jealously. I said, "Come on, sweet pup, we're going to get you a couch to shed all over."

"Don't worry, Rowan," said George as we entered a corridor. "There's an onboard system that sucks up all particulate matter, including pet hair."

"Okay, but I wouldn't put it past my critters to clog it up. And why is Maggie so intently focused? Aren't we out of danger—or at least out of idiocy range for now?"

"Rauc and Win will explain," Tim said as we entered an area with fifties retro-design couches in a pleasing shade of turquoise and what looked like a huge flat-screen TV. The furniture made me think of *The Jetsons* space-age cartoon, and I smiled.

"Would you like a spritzer with our pistachio-cherry liqueur Roger said you liked?" asked Genie.

"Sure. Does it come with a lime slice and spherical ice?"

"All Red Orbiter ice is spherical," she said with a chuckle.

I sat on a couch, Bodie hopped up and curled next to me, and Morris leapt upon a large coffee table in front of us to sniff at various items, including what looked like a remote control. "Is that really a clicker on a spaceship?" I reached for it.

Rowdy plopped down next to me and snatched it from my hand, pressing a button and making the flat-screen on the wall light up.

"Just like a guy. Hogging the remote," I grumped.

"Rowdy, be nice, and you don't have to sit that close to Rowan," said Rauc, appearing on the screen with Win, who gave me a little wave.

I waved back, realizing they must be at Red Orbiter headquarters in Valley of Fire, because the room looked familiar.

Rowdy replied, "I figured I'd need to hold her down when she loses it upon learning we knew we would be attacked at takeoff."

Genie set a red highball glass down in front of me and kicked at Rowdy's feet. "We didn't have confirmation until late this morning, Rowan. Don't worry, it was all carefully orchestrated."

"Yes," said Tim, standing with George to my left. "I made sure my office knew I was headed to the moon on my vacation, and Homeland has unfortunately been gunning for Oz ever since he revealed he was a Red Orbiter. The president and his cronies took this opportunity to try to take us both out, as we expected they would."

"Because everyone already knew about the North Rim of the Grand Canyon being a space launch portal," I murmured, turning to Rowdy and Genie. "And you two were recently in DC gathering intel at that Christmas party."

"And, as expected," said Win from the screen, "the moron-in-chief is already claiming media footage of an MQ-9 Reaper dropping a bomb on you in a national park is fake. Problem is, twenty minutes before it happened, he was busy tweeting." Win read from the phone in his hand. "Bad things are going to happen soon to Red Orbiters and their friends. Explosive things. Many people are saying."

"No way did he spell *explosive* correctly, or *friends*," I said, sipping my delicious drink and feeling quite mellow despite the news.

"The media is now showing footage of the American bomb on the White House doorstep, along with the lasered message," said Rauc. "They also confirmed the drone previously transporting the bomb has crashed at a military bombing range."

"So what's the plan as we head into the seventh-inning stretch?" I asked. "Because I know you wouldn't be sending me to the moonship with my critters if the president could launch another missile at us, right?"

"Affirmative, Copper," said Rauc, and I could see his lips twitch, yummy lips I missed already.

My limbs began to feel like limp noodles, and my head got all woozy. Oh no…

Voice upon voice upon voice crashed into my ears as if blasting from a thousand TVs. I jumped up, sloshing my drink and startling poor Bodie, who hopped from the couch and ran down the corridor as I yelled, "Make it stop! Make the voices stop!"

"I'll get the dog," said Rowdy, chasing after him. "He probably has to pee now, anyway."

Genie and George flanked me, gently pushing me back onto the couch.

"It's okay, Rowan," said George. "You just got too relaxed and didn't block all the aliens out there. We're headed into space, so too many of them are closer than ever."

"Why didn't I think about that when I agreed to go to the moon?" I panted.

"Rowan, listen to me." Genie took hold of my wrists. "Focus inward, and picture your inner ears. Zero in on that spot you can feel throbbing, behind your jaw. Concentrate and flow into the spiral, following it to its center. Let your mind move deeper into the circle, seeking silence."

I breathed deeply, absorbing Genie's words, pushing through the near-painful ear-ringing that crowded in, my defense mechanism. "So I should try to get past the ringing?" I squeezed my eyes shut.

"You won't need the ringing, Rowan, if you can reach the center. Keep trying, and eventually you will," said Rauc. "It may take time, but there are those on the moonship who can help you with this."

I opened my eyes to see Rauc smiling at me from the screen and Genie's Jessica Rabbit curves standing over me. I giggled, remembering how her enormous boobs had once smothered me to shield me from crazed, armed bigots who hated us both.

I didn't hear sweet silence, but the ringing subsided somewhat, and voices and electronic beeping no longer bombarded my ears. Except for one snarky voice that had started it all, this crazy reality in which I lived.

"Oh great, now she's giggly. You didn't zap her with bug juice did you?" said Rowdy as he returned with my precious Bodie, whose tail was now happily wagging.

Chapter 12

"Bodie took just fine to the pet pod, even figured out the doggie door on his own!" said Rowdy as my pup put his head in my lap.

"The pod is great, Rowan, and you'll wish you had one at home, but you will on the moonship as part of your suite," said George. "It simulates the outdoors with bushes and grass for dogs and a sandpit for Morris. And the best part is it has a magnetized pressure-cleaning system every few hours."

"Oh good, because Bodie thinks cat poop is a treat. Speaking of which, there's dog cookies in one of those small bags I brought. I think he wants one, but my legs feel wobbly."

"On it!" said Rowdy heading out of the area. "Did you tell her about the CCS Block going bye-bye yet?"

I looked pointedly at Rauc and Win on-screen. Rauc said, "Their satellite communications blocking device, previously employed against the moonship, has been destroyed. Necessary, because they claimed they would not attempt to use it again to jam transmissions but were in fact planning to do so momentarily."

"Also," said Win, "Maggie is using that marvelous spacecraft you're in to systematically wipe out Space Force satellite communications ability."

"We're obliterating them in space?" I said.

"Only until after the inauguration of our new president and vice president. But the CCS Block definitely is no more."

I looked at Tim, soon to be ex-DHS. "You're okay with this?"

"Yes," he said. "It's an electronic weapon, and it's not nondestructive as claimed. The US doesn't get to control space and everything and everyone in it. We aren't in charge of the universe."

"Wow, you really have come over to the enlightened side," I said.

"It doesn't help when your own country tries to drop a bomb on you. Or uses spy drones intended for warfare overseas against American citizens on US soil. Like you've been trying to tell me, Rowan"—Tim smiled—"Fourth Amendment violations have gotten way out of hand since 9/11, and this administration has taken it to dangerous extremes."

"Along those lines," I said, looking at the screen again. "What are we doing to ensure no more missiles are launched at the moonship or to prevent another bomb aimed at us?"

"Other than a very severe and bizarre windstorm taking place at a certain air base? With vicious dust devils preventing takeoff of MQ-9 Reapers or anything else?" Win chuckled.

"Greens are not happy campers that a bomb was dropped on the spacecraft you're in, Rowan, and you know what vindictive little buggers they can be," said Rowdy, returning with two dog cookies for Bodie.

"Are Greens also abducting paramilitary thugs like those that nabbed me and Mom?"

Win nodded. "Systematically, in cities across the country, wherever they're used to wreak terror. And any and all ammunition, including rubber bullets and tear gas. All weapons frowned upon by the Geneva Conventions are being confiscated," he said.

"Yikes. What's happening to the thugs? Are their minds being messed with?"

"Can't say for sure at this point, because we don't control Greens either." Win grinned at Tim. "The first few that returned clearly did not have their short-term memories erased, as they told terrifying tales of capture by little green forest people, followed by interrogation and probing by evil gray creatures. No one believes them, of course, and thinks they're delusional."

"As for your missile concerns, Copper," said Rauc, smiling at me from the screen in a way that made me wish we were alone, "it was necessary for Red Orbiters to intervene, though you know we don't do so unless the situation is critical."

"Please tell me Greens aren't snatching missiles too," I said, gripping Bodie's fur.

"No. But all launch codes have been scrambled and changed, and will be regularly until the inauguration. Also, those MQ-9 Reapers, or the ones that survive the Greens' dust devil attack, will no longer be remotely controllable in any capacity by any entity in the US. They are grounded, indefinitely, from Earth's airspace."

"Wow. Our nation really has become persona non grata. So much for the Space Farce's attempt at galaxy domination. Will we ever learn?" I shook my head and drained my cocktail.

"In the US's defense, it isn't only us being stupid," said Tim. "But we're supposed to be leaders, not conquerors."

"That's where you come in, Copper, and a key reason you're headed to the moonship with George and Tim. Your nation is in violation of the 1967 Outer Space Treaty and needs your help in persuading the government on how best to remedy the situation," said Rauc.

"And to determine the future fate of Space Force," added Win. "So get out your mighty pen and your intergalactic diplomacy hat."

"Or a baseball bat," snarked Rowdy.

Chapter 13

"This is a lot to take in, Rowan," said George. "Do you want me to show you to your room? It has a bed so you can lie down."

"I'd just end up researching this treaty Rauc mentioned, which I have no clue about so how am I supposed to help? And I've got too many questions bouncing around my brain."

Rauc smiled. "That can wait until you get settled on the moonship, Copper."

"About that three-strikes thing"—I frowned—"if today's bombing attempt was three, what were the first two? The missile at the moonship was strike one, right? But snatching me and Mom wasn't really on the same level as those two maniacal crimes, so what was strike two?"

Rauc and Win looked at each other, Rauc with unease, Win with his usual poker face. Rowdy said, "Ruh-roh!"

"Remember the protesters outside during the Omni convention?" said Rauc.

"I never saw them, but yes, I knew they were there. Part of the armed anti-alien vigilantes, right?"

"Yes, a mix of that and others frenzied into action by the president's brother and others."

"Okay, what happened and why didn't you tell me? You Red Orbiters and your secrets!" I huffed as Genie brought me another cocktail, saying, "Red Orbiter *male* secrets. I told them we should tell you, but did they listen to me?"

"Because there was nothing to tell," said Rowdy, giving Genie the evil eye. "It was during your speech to introduce Warren O'Neill as the next vice president, Rowan. Win, Roger, and I took them down before anything could happen. We had intel on the inside, remember?"

"Yes, you had eyes and ears inside the Executive Office Building and White House. So what was their aim if this was no big deal?" I sipped my drink.

Rowdy had the wherewithal to flinch, which was somewhat gratifying.

Win spoke up from on-screen, his voice steely, "Two of them were tasked to kill Congressman O'Neill. And Cassandra—Senator Rojas-Ortiz. They were standing together backstage listening to your speech."

My stomach lurched. "I always wondered why nothing happened during the convention, what with the president being so tweaked about anyone daring to run against him, not to mention diverse, otherworldly candidates."

"He's even more desperate now that he lost the election and is facing multiple criminal indictments," said Tim, pacing the room. "That's why he tried to use you. A last-ditch attempt to remain in office."

"How on earth was I going to enable that?" I took another sip of my cocktail. "And I'd better eat something soon or you'll have to carry me onto the moonship."

"His twisted psychosis sought to use your imprisonment to force O'Neill and the president-elect to announce they cheated in the election—then he'd claim he actually won," explained Win.

"More projection from the pathological liar! And how dare that scumbag think he was going to put me in jail. What was the plan, some sort of military prison? And my mother too? Has the Air Force no shame?" I shifted on the couch, my knees bumping Rowdy and making Bodie hop down.

"We would never have let them get you behind bars, Copper," said Rauc.

"Do you want another CBD capsule?" asked George, hovering over me.

"No! At this point I might start hallucinating. No wonder I'm being shuttled off to the moon. No telling how many HUMANS FIRST! militias are also at the ready to do the president's bidding and try to scoop me up. Does anyone have any good news, anything not alarming or unnerving, making me want to run screaming away from reality?" I said frantically, then lowered my voice so as to not rouse my critters. "Oh wait! I'm already sort of doing that by flying to the moon."

"Well, there is more to the story," said Win, grinning. "And part of it you might like. The narcissist-in-chief also wanted to force Senator Rojas-Ortiz to resign and leave Washington. Because she's slated to become the next attorney general of the United States, who will preside over his prosecution, and her predecessor's."

"Well, that's certainly worth toasting!"

"The other good news is we have pizza and eggplant parmesan that Octavius provided from his Oregano Wortnik bistro, along with Red Orbiter red wine!" said Genie.

"Red Orbiters have their own wine? You've been holding out on me again." I frowned at Rauc on-screen.

"No, I haven't, Copper. O.W. recently expanded his illustrious enterprises beyond Planet Wynne and bought a vineyard and winery. Now get your sassy butt to the dining area and eat something," Rauc said, looking like he wished he could get his hands on me.

"We are so going wine-tasting when I get back from the moon!" I said.

Chapter 14

Maggie joined us for a meal on what looked like a retro fifties kitchen table with aluminum legs, but it was pale green, not pink like the one in my craft room, which actually did come from the fifties and a Maryland farmhouse.

"What do you think, Rowan? I figured you might get a kick out of the theme."

"It reminds me of that cartoon, *The Jetsons*. And I love the color scheme. Are you reliving the fabulous fifties in some capacity?" I had to tease Maggie, because she was also 125 years old but chose to stall in her thirties like her brother, Roger.

"Certainly not when it comes to the limited role of women back then!" said Genie.

"Boy howdy," I said.

"Hey, don't knock Mrs. Jetson! She was hot for a housewife! And they did, after all, have red hair!" said Rowdy.

"Please don't tell me that in addition to being Superman and Roger Ramjet, Roger was also the alien who inspired George Jetson?"

"Not hardly." Genie snorted. "Can you imagine Roger married with children? I shudder to think!" Genie and Roger were once an item.

"Why is that so hard to picture?" said Rowdy. "So what if he decides to have kids?"

Genie touched Rowdy's forehead. "You're beginning to worry me, Rowdy. Were you abducted and replaced with a normal male?"

Rowdy swatted her hand away. "Too bad Roger isn't here to help me defend our honor. And the Jetsons *were* patterned after Red Orbiters. So there."

"Who are the Jetsons?" asked Tim, taking a bite of pizza.

"Seriously, Maggie, you need to teach your millennial male here all the cool things from days gone by," I said. "But I need to clarify, I was a baby when that show was originally on. I saw reruns."

"By cool things, you mean like Star Wars?" asked Tim.

I touched my hand to Tim's forehead. "Now I'm beginning to worry about you. There will be no worshipping of Darth Vader in my presence."

George said to me, "Remember watching the show and thinking how wild it was that Mrs. Jetson pulled prepared food from a little door in a wall? Hello, microwave oven!"

"Yes, but wasn't she still wearing a 'little woman' apron? At least they had martinis. And a dog!" I said, petting Bodie who was underneath the table, begging for scraps. "What was that big dog's name?"

"Astro," said George.

"That's my cat's name!" said Tim, beaming. "See, I'm with it!"

"Now you sound like my mother. I am exceedingly concerned," I said, sipping wine.

"Speaking of your mom," said Genie, "are you well-fortified enough with this delish Cabernet to hear who was behind you getting grabbed off the curb in Vegas?"

"I don't know, am I?" I said, peering into my glass and wondering about wine. "Who first made wine in the universe? Is it debated like it is on Earth?"

"Red Orbiters for sure," said Genie. "And not just from grapes!"

"Okay, I'm ready. Hit me with more bad news."

"It was the attorney general who authorized and orchestrated your arrest and detainment," said Rowdy, sounding serious, which was disturbing.

"Except I wasn't actually arrested! I heard not one word of Miranda, and I know there's no way they had a warrant! That fat fascist is a master Pinocchio puppeteer! It's he who wants to remain in power!"

"Are you sure you don't want another CBD?" asked George.

I glared at my friend and then giggled, realizing he was being funny. "Maybe I could use a little more wine. And hey"—I looked at Genie and Rowdy—"is that why you nailed his butt at that Christmas party? I figured you were after the vice president because of his constant refrain about anyone with alien DNA being an affront to God and against the laws of nature."

"The VP *is* an abomination of nature," said Genie. "But no, we were there merely to listen, at least that was the plan. The rest was pure karma—or payback justice. And what we learned was they were planning to nab you; we just didn't know when. And we learned why."

"Do I want to know? It was something I wrote, wasn't it?"

"Boy howdy!" Rowdy mimicked me. "All your newspaper columns about legal professional ethics being violated by White House lawyers and the DOJ under this particular attorney general, including FBI violations of the Fourth Amendment. Apparently he read them."

"And got triggered," I said. "Because we all know he has no professional ethics. I also wrote columns about him protecting his twenty-two million dollars. And about how as attorney general, he was supposed to be America's top lawyer and crime fighter, not the president's personal fixer and partner in crime."

"Well, at least one of his crimes is now being splashed across the news," said Genie, touching her throat.

"Oh gosh," I gasped. "I never asked if you were okay after being attacked!"

"Please," scoffed Genie. "You should have seen the other guy. Especially after Rowdy explained it wasn't manly for sanctimonious members of the Conservative Society of hypocritical bible-quoting fiends to attack women who say no to their sexual advances."

Before we left the table, Oz popped into my ear from the control room. "Rowan, come take a gander at what it looks like in space, and I want to chat with you, just us. And tell the others they better save me some pizza."

I stood. "Oz wants me to come see outer space. Doesn't it just look all dark and scary?"

"It will be fine. You'll get to see Earth, and later the moonship as we approach," said Maggie. "And tell Oz I've safeguarded half a pizza and some eggplant parmesan for him."

Okay, so it was creepy to realize Maggie heard Oz in *my* ear. Was she some sort of super alien like her brother?

Chapter 15

I wound my way through corridors back to the control room, surprised I didn't get lost, but Bodie and Morris inevitably followed me, and probably already knew the way. Oz was in the pilot's seat and beckoned me to sit next to him.

"Here ya go, kiddo. Take a look at your home planet!"

I sat and stared at the swirling deep-blue greens of Earth. Tears filled my eyes as I gripped Oz's arm. "Who would have ever thought I'd be sitting here with a renowned astronaut, out in space, staring at Earth?"

"You are worthy of this sight, Rowan, and important. That's why I wanted to talk to you alone. You need to stop selling yourself short, and believe in your abilities. We need you."

"You mean my hearing capabilities? I don't even know how to fully use those yet, and it still wigs me out most of the time."

"That's not what I mean at all," said Oz, his own huge ears waggling when he turned to me, turquoise eyes intense. "It's about your writing skills, your background as a lawyer, and your passionate public speaking abilities."

"Oh no," I said, shaking my head. "Not the lawyer thing. That was for the military, and my area was environmental law. Not whatever this space law stuff is they've cooked up."

"Rowan." Oz grasped my hands, and I wondered if he was still paying attention to flying this spacecraft. "NASA astronauts were always considered to be a kind of ambassador, even though they never dealt with other life forms while in space—or not that they knew of anyway." The elder Red Orbiter winked, and I giggled. "You have the opportunity to be an ambassador as well. For Earth, working matters of diplomacy on the moonship."

"But I was a just a little kid when that outer space treaty Rauc referred to took place. What do I know about it?"

"The Constitution was ratified centuries before you were born, but you know a great deal about it."

"What are you getting at, Oz? Aren't there thousands of skilled lawyers who could do whatever needs doing on the moonship?"

"There are plenty of lawyers. But you're only the third American lawyer to go aboard."

"How's that possible?" I racked my brain and realized both Oliver Warnock, my law professor who started the Other Worldly Coalition, and his daughter, Olivia, who was married to a Red Orbiter physicist, had traveled to the moon.

"Olivia Warnock would do it if she could, but she just won her senate race in Maryland and is on her way to Congress," said Oz. "Oliver thinks you should do this. He said, and I quote, 'We don't need some hotshot litigator for this role. We want someone with heart and passion and dedication to the cause.'"

"The cause?" I swallowed, flattered and flabbergasted.

"The cause you took up since day one in your newspaper columns, then in your personal dealings with Red Orbiters: helping humans on Earth understand their extraterrestrial heritage."

"And not be hellbent on annihilating aliens?" I added, smiling.

"Boy howdy," said Oz, waggling his bushy white eyebrows.

Morris leapt onto the rim of a panel of controls near another screen. "Um, Oz? My cat's sitting on a big red button. Please tell me it's not a problem."

He laughed. "That rolls back a layer of the roof, like our orbs. Now everyone in the lounge area can see space up above."

"Like a moon roof in a car," I said. "Except we can't stick our heads out."

I returned to the aforementioned lounge to find Rowdy, George, and Tim sprawled on the couches watching not outer space above, but the big screen, now showing a movie.

"I can't believe you're watching *Spaceballs* while we're headed to the moon," I said.

"What?" said Rowdy, his all-innocence face firmly in place. "We told you that's how Rauc and I learned your language, watching movies."

I rolled my eyes as George hopped up, grinning. "Why don't I show you where your room is, so you can nap if you want? Genie's resting, and I might too, after I take a peek at Earth as well. Was it amazing?"

"You'll love it. Do show me my room, because I want to check my phone. But I don't know if I can lie down."

"Why do you look so worried?" He asked in the corridor.

"It's silly," I said as George showed me into a suite not unlike a hotel room, with bed and bathroom, though the main door had a built-in pet panel.

Bodie leapt on the bed and rolled over, splayed out. I sat and rubbed his belly.

"What is it, Rowan?" said George.

"It's just that, on planes, if it's dark and I fall asleep, I wake up freaking out when I realize I'm traveling way up in the sky and could come plummeting down at any minute."

George chuckled and sat next to me, petting Morris, who caterwauled for attention.

"Hey! I'm not like you, Mr. Super Physicist. I've never fully understood how a plane can remain in open air without dropping—but don't you dare explain to me how it works!"

George laughed, blond dreadlocks swaying. "Good thing I brought CBD for the moonship. You're a kick, Rowan. Here I thought you were worried about hearing voices again."

"That too," I grumped. "And how much do you know about whatever it is they want us to do up there? How do you feel about this role of space ambassador?"

George shrugged. "It's my military background, and yours too. Although I was merely in the Navy. You were a lawyer for the very entity we're dealing with in this Space Force fiasco."

"The Air Force?" I snorted. "I'm not sure I can be diplomatic about them. I have issues."

George cracked up.

"I mean it! I have no patience for being a diplomat. You know I'm as likely to inform someone that yes, they do have *stupid* written all over their face as I am to placate or disarm."

George, still chuckling, said, "Did you ever hear about how I got myself and my men kicked off of Diego Garcia when I was a Navy commander?"

"Yes," I said, dying for him to finally reveal what I'd wondered about for years.

"Well, I still can't tell you why. Suffice to say it involved a lack of diplomacy. But apparently it's not being held against me on the moonship, so let's just go with the flow. I mean, would you have thought you'd also be working with a DHS agent? Plus, I can't wait to meet exotic alien women."

As he spoke, an exotic-looking calico cat strolled in through the pet door. The sound of my critters reacting was ear-piercing, but I could hear Tim calling. "Astro! Where'd you go?"

Chapter 16

Astro the kitty took one look at Morris, hissing and arching, plus Bodie leaping off the bed in her direction, and hightailed it back out the pet door in a multicolored streak. She was followed by my multicolor border collie mix and orange-and-white tabby.

George and I flew out the door and ran into a frazzled Tim.

"They're headed for the pet pod. And Astro probably thinks it's her safe sanctuary," he panted.

"Whoa ho!" Rowdy said from down the corridor. "If it isn't O.K. Critter Corral in space, a true Animal Planet smackdown!"

We ran toward his voice and found him peering through a transparent wall, grinning.

When I saw the two cats were using Bodie's head for what looked like a punching bag with their paws, I screeched, "Rowdy Wilde, you go in there and get my poor dog! He isn't mean! He only chases kitties when they run!"

"I'm not stomping around in cat poop," said Rowdy. "These are new shoes."

"*Shoes?* You sound like my mom!"

Bodie was now sort of fighting back with his mouth open, nipping and lunging, so I called out, "Bodie, come here boy. Mama's here!"

Bodie looked up and got bopped on the nose.

Rowdy said, "You're making him lose his concentration."

I told Rowdy he was going to lose more than that if he didn't help, so he showed me how to open a human-sized door, and out came Bodie, but he stopped to pee on a bush first.

I knelt down to hug him, but he was all happy, tongue hanging out and tail wagging as if to say, "There's a girl kitty in there!"

Said girl kitty was now circling and squaring off with my boy kitty, making Tim clear his throat. "Uh, Rowan? Is Morris fixed?"

"Yes! He was adopted from a shelter so he came that way."

Genie stumbled into the hall, roused from her nap. "What the hell is going on?" She was wearing nothing but an oversized t-shirt, making all three men stop, dumbstruck.

"Are *you guys* fixed?" I tossed out over my shoulder, taking Bodie back to my room for a cookie, figuring Morris would find his way back when he was ready.

I heard George say, "I think the engineer forgot to factor in indiscriminate use of neighbor's pet doors. And potential promiscuity."

I sat on my bed to read my first text from Mom on the new device, her timing uncanny as usual.

"Doodles, are you there yet??? How are my grandanimals??? Did they like the space ride??? Weather here cloudy and windy. Ugh. How is your weather? Are you resting, my dear??? (dog, cat, moon, cloud, heart, kissy face emoji)"

I texted her back so she wouldn't get anxious. "Not there yet. Morris and Bodie are fine and making friends with another cat onboard. I saw Earth from space and waved to you! Love to you and Dad. (cat, dog, earth, heart, smiley face emoji)"

I fed Bodie and Morris, who'd found his way back inside the room sans Astro, and thought I might try to rest for a spell.

***

I awoke with a jolt, thinking I heard voices, but my ears rang like fire alarms. It took a second to realize I wasn't hearing actual alarms, and then I was hearing Oz's voice in my ear.

"Rowan, dear, time to come take a look at the moon, up close and personal."

My critters scattered as I scrambled from the very comfortable bed, a brilliant alien concoction devoid of springs or foam. Grabbing one of my smaller bags, I unearthed my toothbrush and spent a few minutes in the bathroom, also an alien production involving magnetized pressure as opposed to water.

It had a high-tech version of the potty on Rauc's orb, so I was sort of used to it, but I wondered if I needed to inquire if it was a danger to Morris. The cat had a tendency to stick his paw in the toilet at home while it flushed. Felines were evidently not an overly enlightened alien species despite hailing from another galaxy.

Not bothering to try to untangle my hair, I headed to the control room, meeting George and Tim in the corridor.

"This is really happening!" said Tim, his handsome face looking ten instead of thirty. I knew just how he felt.

George took my hand, giving it a squeeze as we stood in front of a screen filled with the sphere of my beloved moon, the patterns on its surface so familiar. Comforting shades of gray.

Had I known this was my future? Had I been waiting to visit the place I'd spoken to as a child, fervently revealing my truths only to finally learn the moon's inner truth? It was no longer a celestial body due to destructive war millennia ago—the reenactment of which was the very thing I was traveling here to help prevent. I couldn't let my nation's actions—the machinations of a maniacal moron with a sinister agenda—destroy this place.

"We're going to be traveling around it," said Maggie. "So you'll get some unusual views, not visible from Earth."

"Will we see any American flags placed by space crews?"

"Negative," said Maggie. "The US has actually placed a total of six flags on the moon, and they aren't the only nation to do so. But all were in violation of the Outer Space Treaty, given they didn't know the moon is a spaceship."

"That treaty again," I murmured. "I'm really going to have to bone up."

"So what happened to the flags?" asked Tim.

"Removed by residents once the moon was revealed as a spaceship," said Oz.

"So is it going to feel like landing on an aircraft carrier in the middle of an ocean? Will my face feel like it's flying backwards at warp speed?" I asked. "And where are we landing?"

Oz grinned. "I forgot you worked for the Navy, too. You won't feel much at all as we glide slowly into the moonship, where we will hover before touching down. No throttling brakes, no tailhook catching."

"It's getting darker," said Tim.

"Yes, because of where we're landing," said Maggie, smiling.

"Of course!" said George. "We're going where those on Earth cannot see us embark."

"What do you mean?" I asked, peering at the screen, where it was in fact becoming more difficult to see the moon, until Maggie must have engaged some intensely bright headlights.

"Rowan, get ready for a Pink Floyd moment," said George. "We are now entering…the dark side of the moon!"

Chapter 17

Owen Marsden, who I'd probably always think of as Owen the Marine even though he no longer was one, was there to greet us when we emerged from the spaceship into an area nothing like the flight deck of an aircraft carrier because it was enclosed. And quiet.

Quiet except for Morris, who was not happy he'd been wrangled back into his carrier and was letting everyone know it. His caterwauling exacerbated the extreme ringing in my ears, but I didn't care.

"Show me everything! I want to see it all!" I said, hugging Owen, whose black hair was no longer a regulation military crewcut but fell nearly to his shoulders in layered waves.

"Let's get you to your suite first. I'll take you there, and you can meet up with the others later. Is that your luggage? We'll load it into the transpod."

"Transpod? Is everything going to be called a pod here?"

Owen smiled a small, unnervingly sexy smile. Good thing the dude was gay, because with that hair and those azure eyes, he was major interstellar eye candy.

"Transpods come in various sizes and will carry you all over the moonship. Up, down, and around."

"Do they have those little motion sickness bags like on airplanes?" I eyed the vessel we entered and waved goodbye to my space mates traveling in their own transpods, which reminded me of the clear tubes used for drive-through lanes at banks. Except this was the size of a passenger van and had cushy seats, onto which Bodie immediately hopped.

I felt a whoosh as we moved upward, but I didn't feel queasy. We curved onto what was like a highway, with other transpods whizzing by in the opposite direction. Trying to focus on them did make my eyes feel funny, though, so I pet Bodie and looked at Owen. *Be still, my beating heart—and hormones.*

"Your hair sure looks different from the last time I saw you," I said.

His smile suggested secrets swirled in—were they really purple?—eyes underneath what had to be double-rowed eyelashes, which wasn't fair on a guy.

"Our hair grows quickly," he said.

"Our?"

"Labyrinthians. Now, first thing is we need to have you meet with someone who can assist with your ear issues. How soon would you like me to arrange it after your sleep?"

"Oh, I don't feel sleepy, and how'd you know about my ear issues?"

That smile again. "A little birdie must have told me."

"Was the birdie's name Rowdy?"

The doors to the transpod slid open as we stopped. A similar sliding door opened in a wall, and we walked into my suite, which appeared to be an empty space about the size of a small efficiency apartment with an area that resembled a kitchen.

"Why is there no furniture?" I asked, expecting there to at least be a bed.

"You get to pick that out yourself," said Owen. "But yes, you do have a bed. It's in here, next to the bathroom." We walked through an archway to the bedroom.

"That bed is round. And huge," I said. "Bodie and Morris will love it, but sheets are going to be difficult to wrangle onto that mattress."

"It doesn't use sheets and isn't a mattress, not like you're used to anyway. And there's a pressurized cleaning system, which will help with pet hair, for sure. And here's a closet for you, with racks and drawers and shelves. Everything you should need."

"That is one impressive walk-in closet. And the bathroom! Is that lapis lazuli tile?"

"No, it would be too heavy. It's actually a lightweight mineral, similar to corral, from a distant star. In blues and greens, your favorite?" Owen raised his brows at me.

"How did you know that? Another little birdie?"

"Your critters have found the pet pod!" Owen grinned.

"Great, we can literally watch each other pee," I said, because the pet pod shared a transparent window with my bathroom.

Owen laughed. "You need to lie down soon, Rowan."

"But I don't feel all that tired. And I want to get started on this Outer Space Treaty issue. Can you get me a copy of it?"

"You'll have everything you need, but you must sleep. You'll soon be space-lagged. It's adrenaline keeping you upright at the moment."

"Space-lagged? Is that like jet-lagged?"

"Yes, but more intense. You'll sleep about twenty-seven hours or more, adjusting to the distance you traveled and the moon's orbital period."

"Like the twenty-four-hour day-night cycle of the Circadian rhythm? I guess the moon really does continue to orbit, even though it's a spaceship."

"Yes," he smiled, making my lower belly feel tickly. "The ship spins on its axis, like the moon once did, every 27.3 days. It also takes roughly the same amount of time to orbit Earth, which it has to do to not freak out humans like yourself. It's that orbital period that keeps the same side of the moonship facing Earth, keeping it tidally docked."

"And keeps one side of the moon always dark?" I said, yawning.

Owen shook his head. "There's not actually a dark side of the moon. It's the far side, or backside, as in it is farthest from Earth and is not ever seen. But when the moon is between Earth and the sun during the new moon phase, the far side is bathed in daylight. You'll be able to see it from the top deck, which has a transparent roof and is much like an indoor greenhouse. With agricultural fields, parks, even a baseball diamond. You'll exercise Bodie there, or go on romantic picnics," he teased.

"Great, just what I need, romance." I smirked and yawned again, feeling woozy.

"What you need right now is to get in that bed."

"Thash not very romantic." My words slurred. "I have to—"

“I’ll feed the critters, and they’ll likely sleep almost as long as you do. Do you want to change clothes? Shower? If so, you’d better do it soon.”

“Okay, but I freshened up before we—”

Those were the last words I remembered uttering.

Chapter 18

When I awoke, Morris was in my face and Bodie sprawled at my feet chewing on what sounded like a bone but was the color of cheddar cheese, and I was pretty sure I heard a pinging noise from my space phone that had to be a text from Mom. So, pretty normal, but I was in a round bed inside the moonship, fully clothed except for shoes and bra. And if Owen the gorgeous Marine removed my bra, I was not leaving this suite even if I did need furniture.

"What are you chewing on, Bodie?" I said as I unearthed my phone from one of my small suitcases inside my closet.

Sure enough, Mom had texted, "Hi moon girl Doodles! Phil said you would be sleeping, but I thought you'd be awake by now. Do they have coffee? How's the weather? Cold and cloudy here. Ugh. (moon, cloud, coffee cup, heart, smiley face emoji)"

Mom had sure gotten the hang of the new phone quickly. I questioned aloud, "Is there coffee?" Why hadn't I thought to ask about something so important?

"Good morning, Rowan!" said Genie in my ear. "Sorry to pop in, but I was waiting to hear if you'd woken, and yes, there is a coffee maker, similar to what you're used to. I'm also now at your door if you want to let me in."

I stumbled into the living area, Bodie and Morris nearly tripping me as they came along. "How do I open this door?"

"Button on the wall to the right."

I hit the button, and the door slid open to Genie Jessica Rabbit dressed in something red that looked so much like a *Star Trek* uniform, I laughed. Except it had a patch of the moon, not Starfleet.

"I know, right?" she said, strolling in and petting the critters. "But believe me, this is not made out of cheap, Earth-pajama fabric. It breathes, baby! Later I can show you how to program the door to respond to your voice command so you can say, 'Come!' like Captain Picard."

She went to my kitchen area, pointing out a device resembling my Keurig at home.

"Are uniforms color coded like on *Star Trek*? Is red worn by the femme fatale team?"

"Ha! I wish. But it is the color for the security detail. Maggie and Rowdy also wear red."

"And Oz? What will he wear?"

"Kind of a taupe color, for leaders and diplomats. It's what Owen had on yesterday."

"How did I not notice this getup on Owen? I must have been totally out of it." I sighed. "He is too damn yummy, period."

Genie laughed, opening a drawer full of coffee pods. "Here's a variety of flavors for you, and the pods are biodegradable. There's a giant composting facility on the top deck. You'll be amazed at how self-sufficient the moonship is." She handed me coffee that smelled divine in a mug with a moon on it. How tickled was I?

"It's pistachio-cherry flavored, like our Red Orbiter liqueur!" she said.

"This is tasty. And I have so much to learn, but first, please tell me it was you who removed my bra and not Owen the Marine?"

"That's what you call him? Too funny. And yes, it was me, because I figured you wouldn't want to sleep in it, but Owen took off your shoes, after he grabbed you before you hit the floor. He said you fell asleep in midsentence. Then he sent for me to help."

"Mortifying. Do Red Orbiters get space-lagged too?"

"Not really, but I did sleep about ten hours the first night. You slept thirty hours. George and Tim slept a little less than you, so they've been up since before dawn. We'll all meet for an early dinner. And George wants you to help him pick out furniture."

"What's up with the furniture thing? And what day is it?"

"We arrived December 28 around midnight. It took us longer to get here because of Maggie working on taking out that CCS Block, which required us to travel around some in space. Then you slept forever, so it's just after seven in the morning on the thirtieth."

"Oh good, I didn't miss New Year's Eve," I said. "Not that it matters around here."

"For furniture, you get to choose whatever's useful for you. Make it like home, or pick something you'd like to try."

"What do you have?"

"Chaise lounges in bold colors. And a portable kitchen unit, what you call an island, because I like to bake."

"How domesticated of you. I won't want one of those."

"Speaking of domesticated, there's something I need to talk to you about that's really wigging me out."

"I'm intrigued," I said, making myself another cup of coffee. "But I desperately need to shower and detangle my hair."

"We can easily chat while you do so. This hearing gift you have will work in the shower. Haven't you figured that out?"

I paused. "No, and before I knew better, I would've thought any voices I heard could see me and I'd have flipped out."

Genie laughed. "You've flipped out your share of Red Orbiters when they learned you could hear *them*. You're not exactly a typical human."

"I'll take that as a compliment!" I said as I headed for my bathroom, along with the critters, but stopped short. "Wait, I need to walk Bodie."

"Rowdy already did that for you. And brought him that chew toy he's gnawing on. We can take him out again once you're ready."

"Rowdy came in my room? While I was sleeping?" My voice squeaked.

"Calm down. I was with him. We can get in if we need to, especially for security issues, but I asked you to open the door because you were awake. I wouldn't just walk in on you."

Genie stayed in the main area of the suite while I continued into the bathroom. I stepped into the waterless, pressurized shower and said, "So what's got you discombobulated?" The mechanism was strange but efficient and quite pleasant, sort of like a soothing wind massage.

"Rowdy Wilde. He told me yesterday morning over coffee that he's decided he wants babies, and if I'm not interested, he will spend his time aboard the moonship choosing an ideal mother for his offspring."

Chapter 19

"This brings new meaning to the concept of lunacy," I said. "Rowdy's gone batshit crazy on the moon. What did you tell him?"

Genie sounded exasperated while I showered. "I told the lunatic that while his biological clock may be ticking, mine certainly isn't! Besides, no way does he really want kids. He's just got a wild hair up his butt because his sister and my brother are having triplets in the spring."

"He did say Ophelia and Bruce were naming one of them after him, as in Ferus."

"You see? Even his name means 'wild' in Latin! He is not cut out to be anyone's father! And I'm not exactly a poster child for mothering instincts. I'm a *spy*."

"There might be good parenting skills to be gleaned from spy craft."

Genie snorted, and it kind of tickled my ear. "You are not helping, Rowan! You're supposed to be on my side! You didn't choose to have kids, and I'm not sure I ever will either!"

"Okay, no problem. But quick question. Why were you and Rowdy having morning coffee together? A Red Orbiter meeting?" I stepped from the shower and reached for my coconut body butter. The silence from the bedroom was deafening.

"Are you still there, Genie?"

"Yes! And…hell. I slept with Rowdy."

Oh my gosh.

"Are *you* still there?" Genie asked.

"Yes, and now I know why you slept ten hours. I can only imagine how exhausting your evening must have been." I chuckled.

"I'm perfectly capable of wearing you out too, Rowan," drawled Rowdy in my ear. "But it might involve something different, something more in line with your proclivities."

"Rowdy Wilde, get out of my ear, you snooping pervert! I just got out of the shower!"

Genie heard me and yelled, “Rowdy, you swore you would not listen in on our conversations!”

“Then maybe you should stop repeating my name over and over, because you know I’m going to hear that. But I’ll go away now so you can tell Rowan how I rocked your world, Fireball.”

I heard that, and so did Genie apparently. She was standing in front of me, quivering with exasperation, as I headed for my closet.

“Fireball?” I asked.

“His nickname for me. You know Red Orbiters are big on that.” She snorted.

“Damn. No one’s ever called me a fireball.”

“Oh, I seriously doubt it,” said Genie. “We have the same hair, for starters.”

“So what happened? And did he really rock your world?” I was careful not to say Rowdy’s name—and also realized I needed to ask more about that. Could Red Orbiters automatically hear one another when their name was spoken?

“I don’t know how it happened!” Genie flapped her arms as her huge boobs bounced. “All those gigs we did together, and then posing as husband and wife. It just did, okay? And I am not going to elaborate on your other question when he might still be listening.” She crossed her arms. “Oh, what the hell?” She threw up her hands. “It was the most enthralling sex I’ve ever had, and it went on for hours, and then we talked for hours and did it some more, so I didn’t really sleep ten hours!”

“Then he had to ruin it by asking you to have his babies over coffee?”

“That’s the gist of it, yes.” Genie sighed. “I was utterly exhausted.”

She looked like a wilted voluptuous fairy, and I chuckled. “You don’t have to help me shop for furniture, Genie. You should take a nap instead. Plus, Owen was going to show me around the moonship once I woke up.”

“But that all happened yesterday!” Genie rallied. “Maggie wants to come shopping with us, and I told Owen to get you later this afternoon. That man is seriously hot. Too bad he doesn't want me to have *his* babies."

"As if you could! I suppose having Red Orbiter DNA that does not mix well with others can be a liability. Plus, Owen's gay. Wait a minute!" I spun around. "Please tell me *gay* doesn't mean something different on the moonship among Labyrinthians than it does on Earth?" I leashed Bodie, and we entered a transpod outside my door.

"Not that I know of." Genie shrugged. "It's still about preferring one gender over another here, but you know that doesn't mean it has to be exclusively, right? There are bisexuals from other worlds, just like human hybrids on Earth. Plus, what you call aliens can be transexual too. There are even some who haven't chosen one gender."

"Do you mean hermaphrodites?"

"That's an antiquated term. I think humans now call it *intersex*. And yes, it means someone born with reproductive organs of both sexes. Except, unlike on Earth, those babies aren't surgically turned into one gender or another by a parent or doctor's autocratic decision before they can have a say in the matter."

"So there are entities who are both male and female?" I gasped, fascinated, when the doors to our transpod slid open and Bodie bounded out toward what looked like an open field. He also ran into two people apparently waiting for us.

One was Owen. The other was someone who could have been Owen's twin, with flowing, glossy black hair and violet eyes. The difference was her almost translucently pale skin. She was starkly beautiful, if not surreal.

"Rowan, this is someone who can help you learn how to manage and understand your hearing abilities," said Owen.

Chapter 20

"Please call me Byrin," she said, not offering her hand. Handshaking was clearly an Earth thing, and dated at that.

"You mean like Lord Byron?" I asked, feeling like I was babbling because she was so compelling to look at, to be in the presence of.

Thank goodness she smiled. Her gaze was intense. "No, it derives from the word *Labyrinthian*, so it is spelled B-y-r-i-n."

"Ah. That's different, and…pretty," I stammered. "Seems almost Gaelic."

"Thank you. I like your name too, and the Rowan tree itself. I look forward to working with you. Let me know when you are ready." The formal cadence of her speech made clear that Earth's English was not her native tongue.

"Okay, I've got to get furniture today, and eat because I'm about starved at this point, but my dog needed walking, and is this some sort of dog park? And then I want to get with Owen right away—on this treaty thing I'm supposed to work on!" I was babbling like a brook.

Owen and Byrin smiled, making me feel even more foolish.

Genie came to my rescue. "Yes! This is a pet park, here on the top level where it's like the outdoors on Earth and benefits from sunlight through the transparent roof!" Genie was also babbling, and I gaped at her until I heard my phone ping.

"Oh my gosh I forgot to answer my mom's text, and now she'll probably think I never made it to the moon!"

Owen said, "There's a European-style café just across the way with outdoor seating, so you can grab a bite, answer your mom, and watch Bodie play where the area is enclosed for pets, like Genie said. As for the treaty thing"—he turned to me with a laser gaze—"there's someone else from Earth who will be working with us. He arrived late last night and is now sleeping, so let's plan to meet tomorrow. Take today to get situated."

"All right," I said, I wringing my hands. "But who are we working with?"

"You've already met him. Red MacLeod. From Scotland."

"Oh lord," I said.

"Is he in the House of Lords?" asked Byrin.

"Uh, not that I know of. I suppose he could be now. He used to be the US secretary of defense and resigned because of our ignoramus president, but he has a heavy brogue and wears a kilt and carries a dirk, and he might be MI6…" I was at it again with the verbal diarrhea.

"I can't vouch for the MI6 part," said Owen, smiling. "But he's here to represent Britain as well as the US on this issue. Go on and eat, and I'll come get you before dinner."

"Are you sure Bodie will be okay?"

"Absolutely. See look, he's playing with another dog now," said Owen, pointing.

I looked at my dog leaping about with a critter roughly his size, but thinner and tan-colored, with long pointed ears and a big nose. "That's not a dog! That's a coyote!"

"Yes," said Byrin. "Coyotes originate from a distant bright star."

"Wow! Are there Australian dingoes here too? Because Bodie is part Queensland heeler."

"You never know," said Owen, smiling his secret smile as he and Byrin walked away.

"I hope your mom wasn't too worried about you not answering her texts," Genie said as I finished typing on my phone. We were ordering food from devices that looked similar as we sat outside the café.

"She was fine once I told her how long I slept and that I'm having brunch while her granddog plays in a park. She complained about Dad eating all the ice cream and cookies, and is making full use of various moon emoji. So tell me, why were you babbling at Byrin too? And thank goodness there's familiar food on the menu because I'm too hungry to be culinarily adventurous."

"Do we want to order wine? It's French," said Genie, not answering my question.

"Will I still be able to function this afternoon and make it to dinner? Does alcohol affect you differently on the moonship? Because it kind of kicked my butt on the spaceship."

"That's because our Red Orbiter liqueur is like moonshine—no pun intended—when it comes to alcohol content. Plus you were hitting those CBDs and hadn't slept much the night before. Now you've snoozed enough for three people."

We chose crisp white wine, and I had little tea sandwiches like I'd once eaten at Harrods in London, with salmon and watercress. And given it was technically breakfast, I had a couple of pastries on the side—an almond croissant and a layered, cream thing that could easily compete with sex. It was that good.

"We are definitely coming back here for scones and clotted cream. Who knew eating would be so good on the moonship?" I said, finally feeling full. "But why are we the only ones out here? It's kind of creepy, especially since some robotic thing brought our food. And do I need to get Bodie water? He's going at it pretty good with that Westie out there."

"Westie?" asked Genie.

"West Highland terrier. Adorable little white dog."

"Oh," said Genie. "The park has water stations. You haven't noticed because you've been busy sucking up everything like a vacuum cleaner." She grinned. "We are alone out here because it's not a typical dining hour for residents. And don't worry, lots of culinary school students act as servers in the more formal restaurants, like where we'll have dinner."

"So, are you going to answer my question? Because I could tell Byrin made you nervous too. She's pretty intense, but I can't really discern why. It's not like she looks scary or mean."

"She's not," said Genie. "But she is many other things, including intuitive. She's a Labyrinthian, after all. Remember that focusing-and-finding-your-center thing I had you do when you panicked at too many voices? The technique comes from her. It's part of the work she does."

"Is she some sort of reiki practitioner like my friend Oapule?"

"Oh, I remember Oapule from Yearntown! She tried to save Rowdy and me when the idiot police chief opened fire on us in the grocery store parking lot."

"She didn't realize Red Orbiters can block bullets, because you keep that a secret."

"Yes, we do, for good reason. But about my babbling. It was because of what we were discussing when the transpod door opened and there they were, hearing you comment about entities that are both male and female." Genie took a sip of wine.

"You think Owen and Byrin heard me? Is it a bad thing, what we were talking about?"

"Yes, I suspect they heard you. And no, it's not a bad thing. I shouldn't tell you because it's Byrin's story to tell, but it's not a secret. I just don't want them thinking that's who we were talking about when the door opened."

"Why?" I swallowed the last of my croissant. "Oh my gosh, Byrin is both male and female. Is that it?"

Chapter 21

"There you are!" George called out, walking up to our table. "I really need furniture, and I didn't think you'd ever wake up. Owen said you fell asleep in midsentence."

"Owen is as bad a gossip as Rowdy," I grumped. "Are you hungry as usual? They've got European stuff here. You could get bratwurst or some other icky dish you're prone to devour." Skinny George possessed an unfair metabolism and overly brave palate.

"I already ate at a taco stand with far-out spices I'd never had before. On a level with a bunch of shops and restaurants. Where the furniture store is. With stuff to sit on."

"Okay, I get the hint. I'm officially your personal shopping assistant this afternoon."

"We have to meet up with Maggie too," said Genie, who also whispered in my ear, "And yes to your previous question about Byrin. We can talk more later."

The commerce deck, as I learned it was called, was huge, and the area we were in seemed sort of like a mall, but without crowds of loud, rude people and glaring lights and gross smells permeating stuffy air. Trees and other flora grew in giant pots here and there. Savory aromas wafted from a few food carts we passed. And luckily, there were transpods that zipped us from one locale to the next when it was too far to walk.

At a charming furniture boutique my sister and Mom would have loved, George got a couch and a crazy hammock that somehow attached to walls. He selected a kitchen island that looked like a diner counter, complete with a few stools. I went with a more traditional dining set, identical to the one Maggie had selected for the spaceship, with a green top and aluminum legs—or looked like aluminum. No telling what metal it really was. I figured I might as well live like a Jetson while I was here. Plus, Maggie was inordinately pleased.

I selected a teal couch in a microfiber of sorts that I hoped would survive Morris's claws. It was nice and cushiony, but I also got a turquoise-and-white-striped overstuffed chaise lounge that Genie said I'd love.

"Okay," I told her. "But I suspect it will end up being a very fancy dog bed, like a reading chair I once had that got taken over by my last pup. Blue was a black lab. The chair was pale yellow, so you can imagine what it looked like after a few years."

As for a writing desk, I instead got a large coffee table and a couple of end tables, assuming I'd do most of my writing sitting on the couch, like I often did at home. For my walls, I chose prints of amazing photos of the moon and one artistic rendition of Earth from space that enhanced the deep greens and blues of our beautiful planet.

"So how do we get this stuff to our suites?" I asked.

"I've scheduled it to be delivered via freight transpod in a few hours. That gives us time to shop for clothes because I need your help, Rowan," said Maggie.

At the mere mention of girl clothes shopping, George disappeared, saying thanks and he'd see me at dinner.

"How can I be of service?" I said. "And I wouldn't mind finding a few of those flowy tunic-like garments Byrin was wearing. They looked comfortable and beautiful."

"For starters, I want to pick out a dress for New Year's Eve, and then I need outfits that look businesslike, but the closest thing I've ever worn is a Marine Corps uniform."

"New Year's Eve? I thought that wasn't celebrated here."

"It's not, but Tim thought we should throw a New Year's party, and we're arranging for a private space at a restaurant."

"How I love that adorable man of yours," I said. "He is so making up for working for Homeland."

Maggie laughed, and I winced.

"What's wrong, Rowan? Why is your head cocked? You look pained," said Genie.

"It's voices. I think Red Orbiters are arguing about a cake, or cake flavors. Do they have weddings here on the moon? Is that what the deal is?"

"It could be culinary students. You really should meet with Byrin soon. I wouldn't put it off. You don't want to be distracted and overly stressed, and you'll definitely keep getting slammed with voices until you learn coping mechanisms," said Genie.

"She's right," said Maggie.

"Okay, stop ganging up on me. I'll get to it as soon as I start on this treaty thing. Is that why you need frumpy clothes, Maggie? I hope that won't be required of me, because I left constricting suits behind when I stopped being a lawyer."

Maggie smiled, but it was awkward. "No, it's not for that. I've got something else coming up on Earth, but I can't really talk about it yet."

"More Red Orbiter secrets?"

"No, because I don't know about it either," said Genie. "Maybe we can get Maggie drunk and pull details from her at our first girls' night next week."

"Can we use sodium pentothal too?"

Hours later, my feet were throbbing, so I bought flat shoes made of alien material that felt like the softest leather slippers. They looked like pointy skimmers I'd worn in the eighties, and I picked three pairs in bright green, magenta, and a deep purple blue that reminded me of Byrin's and Owen's eyes, though truth be told, I swear his had not been that alluring color when I first met him at OUTWARD in March.

"Are you sure you don't want a dress for New Year's?" asked Genie.

"No, I'm going to wear my teal-and-black one you helped me pick out for the convention. And I'm about shopped out today. I do love my tunics and the dress I got for dinner tonight, my first little party on the moon, and I'm envious of what you gals selected." Genie and Maggie both picked sexy, slinky cocktail dresses in forest green and midnight blue for tomorrow night.

"It's about time to head back for your furniture delivery anyway," said Genie.

"Yep, that's what we're for. Your friendly neighborhood burly guys, ready to arrange!" said Rowdy, strolling up with Owen.

Chapter 22

"There's not much arranging to do," I said to Owen and Rowdy. We were all standing in the suite with the freshly unloaded furniture. "But I'm glad you're here for heavy lifting. And I need to feed the critters before Morris gnaws the furniture."

"Cool artwork," said Rowdy as he hung my selections using a magnetic, hammer-and-nail-free mechanism I wished we had at home. "But you didn't get anything for your bedroom."

"I'm not done spending all of your gambling money. And stay out of my bedroom!" I teased, but sort of meant it. Rowdy was way too tricky of a spy, what with that goofy demeanor.

"Does that edict apply to me too?" asked Owen, smiling his secret smile that made my toes curl in my new shoes. I was starting to wonder how gay he really was.

"I'm out of your hair, gorgeous," said Rowdy, bussing me on the cheek. "But I'll see you at dinner, so do wear something sexy."

"He is such a poser," I said to Owen once Rowdy was gone. "But very good at his act."

"You think it's all an act?" asked Owen, sitting on my new couch, along with Bodie who already had his head in his lap.

"Of course. Rowdy prefers aliens to human hybrids. Plus, word has it he's in the market for someone to bear his children, and I'm not a Red Orbiter."

"Ah," said Owen, looking serious. "The DNA that does not mix well with others."

"I have questions for you." I sat down on the other side of Bodie.

"I was warned about this." Owen chuckled. "Interrogation time. Fire away. But dinner is in an hour."

"Yikes! Time is flying, and I still have to grocery shop."

"You can order stuff online for delivery. I'll show you how, and also how to schedule transpods, but first your questions."

"Great! Well, I know you have a degree in astrophysics, because George told me that's what you taught at the Naval Postgraduate School."

"I also have degrees in geology and geophysics."

"Wow. I love geology and became a bit of a rockhound—and gem hound—in college. It was my best friend's major. And speaking of major, as in your former rank, why did you become a Marine? I mean, I know we learned the Corps originated on Mars, much to everyone's shock, but you didn't know you were from Mars when you signed up."

"Sure I did."

"*What?*" Now I was shocked. "I thought you learned you have less than 1 percent human DNA when you took a spit test like the rest of us."

"No, I always knew I was a Labyrinthian from Mars. And 100 percent so, by the way. I didn't come from Earth, nor did I grow up there. I went to attend college, then became a Marine officer, something I'd always wanted to do."

"Holy moly. I guess you always knew you were gay too?"

Owen grinned, and it was a titillating thing. "You're a wonder."

"I'm no Wonder Woman." I squirmed under his gaze. "Unless these metal gravity bands are magic shields?" I held up my arms.

He full-out laughed, a deep guffaw. "The magic is inside of you, Rowan."

I thought, *I wish you were inside of me*, but what I said was, "I don't want to talk about what's inside of me, or isn't. I'm too old to feel this way." I looked away from him.

"Why? How old do you feel?"

"How old are you?" I blurted. "Sorry, that was rude of me. I'm a little touchy on the subject. I've been down this road before—discussing age with an alien I thought was thirty-three but turned out to be 125."

"Roger Rogers?" said Owen, his brow raised. "I am roughly forty-five in your years. Labyrinthians can't stall the aging process like Red Orbiters, though we age slower than humans. We do other things slowly too, and very thoroughly." His tone turned seductive.

"Major Marsden, are you toying with me?" I fluttered my eyelashes, but inside I was a confused mess.

"Did age matter with Roger? Was he too old or young for you?"

"No! Of course not, as it turned out. But"—I shifted on the couch—"it's the wrists bands, right? Rauc warned me Labyrinthians would be attracted to them."

"Not hardly." He smiled. "You were enticing when you were in law school too. Weren't you about thirty back then?"

"What on earth?" I gasped.

"Yes, it was on Earth. In Maryland. You were a law student in Baltimore, and I was a midshipman at the Naval Academy."

"When my now-ex-husband taught there?" My breath hitched.

"Yes, but he wasn't one of my professors."

"Is that how you knew me back then? This is like Win saying he saw me in Monterey when I was in my twenties," I muttered.

"Oh, I already heard the 'I saw her first' litany from Oswald Winslow," drawled Owen.

"What the hell?"

"It's okay." Owen reached over Bodie to pat my thigh, and I thought I might self-combust. "And it was a paper you wrote in school that drew my attention, other than you being one hot Marine wife."

"Oh great." I smacked my forehead. "Something I wrote again. Maybe I better stop writing. Except it's pretty much all I'm good at."

"Highly unlikely," he said, grinning. "The paper was about the unconstitutional Department of Defense policy disallowing homosexuals and criminally charging them for their sexual orientation. It was brilliant how you came up with that argument on selective prosecution of homosexuals for sodomy, but not heterosexuals—all those married Marines going down on, and getting fellated by, their wives who were never somehow targeted, despite the legal definition of sodomy including oral sex."

"This is a decidedly uncomfortable discussion to be having with you. And I'm gobsmacked. How'd you get your hands on that paper?"

That smile again. "Labyrinthians have their ways—of getting their hands on things."

The implication of his words sizzled in the air, so I commenced babbling for the second time that day. "Well, I know it wasn't from my professor, who was a former Marine and hated that paper. Mostly because I also compared arguments DoD made about homosexuals as being the very same potential 'security' issue claimed against black men in 1948, and later about all women. And if anyone's engaged in so-called witch hunts over the years, it's been the military gunning for lesbians in their ranks."

Owen nodded. "That's why I came out as gay just as I left the Marines. I wanted to drive home the point that it's always been among them, and sexuality is not the problem. Bigotry is."

"Boy howdy!" I yipped, hopping up from the couch and spinning toward Owen. "Okay, I definitely find you appealing too. But I have questions."

Chapter 23

"Why don't you continue your questions while you change for dinner?"

"Change clothes?" My voice cracked. "While you're here?"

"I'll stay out of your bedroom." Owen smiled, and my knees jellied, but I righted myself and headed for my new closet.

"This magnetic clothes-hanging system will take some getting used to, but it sure beats hangers. And I need to unpack my dress for tomorrow night too. Thank you for helping plan a New Year's Eve event. I was bummed to miss it, although I haven't had a good one in years."

"We'll remedy that," said Owen, and I was pretty sure he was smiling that smile.

"I'm going to hop in the shower, so give me a minute."

Once I emerged, I said, "How is it aliens just pop down to Earth and suddenly exist as if they've been there since birth? Do they forge documents?"

"I'll take the Fifth on that forgery accusation," he said, mirth in his tone. "But yes, we create identities, complete with names and backgrounds, like what state we're from. Humans are big on that. But we don't lie about our qualifications or abilities, nor do we claim to be born in the US if we weren't. And to get into college, for instance, we take entrance exams and compete like everyone else."

"Okay, so what's your real name?" I asked, applying fresh eye makeup. "Because I always thought the last name Marsden was too coincidental for someone from Mars, not to mention the *o-w* in Owen."

"Which rhymes with Rowan. There's an *o-w* in your name too."

"Your name?" I repeated.

"Man, you're brutal. It's *Vulcan*," he sighed.

"Like on *Star Trek*?" I squealed while attempting to apply lipstick and had to start over.

"As in the Roman god of fire," corrected Owen.

"Good grief. Red Orbiters like to poke fun at humans for being obsessed with Roman and Greek gods, but aliens sure seem to embrace the same names. I mean, you do actually call your planet Mars, do you not?"

"That's because, as I'm sure you've been told, those entities humans mistook for gods coming down from the heavens were actually aliens. So they appropriated our names, but they can have them. Can you imagine me being a Marine officer with the name Vulcan?"

"I want to talk more about this homosexuality thing," I said, putting on earrings and walking into my living area in my new dress.

"Wow. You look good in olive green. Maybe you should have been a Marine."

"Don't change the subject." I frowned. "When I was in college, guys who said they were bi were really just avoiding admitting they were gay, either to themselves or everyone else. Later, I learned there really were bisexual men, even married with kids and grandkids."

"What are you getting at, Rowan?"

"Are you? Bisexual?"

"Don't you want me to be?" Owen smiled and sauntered toward me. I backed up.

"Stop being cagey! Are you some sort of spy too, because I can feel there are things you're not telling me." I stomped my foot.

"Lookout!" Owen whistled. "The lady's got her hands on her hips."

I glared at him, standing there like one giant question mark.

"No to being a spy," he said. "Yes to wanting to plunge myself inside you. And maybe perform some of those other salacious oral acts the Department of Defense was clueless about."

I swallowed, my throat painfully dry—unlike the rest of me. "You were so quiet when I first met you, so restrained. And I'm not sure that was really an answer."

"It was," he said. "And we need to get going or we'll keep the others waiting, and Rowdy will spread rumors about us."

"Why is it you seem to know what's inside my head? What I'm thinking about but not actually saying. Are you reading my mind?" I floundered for the right words as we entered a transpod after I hugged the critters goodbye.

"No, I'm not a mind reader, but this is best left to another private conversation."

"You're driving me nuts," I said, grinding my teeth.

"You say that like it's a bad thing. And you need to stop fretting, so I'll tell you right now it's an ear thing—something you can relate to. Except Labyrinthians don't hear from long distances like you do. We tend to hear between the lines, so to speak. We hear what you're *not* saying when you voice words aloud. And some of us have more honed capabilities than others."

Chapter 24

I heard the booming brogue of Red MacLeod as we approached the restaurant, and wanted to kick myself for my timing in pushing Owen into divulging a new alien revelation.

"Aren't you supposed to still be sleeping? And where's your kilt?" I asked as the Scotsman enveloped me in a hug after kissing the top of my hand like some dashing prince.

"You know how hearty we Scots are, lass! Plus, I'm famished. And I left the regalia behind in Scotland. Didn't want my manly parts getting drafty here on the moon." He chuckled.

The gang sat around a table, with Owen on my right and Red on my left. I waved across at George and Tim flanking Maggie, asking them how they liked their new digs, but we were soon interrupted by the approach of a lovely dark-haired pixie woman with exotically slanted eyes.

"Greetings, travelers! I am Mazy, culinary student soon to graduate, and I hope to be visiting your fine planet soon. I have prepared the evening's feast at the direction of my mentor, Rose Bergin of Las Vegas. Familiar Cajun dishes with a touch of otherworldly flavor in honor of Tim Rider of New Orleans for his birthday." She nodded toward Tim, who beamed.

"Thank you, Mazy. This is truly a good surprise," he said.

"Yes, it is a surprise. Not only did I not know it was your birthday—how did I miss you being from New Orleans? You have no accent, and I didn't get you a gift," I teased.

"I worked at losing it once I graduated Tulane and set my sights on government work." He winked, slipping into a thick Big Easy drawl. "But I can lay it on thick if you so desire, *chère*. And your dazzling presence gracing my dinner table is all the gift I need."

"Whew. I knew there was something I liked about you, even when you interrupted my lunch that first time we met in person, when your partner claimed I was sending coded text messages via my mom's weather reports and emoji."

As we dined on dishes including eggplant pirogue and shrimp étouffée, I asked George if he'd met anyone special to invite to the New Year's party.

"I don't move as fast as you do," he teased, making Rowdy taunt me with hooting noises. "But now that you mention it, I might have laid eyes on someone this very evening."

"Speaking of that," said Rowdy, "Oz wanted me to extend his apologies for not joining us tonight. He's with a lady friend who will only be here for one night, but he said to tell you he'd see you all tomorrow."

"The astronaut's still got it," said Red, raising his glass. "To Oz, and to women who make us crazy for one night of love."

Owen whispered in my ear, "Speechless at such a deeply romantic toast?"

"No," I hissed between clenched teeth, elbowing him and wishing I hadn't because his chest was a wall of muscle. "I'm not about to say anything out loud and have you *listen between the lines*." His answering chuckle made me squirm.

"You are so full of it, Red," said Genie, seated on his other side. "Been hitting the Scotch a wee too much?"

"Brazen bonnie lass," Red parlayed. "Dinna you ken I was speaking of you?"

"Hey," said Tim, feeling no pain after a few hurricane cocktails. "Does anyone want to regale me with exploits of their thirtieth birthday?"

"Okay, but it's your thirty-first, though who am I to be counting?" said Maggie.

I said, "I was in law school and threw a party at my house where I played rowdy drinking games with Marines who worked with my husband. I think you've got me beat with a dinner party in outer space. But can I just say I didn't look my age any more than you do?"

"You still don't," said Maggie, looking quite relaxed. "I've done some drinking with Marines too, and have had more than my share of birthdays in my thirties. Over and over and over again." She actually giggled, and it was a hell of a sound.

"Yes, but you don't look your age either, darlin'," said Tim, giving her a sloppy kiss.

"And thank goodness for that!" Maggie swatted his roaming hand.

As we left the table, I whispered to Genie, "Is there something between you and Red?"

She snorted. "He and Bruce went to school together in Edinburgh, and his parents and ours grew up as neighbors there. Red is like a very annoying human-hybrid cousin."

"Did you grow up in Scotland too?"

"Not entirely. We moved around, so Bruce tells everyone he was a Navy brat, though neither of our parents were actually in the Navy, but Dad was a Red Orbiter pilot."

"Don't you ladies know it's terribly naughty and rude to whisper?" Rowdy butted in.

"Says the slut king of gossip and intrigue!" Genie scoffed.

I glanced about and saw George, chatting it up with our chef, Mazy.

"Look there, you two," I said. "I think I know who George has his eye on. And doesn't it figure that my friend with the most adventurous stomach ever would fall for an alien with a talent for food preparation?"

Soon after, as Owen left me at my door and hopped back in the transpod, he winked at me with dazzling purple eyes. "I want to hear more about those drinking games with Marines."

Chapter 25

"Sorry I'm late," I said, rushing into the meeting room ten minutes after the hour. "I'm big on punctuality, but I have a terrible sense of direction, just like the transpod that was supposed to bring me here but somehow took me to another residential deck."

"You haven't missed anything. We weren't allowed to start the meeting without the great Rowan Layne!" The snide tone was palpable coming from the one in the room I didn't know.

Oz stood to give me a hug, pulling out a chair next to him. "Rowan, dear, please join us. I just got here myself."

I looked around at Owen, George, Red, Maggie, and Tim—who, unlike the unknown entity, were smiling at me.

"Allow me to more formally introduce myself," said the derisive, diminutive figure dressed in a taupe uniform and sneering at Oz and me. His hair looked like one of those little furballs that rapidly multiplied on an episode of *Star Trek*. He drew himself up in his chair. "I am Tribble—"

"No way!" I blurted. "Oh, sorry. Please continue." I looked at George wanting to say, *See? I told you I wouldn't be good at this diplomacy stuff*. George's eyes were huge behind his wire-rimmed glasses, like he was trying not to laugh out loud.

Tribble glowered at me, his shoulders quaking, before he continued. "I represent residents on the moonship whose ancestral home is Lacerta."

"What we Earth dwellers mistakenly called Venus." I nodded. "My next vice president also hails from your planet, or a great deal of his DNA does, but he was born in Nevada. As was my friend Oapule, who was adopted and has less than 1 percent human DNA. And Karim, a Tunisian Uber driver in Oregon, except his DNA is from Lacerta too." I turned to Tim and Red and George. "Did you guys know *Lacerta* is Latin for 'lizard,' and there's an all-female lizard species from there that reproduces asexually?"

Tribble's furry head bobbled around on his neck, all snippy like. "I assure you, we are not lizards. Nor are we all *female*." He spit the word like it was a sour grape.

"You're also not the actual voice for Lacertans here, because your leader is currently on Earth right now meeting with the vice president-elect Rowan just mentioned, as a courtesy, and to congratulate the first Lacertan human hybrid to hold such high office in the US," said Oz, not without rancor.

"I am second in command!" said Tribble, his tone taking on a squeak.

"No," said Owen. "The second in command is also on Earth, because he's the husband of the *female* Lacertan leader. But let's move on to what we're here for. To discuss the Outer Space Treaty and what role the moonship plays now that it's been revealed as a spaceship, no longer the celestial body that the treaty's drafters and signatories presumed."

"Yes, I'm anxious to better understand what the treaty is about, and how signatories may have violated it," I said.

"You don't know what's in the treaty?" scoffed Tribble. "Then why did we need to wait for you, and why are you here anyway? And dressed like a Labyrinthian woman!" He said those last two words like they tasted badly, so I was hopeful Owen might flatten the toady little bugger by the end of the meeting.

I responded, "What? Is there a rule against my wearing their very comfortable tunics?"

Oz said, "Rowan is here because of her passion for civil rights and her legal background with the US Department of Defense, not to mention her exemplary writing and public speaking skills. The US's Other Worldly Coalition, as well as the head of the North American Red Orbiters, chose her to represent them on this matter."

"Well, it's just that there are four humans here representing Earth, and that seems like an awful lot," huffed Tribble, looking with distaste at the bands on my wrists.

"Aye, it may be," said Red. "But we are not here representing all of Earth, or even all signatories to the treaty. We are here for the US and Great Britain. We do not speak for other nations, any more than any of you speak for other species."

"Yes, and let me make it very clear that this Lacertan here today does not and will never speak for Red Orbiters, either in the moonship or on Earth, which he has never visited," said Maggie, her steely gaze causing Tribble to visibly tremble, but not enough to shut him up.

"I don't need to visit a place to know what is wrong with it, or its species! We on the moonship did not subject ourselves to this treaty. We are not subject to their laws!"

"He'd fit right in, in the town where I used to live," I muttered to Oz, who chuckled. I cleared my throat. "You are correct, Tribble. You are not subject to the laws of Earth. Just as I am neither subject to your highly irrelevant notions of what I should wear, or your subjective opinion on whether I should be here. Yes, I am female, and a human hybrid. I am also an individual who has a great deal of respect and admiration for those I've encountered with Lacertan DNA *on Earth*."

"And on that well-said note"—Owen smiled at me—"let's go over the basics of the treaty. You'll be provided with a copy of its articles to scrutinize and use in drafting remarks to Congress, which may not be aware this treaty was largely based on something called the Declaration of Legal Principles Governing the Activities of States in the Exploration and Use of Outer Space, with added provisions."

"The treaty was opened for signature by the US, the United Kingdom, and the Russian Federation in January 1967 and entered into force that October," said Oz. "It provides the basic framework on international space law and denotes that the moon, as a celestial body, is a global commons. As such, it was deemed legally accessible to all countries but belonging to none. This is why the US or any other nation can't claim ownership simply because it places its flag on the surface of the moon."

"So the problem now is, the moon is actually a spaceship, not a celestial body, which changes the game in terms of who gets to decide legal accessibility," I said. "Plus—"

"We should also change who gets invited here without consulting with those who have a stake in what goes on," Tribble interrupted while glaring at Owen.

"We will definitely be changing who participates in these meetings," said Maggie. This time Tribble did shut his trap. "Would you like to finish, Rowan? I apologize for those who apparently don't realize this is not a forum for airing petty grievances."

"No, that's okay. I think what I have to say is best saved for a different audience. Plus, I'd like to hear what George or Owen thinks on the military aspects."

"One problem," said George, addressing me, "is this treaty does not specifically ban military activities within space, military space forces, or the weaponization of space, with the sole exception of placement of weapons of mass destruction. Article IV also prohibits testing and deployment of any kind of weapon on the moon or other celestial bodies."

"And one critical issue," Tim weighed in. "The treaty denotes all nation-states are responsible for their actions in space as well as any actions of their nongovernmental entities operating in outer space."

"That's part of the issue we've also been dealing with on Mars with those start-up mining outfits," said Owen.

"So, with respect to nations taking responsibility for their actions, although some might try to claim all bets are off with the moon now that's it's not a celestial body, any actions taken against the moonship nonetheless occur in outer space and can still be considered violations of the existing treaty," I said. "Not to mention folks should be far more discerning when it comes to choosing leaders of their nations—and their species."

Tribble harumphed. I responded with a withering glare.

Chapter 26

"Well, that was a total situation FUBAR of a meeting," I said to George and Red. We were eating lunch at a pizzeria that had apparently just opened, making me wonder if Rauc had something to do with instigating it during his time here last spring.

"I'm still astounded by how many extraterrestrial mushrooms there are," said George. "And the meeting wasn't a total waste. We learned there are power-hungry punks everywhere."

"Aye, with oddly appropriate names. But you two weren't paying attention. I dinna ken it's as much about power as it is about unrequited love and the little green monster," said Red, swigging beer from a pint glass.

"What do love or Greens have to do with that toad of a man?" I said, sipping Sangiovese and enjoying my pizza with artichokes and olives from an unpronounceable planet.

"I think he means jealousy," said George, downing his fourth slice of pizza and counting.

"Aye. That little Tribble has a thing for Owen. Not that we won't likely have other trouble with Tribble."

"Well, Tribble sure as tootin' didn't approve of me! He reminded me of this Marine general who didn't cotton to me being a lawyer. As a Marine wife, I was supposed to stay in my place and make babies."

"To be fair," said eternal optimist George, "I don't think he was all that enamored of any of us Earth dwellers."

"Maybe not, but I endured enough misogynist derision working for the military—I know it when I hear it. And if anyone tries to tell me I can catch more flies with honey than vinegar in dealing with this jerk, I might run screaming from the moonship. Is Pluto nice this time of year? No one's talked about Pluto. Is it or is it not a planet?"

Red said to George, "Before I step in it, why she doesn't like that honey-vinegar analogy?"

George said, "I recall her favored response tends along lines of, 'Why would anyone want to catch fucking flies?'"

"Oh aye, that makes sense. So it's like telling a lass she needs to smile more?"

"I'm right here, guys. And I have excellent hearing."

George turned to me. "You did kind of call Tribble a lizard. Don't they catch flies?"

"You don't actually dislike honey, do you lass? Because it's sweet, and bees are special," said Red—with a straight face.

"Stick your bagpipes up your bum, Brigadoon," I said. "And you!" I turned to George. "Whose friend are you?"

"I am eternally devoted only to you, Rowan. Or I am until Mazy shows up at the party tonight when she gets off work. I have to go now and shop for something decent to wear."

"George, you can't leave me alone with the Scotsman. He carries a knife in his skirt. And in all the years I've known you, you saying you have to find something decent to wear was not on my bingo card."

"Do try to play nice with the former secretary of defense, Rowan. It's too soon for us to get kicked off the moonship," George said, blond dreadlocks swaying as he kissed me on the cheek and dashed away.

"Did you just blaspheme bagpipes, dirks, *and* kilts, lass?"

"Yes, but you know I could listen to that brogue of yours accompanied by pipers for at least a hundred years." I batted my baby blues at him.

"Clever, you are. Have another drink with me before you go off to get all gussied up for New Year's and I won't have you all to myself. Not that I don't approve of that lovely purple frock you're wearing, the color of heather in the Highlands. That's the trouble with Tribble. There's just no pleasing them."

"Is it possible we met our first alien mutant today? Because those normally alluring light-green Lacertan eyes did not go well with Tribble's sallow skin tone. And that hair! I'm so glad Maggie seems to have upped her game in the world of Red Orbiter leadership, because I don't think she's going to let him participate anymore."

"Aye, that would be a wise move for all of us. Like you, there are things I'm not comfortable discussing in his presence about our nations."

"Boy howdy. He was a total cockwomble."

"It's settled, lass. You're going to have to marry me."

"I don't think they have wedding chapels here in the moonship like Vegas. Does anyone ever call you Colin instead of Red?"

"Only my mother. But the way you say it with a bit of Scots lilt makes me think I wouldn't be minding if you did. May I ask why you'd want to? Is it because my hair is no longer a vibrant red and you find me unworthy of the title?"

"No, that would be hypocritical of me as I myself am cheating with hair dye. But the name Red makes me think of a crusty old bearded guy, like a Gaelic Santa Claus, and you definitely are not that. More like a blue-eyed Sean Connery, without the whiskers."

Red roared with laughter, then hit me with a lascivious gaze. "You know, that first time I met you when Oz introduced us, you were at the convention in a red dress, looking flushed."

"Yes, well, I was a tad overwhelmed during the Omni convention."

"That's not how I recall it. You looked like a woman who had been well-pleasured."

I was tongue-tied, and mortified. Did he know about the Red Orbiter magic stroke of an orgasm-inducing spot on the back of human women's necks—and that Rauc had done that to me seconds before I shook Red's hand?

"And I thought to myself," Red said, taking his time with a swig of beer, "one day I'd like to be the man making this bonnie lass glow so delightfully."

I felt as if I was glowing bright red now. "Why, Colin, you do know how to flatter a gal."

"Aye, that I do. But dinna be thinking I'm only after a chance to toss up your skirts, because it's your smarts that first captured my attention."

"Let me guess. Something I wrote? In high school perhaps?"

Red laughed, the sound vibrating through my chest. "Win showed me your newspaper columns, and what you wrote for the senator, and I heard your speech introducing the next vice president."

"You made a pretty impressive speech yourself at the convention, so much so I felt bad about harassing you at dinner the night before."

"Did you now? And how would you be wanting to make it up to me?"

"You're a smooth one, Colin MacLeod."

"Like good Scots whiskey," he grinned.

"So, are you one of the people responsible for why I find myself on the moonship?"

"Aye, that I am. And when our work is done here, I want you in Edinburgh, and in London, as it were. To be by my side to address Parliament on how to atone for these treaty issues and repair our image in outer space."

I almost spit my wine but managed to reply, "I don't think I'm qualified for that."

"Didn't you study law in Scotland?"

"For one summer! Nothing about diplomacy! Although I did tour a prison. It's weird that you call your wardens governor."

"Aye, but you're fiery, and a natural. Plus, I will return the favor and be by your side when you address Congress in Washington."

Chapter 27

I went back to my suite, got Bodie and took him to the park, walking around in circles while talking on the phone to my sister.

"I don't know why I thought coming to the moonship would be a diversion from life's complications!"

"But Rauc and Roger or Win aren't there, right?"

"Yes, but Red MacLeod is, and he wants me to go to the UK to address Parliament, and it turns out someone decided I'm going to address Congress too. And Owen the Marine is clearly not exclusively gay like I thought, and you should see him. Talk about Adonis."

"Who is Owen the Marine?"

"Astrophysics professor in Monterey. George's friend. And he's a Martian—or Labyrinthian. There's lots of them here. But there's also a rotten little dude from Venus who doesn't like me. Oh, but I got to select my own furniture, and last night we had a birthday dinner for Tim Rider—the DHS agent dating Maggie, Roger's twin sister? Turns out he's from New Orleans, and he went to Tulane, just like your hubby. And it looks like my friend George is sweet on a Labyrinthian culinary student named Mazy."

"I so want to go to that culinary school." G sighed. "But the moon kind of sounds like a soap opera. You're making my head spin. Are you going to Scotland? Phil and I should come too. We've never golfed at St Andrews."

"You and Phil should plan a trip here. Each restaurant has food from some region or place on Earth in honor of this spacecraft representing its moon."

"Yes, but how do we pull off going to the moon without Mom? Do they have a hair salon? Or a golf course for Dad?"

"I don't know, but they definitely have shoe stores!"

When I got back to my suite I had an email from Maggie:

> Thanks for enduring today's meeting. From here on out, our group will be smaller. Oz is returning to Earth tomorrow to assist Rauc with pressing Red Orbiter issues, and Owen will be sole representation for the moonship until actual Lacertan leadership returns. Just so you know, I heard you talking at lunch today (sorry, but Tim and I were close by getting things ready for the party tonight). You were spot-on in your reference to an alien mutant. Terrible Tribble is only part Lacertan, because his father hailed from the planet you know as Uranus. It didn't turn out to be a stellar genetic combination. I know this might seem like a joke since the degenerate president also has Uranus DNA, but I assure you it's the truth, which I've heard you say is always stranger than fiction. I've attached a copy of the Outer Space Treaty of 1967, but don't you dare start working and be late for the party—where there will be absolutely no shop talk and only fun and merriment free of misogynist mutants. Oh, and Tim wants you to bring Morris over for a playdate with Astro soon. The poor kitty's been lovesick :)

I had my marching orders from a former Marine fighter pilot Red Orbiter, but I still couldn't resist skimming over the treaty articles, and I noted repeated emphasis on maintenance of international peace and security. Article IV flat out stated that the moon and other celestial bodies shall be used exclusively for peaceful purposes. This did not bode well for Space Force and the secretary of the Air Force crowing about "space dominance" last year.

Morris was howling for dinner, so we tried out some of the moonship pet food I'd ordered, and it was a shocker he liked it because it was healthy and didn't contain meat. Bodie had all vegetables in his food, and he scarfed it down.

Next, a text from Mom. "Happy New Year's Eve Doodles!!! Do you have black-eyed peas to eat tomorrow for good luck??? How are my grandanimals??? We are supposed to get an ice storm!!! Ugh. Dad sends his love. (heart, dog, cat, moon, New Year's fireworks emoji)"

I texted as I headed for the shower, "Not sure about black-eyed peas. Lots of good restaurants though! And Morris and Bodie love their fancy new food. I got three pairs of shoes yesterday! (moon, dog, cat, three shoe emoji)"

After my shower I struggled with my hair, so maybe I should have scoped out a salon for a festive New Year's Eve 'do. Slipping into my retro 1950s-style teal-and-black dress with its full skirt, I realized I was definitely rocking that Jetson vibe. As I put on my blue-diamond shooting-star earrings Rauc bought me to go with the dress, I grew maudlin, missing him.

As if on cue, the phone he had given me vibrated. "Hello, my most wonderful, handsomest alien in the galaxy!"

"I'm sorry I won't be there to kiss you at midnight, Copper."

"It's okay. I know you have a lot on your plate, being the new boss man."

"It has been nuts. Thankfully, I have a great predecessor in Oz to help me out. How are you doing up there?"

"So far, so good, except for one little bastard who doesn't like me much. But he's kind of an equal opportunity bigot, in that he seems to abhor most Earth dwellers."

"I heard. Oz was not pleased. Nor was Maggie. So you don't have to worry about him being at the party tonight."

"Thank goodness. Hey, I have a question."

"First, I have one for you. I've noticed you never use the term Earthling. Why?"

"Once I learned that's how Greens refer to themselves, it didn't feel appropriate."

"Yes, but you still come from Earth, and the rest of the world doesn't know Greens aren't extraterrestrial."

"Well, we damn well knew we weren't first in time in North America, but that hasn't stopped folks from thinking they're entitled to take over space like we did Earth. I just read over the Outer Space Treaty, and I'm appalled at our astounding arrogance in presuming space was devoid of other beings and is simply a bunch of empty planets to be exploited for human gain."

"Yes, I've considered that we should have revealed the truth about aliens sooner, but what was your question, before you get too worked up? I want you to enjoy your party, and I'm not there to take care of reducing your stress level."

"My question? What was my question? Can I touch the back of my own neck and get the same results?" I chuckled. "But what I wanted to know was about how you told me the gods who everything seems to be named after were actually extraterrestrials, but not from planets in our solar system. If so, why is Mars called Mars?"

"I may have misspoken, although I think we were talking about the Latin language as well as Greek gods at the time, who did come from elsewhere. But most of those mistaken for Roman gods happen to have been from Mars."

"Yikes. No wonder the Marine Corps originated there. Mars is the Roman god of war, after all. And there you go again, proving you're an alien and not a human male by claiming you might have misspoken."

"Careful, Copper. A few of those so-called Roman gods also hailed from Jupiter, the planet my kind calls Cumulus. Don't forget my real name is Romulus. And I miss getting my hands on that sassy behind of yours."

Chapter 28

I walked into the party room through festive silver streamers hanging from the ceiling. The song "Moondance" played in the background as Tim and Maggie greeted me.

"You've outdone yourselves. Is that a red mirror ball? You found a disco ball on the moonship?"

"Hey, that's a *red orb* disco ball," said Genie, approaching in her sparkly green dress. It wasn't fair there were women who look like Genie, alien or otherwise.

Tim said, "We even have a DJ who will play moon-themed songs all night!"

"And don't forget we can sing karaoke, which I excel at," said Rowdy, smooching me on the cheek. "I'm sure glad I didn't have to pay for those earrings, but you look smashing."

"You're pulling off that tuxedo quite well yourself. Pretty fancy for a guy who used to favor Wrangler jeans and Ropers."

"Tim decided the theme of the party would be the Bond film *Moonraker*, and we got tuxedos from different Bond films. They have a great clothing rental place because the moonship loves to celebrate Halloween."

"Of course it does. So which Bond are you? Let me guess, Daniel Craig? Be still my heart."

"Yes, and Owen is coming as Pierce Brosnan because of that sexy black hair," said Rowdy.

"I can also do a pretty decent Irish accent if I drink enough whiskey," replied Owen, entering in an exceedingly well-cut black tuxedo.

"Oh my," I breathed. "And, Tim, who are you tonight?"

"Timothy Dalton in *License to Kill*. I'm going to kill it on the dance floor with my Bond girl, Maggie."

"I'm no Bond girl. I'm Dame Judi Dench as M," said Maggie in her midnight-blue dress and classic ponytail, looking sleek and stunning.

"That's okay, I'm enough of a Bond girl for all of us!" said Genie. "I'm Dr. Holly Goodhead from *Moonraker*."

"That you are," drawled Rowdy. "But shouldn't you really be a Bond villain?"

Luckily Red strode up at that moment.

"Well, I have no doubt who you are, and don't you look splendid? Although I do miss that kilt," I said. "Didn't they make Sean Connery a knight, too? Should I call you sir?"

"Stirred, not shaken," said Red, handing me a martini I presumed was botanical gin from Saturn, a new favorite of mine. "And you can wait until my accolade to call me sir, lass."

I almost dropped my drink. "You're kidding, right?"

Before Red could answer, George strolled up in a black suit, reminiscent of the sixties, with skinny pant legs. Perfect.

"James Bond with dreadlocks would be a genetic mutation. So I went with another Brit, a musical fellow with my name, George Harrison. Representing the 1964 Beatles song 'Mr. Moonlight.' But I also think that yellow submarine was an alien spacecraft."

"You look fab!" I said. "So who am I going to be? M's already taken, darn it."

"You, lass, are Jill St. John as Tiffany Case, redheaded American who starred with Sean Connery in *Diamonds Are Forever*."

"Good thing I wore my diamonds," I quipped. "And where's Oz?"

"I'm over here, but call me Roger Moore, the star of *Moonraker* and old coot of a James Bond!" said Oz in a white tuxedo from across the room, standing with an older couple I didn't know.

"Moon River" now played in the background, a little tame for the mood of this crowd. "I hope you're not going to sing this tune for karaoke," I told Rowdy.

"No, but 'Bad Moon Rising' for sure!" He sailed off to argue with Genie.

I turned to Red and said, "I need to sit because I won't last forever in these shoes, but I want to hear about this accolade thing."

"Aye, I remember those sexy heels fondly, and that dress at the convention. We have a bar we can belly up to, so let's get to it."

"Will you join us, Owen? And will Byrin be coming tonight?"

"Byrin is more of a one-on-one type of socializer. But you really should arrange a meet-up soon so she can help you out," said Owen.

"I know, I know. I'll get there. My ears haven't been too bad so far."

"I'll hold you to it. And I'll come holler at you in a while. I need to talk to Oz."

"Okay but Maggie said no shoptalk tonight. And I also want to hold you to telling me more about these Labyrinthian skills."

I sat at the bar with Red on a swivel stool that had nice back support and eyed trays of interesting-looking appetizers as I sipped my martini and felt like I was in a movie. The DJ played "Walking on the Moon" by the Police.

"So, are you really going to become Sir Colin MacLeod, knight in shining armor?"

"It would seem to be in the cards, lass." He grinned. "But I want the rundown on your ears. Tell me what makes you so special to aliens. They're like a moth to a flame with you."

"Funny you should say that, because, in a nutshell, I hear voices over great distances, like a moth, and those voices belong to Red Orbiters. I also hear high-frequency sounds other humans can't. And because I never knew what it was, I apparently developed my own version of tinnitus. The ringing is a defense against being bombarded with voices, because it tends to freak me out. Apparently Labyrinthians, or one in particular here on the moonship, can help me cope and learn to manage it."

"It's in your DNA then? You have Red Orbiter DNA?"

"From my 42 percent that hails from Jupiter's moon Elara—actually called Actius, for the Luna moth, or *Actius Luna* in Latin. Red Orbiters are big on Latin. Did you know that? Apparently their language is similar, which is why they call Jupiter, Cumulus."

"Yes because we're big on clouds too," said Rowdy, striding up to the bar. "You look like you could use a refill on that martini."

"Rowdy Wilde, I don't care how many drinks you ply me with, I am not going to sing karaoke with you."

"Not even 'Fly Me to the Moon?'" Rowdy pouted, which was kind of alarming.

"Let's be clear here on who flew you to the moon," said Maggie. "Did you try the shrimp puffs yet? And there's cheese fondue I heard you love, with OW apple slices."

"Great, I might need a bib to cover this dress," I said. "And do you know if there's a Southern-style soul food restaurant here? My mom will hound me if I don't eat black-eyed peas for good luck tomorrow."

"Already on it!" said Tim. "My mom's from Texas too. There's a place we could go, say late afternoon? They supposedly have killer cornbread."

"They do. And collard greens from Cultura, or Saturn in your world," said Mazy, walking up with George in a tight, shimmery Asian-style dress that complimented golden skin, her previously braided black hair now flowing to her waist.

"I'm game!" said George.

"Of course you are," I said. "This moonship is better than being on a cruise. Here's to galactic gastronomy. Cheers!"

Chapter 29

While Genie asked Mazy for culinary pointers, "Sail to the Moon" by Radiohead played in the background and I chatted with George.

"So why do we think Tim picked a James Bond theme for this party? Is it his next line of work, post Homeland?"

"You were correct in wondering if he would be OUTWARD's latest recruit," said George, dipping into something that looked too much like horseradish for me to stomach.

"I'll be working for the new acoustics facility in Las Vegas," said Tim, approaching us at a table laden with food Mazy had brought for us to sample. "I believe I told you over our pseudo-whistleblower dinner that I hear things too?"

"Okay, great." I laughed. "But what does that have to do with James Bond? Oh my gosh!" I was a bit slow on the uptake. "You're working intel issues! How could I not realize that was part of acoustics?"

"Why else would Win be in charge of the new facility?" asked George. "And once Bruce tested your ears and Tim had us test him too, there were similarities in your auditory abilities, but also anomalies. Based on the law of averages, we realized there had to be more of you, roaming Earth, wondering if you're crazy because you hear voices." He grinned and dug into more dip.

"Or in my case," said Tim, "being drawn to a field of work where my abilities could help as oppose to hinder as a stigma. Though I did have to keep it a secret from the government while working for them."

"Ya think?" I snarked. "But please tell me this isn't going to turn into some invasive, NSA-like operation."

"Not to worry." George patted my shoulder. "OUTWARD is about advances in new technology, but we're going to go about it differently. We've now realized we have a unique opportunity to help human hybrids identify and explore their misunderstood abilities. Turns out we are the first-ever company, just as the Other Worldly Coalition was the first organization, knowingly operated by and with human hybrids and multiple species of other origins teamed together for intergalactic outreach and understanding."

"So that's what the *Other* and *Universal* in the acronym stand for," I said.

"You got it!" said George. "But you also know, like any good R&D company, we have to be concerned about industrial spies, and in our case all the anti-alien vigilantes, including those working for the government. So we need our own counterintelligence operations to stay one step ahead of our enemies."

"Are you guys talking shop?" said Maggie, slipping her arms around Tim.

"Absolutely not!" I responded. "Not one word about that patriarchal treaty has been spoken! But I am learning that maybe Tim and I can become a superhero like your brother, or you, because you're my Luna Moth Woman ideal. So, Tim, what did your results reveal?"

"Like you," he said, "I seem to hear those most closely aligned with my DNA origins, which I told you I suspected. It's why I heard George. We both have predominant DNA from Neptune."

"Galilei," corrected George, ever the proud physicist.

"Yes, Galilei. I have to get used to that name. But unlike you, Rowan, I don't hear high-frequency communication, at least not with an unaided ear." Tim smiled. "Nor do I hear from great distances. I don't have your hairless cochlea."

"Lucky you." I sighed. "So when you heard George talking about the new Red Orbiter spacecraft design and our Iridescent Insect War plans, you were actually in Washington State, trying to spy on OUTWARD headquarters?"

"Yes, unfortunately. But of course I was the only one who learned anything, and I didn't share it with my Homeland bosses."

"And I forgave him!" George beamed as he was still eating, but now something purple.

"I forgive you too, for all those times you listened in on me, Rowan," snarked Rowdy. "Now will somebody please sing karaoke with me?"

"Come on, scamp nephew," said Oz, approaching Rowdy from behind and grabbing him by the shoulders. "We'll sing 'Rocket Man' again, but I swear it's the last damn time."

"Want to dance with me to 'Rocket Man'?" Maggie asked Tim.

"I'm going to be brave now and go ask Mazy to dance with me too," said George.

Genie grabbed my arm and said, "Let's sit for a spell and girl gossip," which meant she wanted to grouse about Rowdy.

"That crazy-ass Red Orbiter is out of control on this ultimate mommy quest of his," Genie said as we listened to him howling at the microphone with Oz. "I swear he's out to torture me for telling him I'm not ready to have kids with anyone right now."

"Did he have something to do with the redheaded women that seem to be arriving to this party in droves?"

Genie made a face. "Rowdy invited them. Red Orbiters from the flight school, the culinary school, from all over the damn moonship. Mark my words, he'll manage to sleep with most of them before we leave here, whether they have his babies or not." She downed her martini and still managed to look glamorous despite her ire.

"So…what's with all the dudes joining the party too? Because it's starting to look like some sort of recessive-gene convention, what with all the red hair and green eyes on the dance floor under that red-orb disco ball." The Talking Heads song "Moon Rocks" was playing.

"My countermove." Genie smirked. "Every time I heard him invite females, I recruited guys. With any luck, they'll pair off and go make Red Orbiter babies elsewhere."

"Brilliant." I kicked back the rest of my martini. "But please tell me you did not invite that squat dude with fluffy hair?"

"Definitely not," Genie said as we watched Tribble waddle into the room, toes pointing outward like a duck. He was immediately approached by Owen with Maggie on his heels, coming off the dance floor like a guided missile when she spotted him.

Chapter 30

"You need to leave. This is a private Red Orbiter party, and you were not invited," said Maggie to toady Tribble.

He was still in his taupe uniform, which on him really did look like rumpled pajamas, and attempted to draw himself up to compete with her intimidating height. "But Owen is here—and a bunch of nasty humans!" He sneered at me.

"That's because they are not blowhard bigots," said Maggie, making me proud of her alliterative wordplay.

"But I have a right to be here! I am a leader on this moonship, and it is my job, my *prerogative* to know what subversive activity is occurring!"

"The lady asked you to leave. Am I going to have to help you with that?" said Owen, his tone making me quiver and scope out the nearest bathroom.

Oz walked up, putting his tall form between Tribble and the rest of us. "You're no leader, and piss on your so-called prerogative. You're not welcome at this party, and you *are* leaving. Right now."

"I've got a bad feeling about this," said Maggie as Tribble quaked with huffiness but turned and walked from the room.

"Me too," I murmured. "Especially after hearing him call humans by the president's favorite word for women or aliens—*nasty*. Uncanny."

The DJ chose that moment to play "Concentration Moon" by Frank Zappa's Mothers of Invention, a song intended as part of the group's takedown of right-wing politics back in the day.

Oz said, "Come on, folks. Let's not let this ruin a great party. We've got a little more than an hour before midnight, so freshen your drinks and get ready to pucker up!"

When Genie and I emerged from the restroom with fresh lipstick, karaoke started up again. Tim sang Sting's "Moon Over Bourbon Street," and Rowdy unfortunately followed with Ozzy Osbourne's "Bark at the Moon." Oz declined to join in.

Maggie said to Genie and me, "I've got us signed up for a song together. Fleetwood Mac's 'Sisters of the Moon'!"

"I suck at karaoke," I said. "But I love Stevie Nicks, so let me at that microphone."

After that, the DJ took over again, and Owen asked me to dance, making Genie's green eyes grow almost as big as her boobs.

The song was "Blue Moon," and Owen softly crooned the lyrics in my ear as we slow danced and my hands kept slipping down to his biceps.

"My last dog was named Blue Moon, and I used to sing this to her, but I never sounded as good as you do," I said. "I miss that sweet pup."

"Don't be blue tonight, Rowan. You feel so good in my arms."

I wanted to say the same but was afraid it would sound cheesy, given my grip on his biceps, not to mention his ability to "listen between the lines." Instead I said, "You know, the first time we met at OUTWARD, I don't remember your eyes being so—"

"Strangely purple?"

"Yes, but they're beautiful."

"Thank you." He smiled that secret smile. "And your powers of observation haven't failed you. On Earth I tend to wear contacts in public so my eyes appear a normal dark brown. It makes me look less like some fantasy man in a historical romance novel. You know how they always describe eyes as being the color of gemstones, like amethysts?"

I laughed. "But Red Orbiters have emerald eyes for sure, or green tourmaline. Not to mention Roger's that change to an unnatural green. And you definitely have amethyst eyes, or maybe more like an alexandrite."

"You know your gemstones. That's a very special one you're wearing," he said, touching the clear stone at my throat, and I'll be damned if it didn't heat up again.

"It's from Proxima Centauri b. It's supposed to be protective, and Roger told me to wear it at all times. Even in the shower."

Owen's eyes widened, and I wished I hadn't mentioned being in the shower, because I also imagined him in the shower with me, and what were the odds he'd detect what I was thinking? But he only said, "Yes. That's good."

"How is it an astrophysicist knows about romance novels?" I changed the subject.

"I read a lot." His smile grew mischievous. "I'd like to read more about this amazing Luna Moth Woman character and her adventures. I bet she has beautiful blue-green eyes. Kind of like those diamonds in your ears."

Then he kissed me.

It was so surprising and consuming and delicious, all I could utter when it was over was, "But it's not yet midnight."

"Marines go first," Owen responded.

The dance floor was crowded with Red Orbiter invitees of Rowdy and Genie, so I had hopes this kiss would remain our secret. But as we walked off, Genie intercepted me on the way to the bathroom.

"I want to know what he tastes like," she demanded, gripping my arm. "I'll bet blackberries, given that hair and those eyes. And that smile of his after he kissed you! Is this what a hot flash feels like, because I think I'm melting."

"I had no idea it would happen! That guy is one stealth bomber. It's always the quiet ones you have to worry about in that regard. What is it with me? I can't even get away from Marines when they're actually a flipping Martian," I muttered.

"You know you're supposed to call them Lab—"

"Yes, Jessica Rabbit, I know! I'm just a little discombobulated right now!"

"What did you call me?"

"Crap, I said that out loud, didn't I? It's a compliment, I swear!"

"I love it!" she said. "It's so much better than a Bond girl!" She put her hand on her hip and struck a pose. "I'm not bad, I'm just drawn that way!"

"I've created a monster," I said. "And I can't believe I'm the first one to make that comparison. Let's get champagne. We don't want to miss midnight!"

"But you've already been kissed. And from the looks of you, it was a whopper!"

We headed back to our little group, and Red handed me a glass of champagne as "Midnight Moon" by the Firm from the eighties played, which I only knew because that's what the DJ said it was. There was a countdown, and they lowered the red-orb mirror ball. It swirled, scattering twinkling light throughout the room.

"Happy New Year!" We all toasted, and Maggie and Tim kissed, which was sweet, their first New Year's together, and Rowdy grabbed Genie by the back of her neck and reeled her in for a lip lock, which didn't look so sweet, but at least she didn't deck him.

Red looked down at me and said, "It's customary to kiss now, is it not, lass?"

"It is. But all I need is for Rowdy to see us and blab to Rauc and the rest of the universe."

"Aye. Dinna fash yourself. The first time I kiss you, Rowan Layne, it will be in Scotland."

Which is why my mouth was wide open, dumbstruck, when Oz swooped in and laid one on me.

To be fair, I think he kissed many of us in the next few minutes, but hey, how many Earth gals can say they were kissed on the moon by a NASA astronaut who also happened to be an alien and no telling how old he really was?

Rowdy soon insisted on one last karaoke song. George said he should sing "Yellow Submarine," so Rowdy decided they needed four Beatles for the gig, and they roped in Tim and Owen. Owen tried to bow out and say it should be Red, he being from Great Britain and all.

Red replied, "I don't do Beatle. I am a Scot, not some bloke from bloody Liverpool." He was grinning when he said it, chugging Scotch.

Oz whispered to me, "George wasn't far off with his theory about the yellow submarine being an alien spacecraft." I wasn't sure if he was joshing because he was three sheets to the wind. But George's theories often proved to be true.

Afterward the DJ played Tom Waits' "Drunk on the Moon," a fitting end to the night.

Chapter 31

I had no business partying past midnight, because the holiday mattered not to a dog and cat who wanted their breakfast at zero dark thirty. At least I didn't have to let Bodie out to pee. I needed a pet pod installed at my house when I got back.

I returned to bed for a few hours after feeding the critters, then rallied to take Bodie to the park. Because we'd be out in public, I fixed my hair and face, which still had mascara smears.

I sat at the same café and ordered scones. A bowl of clotted cream appeased my grumpy resentment of my pals, who still slept. I called Mom and filled her in on the party. She wanted to know what all the women were wearing and what we ate and did I jitterbug?

My plan was to call Win as well, but I waited to return to the suite, worried about potential prying eyes and ears after last night's Tribble drama.

"Happy New Year, sweet pea," he said when I called. "You weren't here at midnight, so I imagined kissing you—among other things. Like watching you breathe in lowcut necklines."

"Don't start with me," I panted. "It's only January first, and I am already officially overwhelmed and on info overload. I had a bomb dropped on me before we even got here, and I've already learned about lunar stuff, Mars stuff, intersex stuff, Labyrinthian stuff—and boy howdy, is that strange—a treaty from 1967 the US has apparently chosen to ignore, *and* dealt with a mixed-species, Lacerta-Uranus alien who could easily win a small-man complex contest on Earth. What's next? Flying monkeys? Because someone on board has a coyote for a pet."

"What was that bit about sex?"

"*That's* all you got from that? You have too much testosterone. I said *intersex*."

Win was laughing. "I know, sweet pea. With all that, it's good you're getting a break from social media mania. And remember, Uranus is actually called Glacies."

"It ought to be called *Feces*. And I'm only staying off Twitter because you and the other bossy men said I should lay low while on the moonship," I grumped. "But I shudder to think what the president is tweeting these days."

"The usual lying, projection, and illiteracy. Even more desperately deranged as his dethroning approaches. He still says he never ordered a missile fired at the moon, or a bomb dropped into the Grand Canyon. It was all a devious alien plot to make him look bad."

"At least he didn't claim it never happened."

"Oh, he did that too. But there was too much media footage of the Grand Canyon debacle. With an MQ-9 Reaper no one in their right mind mistook for a UFO."

"And the AG and VP? What do those diabolical dotards have to say for themselves?"

"The usual entrapment claims. They were set up by aliens, or Democrats, or both. The vice went on a rant about jezebels and loose women who prey on decent men of God."

"So, the usual misogyny and hypocrisy. It used to be political figures had the good sense to resign over stuff this bad. Now they blame it on aliens."

"Considering the only outfit that will likely hire the vice after this is the Everlasting Evangelical Ministry, he's as desperate as the president. But you called me, sweet pea, so I know you must have questions."

"What if I just wanted to wish you a Happy New Year?"

Total silence. Like I thought I was going to slip one by Mr. Superspy?

"Okay, fine! Someone got a wild hair that I was going to address Congress on this treaty and Space *Farce* stupidity, but they forgot to tell me, or at least waited to spring it on me once I got here. I still have no clue what that entails. I thought I'd have a call from Senator Rojas-Ortiz by now at least. And why didn't you tell me your best buddy Red MacLeod would be here? And he wants me to address Parliament with him. *Parliament*."

"I didn't know about Red because he didn't tell me until he was on his way from Scotland. I can tell Cassandra you're anxious to speak with her, but remember, she's going to be the US attorney general by the time you're on Capitol Hill to tell them they'd better play nice in the outer space sandbox."

"You're calling the senator by her first name. Is that because you're seeing her again?"

"No, I am not romantically involved with Senator Rojas-Ortiz. But yes, we remain friends, as you well know, because she is your friend too, and a good one to have."

"Okay, but I need information. This is kind of a big deal."

"And I have no doubt you will get it. Cassandra was planning on reaching out to you, and you'll likely hear from others as well."

"Others?" I squeaked. "Who?"

"Hey, I'm not actually in charge of this, sweet pea. Just chill and do your stuff."

I googled for a few hours, looking up fun facts about the moon and historical bits on the Outer Space Treaty. Then I got dressed in another of my new tunics in a periwinkle-blue-and-lime-green swirly pattern, slipped on my green skimmers, and dragged myself to meet Tim and Maggie for our planned three p.m. early dinner—or late lunch.

"It's more like breakfast for me," said Tim.

"No fair," I said. "How come Astro didn't wake you to be fed?"

"She woke me," said Maggie, sounding none too pleased about it.

George arrived as we sat, because although he was from Northern California and not in need of black-eyed peas, he wasn't going to miss vegan soul food in the moon. Mazy was working and couldn't join us but would have, so apparently their first date went well. I was surprised we hadn't scared her off with karaoke.

I lasted one hour and most definitely did not have any hair of the dog. But I did take cornbread back to my suite for breakfast tomorrow.

I lasted another hour trying to skim over salient sections of the Outer Space Treaty and related documents that Maggie had sent, but my eyes couldn't focus and my brain was mush, plus none of my pens would work when I tried to take notes. Maddening.

I am officially old, I thought as I crawled into bed at five thirty p.m. and the critters joined me. At least until I awoke screaming in a cold sweat at two thirty a.m., whereupon Bodie and Morris scattered.

Within seconds, Rowdy Wilde strolled into my bedroom, Bodie yipping behind him.

Chapter 32

"What's up with the screaming?" Rowdy said as I sat up, wigged out. "Did you dream the moonship fell out of the sky? I heard you talking to George about your phobia."

"No." I racked my fogged brain. "I dreamed the moonship was under attack. That we were under attack. And there were different colors. And why is it you in particular always seem to hear what I say?" I rubbed my eyes.

"What was that about colors? Are you still drunk from New Year's?" He sat on the bed.

"Give me a break, Rowdy. I don't think I'm fully awake yet. And why isn't Genie here? Wouldn't she hear me scream too?"

"I think she's in some wanker's bed on another deck. And once she hears I've come to your rescue, she'll likely stay away because she's holding a grudge."

"Oh. How do you feel about that, the wanker part?"

"Like I want to smash something."

"You're in love with her."

"But the daft woman won't realize it. She's also kidding herself about not wanting kids. She's just scared."

"Funny, she said the same thing about you wanting kids. Are you? Kidding yourself?"

"Hell, I don't know." He raked a hand through wild light-red hair. "Let's talk about something else. Like your screwed-up love life."

I winced, knowing he was only kidding, but still. "I think that's part of why I had a nightmare tonight. It's been one year since Lucas left Yearntown without a word. I was really upset at first, but that's crazy because it was such a relief. I've had a year to realize the situation with him was so much worse than I'd ever admitted to myself, or anyone else. A nightmare." I wrapped my arms around my middle.

"You're making me want to smash things again," said Rowdy. "One skull in particular."

"Me too. Or I used to want to. Now I just want to get past the rage, and the guilt."

"You can, and already are, whether you realize it or not. You're strong."

"It's weird, knowing Roger and you were listening in on my last few fights with him."

"Think of it as witnesses, if you'd ever need them."

"Too bad I couldn't have stalled in my forties, like you. While I was sowing middle-aged wild oats without much care, unburdened by violent rage and never-ending verbal abuse."

"Wild oats," said Rowdy, sounding regretful. "My specialty. You really should talk to Byrin about this. It's kind of her specialty."

"What? Is she some sort of shrink? Is that why everyone's pushing me to talk to Byrin? Do you all think I'm crazy?" I gripped the back of my neck, wondering if they had masseuses aboard the moonship.

"*Hell-o?* You're talking to Rowdy here. You are not crazy. And Byrin is not a traditional psychologist. But are you trying to touch that spot on the back of your neck? Do you need something, gorgeous?"

"I am *not* having this conversation with you in bed. Let's go into the other room."

"Okay, but I want to make sure you realize you can't do it to yourself." He grinned and motioned like he was reaching for my neck.

"Back off, wily spook," I said.

"You know you want me to."

"I most certainly do not! Won't it mean we kind of had sex? And you take the couch. I'm sitting over here in my reading chair, away from you, you letch! I've got enough complications."

"We don't have to have sex, unless you're hankering to check me out." He waggled his rust-red eyebrows and plopped onto my couch. Bodie hopped up next to him.

"You're a total perv. I know you prefer aliens to humans. And I feel bad that I rattled my critters. They went through a lot with me and don't need to hear me scream."

"They seem fine," he said, petting Bodie and then Morris, who hopped in his lap to investigate, purring loudly. "It's true about my preference, but maybe I hadn't met anyone like you yet. And what's up with all the colored-ink pens?" He nodded to my coffee table.

"Pens are what I use to draft my thoughts. But they won't work." I sighed.

"Your dreams *and* your thoughts are color coded?" Rowdy quipped. "Your ink pens don't work in the moonship's magnetized gravity. The ink doesn't get pushed onto a surface. You need a specially magnetized ink cartridge. They have them here, but the moonship isn't big on paper. There's a very cool device we can hook you up with. It has a type of pen that writes on a screen, and you can write in different colors to your heart's content."

"Gravity again!" I huffed. "Gravity bites. I don't see lack of gravity keeping my boobs from sagging on the moonship, now, do I? You'd think these metal wristbands would help with that! And why didn't your brother tell me? Rauc even asked me why I was bringing these pens!"

"My guess is he likely tried to tell you," said Rowdy, chuckling. "And I wouldn't know about your boobs because you don't want to have sex with me. Now, would you like me to stay on this couch until it's time to start the day, so you can try to get back to sleep?"

"No, I'll be fine. I appreciate you coming to check on me. But hey, I have a question."

"I have an answer."

"You're such a butthead."

"Not a question, even if true. Are you sure you don't need me to stroke the back of your neck? Or I could fetch another Red Orbiter. There were more than a few curious about you at the party. Did you hear them talking about you?"

"No! And no, thank you," I snipped. "My question is, I'm sure you didn't donate half a million of your gambling windfalls to the Conservative Society without knowing for sure they couldn't keep it.

But you didn't know the attorney general would proposition Genie as Scarlet Fitzgerald at that Christmas party, so what was the original plan?"

"The AG is currently under investigation for embezzlement of Conservative Society funds. I donated knowing the money would end up in one of his offshore accounts, evidence of his fraudulent activity. But that story hasn't broken yet, and I got my money back earlier than expected, so you can buy whatever you want here on the moonship." Rowdy winked. "And you'll also be happy to know his indictment is imminent."

Chapter 33

I woke a few hours after Rowdy left to the sound of two pings from my phone. The first was a text from Mom.

"Will you find out if those moon shoe shops have my narrow size? And I want black flats with a little cushioning, not in any tacky colors. (three shoe emoji)"

The shoe emoji were pink, not black, because Mom couldn't control emoji color. The second text was my sister.

"Thank you sooo much for telling Mom you got new shoes on the moon. What were you thinking? (six screaming faces, three crazy faces, face sticking out tongue emoji)"

I replied to G, "I thought Mom's foot wasn't so narrow anymore, after she gained ten pounds. Oh the horror. (foot and shocked face emoji)"

G texted, "I am not speaking to you right now. You'll be lucky if Phil doesn't find a way to send her up there while you're there. Good luck with that. She will befriend the entire population and come back bragging about all her 'peeps' on the moon. And heaven help them if they don't have her shoe size. (no emoji)"

I crawled from bed, intent on getting coffee, only to stop dead in my tracks. Owen the Marine was in my reading chair fixing to bite into one of my apples.

He looked up and said, "Rowdy told me what happened."

"Good grief," I grumped, heading for my coffee maker to try out the moon version of cinnamon spice coffee. And between Rowdy and Owen popping in, it's a good thing I wore pajamas to bed these days.

Owen continued, "I asked him to let me know if you had any such outbursts, or issues with your ears." He rose and walked toward me, which I should not have watched. He wore that taupe uniform all too well.

"But it was only a nightmare. I wasn't hearing voices."

"What about high-frequency communications?"

"I…I don't know." I pondered, sipping marvelous coffee. "Even if I did, I wouldn't have known what was being said. But I guess that could be agitating, leading me to feel attacked."

"So you really did dream the moon was under attack like Rowdy said?" Owen's deep-purple eyes were so intense, I held my breath. "Breathe, Rowan, and talk to me. Let's sit down."

"Okay, but do you want coffee? You sound kind of mad at me."

"No, thanks. I'm good with an apple. And I'm merely concerned. Can you describe your dream to me, the parts most vivid?"

We sat together on the couch, so Bodie took the fancy chaise lounge. Probably the beginning of the end for it remaining my reading chair.

I swallowed, adrenaline coursing through me as I recalled my nightmare. "Gunfire. Lots of gunfire. But only several men. And shouting. Flashes of bright light. Was that where the colors came from? Green…red…"

"Were these men after you? Or someone else, do you think?"

"Me, for sure. Maybe others too."

"And then you woke screaming?"

"I guess so, I don't remember hearing myself scream, but I suppose I must have."

"Okay, Rowan." Owen leaned in and put a hand on my shoulder, pinning me with those formidable eyes. "Here's what's going to happen, if not today, then tomorrow. No more putting it off. You're meeting with Byrin."

"But what does talking to Byrin about my ears have to do with a nightmare? I didn't hear voices last night."

"Byrin is an empath, in addition to being a labyrinth specialist. She's like an alternative medicine doctor, both mental and physical. And you're clearly stressed, or—"

"What? You think I need therapy too?"

"Please don't be defensive, babe. Hear me out."

"But you're being kind of autocratic."

He smiled, and I shivered.

"Have you ever had nightmares, or any type of dream, that ended up occurring in some capacity?" Owen asked.

I sipped coffee. "Yes, but I've dreamt about things that didn't eventually happen."

"Yet I know you've pondered on the meaning of your dreams."

"How did you—oh. Hearing between the lines. That thing you do." I frowned.

"That thing we do makes Labyrinthians like Byrin great at psychotherapy, and makes some of us adept at interrogation. I know you're keeping something from me."

"Nothing relevant." I put down my coffee and crossed my arms over my chest, then dropped them when I realized it was likely a defensive tell.

Owen didn't smile. "Not relevant? You sure about that?"

"Now you sound like Roger." I sighed. "Look, if it makes you feel better, I did have a dream that might have been about you. It was more than a year ago, but I remember it well."

"Tell me about this dream."

I eyed the apple in his hand, both red and green like Honeycrisps, my favorite. "Just before I left for Monterey, where the spaceship ended up landing and shocking the world, I dreamt of my ex-husband and me, wearing the full dress Marine Corps uniform."

"And you wondered at potential symbolism?"

"Yes, but it didn't make sense, especially because I was never a Marine. But my ex-husband had black hair, like you, with the same military buzzcut. And those long, double-rowed eyelashes. You also have them."

"It's a Labyrinthian trait. Has your ex-husband had his DNA tested?"

"I don't know. But within days of my dream, there you were, on TV talking about Mars being like a phoenix. Wearing the Marine full dress uniform. And one more thing. My dream included Honeycrisp apples," I said as Owen flinched, his arm stopping in midair with the apple he intended to take a bite of.

"I'd wondered," I continued, "if the dream was like a strange Adam-and-Eve-based allegory blaming women for everything. Or a physics thing. You know, Newton's apple. I can't seem to get away from Marines—or physicists."

Owen put the apple on my coffee table and turned to me, taking my hands in his.

"I had a dream about you too, after meeting you at OUTWARD in March."

"Oh boy." I breathed.

"In my dream you were here in the moonship. Someone was trying to hurt you."

I started to tremble and tried to keep tears from gushing forth. "And you eventually thought it was just that the president was after me, because that's why I ended up here?"

"I did until you had this nightmare that an attack was taking place on the moonship."

"That thing you thought I wasn't telling you?" I pulled my hands from his, digging my fingers into my thighs. "One of the attackers in my nightmare—I know him. And it wasn't the president."

Chapter 34

"All right, I will meet with Byrin today. But seriously, Owen, this guy Lucas is someone I've had nightmare flashbacks about for a year now because he was literally a living nightmare when he occupied my home before he left, exactly one year ago. The problem is he went to join up with one of those mining outfits on Mars that's causing problems. But they aren't allowed to come to the moonship, right?"

"True," said Owen, looking preoccupied. "Does anyone have intel on this Lucas guy?"

"Roger, and Rowdy, because they spied on me and anti-alien groups in Yearntown that Lucas apparently became a part of. And you should know, he was a combat Marine and his DNA turned out to be predominantly from Mars. But he's pretty much out of his mind, especially when drinking heavily, which is most of the time."

"I'm going to go talk to Rowdy. You stay put. Byrin will come to you here," he said, pulling me to him and touching the clear stone at my throat, which emitted heat when he did so. "Keep this on."

"I will, and have. But is it going to protect me from potential armed intruders?"

"It doesn't work that way. But it will warn of danger to you," he said, slipping out the door before I could ask more questions or spend too much time fretting about why he hadn't kissed me again.

Byrin arrived a half hour later, and I learned I had a door chime to alert me to visitors—the five-tone sequence from *Close Encounters of the Third Kind*, likely a Rowdy prank.

As my door slid open, I blurted, "I want you to know Genie and I were not talking about you before I met you the other day!"

Byrin glided in, long black hair flowing, wearing a tunic of deep greens and blues and a winsome smile that made her violet eyes dance. "Yes, but it was ironic timing, was it not?"

"I guess so. When you think about it, your name is kind of ironic, beginning with B-y, which sounds like *bi*, which is a shortened slang term for 'bisexual.'" I popped my hand over my mouth, my eyes feeling huge in my head.

Thank goodness Byrin continued to smile as she sat in my reading chair. I hoped she didn't end up with critter hair all over her. Luckily Bodie didn't leap on her when she arrived. Instead he stood by, tail wagging, staring at her. Kind of like I was doing.

"It is not actually about sex partners, Rowan. It is about how I identify."

I sighed and sat on the couch. "I know, but you make me babble. Or make me feel nervous. I don't know." I wrung my hands, wanting to bite my nails. "And where are my manners? Can I offer you a beverage? Something to snack on? I have apples!"

"Thank you, I am fine for now. I have heard that humans often resort to joking when they feel uncomfortable, and though I do not want you to feel awkward around me, it is understandable. I expect I am unlike anyone you have encountered." Bodie lay on the floor next to Byrin's feet, which were in blue skimmers like the ones I'd recently bought.

"You've heard? Have you not dealt with many humans? Surely you've been to Earth?"

"Do not call me Shirley," Byrin said with a mock straight face before she giggled.

"Oh my gosh. You learned English from watching movies too?"

"Partly, and I have been to Earth, but not a populated area, and not to the States. I have deduced that my kind is not so welcome or accepted there." She smiled wryly.

Did Byrin go by *she*? That's how I'd been thinking of her. Would she let me know how to refer to her? And my heart plummeted at her expression, a kind of weariness in those striking eyes. I wanted to deny her observation about the States, even as I knew it to be all too true. Instead I asked, "Where did you travel on Earth?"

"Antarctica. To see the penguins." Byrin's smile was pure joy. "Penguins are extraordinarily resilient and endearing creatures, and also odd in their physiology."

"Yes, they are. Are penguins indigenous to Earth?"

Byrin nodded. "It's strange to have a human ask me that. There's so much you don't know because many of your species don't want to know." Her eyes grew sorrowful.

"Fear and willful ignorance. It's gotten worse upon finally learning aliens are among us," I murmured. "Though I'm embracing it as much as I can. I managed to come to the moon, but I've never been to Antarctica. I'm envious, though I bet it was frigid cold."

"Not colder than being outside the moonship." Byrin full-on grinned.

"Yikes," I said. "But there's something I still don't know, which is how to refer to you. On Earth there's a movement to have pronouns announced during introductions, such as *he*, *she*, *they*. Something for my generation to adjust to, and learn from."

"I have heard about that too. But for me, I dress as a female because that is how I most identify and how I am comfortable. So *she* would be my pronoun, would it not?" She tilted her head, purple eyes mischievous and merry. It was a wondrous thing.

"I'm sorry if I'm being rude by staring. I'm starting to question if I've developed bisexual tendencies of my own. You are simply the most beautiful creature I've ever seen. And I'm babbling again, aren't I?"

"Yes." She laughed. "It is actually about Owen, is it not? This sudden focus of yours on bisexuality? He has gotten you all… What is your expression? Twisted in knots?"

"Yes!" I squealed. "I thought he was gay, and then he goes and lays a kiss on me on New Year's, and now when I'm near him, I feel things I shouldn't. At my age you'd think I'd have gotten past that. I sure thought I had, until I started interacting with exasperating alien males."

"If it makes you feel better, he is doing some twisting of his own, about you. Especially after this nightmare of yours, which he explained to me, so you do not have to relive it. This brings me to what I would like to discuss with you today, other than our delightful introductory banter."

"You've been delightful. I've been a nut wing!" I snorted.

"Nut wing? That is a new one. Maybe we can explore that next time." She grinned again. "And next time we will get more technical and delve into labyrinth details so I can help you with your auditory challenges. But today, let me reveal to you why Owen focused on your dreams, and this nightmare."

Morris chose that moment to awaken and leap onto Byrin's lap. "Oh my gosh, I'm sorry! They tend to have minds of their own!" I reached for my cat.

"As well they should. It is quite all right." She stroked Morris with her pale delicate fingertips. "My, his tail is long! And he is a talker, this one."

Apparently Byrin made Morris babble too, because he chattered as if telling her a story.

"Yes, Morris is noisy with an extra-long tail and an ultra-stubborn disposition. But I love the little varmint to pieces, and my puppy dog too. Bodie is being on his best behavior with you. Actually, he's never behaved this well."

Byrin leaned down to pet Bodie. "Hello there, handsome fellow," she said, making him gaze at her adoringly. "You have DNA from Sirius," she said to me, "the same place of origin as canines like Bodie, do you not?" she asked.

"Yes, 5 percent."

"And your Mars DNA?"

"Only 4 percent, the smallest of my alien percentages, actually. But Mars is my ruling planet for my zodiac sign, Aries. Do you know about those, about horoscopes?"

"Yes, they can sometimes be uncanny, can they not?" She tilted her head, peering at me.

"Did you use that word *uncanny* because you somehow know I use it a lot?"

"Perhaps. It could be why it seems to be floating about in my head. But horoscopes, like dreams, can often have great significance or accuracy. Other times, it is as if they have no direct applicability to any given daily occurrence."

"So how do you tell the difference—how do I determine if a dream or a horoscope is actually going to happen?"

"You do not. That is why anything telling you your future should be approached with a grain of caution, or skepticism. Everything in the universe is subject to change. There are many different forces, different sources of energy at work."

"So this recent nightmare of mine? Why is Owen so worried about it?"

"Your Mars DNA, which is Labyrinthian, may be a small percentage in comparison to your other DNA, but it is nonetheless significant because of what it reflects in you. The intuitive nature of Labyrinthians includes what some on Earth deem psychic. This means that while most of your dreams are mere manifestations of your subconscious and a reaction to past experiences, a small percentage of them contain details that are definitive premonitions. Like the one you described to Owen, about Marine uniforms and apples."

"He thinks my nightmare is really going to happen?" I thought I'd said it calmly, but Bodie leapt up and put his head in my lap, and Morris woke from slumbering in Byrin's lap to gaze at me in a most enigmatic manner as I hyperventilated.

"Rowan, your biorhythms are still adjusting to being in space, where they have never been before. Take deep breaths, and let us look at this from all angles. Your nightmare could be like others about this man, simply the result of your agitated state. You recently were abducted on Earth by armed men, as I understand. And then your spaceship was under attack upon launch for the moonship."

"Yes, because the US president is a vindictive criminal, not to mention his fascist greed-mongering attorney general. But what if Owen's instincts are correct?"

"He is fully preparing for that contingency. And you revealing your nightmare to him has enabled him to do so, to be aware and ready. This is good, is it not?"

Chapter 35

Owen returned to my suite after Byrin left. "How'd it go? You feeling calmer?"

I showed great restraint at not thumping him in his perfectly formed pectoral muscles.

"I suppose I might feel calmer, if I wasn't so frustrated at Red Orbiters for constantly keeping things from me, and now you! Does everyone assume if I'm not asking a direct question, I don't need answers to vital details about what the hell is going on? Like maybe telling me when my spacecraft is going to be attacked because the president is a psychopath?"

"Let's—"

"I mean, Red Orbiters always manage to pop into my ears at their whim, but it never seems to be to impart pertinent, *critical information*, now, does it?"

"Why don't we—"

"I don't want to sit down! What I want to know is what this bleeping necklace is for. I'm fed up with half answers, subterfuge, and outright obfuscation," I said, my tone seething because I was trying not to yell again for the critters' sake. "You know, for highly evolved beings who spend their lives observing and listening, it is mindboggling how much Red Orbiter males can't seem to elaborate out loud!"

"You're tense and on edge, and yet you still use words like a pro. You're also afraid, and I get that. The stone in the necklace will warn those who touch it of impending danger to the wearer. You've touched it, so you'll know too."

I sat on my couch, feeling small. "But don't I just have to speak out loud to let Red Orbiters know I'm in danger?"

"I suspect the necklace was in case you aren't able to do that."

"Lovely. This is crazy. This whole situation is crazy." I shook my head and reached to pet Bodie.

Owen said, "Can I sit? Because I have something to tell you. I don't want to rile you or frighten you further, but I'm not about to withhold it from you at this point."

"Yes, and I'm sorry. I shouldn't take my frustrations with Red Orbiters out on you. I know this isn't your fault."

"That may be so, but I think we've all been so worried about protecting you, we didn't consider how keeping things from you makes the situation more difficult."

"Ya think?" I snorted, sniffling.

Owen sat on the arm of the couch, because Bodie hogged the half I wasn't sitting on. "After talking with Rowdy, I was able to put it together. I know Lucas Rawlins, or at least I did."

My stomach did a somersault. "From the Marines? Were you recon too?"

"Yes. And I'm going to come out with it, though it's not usually said about a fellow Marine. He was *not* a good guy, and it wasn't as a result of his head injury. In fact, it's part of the reason he was wounded in combat to begin with."

"I always wondered why he wasn't awarded a Purple Heart," I murmured.

"I know you want full disclosure. But the details of what happened are classified. What I can tell you is that on Mars, he's played a part in problems we've had with the company he works for. And it involves some of the same issues he had in the Corps. Drunkenness, violent outbursts, erratic, reckless behavior."

"All too familiar to me. But despite my nightmare, my gut instinct tells me Lucas is not out to get me. At least not in the way the president and his cult morons are. He went to Mars to escape his demons, but they went right along with him."

Owen turned my shoulders to him, his touch somehow comforting and evocative. "My instincts tell me the same thing, Rowan. But I still want to be prepared. Moonship security will be on our highest alert level until I can shake this feeling. And Rowdy is sending a couple of Red Orbiters to Mars for some of that focused observation and listening you're ready to choke them over." Owen grinned, and I felt tension drain from me.

"If I said, out loud, what I was thinking, you wouldn't need to hear between the lines?"

"Yes." He smiled that smile.

"Well, okay then. Why did you kiss me?"

Owen leaned down, those purple eyes inches from mine. "Because I wanted to. But what you're really wondering is, why haven't I done it again?" His lips captured mine, right there on the arm of my moonship couch.

I kept my eyes wide open, and so did Owen. It went on for a while, with only our lips touching, and touch they did.

When Owen finally pulled away and stood, I felt a sense of inner calm despite my heart rapidly thumping in my ears.

"I'd like to stay and continue this to wherever it might lead—I truly would. But I have more work to do in securing the ship. It may not be relevant, but Tribble is missing. And I'm telling you so you don't think it's being deliberately kept from you, even though I'm concerned it may cause unnecessary worry."

"What do you mean by missing?"

"Tribble fraudulently commandeered a saucer by claiming he was head of Lacertans and departed the moonship not long after we kicked him out of the New Year's party. It could just be a hissy fit, like a bratty kid pretending to run away to worry everyone. But he has not yet returned. We're working to determine where he might be, and why."

Chapter 36

I stayed in my suite all day after Owen left, trying not to stew, not wanting to call anyone. I wasn't going to worry my family and was afraid I'd scream at Rauc or Win like I had Owen. Roger hadn't left me with a method of contacting him, other than the necklace. Why was that?

Worse, I had no appetite and no working ink pens. My mind had too much time to contemplate why I had such a delayed reaction to not being told about the attack on the spaceship. Maybe I'd been juggling too many balls in the air, as in orbs. As in Red Orbiters.

But it was only January second, and I couldn't stay holed up in my suite forever.

By the time my door chimed around five p.m., hours after I'd eaten the leftover cornbread, I was finally feeling hunger pangs and pretty much stir crazy. My door slid open to Red MacLeod, complete with a West Highland terrier in his arms.

"Was that your dog Genie and I saw at the park? She is adorable!" I said.

Bodie careened into my legs in an effort to get to the Westie, yipping and squealing, which answered my question, but Red said, "Yes, it appears she's the dog. This is my Rosie. Someone walked her for me while I was sleeping upon arrival. I'm headed out to the dog park and thought you might like to come along with your pup. We could get a bite at that café with scones you told me about." He pronounced it *scons* in the Scots' way.

"Yes! Let me get Bodie's leash and change my shoes," I said. I sounded like Mom.

As we departed the transpod on the upper deck, Red took my arm. "Owen told me about the potential threat he's dealing with, but I'd already planned to ask you to join me. I dinna want you thinking this was some sort of set up to get you out of your suite."

"And out of my funk? I appreciate that, and I did need to get out. So did Bodie."

"You are safe with me, lass. Although I suspect the only reason Owen didn't disapprove of me taking you out was my Royal Marine background. He is protective of you."

"I'd love to hear details of your military life, perhaps when I'm not so anxious. I also want to know what it was like to be secretary of defense."

Due to the hour, no sunlight beamed through the transparent roof. Our table had a candle of sorts, not a flame, but not a battery bulb like on Earth either. I ordered scones again because, although hungry, my stomach was still in queasy knots. Red got fish and chips and ended up feeding me as many bites as he took.

"Bodie and Rosie look to be in love," I said, watching them frolic in the park. "Morris already has Tim's cat for a girlfriend, so I guess it's only fair."

"I'm getting a cat soon too," said Red. "Have you heard of a Scottish fold?"

"Those cats that look like the cutest stuffed animals in the world, with folded-down ears? I've always wanted one, but you don't see them at rescue shelters."

"Mine will come from a litter of a friend's cat. They tend to have great personalities. Like someone else I know." Red smiled, looking into my eyes.

"I'm afraid my personality has tended toward harpy today." I fidgeted with unused flatware on the table. "It's great there's no throwaway plastic utensils on the moonship. How do you suppose this little candle is powered? And those lamplights in the dog park?"

"The moonship surface is directly exposed to intense and constant solar wind. There's technology on the far side that harnesses its power."

"A windfarm on the far side of the moon?" I cocked my head. "Wouldn't that make a great song?"

Red laughed. "It doesn't look or operate like wind energy on Earth, but it is very effective. A fine work of engineering genius."

"Yikes! Engineering. Genie said you went to school with her brother Bruce in Edinburgh. Is that what your degree is in?"

"Chemical engineering. In fact, one of the things I want to study while I'm here is the pressurized sewage system, which transforms waste into renewable energy."

"Yuck. I'm glad we're done eating!" I wrinkled my nose. "And please don't try to explain how it works. I don't possess the engineering or science genes."

"I promise I won't mansplain how your toilet suctions, lass." He chuckled. "But I suspect the environmental attorney in you would be fascinated to learn how all waste aboard ship is processed into renewable energy or products. It is a far more advanced technique than recycling aboard naval aircraft carriers, for instance, but there are some similarities."

My throat grew warm, and I knew I wasn't having a hot flash over our discussion. As I touched the necklace where heat emanated, I was hit with intense panic, as if the word *danger* were erupting in my head.

I leaned toward Red and said in rush, "Please touch my necklace and tell me what happens?"

Red didn't hesitate. His blue eyes grew wide as he touched the stone. "Danger," he said. "Imminent." He stood abruptly and took my arm before I could give in to the reflexive urge to dive under the table.

"Oh my gosh!" I shouted. "I've got to get to Bodie!"

Red was practically carrying me in that direction. We were inside the park, and I had Bodie on a leash within seconds, feeling immense relief, until sirens blared and Rowdy's voice blasted in my ear.

"*Critical information* coming at you, Rowan! A protective shield has been activated around the perimeter of the park. Do not leave. Repeat. Do not leave!"

The next voice was Owen's, over some sort of booming intercom. "Security breach in landing hanger six. Gunfire. All Red Orbiter security personnel, mobilize now."

What seemed like a swarming horde of red uniforms appeared from all directions, including two who'd been dining at a table near ours. Minutes passed, and through a sea of red, I saw movement, flashes of dark green and blaring light in the gaps between security personnel storming toward the transpod depot. Then I heard gunfire, not distant, but mere yards away.

Ringing in my ears became so painful, tears stung my eyes. I wanted to bolt, but my legs felt heavy and weak, as if encased in the panicked sludge of my mind. My heart raced, and my breathing constricted. *I have to get to Morris too!*

I tried to lunge toward the perimeter. But why was Red's arm wrapped around me?

I held on to him as he held Rosie in his other arm, feeling Bodie at my knees. Genie's voice broke through my ears, "Rowan, please stop struggling and stay put! Your kitty will be fine. There's a protective shield around your suite too. It's going to be okay. Please stop!"

And another familiar domineering voice in my ear, soon after: "We've got this, beautiful."

Those were the last words I remembered hearing.

Chapter 37

"That is the only time in my life I have ever fainted," I said. "Like some twit in a cheesy romance novel. Jeez."

"Yes, but how many romance-novel twits are caught before they hit the ground by a Scottish Royal Marine former secretary of defense spy soon to be knighted?" said Genie.

"How did you know that? And is Red really with MI6? Can you confirm that?"

"You babbled it as we brought you back to your suite. How he was your knight in shining armor. Kind of like you were babbling, or more like screaming, about how you had to get to Morris, which is why Red had to grab you to keep you from careening out of the dog park, and why I had to pop in your ear to beg you to come back from crazy town. I don't know if Red's MI6. Why don't you just ask him?"

"So where is everyone? Is everyone okay? Was anyone hurt in the attack?" I tried to sit up on my chaise lounge, but Genie leaned over me.

"You might not want to do that. You said you were feeling pukey in the transpod."

I felt the room spin and lay back down but spied Bodie on the couch. "Bodie! Come here, sweet boy." I struggled to sit up, but Bodie leapt onto the chaise, and we both fell backward. "My sweet pup, I'm so glad you're okay."

Genie said, "Everyone is fine and dealing with the situation, and its aftermath. Did you know these chaise lounges were also called fainting couches back the day?" Genie chuckled.

My head felt fuzzy. "You're laughing at me, so everything must be okay. Unless you're making jokes to cover for something. Did I hear Roger too?"

"Yes, you did. He arrived to help flatten the guys with AK-47s. Not a pretty sight, or sound. There was no calming bug juice involved in the takedown. But poor little Tribble screamed loudest when he saw Owen coming at him. I believe Marines call it a full-frontal assault? He panicked and waved around a gun he had no idea how to use, which means bullets sprayed, so Maggie ultimately tackled him, squashing the little schemer like a bug."

"So Tribble was with the armed invaders? Did you say *squashed*? Is he dead?"

"No." Genie snorted. "But he may wish he was once Owen is done interrogating him."

"I need you to start from the beginning. My head's kind of fuzzy," I said.

"That's just it. I can't tell you much of anything until Owen learns what was behind this. He said to tell you you'll know when he knows."

"But you saw the men with guns?"

"Yes, three human dudes in old woodland-pattern camouflage, the kind once used by your army. They came out of the transpod onto the upper deck, guns blazing, but were met with a wall of Red Orbiter security personnel who blocked the bullets, much to their surprise."

"But Tribble hates humans, and doesn't he know Red Orbiters can block bullets?"

"Yes, but apparently he didn't tell his cohorts in crime, or if he did, they didn't believe him because it freaked them out."

I shut my eyes, remembering gunfire and screams.

"Hey," said Genie. "Are you okay? You don't look so good."

"I think I'm going to be sick," I said, struggling to get up from the chair.

"I've got you," said Genie, taking my arm and letting me lean on her until I could reach the bathroom, where the poor woman had to hold me while I vomited.

"I know you might think this is awkward," she teased as she helped me up. "But better me than your knight, or Owen."

"Or Rowdy, perish the thought," I said as I gulped water from a flask Genie handed me. "This is when he would pop in my ear if he heard me. Is he okay? Why hasn't Rowdy said something snarky yet? Or Roger? Why isn't he trying to boss me around?" I sat in my chair and lay back, grateful it was a chaise. Bodie rested his head on my thigh.

"We didn't want to overwhelm you. Rowdy's lying low, as is Roger. But I know everyone is anxious to hear you're okay, so you might want to let them know."

"I'm okay," I said weakly.

"Not terribly convincing," drawled Roger in my ear. "But I'm on my way to Mars, beautiful, so I can't make sure you are as you say."

"I felt the necklace give off heat and knew I was in danger," I said.

"Good. It worked as it should. It alerted me and Rauc, and especially gave Owen a head's-up that trouble had arrived, headed for you. I will speak with you soon, beautiful, whether you want me to or not." And just like that, Roger was gone from my ear, and I realized why he and Rowdy were lying low.

"I'm in trouble. They heard me talking to Owen when I was ranting about Red Orbiters, didn't they?" I asked Genie.

"Yes. Maggie and I did too, but we understand, Rowan. And Maggie says you can ask us whatever you want at girls' night next week."

"Great. I'm just glad everyone is okay."

My door chimed the five-tone *Close Encounters* sequence. Genie said, "Sounds like a Rowdy prank," before she went to the door. "It's your knight, Rowan. Should I let him in?" She chuckled as Red walked into the room, without his dog.

"Is Rosie all right?" I asked.

"Aye, she's fine. Bodie was a bit skittish, but now he sees you're okay." Bodie trotted to Red, who reached down to pet him. "Why does your door chime sound like *Close Encounters of the Third Kind*? No fair." Red made a pouty face. I laughed as Morris leapt into my lap.

"It's good to hear you laugh, lass. I was worried about you."

"Thanks for catching me so I didn't fall on my head. I kind of feel like I did anyway, but I know it could be worse!"

“Yes, it could have been,” said Owen, strolling in with George. “But it wasn’t bad at all. It really wasn’t, Rowan. Lucas was not one of the armed men.”

Chapter 38

"I should have gotten more chairs at the furniture store," I said. With Red and Genie also in my suite, there wasn't enough room for everyone to sit.

George came and hugged me before sitting next to Red on my couch.

"I'll stand so you can sit," Red said to Owen. "You've been working pretty hard."

"Thanks, but I've still got adrenaline pumping, so I'm good with standing," he said.

"Or pacing," I muttered, watching him move in the small space like a caged panther.

"Sorry." Owen stopped and dropped down, squatting next to me on the chaise, his hand resting on my thigh. "How the hell are ya, babe?"

"Oh, just lounging, eating bonbons, waiting to hear about the terrible trouble with Tribble," I said, trying to keep a straight face but ruining it with a giggle.

"And terrible trouble Tribble is, along with being quite adept at finding it. When he left here with a saucer he was not authorized to fly, he headed for Mars, seeking those he heard me say were causing issues there, thinking he might use them to get revenge for being booted from the party and further meetings."

Genie said, "Can I get anyone a beverage for this terrible Tribble tale? And we can use some of your dining chairs, Rowan."

"I think all I have is that bottle of Red Orbiter liqueur you had delivered to me," I said as George hopped up to help Genie drag two chairs near the couch.

"Great, I'm making cocktails. Keep talking, Owen," said Genie, headed to my minibar.

"Meanwhile," Owen continued, "on Mars was a group of three men—at least. If there's more, Rowdy and Roger will learn who they are. These guys were part of the gung-ho Rambo wannabes gallivanting about the US with automatic weapons seeking to intimidate anyone who doesn't worship the president, but apparently they took time out to come to Mars thinking they were going to strike gold, or oil. They weren't sure and didn't seem to realize it's diamonds being mined there."

"They're not too bright," I said. "I dealt with too many of them in Yearntown."

"Instead of getting rich, they got roped into a scheme by cronies of the president, several of whom are running these start-up outfits on Mars but ignoring all rules and protocols. This scheme was originally supposed to avenge the failed attempt to kidnap you. Because when Greens used a flying saucer to rescue you and your mother, the president and his pals assumed it was a Martian craft, so they were gunning for yours truly."

"Why you?" I asked.

"I'm the only *Martian*"—Owen made air quotes with his hands—"they know who was on Earth as a Marine, so they'd been after me, just like they were Tim and Oz in the spaceship."

"And me, as it turns out," said George.

"Good grief," I said.

"The problem with their plan was they hadn't yet figured out a way to board the moonship, since they were banned. Then, along came Tribble."

"And he spilled that I was on the moonship along with you?" I said.

"And Red," said Owen. "Which of course these guys thought would be quite a coup once Tribble weaved a tale of how Red had been the secretary of defense but was fired because he wasn't loyal to the president. They sucked it up like chewing tobacco."

"Because they don't read or listen to anything but Jax Smith on SlayNews."

"Exactly," said Owen. "So, within hours, they got suited up in their pseudo-soldier outfits, armed to the teeth with guns supplied by their feckless employers on Mars, and they hopped into the saucer with Tribble and headed for the moonship."

"And they gave Tribble a gun," I added.

"Yes, which was perhaps Tribble's biggest personal error among his many miscalculations in terms of his future, because guns are not allowed on the moonship."

"Aye, for good reason," said Red, muttering. "Costumed cockwombles."

"They arrived in the hangar, which is when your necklace alerted me to danger, even before they disembarked and opened fire," continued Owen.

"At absolutely nothing but walls," interjected Genie, handing us all spritzers with spherical ice. "Because they had no clue about the moonship, how it works, or anything else."

"Tribble didn't tell them?" I asked.

"Tribble was a fool who thought he could control three armed men who hate aliens," said Owen. "They weren't about to take orders from him, but he managed to stop them from shooting up the empty hangar long enough to get them into a transpod, headed to the top deck to begin looking for you, Tim, Oz, George, me, or Red. Because they also had to avenge the embarrassingly thwarted bombing attempt to take out Tim and Oz."

"That little pincher actually thought he was going to traipse all over this ship with those armed idiots and not be noticed?" said Genie.

"I dinna suppose Tribble *thinking* had anything to do with it," said Red.

Owen nodded. "He told me that's what the guns were for, to intimidate each person into going back to the saucer. Tribble didn't factor in itchy trigger fingers, or their alternative agenda. Those guys wanted to wreak havoc because they'd been cooped up on Mars. But they were out of their element. At least Tribble didn't give them intel on what to expect."

"I suppose they likely didn't ask," I said. "So where are they now?"

"Rowdy and Maggie are escorting the men back to Mars because we have no jail, where they'll be detained until after the inauguration, when they'll return to Earth for criminal prosecution. I'm ensuring the outfit they worked for will be permanently banned from Mars, and Tim is busy filing a report with Homeland about the men and their employer, which was already one of several under investigation."

"And Tribble, what will happen to him?"

"Tribble is confined to his residence, with magnetic monitors to ensure he stays put until his fate is determined by moonship residents," said Owen, not without heat.

I turned to Genie. "Roger said he was headed to Mars too?"

"Roger flew there ahead of Rowdy and Maggie to flush out any more of these anti-alien vigilantes doing the president's bidding."

"It's the ultimate hypocrisy," I said. "They hate aliens, but not enough to refrain from attempting to exploit their planetary resources."

"And Tribble joined forces with hated humans to further his own ends. Hypocrisy is not a trait limited to one species, it would seem," said Red, shaking his head.

"Unfortunately, it isn't," said Owen. "But I need to head out and confer with Tim, who said to tell you he's sorry he couldn't pop in to see you too."

"We should all clear out and let Rowan rest," said Genie. "Are you okay with being alone? Because I don't mind hanging out."

"That's not necessary. I'll be here with Rowan for the night," said Raucous Wilde, walking in with a pizza box and wearing his Red Orbiter flight suit. The sight of him took my breath away.

"I think I might faint again."

Chapter 39

"How did you get here so quickly?" I asked once the others had scattered and Rauc lifted me from the chair, bestowing a kiss as he carried me to bed.

"I was already on my way soon after Rowdy told me you woke screaming from a nightmare about a moonship attack. I'm very concerned about you, Copper," he said, stripping out of his flight suit and turning to me.

My breath left me again. "I suppose Rowdy also ratted me out about my frustrations with Red Orbiters. Because I know he heard me."

"Why don't we get you out of those clothes?" Rauc sat next to me on the bed. "It would appear we've both been a bit frustrated with each other."

"Please don't be mad at me!" I said, pulling my tunic over my head. "It's been a wild ride here so far."

"Damn it, Copper." Rauc took my chin in hand. "That's one of the reasons I agreed to send you to the moonship where I knew you could get help with why you have these nightmares. And with your hearing abilities, which I know you wanted my help with. But you need assistance I can't give you, and you can get it here. If you weren't so stubborn about getting help. Have you even met with Byrin yet?"

"Yes! Today!" I pulled my chin away from his grip. "And I'm meeting with her tomorrow too! Or the next day! Right now I don't know what damn day it is, okay?"

"You taking that tone with me makes me want to turn you over my knee and calm your ass down."

I smiled inwardly, because Rauc's tone was filled with exasperation, yet wholly nonthreatening. Now naked, I curled against him and heard his sigh of contentment.

"How is it you can be here, with me? I know you must be busy dealing with the president's attack on a Red Orbiter vessel, and on Oz."

"And on you, Copper. But Oz is filling in for me, though I can't stay away longer than this night. So I intend to make the most of it."

After several hours of love play followed by sleep, we were snacking on pizza in bed.

"Octavius insisted I bring this for you from his Oregano Wortnik bistro," said Rauc.

"It's yummy, but isn't it going to leave some uncomfortable crumbs?" I asked.

"No, the pressurized cleaning system will take care of it."

"While we're in bed?" I squeaked.

"Good point," said Rauc, grinning. "Let's go make use of that chaise lounge I'm sure was Genie's idea."

Afterward, I realized why Genie liked that style of chair so much. And we had to kick poor Bodie off of it beforehand.

"I have a question," I said, making Rauc smile as we headed back to bed. "Yesterday I was looking up stuff about Luna moths to keep me occupied, seeing as how I'm sort of in the moon and Luna is the Roman moon goddess."

Rauc grinned. "Yes, she is. What's your question?"

"I think I spelled *Actius* wrong when writing the *Adventures of Luna Moth Woman* and the moon she hails from. I've been spelling it with a *u-s*, but it turns out the Latin term for a Luna moth, *Actias Luna*, is spelled with an *a-s*."

"Not to worry, Copper. The Latin name humans came up with may be spelled that way, but the actual moon where some of your DNA comes from, as well as entities from whom the Luna moth derives, is spelled with a *u-s*. Same as Romulus," he said, reminding me of his formidable given name.

"Well, that's a relief," I said, resting my elbow on Rauc's chest, propping my chin with my hand. "But all this Latin reminds me too much of law school."

"In your recent research, did you happen to learn about the Luna moth's defense mechanism?" he asked.

"What do you mean?"

"While in the larval stage, they emit clicks as a warning sign to deter predators."

My mouth fell open. "Like the clicks in my head as part of my tinnitus to block out voices? Or like the clicks of electronic communications?"

"You tell me," said Rauc, smiling. "But right now, I have things I want to do with this lush body of yours."

Chapter 40

When Rauc and I awakened again, it was full-on morning, and I felt like Shakespeare's Juliet because I didn't want it to be.

"Before you have to go off and be a big bad Red Orbiter leader, I have something to say."

"Okay, but is it going to make me want to paddle your ass again?"

I swatted his chest, and he swatted my butt.

"Maybe." I smiled. "But I want to get this out. I know you think you couldn't help me with my ear issues, but there's things you probably didn't realize would be helpful. Things I didn't necessarily know to ask about. For instance, Red Orbiters can apparently hear when another Red Orbiter speaks their name? But they don't have to be zoning in, as I've heard you put it, or actively listening?"

"Yes, Copper. If a Red Orbiter says my name, the voice will come to me."

"Not just in calling out for help or to get your attention? You hear your name spoken when someone is simply speaking of you?"

"Yes, but you're not a Red Orbiter, so why is this relevant?"

"What about me? If I say your name? Don't you hear it?"

Rauc paused before he answered, his teal eyes boring into me. "Come to think of it, yes."

"Well, this is enormously helpful. Because so many times when I've heard Red Orbiters speaking from afar, it's because they spoke my name. I'm sure of it. Sometimes that's not the case, because I'm merely in closer proximity to a Red Orbiter and that's why I hear them. But from afar? It's because they're speaking my name in conversation."

"I'm proud of you for figuring this out, Copper, based on what you've heard, and when. I wasn't trying to keep anything from you, because I'm not aware of what you're actually hearing."

"But this is where you can help me. By understanding your abilities better, you help me understand mine."

"I will try to do better, but I'm also aware it's suppression of your auditory abilities that's hurting you. Because voices are not the only thing you block. It's why I wanted you to get help. I'd love to fix what torments you, but I can't."

"I appreciate that," I said, kissing him. "And I promise to learn as much as I can from Byrin. No more procrastinating."

"Good, because I'll take it out on your hide if you don't." He flipped me over, covering me with his body.

"Okay, but wait! Ro—someone—told me how Red Orbiters might also hear another Red Orbiter at the moment they think of them. I just want you to know—so you don't have to worry—that I can't do that. But I do think of you all the time."

"Now I really am going to have to tan your behind."

As Rauc redonned his flight suit, he said, "Before I go, I want to fill you in on what I've been doing back on Earth."

I leapt from bed to kiss him.

"Mmm…I may never make it off this ship, so put some clothes on and let's have coffee. Have you bought a bunch of mugs with moons and planets on them?" He grinned.

"No, I still have lots of shopping to do!" I said, throwing on my tunic from yesterday.

Bodie and Morris pawed over Rauc on the couch as he spoke. "I know you're aware that Lacertan leaders residing in the moonship went to Earth to meet with Vice President-Elect O'Neill. But what you didn't know was I was with them for that meeting."

"Cool! I know it's a big deal having a human hybrid with predominant Lacertan DNA elected to high office. Oz said it's the highest office so far."

"It's the highest office for a Lacertan, or someone like O'Neill who is nearly 100 percent so, to be *knowingly* elected as an otherworldly individual," corrected Rauc.

"What are you saying?"

"A higher office was once held by someone who was 100 percent extraterrestrial, yet born in the US."

I almost spilled coffee on my fancy chaise lounge.

Rauc continued, “I was at that meeting to provide information to both the vice president-elect and the president-elect about aliens who have been famous figures in American history.”

“No fair you got to meet our first female president, but please tell me what you’re getting at because it is flipping fantastic. And don’t you dare tell me I can’t put it in the book!”

“I’m telling you *for* the book, Copper. But first I want you to know there have been other prominent figures with origins not of Earth. Such as a Founding Father and various inventors. Orville and Wilbur Wright, for instance, both had less than 1 percent human DNA.” Rauc paused and smiled. “But let me ask you, do you have an absolute favorite individual, a signatory to the US Constitution? The signer who was known throughout the world and was, coincidentally, about as wild and snarky as Rowdy?”

“Benjamin Franklin.” I breathed the words. “I’m so loving this.”

“You’ll love it even more when I tell you he was a Red Orbiter.”

“This is so great! And the president? No, wait, I already know. It was Thomas Jefferson, wasn’t it?”

“Born in Virginia, to parents from Proxima Centauri b.”

Chapter 41

"I've got something to tell you about the man who founded that alma mater of yours," I said to my sister after Rauc left. He'd said it was okay if I blabbed to one person about Thomas Jefferson, who founded the University of Virginia. At least until I told everyone with the official reveal of the book, that is.

After G plotzed, I also told her about the attack on the moonship, and we agreed to not tell Mom and Dad.

I needed to take Bodie out, but first confirmed via email with Byrin that I was meeting her again tomorrow. Then I snagged my usual seat at the café and ordered tea while Bodie played with a few dogs, plus a jackrabbit, a wolf, and that coyote again. It felt like I was in a Native American totem fantasy. And how much did I love those long, jackrabbit ears?

"May I join you?" said Owen, standing over me at the table.

"Sure," I said. "I know I should try a different eatery at some point, but right now I don't have the energy to figure it out."

Owen took the chair opposite me. "I admit to being envious it was Rauc and not me in your bed last night, draining your energy. But at least it wasn't Rowdy."

I looked into those purple eyes. "You're attracted to Rowdy?"

"Look at you, being all intuitive like a Labyrinthian! But yes, very."

I grinned. "Apparently Rowdy confuses human folks into presuming he's gay. Kind of like his goofy act."

"You know he can probably hear you," Owen warned, but also grinned.

"I suppose Red Orbiters could keep some of us in the universe a bit more honest, what with their abilities. Do you think that's why it doesn't seem possible to block them from listening?"

"They only hear the parts we say out loud. Folks can still keep lies in their heads, their thoughts hidden."

"Except from certain Labyrinthians."

"Even then. Not everyone is easy to read," said Owen.

"I don't suppose those intriguing alexandrite eyes of yours can also change color and put words in people's heads?"

"That sounds like a Roger Rogers specialty, of which he has many."

"Don't tell me you're attracted to Roger too?"

"Not in the way you are. But I do admit to being curious." Owen's eyes took on a mischievous glint.

"Do I dare speak out loud and ask what about?"

Owen leaned in, his face inches from mine. "What's it like being intimate with Superman?"

I swatted his hand resting on the table. "You have to hear between the lines on that one, but it's even more intense than flying through the sky with him. Like I'm Lois Lane." I laughed.

"That giggle of yours makes me want to do all sorts of things with you, which I will keep in my head and won't say out loud." He smiled and looked over at Bodie in the park. "That's a great pup you've got there."

I looked at my dog, now resting on his back, legs stretched high in the air, not a care in the moonship. "I mistakenly thought I once wanted a cowboy. As it turns out, I ended up with a much better deal. A cowboy dog. The best kind of mixed breed. A herder with a sweet soul and a little bit of wild."

"Sounds like you," said Owen, smiling before his expression turned serious. "I wasn't sure if you wanted to talk about Lucas not being part of the attack yesterday, but since you brought him up, is there anything you want to discuss?"

"I don't know." I looked away. "I'm glad he wasn't part of it, that he left the anti-alien political craziness behind in Yearntown. It's weird that he was in my dream, though."

"You still need to process what you went through with him. I will listen all you want, but know that Byrin is a safe and ideal harbor for that journey. She won't want to avenge your honor as much as I so badly want to."

I smiled and reached for his hand. "I am lucky to call you friend. And you're also a safe harbor for me. For instance, I feel safe asking you to mansplain—but only this one time!—how it is that guns can be fired in outer space? Isn't there a gravity issue? And is that what the flashing lights I saw were?"

"Yes to the flashes. At night, like it was during the attack, gunfire tends to look like fireworks. And with guns, it's not about gravity. They can be fired aboard a spaceship, but they can also be fired outside, in the open vacuum of space, an oxygen-free environment. Because while fires can't burn without oxygen, modern ammunition contains an oxidizer, a chemical that will trigger the explosion of gunpowder, thus firing a bullet, wherever you are in the universe. No atmospheric oxygen required."

"And no oxygen to the brain needed either, for far too many who wield guns."

"Speaking of that, Maggie's returned from escorting the armed idiots back to Mars and thinks we should all get together for a debrief dinner. She knows you'll have questions."

"So Rowdy stayed behind to work with Roger?"

"Yes, and Oz is still gone, helping Rauc. But George is anxious to see you again and see for himself you're really okay. And Maggie is letting Red pick the restaurant, so no telling where we'll end up, given he's been all over the world."

"Could be interesting, assuming we don't have to eat haggis."

Chapter 42

Before I left for dinner, Win called. "I figured you could use some comic relief."

"Ya think? But it's good to hear your voice."

"Do you miss me, sweet pea?"

"Depends on how soon you deliver that comic relief."

"Funny you should use the word *deliver*, because the president has a five-hundred-pound peccadillo and is doing a slow, combustible burn over it."

I pondered this. "Five hundred pounds? The MQ-9 Reaper bomb?"

"Well, it is blocking the door he normally uses to enter the White House. You know, the one guarded by Marines? Except they aren't there. Only the bomb Roger delivered is."

"No one could figure out how to move it?" I bent down to give Bodie a belly rub, which he always seemed to need the minute I got on the phone.

"That, and no one will. He demanded Space Force take it away, but they don't have access to the heavy equipment needed."

"And the president has no secretary of defense. Wonder why that is?" I snarked as Morris leapt into my lap to keep me from giving Bodie attention.

"Plus, most recently the Army, Navy, and Marines all claimed to be too busy celebrating the New Year's holiday. Now they're saying, why would the president want a bunch of losers, as he called them, to solve his problems?"

"Ouch. The media must be having a field day."

"Oh, they are, despite the poser-in-chief banning them from the White House. He's ranting on Twitter about leakers. Especially because that 'You were stupid' message Roger left keeps getting airtime because it's still on the lawn, clear as day."

"What's the Twitter universe said about this? What did Alamogordo61 say?" I referred to Win's incognito handle.

"My tweet was in your honor, sweet pea. I said that perhaps the Air Force has a weather balloon they could use to move it, like the ones so very popular back in Roswell in 1947."

"Yes, I do miss you very much." Bodie shoved his nose into Morris's butt, making the cat leap to floor, meowing his disgruntled displeasure.

"Another tweet suggested the president straddle the bomb and ride it from the White House on Inauguration Day, like Slim Pickens's character in *Dr. Strangelove*."

I chuckled. "Sounds like Rowdy."

"It was Roger, but I don't want you missing him too much."

"So what's next?" Bodie rolled over for more belly rubbing.

"The president is now threatening to issue an executive order abolishing Space Force if they don't remove it."

"Have at it. Too bad he can't actually do that with an executive order."

"Never stopped him from wasting ink before."

"So, is Roger going to have to remove the bomb?" I asked, picturing it in my head.

"Yeah, it was inevitable. He'll pick it up during the night before inauguration, and remove the message lasered on the White House lawn. I'm coordinating with Greens, who have agreed to dismantle it and do their scrap-metal-recycle thing in the Sandia Mountains."

I giggled.

"You laugh, but it's pretty impressive what those little dudes can do—and quickly."

"Don't I know it!"

"You should know Greens will continue to be involved, with logistics still to be determined as the situation gets increasingly dire for the president."

"Will they abduct him?"

"We're waiting to see what he does. Right now he's claiming he won't leave the White House on Inauguration Day. Oh, and he's decided because he can't destroy the moon, he'll buy it—with US taxpayer dollars. Then he plans to put his name in huge neon lights on its surface."

"That's not comic relief," I said.

"Here's a jocular riddle. What's the difference between NASA and Space Force?"

"Is this an Oz joke?"

"Yes, and the punchline is: Intelligence versus aggression. And while what's happening may not be funny, make no mistake, sweet pea—the treasonous trash will be removed from the White House, one way or another."

Chapter 43

Other than Red, I was first to arrive for dinner.

"Welcome to Southeast Asian dining. Light, fruitful fare with a spicy flair. A little lime, coconut, basil here and there, and mango sticky rice for a sweet, or fried bananas with coconut ice cream. Sugarcane shrimp, Vietnamese style, and the best fisherman's rice this side of Bangkok."

"You sound like a chef. What's up with that?"

"Culinary arts is my hobby," said Red, pulling out a chair for me at the round table. "I find it relaxing."

"You sound like my sister. You're both wackadoodle." I shook my head.

Red leaned down, his lips at my ear. "Did you say I should whack a Doodles? I hear that's your nickname."

I stared into his laughing blue eyes. "Have you been spying on me like Homeland by reading my mom's tweets? Jeez, you must be with MI6."

"Not anymore."

"Holy spooks! *I knew it!* There really was a James Bond at our New Year's party."

"I knew that!" said Tim, joining us at the table with Maggie.

"Knew what?" said George, close behind, followed by Owen.

"What? I don't qualify?" Genie strutted in.

"And don't forget Rowdy," said Tim.

"I have no problem with forgetting Rowdy," grumped Genie.

"I am not about to say anything on that out loud," I quipped.

"Very wise, lass. Please, everyone sit. I was just telling Rowan where we are traveling in the world of Earth for tonight's grand culinary experience."

"Why does Red suddenly sound kind of gay?" Owen whispered in my ear as he sat next to me.

"You should have heard him before. Maybe we should sing show tunes. I vote for *South Pacific* and *Brigadoon*," I whispered back.

"I heard that," said Red, seated on my other side, his voice low. "And you're within whacking distance. Your nickname is not all I know about you, lass." He winked.

"My psyche is stirred by the news but not shaken." I blew him a kiss.

George said from across the table, "I heard you had a bit of a gravity problem with ink pens. Tomorrow morning I'm taking you shopping to get what you need. We can't have our favorite writer unable to spin her craft!"

"Rowdy blabbed. But I'm interested in seeing this device he mentioned."

"Once you get the hang of it," said Owen, "I think you'll love it."

As we started with spring rolls, Maggie said, "Rowan, I can feel questions coming off you in waves over there."

"Busted." I smiled. "What's got me puzzled is why Red Orbiters didn't have intel on what was going down. There were known problems on Mars, so was anyone actively observing or surveilling them?"

"We had limited security personnel there, and we certainly have more now, including Roger and Rowdy. But those guys had only been planning their attack for a few days with maybe a couple of meetings before Tribble arrived. Their discussions were not overheard. It's often a crapshoot when it comes to timing and focus." Maggie shrugged.

"Plus," interjected Owen, "in defense of Red Orbiters, who can't be everywhere at all times listening to everyone, our previous problems involved drunken fights and failure to follow mining safety guidelines and extraction rules, not threats of storming a place they were already banned from. Hence, they weren't deemed a potential security threat for the moonship, on which they would never have been able to land had they not been in a Labyrinthian spacecraft."

"I get it now," I said. "That's the trouble with Tribble. And I wasn't being critical. You Red Orbiters are kind of my superheroes."

"I sure hope Rowdy didn't hear you say that. You'll never hear the end of it," said Genie.

"Yikes! I'll change the subject. What is it with these dumbasses wearing desert camouflage in urban cities and that old woodland pattern to attack a spaceship? They look ridiculous." I bit into a delicious eggroll—at least, I thought that's what it was.

"They *are* ridiculous," said Maggie. "But it's worse than that. Those punks who attacked the moonship actually claimed it was their Second Amendment right to do so. Because, and I quote, they 'are a *militia* and the US is going to *dominate space*.'"

"Second Amendment? In *outer space*?" I shook my head. "From the sound of their screams when their guns didn't work on Red Orbiters, they couldn't dominate a miniature poodle," I said. "But won't they spew to the president and everyone else about you being able to repel bullets with your bodies? That can't be good."

"They think it was some short of shield, a defensive object, same as the pissant vigilantes who attacked you assumed," said Genie. "They have no clue it has to do with our physiology."

"No more than they grasp the meaning of 'well regulated' in the Second Amendment," said Tim.

"Or that the Constitution doesn't apply in outer space, or anywhere else on Earth but the US. Nor does our military—much less a bunch of posers playing army—have the right to dominate anything up here," I said. "Something Space Farce also can't seem to comprehend."

Once we reached dessert, Maggie dinged her aperitif glass with a spoon.

"If I could say a few words, something's come up that's made me realize how much I'm going to need friends on Earth—and the moonship." She smiled at Owen. "And I'm grateful to be able to call you my friends, especially this guy right here." She held up Tim's hand clasping hers. "Tim has agreed to stick with me through this, which is very chivalrous of him. Because it also means I'll leave here earlier than planned. For Washington, DC."

"Are you going to take Roger's place to guard Senator Rojas-Ortiz when she becomes attorney general?" I asked.

"No," said Maggie, taking a deep breath. "It looks like I'm going to be taking her place as a senator for the Battle Born State of Nevada."

Chapter 44

"This calls for a champagne toast!" said Red, sounding disturbingly like Mom.

"Yes, this is fantastic news, other than the part about you leaving early. We haven't even been here a week," I said. "And no wonder you needed to shop for pantsuits."

"We've got another week or so," said Maggie. "I'm not sure when I'm leaving. We can still have girls' night, which I definitely need now! And don't worry, Rowan. Oz will come back to fly you home. And both Genie and Rowdy are trained on the new spacecraft."

"Sounds like a party," I said. "So tell us how this is all coming down. It's the governor who appoints someone to replace a senator, right?"

"Yes, and they must choose from the same political party. Like Cassandra, I'm a member of the Omni Party, and was previously a Democrat. Although I haven't held office before, and she was Nevada's attorney general before she became a US senator. But you know how folks love their combat veterans in Congress!"

"You're certainly old enough. The Constitution says you only have to be thirty," I said.

"Yes." Maggie grinned wryly. "I'll be one of the youngest senators currently serving, at age thirty-three—and also the oldest at 125."

"And the first former Marine female fighter pilot, though not the first Red Orbiter," said Tim.

"Well, I will be the first Red Orbiter *pilot and observer* in Congress." She smiled.

"Look out! They'll never know what hit 'em. Does the governor know this? Don't tell me he's a Red Orbiter too?" I sipped champagne from a flute passed around by Red.

"No, he isn't. And he hasn't revealed his alien DNA percentage yet but plans to after the inauguration, like many who've been reluctant to be a target of bigotry by this administration," said Maggie. "But the governor's wife, the woman he recently married? She's Labyrinthian and lived for a while on the moonship. And remember before Oz left, a woman came to see him for one night here? She's his longtime lady friend who works for the governor. She arranged for Oz to meet with the governor along with Cassandra and Rauc," said Maggie.

"Rauc also got to meet with our president-elect," I said. "I guess you will now too."

"You'll be visiting Washington before long, Rowan, so you never know who you'll meet. I know Vice President-Elect O'Neill wants to see you again."

"As long as no one expects me to replace him in Congress. I already paid my dues by growing up in that region—and working for the Pentagon."

Tim laughed. "Maggie tried to talk me out of coming with her, but I'm going to Washington too—although she's making me stay on the moonship to work with you on treaty issues, so you're still stuck with me, but not for girls' night." He grinned, looking ten years old.

"I just thought you wouldn't want to return there and would be happier in Vegas," said Maggie.

"I am happy in Vegas—with you," said Tim. "Where we will still be, some of the time."

"So will Roger guard you when you're in Nevada like he did Senator Rojas-Ortiz?" I asked. "Although now I wonder why that was necessary. I know she doesn't have observer capabilities, but can't she repel bullets too?"

"Yes, but up until the convention, no one knew she was a Red Orbiter," said Genie. "It would have looked bizarre if she repelled attacks against her, unaided. Plus, it left her to focus on public appearances and other work at home without having to worry about her security."

"To answer your question, Rowan, I'm not going to have my brother guard me," said Maggie. "I really don't need him to. Plus, it looks like he might be wanting to phase out of personal security."

Wow. This news about Roger was almost as big as Maggie's. I couldn't imagine him not working as a bodyguard because that's how I'd always known him. I wanted to ask Genie if she knew what was up with that but figured I'd wait for girls' night.

Instead I asked Tim, "What are you going to do about your spook work at the new OUTWARD acoustics facility in Vegas?"

"I've already talked to Win, and he's thrilled I'll be in DC. It's perfect for what I'll be doing, and this way he can focus on Vegas and elsewhere. And he took his Virginia townhouse off the market, so Maggie and I and Astro will have a place to live while she kicks butt in Congress." Tim gave Maggie a peck on the lips.

"So just what *are* you going to be doing, Tim?" I teased. "We won't have to worry about keeping tabs on this dangerous president for too much longer."

"Yes, but you know there'll still be plenty of anti-alien fanatics fighting inevitable change, in Congress and elsewhere," he said. "There will always be enemies to stay one step ahead of."

"Don't remind me," I sighed.

"Enough talk of enemies. Let's have a toast," said Red, raising his flute. "To our friend, soon-to-be Senator Maggie Rogers. May the best you've ever seen be the worst you'll ever see. *Slàinte Mhath!*"

As I sat there thinking what a lovely evening this was and how unusual not to have Rowdy or another Red Orbiter popping into my ear, I thought too soon.

"Don't think I didn't hear you talking about me, beautiful. But I'm glad I'm on your mind. I'll stop at the moonship on my way back from Mars, so I will see you soon. We have things to talk about…and things to do."

And how was it Roger could hear me from Mars? Wasn't it too far away, like Earth?

Chapter 45

"Here's one I thought perfect for you. It's the size of a sheet of notebook paper, and it even has lines on the screen," said George. We were in a type of store I'd normally avoid like the plague, full of electronic devices and all manner of computerized equipment.

I picked up the stylus that came with the device and was pleased to discover it was available in fine point or medium point, like pens. I'm a medium gal.

"It runs on the moonship's solar wind energy, and each page saves on its own as you write. You can set up files, like on your laptop, or leave your work to scroll through, like you would a notepad."

"This is great. Morris won't have paper to chew on and destroy my notes."

With that critical purchase made, George asked if I'd like to check out the art galleries.

"I want to get something for my walls," he said. "We can either rent pieces or buy them to take back to Earth with us. There are artisan crafts from all over the galaxy in just about any medium imaginable!"

At the first place, the pottery was right up my alley. I got a set of mugs, each depicting planets of our solar system, of which Pluto was included, thank you very much. The colors alone made them works of art, almost too precious for coffee.

When we entered a large gallery with wall art and sculptures, George went bonkers over a huge painting that had to do with string theory, or the big bang theory. Some crazed physics thing that was beyond me. But it made him happy. As he arranged to have it delivered to his suite, I was dumbstruck by an actual quilt on a wall, like the colorful textile art back home.

Its background was indigo blue, and the pattern depicted Earth's solar system, including all planets and moons. A mosaic comprised of myriad fabrics in bright colors, and I could not stop staring at it.

I said over my shoulder to George, "I would so love to have this and be able to look at it while I'm writing, here and at home, but it's way too costly, though worth every penny. I just wouldn't feel right spending so much of Rauc and Rowdy's money."

"I will get it for you," said Owen, who suddenly appeared next to me, stealthy as ever. "It would give me great pleasure to do so, so no arguing."

"But I can't let you—"

"What did I just say?" Owen said over his shoulder, heading toward George, apparently to buy the quilt for me.

"But in Earth currency, it's thousands of dollars," I said, putting a hand on his arm.

He looked at me with those purple eyes, and my heart thumped. "You are such a minx," he said. "Did you happen to notice who the artist was who made this? It's Byrin, and I know she would be honored for you to have it."

"Byrin made this? It's amazing."

"Byrin is a true artist. And the reason I came looking for you this morning," said Owen. "She would like you to come to her place for your meeting this afternoon. I'll take you, so you don't have to find it on your own."

"It is a wondrous work of art," said George, gazing at the quilt.

"Okay, but how do I hang it? Rowdy put up my other stuff using the magnetic system here, which I have no clue about."

***

Once Owen got my quilt displayed where it was in full view from my couch and I could now gaze at my Earth art from my bed, he said, "The Lacertan leaders are returning this evening, so I'm going to be holed up the next couple days working on the Tribble issue, as well as the Mars issues. But so far, Roger and Rowdy have not turned up any more of these militia types, and it will soon be a moot issue for Mars. All three private mining companies are being banned, along with anyone working for them."

"So Lucas will return to Earth?"

"Yes, and I didn't know how you'd feel about it but thought you should know."

"Thanks. If he goes back to Nevada, it'll be the Reno area." I turned away from my new quilt, feeling my stomach twinge. "He doesn't know I'm in Vegas. I don't know how I feel, except to realize it's all very sad. Or at least it seems sad when I'm not remembering how horrific it was." I sighed.

"I'm glad you're meeting with Byrin. Let's have dinner later in the week, and I'll look forward to hearing how it's going. And we need to get going to Byrin's."

We took a transpod to the upper deck, not in the area where the pet park was, though bright sunlight still shone through. "I didn't know there were residences up here. Or is this Byrin's work space?"

"A bit of both, and she is one of few who reside here. Mostly this area is agriculture, and Byrin is in charge of herb and wildflower cultivation."

The transpod stopped in front of a cottage with a curved, thatched roof and gated garden overflowing with bright, colorful flowers and twisting, leafy vines. A scene straight out of a Northern England village.

"Has Red seen this? Because he's not going to believe it," I said as we walked up the stone path to the door, which was painted azure purple and flanked by fragrant, blossoming rosemary bushes. "Are those actually honeybees buzzing around?"

"Yes. That's who the wildflowers are for." Owen grinned as Byrin opened her door wearing a tunic of many colors.

"Welcome to my space. Rowan, please come in."

Owen said, "I'll be in touch," kissing me on the cheek before departing.

We walked into a cottage that could easily have been mine, with quilts on the walls and antique trunks and trinkets scattered everywhere, including fascinating geological treasures. But the one thing I didn't expect was the jackrabbit from the park.

I spun around to Byrin, and there was the coyote, standing next to her. It stared at me, its eyes not wary but curious.

Chapter 46

"This is Sky," said Byrin, gesturing to the long-eared jackrabbit.

"Sky? Like earth and sky?"

"It sounds like sky in your language, but it's actually a word from mine that means 'friend,' or 'companion.' Sky had an inner-ear problem affecting her equilibrium, and she latched on to me while I was visiting her planet. I helped her heal, intending to return her home, but she chose to stay with me. As did this scrappy fellow." She stroked the coyote behind his ears.

"I call Bodie a scrappy fellow too! What's his name?"

Byrin smiled. "Every time I asked, he had a different answer. So I call him Wily. He doesn't seem to mind."

"Oh my gosh. Wile E. Coyote! Good thing Sky isn't a roadrunner!"

"There are a couple of those onboard. But Wily doesn't chase them." She grinned. "My companions are part of the reason I asked you here today. Sky and Wily can make it easier for you to unburden yourself."

"Yes, I imagine so. I find both of their species fascinating. Every time I've seen coyotes on Earth, it's strange. They always stop. One actually stared at me for some time. And I swore they were talking to me, or trying to."

"They likely were. Coyotes are very verbal creatures."

"Wait? So you can *talk* to them?"

"Like Dr. Dolittle." She grinned again. "We understand each other on many levels."

"Is the wolf I saw in the park your companion too?"

"He is Owen's. She chose him as well."

"On Earth?"

"Sirius. Like your domesticated canines, that's where wolves originated."

We sat on matching cozy loveseats. "I think I've learned more from you in ten minutes than in months from alien males. It's like pulling teeth to get information."

Byrin laughed. "Have you read that book *Men Are from Mars, Women Are from Venus*? It makes many salient points."

"I have, but I can't believe you have!"

"I tend to read a lot of gender-based material. Can you imagine how splintered it can feel to be both, to have tendencies of both genders that often manifest when least expected?"

"I'm glad you said it, so I didn't have to feel rude asking. For me, it's bad enough hearing a bunch of different voices. On Earth, they often diagnose such things as schizophrenic, or downright crazy."

"Many like to demonize what they do not understand. But let us talk about those ears of yours, and the voices they make possible. I am going to be a bit technical in the beginning, so it may sound like mansplaining if there is something you already know." She winked.

"I so love you already," I said. Wily the coyote yipped, his eyes narrowing.

"It is okay, Wily," Byrin said. "He can be a little possessive. Would you like tea?"

Of course we had to have tea, with lemon and honey, in this snug English-seeming cottage, though there was no fireplace or chimney.

"I love your quilts and other artwork," I said as we sipped an intriguing spiced tea. "I have to tell you I fell in love with your amazing solar system quilt this morning. Owen bought it for me."

"I am honored. I made it from many fabrics and fibers brought to me from all over the galaxy, and I am so pleased it has found an adoring home. That cousin of mine is such a dear, is he not?"

"Owen is your cousin? He didn't tell me. Just like a male." I sighed. "Okay, I'm ready for technical mansplaining!"

"In terms of the anatomy of your ears," Byrin began, "the labyrinth is a complex structure in the inner ear, which contains organs of hearing and balance. The bony labyrinth, a cavity of the temporal bone, is divided into the three sections: the vestibule, the semicircular canals, and the cochlea."

"The cochlea's the part I know, and mine are hairless."

"The cochlea houses the cochlea duct of the membranous labyrinth. Yours being hairless is unusual in humans but perfectly in keeping with your Red Orbiter DNA that derives from Cumulus's Actius moon, or Jupiter's moon Elara, correct?"

"Yes. A whopping 42 percent, the greatest of my alien DNA by far, and much more than my human DNA, which is 17 percent."

"This accounts for why you hear voices from a distance like many Red Orbiters can, and seems to explain why it is their voices you hear. But your cochlea also enables you to hear high frequencies, like many animal species, which is likely derived from other DNA including Mars and Sirius. And you also have DNA from Mercury, do you not?"

"Yes, 12 percent. I learned hummingbirds are from Mercury, and I swear they've been chirping at me for years. I'd love to know what they're saying."

Byrin smiled. "I am sure it is good things, if they speak to you. They would not bother with you otherwise."

"I feel like I've entered *The Twilight Zone*," I said. "Or *The X-Files*."

"TV shows, are they not? But reality can be so much more delightful than fiction. Let us go back to this word, labyrinth, as you are a word person. *Labyrinth* is defined as 'a complicated, irregular network of passages or paths in which it is difficult to find one's way.' A common synonym used on Earth for labyrinth is *maze*."

"Is that how chef Mazy got her name?"

"Yes." Byrin smiled. "It is a popular name for Labyrinthians."

"Interesting. And sorry I keep interrupting."

"That is most acceptable and expected, even from those not prone to questions. You must ask in order to learn and grow, and to heal. So let us get to the more esoteric, but also pertinent portion of this discussion. This is what I want you to spend time considering. We can meet again tomorrow, if you like, to take this further."

"Is this about finding my center, in my ears? Genie tried to get me started on the trip here." I suddenly felt anxious. Sky hopped up next to me on the loveseat, and Wily came to lie at my feet.

"Yes, Rowan." Byrin's eyes seemed to glow. "The labyrinth is an ancient symbol that relates to wholeness. It combines imagery of the circle and the spiral into a meandering but purposeful path. The labyrinth represents a journey to our own center and back out into the world."

Chapter 47

I spent the rest of the day into the next morning pondering this labyrinth journey, doing research. I learned how the labyrinth pattern, or maze, appeared on ancient coins in 400 to 200 BCE, on Roman floor mosaics, in body art, as designs on pottery and basketry, and in etchings on cave walls and churches.

Labyrinths tend to have more than one path to their center, providing a navigational challenge. But there are unicursal labyrinths with only a single path to the center, patterns used historically in group rituals and private meditation.

Could the spiral-patterned Anasazi petroglyph in the American Southwest, speculated to depict water but which I thought could indicate sound or auditory messages due to the spiral-shaped cochlea, represent a unicursal maze?

As a result of my findings, I headed back to the art galleries, seeing numerous works depicting labyrinths. I bought a bowl and a mug and a small framed watercolor by Byrin. When I saw her artisan jewelry in various metals twisted into the spiral coiled within a circle or rounded square, I chose earrings that looked copper—and heard shoppers speaking in what sounded like Italian, just as Win said I would.

I looked around at two young Labyrinthian women and realized too late that I was staring. They noticed. They had long black hair and alluring tilted eyes—like Mazy—which immediately dropped to my metal wristbands. I froze. But they smiled and nodded and went about their way, and I started breathing again.

Later I researched quilts, because I had many at home including one with a repeated red-star pattern and one over my bed depicting blue irises, but the quilt in my living room made me think of Earth's sun. It was in what was called the lone star pattern in graduated shades of red, orange, and yellow fabric.

Quilting is thought to have originated on Earth in thirteenth-century England. And the word *quilt* is linked to the Latin word *culcita.* Most interesting was in quilt stories from the 1840s, they symbolized the domestic sphere of all acceptable womanly endeavors. Quilts were cherished objects, with quilters perceived as kind and loving, representing all that was wonderful about a woman. No wonder Byrin made quilts as part of her artistry. It was a gender-based endeavor.

I mentioned this to her the next afternoon when we met in her cottage with her critters.

"I tried glassblowing too," she said, "which I believe was a traditionally male craft. But I did not enjoy it as much."

From there she jumped right into a subject I hadn't expected—and wasn't sure I was ready for. We hadn't yet had tea.

"Let us talk about your defense mechanism, this ringing in your ears you developed to cope with voices you hear. It is something that concerns my cousin and others who care about you, does it not? Because you also are having traumatic nightmares."

"Yes, but I wasn't entirely certain they are connected."

"They are," Byrin said but at least softened it with a smile. "This blocking mechanism of yours, your self-induced tinnitus, is similar to how you deal with traumatic events or experiences. You block emotions or reactions while they occur as a defense against how they make you feel, or to keep from breaking down, and to protect against vulnerability."

I leaned over to pet Wily, who came to sit at my feet and stare into my soul. I looked back into his coyote eyes and began to cry. "You're talking about how I dealt with the abusive relationship I was in."

"And there have been other traumas, have there not? A historic American event in which you were involved?"

"The Pentagon. 9/11." I felt my throat tighten as intense ringing settled in my ears.

"That trauma also resulted in sound-related triggers? You have problems with loud noises and crowd-related noise, do you not?"

"Even after all these years. I thought it would get better."

"I suspect it did begin to get better over time. But was there also noise-related trauma associated with this more recent bad relationship you were in?"

"Very much so," I said.

Byrin came from her loveseat to mine, taking my hands. There were tears in her eyes.

"I will be very direct out of respect for what you endured with bravery and fortitude. Your protective defenses were natural because you were in survival mode. You blocked emotion just as you have blocked out voices over the years because they frightened you. We often are frightened by what we don't understand or cannot control. This was necessary at the time."

"But now it's eating me alive?" My voice quavered.

"Yes. While the blocking you do may help you in the moment, it delays an inevitable emotional reaction to what has occurred, and sometimes that reaction is a nightmare that makes you scream, makes you react. Other times it might be a—what is the expression?—a kneejerk response to something that triggers these traumatic memories and stirs up feelings of angst or anger. The truth is, we must all eventually deal with our emotions, one way or another. There is no escaping this. Your emotional responses should not stay repressed, trapped as if in a maze from which there is no exit."

"That's a nightmare in itself," I said. "Feeling trapped, like there is no escape, no solution."

Byrin nodded. "This is because when we block out negative thoughts, feelings, or experiences, we are repressing a part of ourselves that needs to be seen, heard, processed. When we repress emotions, these deeply personal parts of our beings, they do not go away so much as get buried deep within us, within our maze. And they will often come out when least expected."

"Boy howdy," I murmured. "I've been really grumpy at Red Orbiter males lately."

Byrin smiled, patting my hand. "I suspect that is to be expected when dealing with Roger, in particular."

"You know Roger? Did you know he was the impetus for Superman?"

"Yes, and he is in many ways. But because of that, he can be quite a challenge to deal with on a personal level."

"Ya think?" I said.

"Here is what I want you to think about, until we next meet, which can be as soon as you so choose. Instead of blocking, either emotions or voices, if we allow ourselves to be fully who we are, honoring all of our thoughts, moods, messages, and feelings that pass through us, we can simply observe and let them go. Things get trapped—we get trapped—when we push them down where they lodge into our unconscious mind, making us fearful of our own consciousness."

"Like I've been afraid of all of the voices I hear, and having them overwhelm me?"

"Exactly. Instead, we should develop a friendlier attitude toward ourselves and our inherent abilities. You must trust in yourself, Rowan. In your goodness, in your special gifts. When we recognize our true worth, a few dark clouds or strange voices passing through our minds will not intimidate us."

"I've been alternately suppressing frustration and lashing out at Red Orbiters because their abilities are so closely aligned with mine and I don't understand them."

"It scares you. They scare you, on some level. You are reticent to trust, making you blame them for your frustrations as you fight against your abilities. But once you accept what you can do, you will come to understand it. Blocking means denying an opportunity to find peace—and enlightenment."

"So I ultimately have to stop blocking these voices, as opposed to finding a way to do so without this ringing in my ears?"

"Protecting yourself, such as you do with your tinnitus, is one thing. Complete suppression, such as your denial and anger at what you don't understand about yourself and your abilities, is another. We need to find your balance. Find your center. The center of your labyrinth."

Chapter 48

"This was good timing for girls' night," I said to Genie and Maggie as I exited the transpod onto the commerce deck.

"Did it go okay, with Byrin?" asked Genie.

"It was very good but intense."

Maggie said, "You know it will take time, right? Red Orbiters have had our whole lives to grow into and accept our abilities. You've only come to understand yours recently."

"Kind of makes it hard for me to flourish in my special gift." I smiled wanly.

"I'll help you!" said Genie. "Byrin said it would be good for me to practice the centering process with you, once you understand it, out here in the real world among all the voices."

"This is one hell of a nightclub." I was astonished by the interior of the bar we entered.

"It's a wine bar," said Maggie. "We picked it just for you."

"It sure is. With an actual vineyard in it." Rows of vines grew between each table.

"Did you see the vineyards on the top deck, near Byrin's space?" asked Maggie.

"Yes, but inside a bar, on a lower level? How is this possible?"

"They're experimenting with a special type of lighting, to see how it affects the process and the end product—as in wine! Let the tasting begin!" said Genie.

We got to choose from flights of wine from all over Earth, and some not of Earth.

"I may never leave the moonship at this rate," I said, trying to decide between reds of Italy and Spain before giving up and getting both. As well as a few selections from Saturn, also known as Cultura. Not to mention tasty cheeses made not from animal milk, but from OW plants and minerals.

"I don't want to get into the no-fun parts of my session with Byrin today, but I am dying to share with you something I find uncanny. Can I read you the yearly horoscope forecast my mom gave me from a magazine?"

"Sure," Genie and Maggie said in unison.

I pulled out the rumpled scrap of paper I'd written it on and read aloud, "Be present in your life! Open yourself to your inner voice to assess choices you make. Reconnect to avoid feeling overwhelmed by the intricate maze of your life, to understand the very purpose of your existence. Advance toward the center of your own life, rather than hovering like a moon around a planet."

"Wow," said Maggie. "Spot on. I'm not always sure about the validity of these things, but this makes me wonder what my annual horoscope was, given the year I'm having so far."

"I'm Aries, and my ruling planet is Mars. Even more uncanny, given all the happenings, right?"

"Aries?" squeaked Maggie, and Maggie squeaking was like a genetic mutation. "Isn't that the sign for those born in April?"

"Partly. It starts in late March and ends April 19. When were you born?"

"In the spring," said Maggie. "April 17. And did I see lucky numbers at the end of what you were reading from?"

"Yes, but I haven't figured out any significance for those yet. Last year my lucky numbers turned out to be my exact alien DNA percentages, which was mind-blowing."

"Let me see that paper," said Maggie. I handed it to her, and she read them aloud. "Two, thirty-eight, eight, fifty-five." She read the numbers, her eyes narrowing as she thought about them. She repeated them and looked up. "The moon is exactly 238,855 miles from Earth."

"We are now entering the Twilight Zone," said Genie in a deep, ominous voice. "And we need more wine."

After trying tasty pseudo-fried eggplant and zucchini with an OW spice, paired with a Nebbiolo, I said, "I would like to toast Maggie, soon to be a senator, yes, but here's to taking down Tribble. Word has it you squashed him like a bug." I raised my wineglass.

"It wasn't much of a challenge." Maggie grinned, and Genie hooted, Rowdy style. "But in the spirit of full disclosure, and given your previous comments about superheroes and Luna Moth Woman, I want to share something with you."

"Okay," I said, excited. "But can I guess first? Can you hear Red Orbiter voices in other people's ears, like mine?"

"Yes." Maggie smiled. "And I think you have superpowers of observation. But there's more. While I can't fly or do other things my twin brother can, I have one very valuable and rare gift. I can detect impending danger, evil intent, in the voices of others."

"Wow," I said. "I bet you heard it in Tribble."

"As did you, in your own way," said Maggie. "I want you to remember that as you go on this journey to your center. You have gifts too, and you should embrace them."

"Now you sound like Byrin." I smiled.

"Thank you," Maggie said. "I know something about struggling with abilities. It's not so much that I wanted to keep my powers a secret as it has been about being discrete, humble. I've never felt comfortable broadcasting them, but I'm here to tell you, sometimes it's okay to toot your own horn, Rowan."

"Okay, but no Superwoman tattoos!"

"I'll toast to that!" said Genie. "And I have an announcement too. I've decided my special superpower is going to be cornering the market on dog cookies!"

I spit my wine, Mom-style. "What on earth?"

"Yes, it will be on Earth, because you humans are in love with your dogs and spend extravagant sums on treats. Not that doggies aren't totally worth it. One of the best things about humans is how much they love their pets. It's why I've experimented with baking the ultimate dog cookie—as I heard you call them—which helped spark the idea. I was trying to come up with something healthy for humans and realized my end result was ideal for dogs."

"So what's in this cookie?" asked Maggie.

"Beans and a tiny bit of pistachio, for texture," said Genie. "I read how dogs love green beans and are fed canned ones for weight loss. But my beans are fresh!"

"Do you want to use Bodie for a taste test?"

"I sure do. When I get this going, can he be my mascot?"

"I think he'll be honored," I said. "But I just had a thought. You and Rowdy should get a dog together! Humans often do as a trial run to see if they can handle kids."

Genie's face squinched like a mean kewpie doll. "I'm not sure I like you very much right now, Rowan. But I still love your dog."

Maggie was laughing harder than I've ever seen her. "I so needed this," she said, wiping her eyes.

"I have a question. Do you two have science degrees like most Red Orbiters seem to? Or engineering? I know Rauc is an aeronautical engineer."

"No, he's a pilot, but he studied anthropology, I think it was," said Maggie. "And my degree's in history. I thought about law school but went Marine Corps instead."

"Okay, so I made a huge assumption I can't blame on Rauc." I sighed. "What did Rowdy study? Gambling?"

Genie laughed. "Statistics. And my major was chemistry."

"That blows my mind. Maybe you should make wine instead of dog cookies!"

Before we left, I said to Genie, "I think you might have been fibbing about Red Orbiters being the first to make vino. Seems like it was likely folks from Saturn and not Jupiter who came up with the gift of the grape."

"Fighting words!" said Genie. "Maggie, strut your stuff and squash Rowan like a bug."

Chapter 49

I spent most of the next day getting the hang of my fabulous solar-wind-powered scratch pad, as I liked to call it, jotting down observations about the moonship as well as conversations with friends, thoughts on my journey to the center of my labyrinth and what that would mean, and…my feelings. For the first time ever, it felt like I was writing in a journal.

I also researched potential famous quotes to use in writing the treaty presentation, hoping it would organize my thoughts. Tim called an impromptu brainstorming session on the treaty at his and Maggie's suite for late that afternoon, saying I should bring Morris.

So there we were. Me, Tim, Maggie, Owen, George, and Red, with the unexpected addition of Rowdy and Genie. At least their suite was larger than mine, sized for a couple. And Maggie and I clearly favored the same furniture hues. Morris and Astro provided a cacophonous backdrop, having quite the reunion and love play session, currently in progress.

Owen explained, "Rowdy is filling in for Oz while he's away, and Genie will take on Maggie's role in our little group once she leaves to be a superstar in the senate."

"No pressure there." Maggie smirked.

"Yeah, for me too, having to take Superwoman's place," said Genie.

"I just realized you'll now be in the audience for our Congressional presentation. No pressure there for Red and me!" I said. "Actually, I'm over the moon about it." I waggled my eyebrows.

Groans erupted at my moon pun. "Hey!" I said, "Here I am in meetings with military-minded folk again. And believe me, those guys were the kings of puns and trite phrases. Do you know how many times I had to hear, 'We'll blow their socks off,' or 'Been there, done that, got the t-shirt.'" I rolled my eyes.

“I can vouch for hearing those repeatedly from Marines,” said Owen.

“Thank you!” I said. “But at least they seemed somewhat in keeping with gruesome elements of battle and the overseas element of conflict. Unlike their popular expression, ‘We screwed the pooch on that one!’ It’s kind of disturbing if you think too much about it.”

“That’s just wrong,” said Genie, but Owen was laughing along with the others.

Rowdy said, “Hold on there, Rowan. I seem to remember hearing you use that phrase yourself, accusing Rauc while juiced up on bug spray. After he snatched you from Las Vegas Boulevard. And right before he put you over his knee.”

“Rowdy Wilde, you zip it!” I gasped.

“Now you sound like Rauc.” Rowdy smirked.

“Why don’t we begin our treaty brainstorming?” said Maggie, thank my stars. I could feel my face turning as red as an orb.

“Yes, because Space Force sure screwed the pooch on treaty compliance!” said Tim.

“Not to mention the president,” said Owen. He’d been looking at me speculatively, making me want to run screaming from the room. Or faint again. Fainting could be good to escape this mortification.

“The president first violated the treaty by shooting a missile at the moon, which if you recall, is why I resigned as secretary of defense,” said Red. “But now he’s got Space Force lawyers claiming that because it’s a spaceship and not a celestial body, there is no violation.”

“The flaw in that argument,” I said, “is regardless of the status of the moon, anything occurring here is in outer space, so the ‘exclusively for peaceful purposes’ use clause of the treaty most certainly does apply, not to mention maintenance of international peace and security.”

“Bingo,” said George, beaming at me. “Our lawyer has spoken.”

“There are a lot of inherent contradictions and narcissistic presumptions throughout the terms of this treaty that remind me of heavy-handed first-in-time hypocritical tenets of American property law. I plan to draw parallels for my presentation.” I turned to Red with a cheeky smile. "And you can cut and paste as you will, making it apply to British marauding imperialism."

Red frowned, squinting at me. "Now I know how Rauc must have felt when you told him he sure screwed the pooch, and why Rowdy said he—"

At that moment, Morris and Astro erupted into howls of what sounded like an excruciatingly intense sexual encounter. Saving me from further intense embarrassment.

Once we adjourned the meeting an hour later, Owen and I were headed off for our dinner date, and he told me in the transpod he had a special surprise waiting at his place.

"Do you think it will look bad, us going off to dinner together alone, and in your residence as opposed to a restaurant?"

"I don't know," said Owen, "but it's good we'll be at my place and not in public, considering what I now want to discuss with you."

"Why do you sound mad at me?"

"Not mad. Curious. You seem overly concerned about what others might think or say. That's not the brazen Rowan Layne I know."

"Well, Rowdy is a huge gossip, and half the people in that room deal in spy craft."

"They are all your friends and would do anything for you, Rowan. No one in that room is out to get you, or hurt you."

We left the transpod and entered his condo, or what passed as one on a residential deck of the moonship. It was, as I expected, very open and masculine and organized. What I didn't anticipate was the color scheme, in shades of purple from the palest lavender on the walls to the deepest of violets in furniture. On the wall was a quilt, not unlike mine. It depicted Mars and its two moons in a pleasing array of red, violet, and blue hues. Clearly another of Byrin's works. I stopped and looked at Owen.

"I like purple," he said, smiling that smile.

"You are so gay," I said, laughing. Until he swatted my butt.

I turned to him, wide-eyed, adrenaline coursing through me. "Did you do that because of what Rowdy said at the meeting?"

"I did that because you're a smartass—and because I wanted to."

"And because you knew I would like it on some level?" I squared off with him, hands on hips.

Chapter 50

"Why don't you let me show you my dinner surprise, and then we'll talk?" said Owen, headed for his kitchen, neat and modern, like the rest of his place. Lots of black appliances.

He poured me a glass of Sauvignon Blanc that smelled deliciously lemony. I took a seat at his table and told myself to chill out. Even his pottery dinner plates were purple.

"We don't have a restaurant specifically for Maryland seafood onboard," he said. "So I asked Mazy to prepare a few treats. We have Chesapeake Bay blue crab cakes, steamed shrimp with Old Bay Seasoning, plus boardwalk fries with the same. For dessert, Smith Island cake."

"You and Mazy have my undying gratitude. We used to go to beach week in high school in Ocean City—where I first had fries with Old Bay. And then I'd order them at movie theaters in Annapolis."

"I first had them at the movies too. Did you fulfill any lifeguard fantasies in your beach-week exploits?"

"As a matter of fact, I did," I said, smiling and peeling a shrimp.

"And did you tell anyone about it? Or was it a shameful secret to be locked away?" Owen bit into a fry.

"Where are you going with this? Are you telling me I shouldn't be embarrassed that Rowdy blurted out details of my sex life at a work meeting? Things everyone probably suspected anyway because of Roger and Rowdy digging up every little salacious detail about me?" I gulped wine.

Owen took the glass from my hand, setting it down. "I concede that Rowdy doesn't have typical social boundaries. But it wasn't a formal work meeting, and, like I said before, you were among friends."

"It was still embarrassing. Mortifyingly so." I reached for my wine glass, but Owen grabbed my wrist.

"Why was it embarrassing?" he said. I tried to pull away, but Owen held fast. "You want those crab cakes, you have to answer me."

"I don't have an answer," I said, sounding small.

"Okay then. I'll feed you some crab and you can have your wine back if you'll listen to what I have to say. Deal?" He held up a fork full of lump crab meat, and I melted like the butter in a crock on the table. I took a bite and closed my eyes and chewed. Ecstasy.

"I never thought I'd be jealous of a crab cake," said Owen, chuckling.

I said in a rush, "I spent too many years being afraid others would find out about my fantasy, but at the same time feeling immense frustration when I revealed it to men who didn't understand and made me feel like there was something wrong with me."

"See there? You answered my question. You get an extra crab cake. And I think you need more wine to account for those clueless men." Owen poured white wine into my glass, which wasn't purple, but the water glass I gulped from was.

"What I'm really getting at is it's not a crime to have a sexual fantasy, or to engage in sexual fetish safely among consenting adults, despite what the Department of Defense claimed and too many sanctimonious fanatics believe," he said. "Aren't you letting them win if you treat your own sexuality this way? Like some dirty secret to be ashamed of?"

"I suppose that's true. It's bad enough having the president and his cronies make constant cracks about humans having sex with aliens. Not to mention the evangelical mindset." I couldn't look into those purple eyes, so I peeled more shrimp. "I just wish my own activities didn't have to be so *out there*. Being involved with so many spies has made that impossible."

Owen got up and came to my side of the table, lifting my chin. "But don't you want, and need, for those you're intimate with to be aware of it? Hasn't it often been difficult finding the words to speak out loud and make that happen?"

I nodded. Owen went back to his seat at the table and fed me more crab cake. "Red Orbiters, with their heightened observation skills, are a big part of your world now, and they hear and know pretty much anything they want. But they don't seem to be holding your interests against you, or think there's anything wrong with them, or you. Quite the opposite."

"But does everybody else have to know? You and Red and—"

"I solemnly swear not to share what I know with anyone. But I want to hear about that Ocean City lifeguard, because it's one of my fantasies too. And I also want to ask, did you develop your fantasies from reading certain romance novels?"

"Maybe that's why I always wanted to be a writer." I smiled.

Over eight-layer yellow cake with chocolate frosting, Owen said, "I want to thank you for submitting—pun intended—to this discussion with me tonight, and for so graciously joining me in my home for dinner. I don't think I ever enjoyed crab cakes and fries this much as a midshipman. So here is my confession to you. I had very vivid and erotic fantasies about you in Maryland, when you were a law student and a Marine wife. It was the first time I ever intensely desired a woman."

"I am never going to get to sleep tonight," I breathed, staring into his eyes and feeling thirty years old.

"When the time comes, and I feel it will, we will not be sleeping much either."

I was afraid to speak, knowing he might hear between the lines and detect my own fantasies—about him.

"I'm not reading your mind, Rowan, but I can tell by your face that you're concerned about it. You have nothing to fear, only to anticipate. And remember, your secret is safe with me." He smiled that smile, and I thought I might have trouble walking out the door and to the transpod.

But I rallied, tossing my head and throwing some sass. "Oh sure! Some secret it is now!" I went to swat at his chest, but Owen caught my wrist with an enticingly firm grip.

"Careful." His voice vibrated through my chest. "I said your secret is safe. I didn't say you'd be safe from me when it comes to your secret."

Chapter 51

I called my sister the next morning. "I had crab cakes last night, and coming here has sure turned out to be so much more than getting away from the president's goons. I've run headlong into facing past trauma, thanks to talking to Byrin."

"Which guy is Byrin?"

"Byrin isn't one of the guys. She's a *she*—well she's both. Remember I told you about meeting with a Labyrinthian to help me with my ears? Turns out she's helping me with a whole lot more, including my nightmares."

"Thank goodness," said G.

"You too? You were worried about me?"

"For a long while now. I am your big sister, remember? Especially given what you went through with that monster who will not be named. To use a Mom phrase, 'He is discussed, and cussed.' But who did you have crab cakes with?"

"Owen the Marine. Astrophysicist. Also a Labyrinthian, with purple eyes. And things seem to be heating up with Red too."

"Red is the one from Scotland who's going to be knighted?"

"Yes! You're catching on!"

"Did you find Mom shoes yet?" G said with a devious tone.

"No. But I got an amazing quilt and had girls' night in a wine bar with grape vines. And Rauc came to see me for one wonderful night."

"I think you buried the lead, as you journalists say," said G.

"And Roger came to deal with the attack and is now on Mars but is stopping by on his way back to Earth."

"When is your next meeting with this Byrin?"

"This morning. And I'm going to ask Genie if there's a spa here. I could use a massage. I'm a little tense."

"Ya think?" G snorted.

"Are you mocking me?"

"Yes. Do you want to hear social news from Portland? I'm assuming you only get weather reports from Mom. We're throwing a baby shower for Ophelia and Bruce. It'll be in early March since the triplets are due early April."

"That's great. But is Mom now closer friends with Rauc and Rowdy's sister than I am?"

"She calls them her Red *Orator* peeps and holds the status of honorary grandmother."

"And she's okay with that? But do make sure all party decorations and favors are not black. That would be a downer for a baby shower."

Before I left to meet with Byrin, I had a text from Mom. "Did you find out about shoes? Are you busy writing the book about Red Orators? Cloudy here, but no snow. (six shoe emoji)"

I supposed I wouldn't get heart or kissy face emoji again until she got shoes.

I quickly answered, fibbing that I'd been too busy to shop. I texted instead how I might get a pedicure, which should make her happy. But I didn't lie that I was working on the book. Because I hadn't been. And it flat-out bugged me.

Stuff kept getting in the way and rearranging my priorities, like this treaty thing. But procrastination didn't use to be in my vocabulary. And it wasn't like I didn't have plenty of free hours to write up here. What was my problem?

"Genie," I said as I stepped into the transpod headed for the upper deck. "Is there a spa where we could get massages, and maybe facials or pedicures this afternoon?"

Popping into my ear, Genie said, "I'm on it. Give me a shout after your meet with Byrin."

Did *everyone* know my personal schedule in addition to my sexual proclivities?

As I arrived at Byrin's space, she awaited me in her wildflower garden with Sky and Wily. "Our time together will be outdoors today, where you can smell herbs and flowers and listen to bees." We walked around to the backyard, equally overflowing with plant life and a large hammock between two lemon trees. "Did you ever daydream in a hammock in your youth?"

"Yes, at the lakefront house of dear family friends," I said.

"And it was a happy memory, was it not?"

"Sure, except when my sister tried to flip me out of the hammock."

Byrin laughed, a singsong sound. "I will make sure Wily does not try that."

I climbed in the hammock and swung for a moment, getting the feel of it.

"Close your eyes or look up at the sky, whatever makes you most comforted. Focus inward while listening to sounds closest to you. The rustle of leaves, the buzz of bees, the flutter of Sky hopping about. Listen and make them your world. There are no other sounds to be heard, no voices, other than mine and that which you choose to hear."

I floated on the rhythm and flow of Byrin's voice and nature surrounding me like a cocoon.

"Focus on your inner ear, traveling into the labyrinth. Concentrate and flow with the spiral, following it to its center. Let your mind move deeper into the maze, finding your path to peace. Breathe deeply, hearing only that which you choose to hear."

I wandered into the maze of my mind, of my ears, and thought I must have fallen asleep. There was no ringing in my consciousness, no voices, no synthetic beeps. Only the sounds of nature, of rushing air and fluttering leaves.

I came back to the sweet sound of Byrin's voice. "You did very well today, Rowan. Each time you will grow, and soon you will bring yourself to this center of safety, of calm, whenever you need to. And should you choose to focus on voices, you will follow a different path to your center so that you may listen without interference, without fear. You will practice this until it becomes second nature, like blinking your eyes."

"Thank you. I feel as if I've awakened from a deep but replenishing sleep."

"You traveled for some time, but you were not really asleep. When you sleep tonight, some of your journey today may return to you. But it will be peaceful, unharmful, knowledge bearing."

Chapter 52

"Genie, what were you able to find out?" I said, stepping into a transpod.

"Massage, then facial and pedicure, in one hour," she answered in my ear. "You sure you don't want a manicure?"

"No. I tried to stop biting my nails for the umpteenth time, but the moonship attack foiled my plans. I'm now headed to the commerce deck to see if the shoe store we went to has anything in my mom's scrawny size."

"I'll meet you there."

I was waiting to hear if they might somehow have black flats, size virtually-impossible-to-obtain, when Genie arrived. "Your mom's a hoot. I'm a 6 1/2 narrow. What's her size?"

"She's a flipping triple A narrow size 7, and we cannot tell her your close foot size because she will make you try on shoes for her the rest of our time here."

Genie chuckled. She didn't realize I wasn't kidding.

We learned they had not a single black shoe in size 7 but did have one pair of four-inch-heeled pumps. I sat in a chair and texted Mom. "Only one pair of high-heeled pumps in size 7A, but royal blue. On a happy note, both your granddog and grandcat have girlfriends! (dog, cat, heart emoji)"

I eyed possible sandals for wearing after my pedicure, waiting for the inevitable ping. And yet I still jumped when it arrived. "Tacky, tacky!!! What is wrong with that shoe store??? They are out of it!!! (no emoji, no weather report)"

Genie read her text over my shoulder. "Does she mean the store is out of shoes?"

"No. In Mom's universe, you are either with it or totally out of it."

My phone pinged again. The text contained three angry face emoji but at least no flipped birds. I had a rubber stamp for paper crafting that said, “A woman’s right to shoes,” but Mom took the obsession into the stratosphere.

The visit wasn’t a total loss because I got copper metallic sandals with cool ankle straps, and Genie got the pumps in bright purple.

The salon was remarkably similar to those at home, including the massage table. But the masseuse gave me heart palpitations. To begin with, he was male. And young. And buff.

But I got myself naked and lay down on the table with a modest sheet covering. When Hung came in—yes, that was his name, or what it sounded like when he spoke it—I said, “The very tight tendons you’ll find in my neck come from my mother.”

Hung was so strong, and thorough and quiet, I thought I’d need to be removed from the table with a giant spatula. Getting a massage was risky—I was worried I’d get so relaxed, I’d let in a cacophony of voices and end up panicking. But I had definitely focused on my center like Byrin taught by about halfway into the massage, though it might have been lower than some would think.

In contrast, the woman who did my facial had a light touch but chattered the entire time about her boyfriend who didn’t talk much but was so fantastic in bed, she figured communication was overrated. I was fixing to tell her that might be a misguided compromise when she said he was a masseuse named Hung at the salon. Her name sounded like Blonde, which she was, so there’s that. She was from Lacerta and had the light-green eyes with black ring around the iris to prove it.

Genie and I then got side-by-side pedicures, an entirely bizarre experience because the process was performed by a machine you stuck your foot into that didn’t involve water, complete with a fast-drying mechanism. I hadn’t needed to worry about having open-toed sandals.

Genie cut her eyes at me after I selected my color. “That polish looks like Owen’s eyes.”

“You got purple shoes!” I said. “And hey, Miss Dog Cookie Inventor, have aliens managed to come up with anything snazzy to replace magnifying mirrors and tweezers yet? Something not involving hot wax that I told the facialist not to apply because it makes me swell up like a festering boil. I tried it once with my eyebrows. You should have seen me."

"Isn't that a lovely visual. And why are you dissing aliens? I'm baking for your dog."

"Trust me, you'll appreciate what I'm suggesting once you hit menopause."

"You're making me think maybe I should stall my age to delay that experience," said Genie, pouting like my sister in Gigi mode.

"I guess Red Orbiters probably can't be masseuses, am I right? Because the minute they touch the back of your neck, it would be naughty massage parlor city!" I cracked myself up.

"I want details of your cozy little dinner with Owen the Marvelous. Is that why you're being goofy? You remind me of Rowdy."

"It's the massage," I said. "I didn't think it was possible to get so relaxed and not flip out about voices."

"That's very exciting. A breakthrough," Genie said, sounding sincere. "But I still haven't heard about last night with Owen."

"And you're not going to! Especially out in public with so many potentially listening ears. And after you just said you-know-who's name aloud!"

"And who would you-know-who be?" said Rowdy, popping into my ear.

I jumped. "Rowdy's back."

"Crap on a cracker," muttered Genie, making me giggle at her mutinous expression.

As we left the salon, me in my fancy new sandals, Owen approached. "You have an important caller trying to reach you. Do you have your phone with you?"

"Yes, but I turned off the ringer during my massage and facial and forgot to turn it back on," I said. "Who's trying to call? Is my family okay? I was just texting with my mother."

"It's not your family. Hold on," said Owen, getting on his phone. "I found her. Yes, she can be available in ten minutes." I looked at Genie in confusion. She shrugged, wide-eyed.

“Come.” Owen took me by my arm. “We can pop over to my place for the call. It’s closer, with a secured room. Genie, you come too.”

“But who is calling me?” I said as we stepped into a transpod.

“I don’t want to ruin the surprise,” said Owen, smiling. He looked down at my feet, and his smile widened. “Nice purple toes. And killer sandals.”

We rushed into Owen’s condo to his office room, and I sat in a big ergonomic chair, holding my phone, my heart racing.

“Maybe now’s a good time to practice finding your center,” said Genie, just as my phone rang.

I answered with a tremulous “Hello?”

“Is this Rowan Layne speaking? Please confirm.”

“Yes, this is Rowan Layne.”

“Please hold for Vice President-Elect Warren O’Neill.”

Chapter 53

"Rowan Layne, how are you doing up there on the moonship?" said the vice president-elect in a booming voice that startled me.

"I'm doing pretty well, sir—I think. This call from you has my heart beating a bit too fast."

Warren O'Neill laughed before his tone turned serious. "I want to unofficially apologize, until I'm in a position to do so officially, for the attack on you and your mother in Las Vegas, as well as on your spaceship. The president-elect and I appreciate the work you're doing on the moonship with regard to Space Force issues. We look forward to your address to Congress."

"Thank you, sir. I am so very relieved and thrilled that you and President-Elect Harrison will soon be leading our nation."

"Thank *you*, Ms. Layne, for your vote and your voice. As a result of your convention speech about my first job as a lifeguard, I still have people coming up to me saying 'Mr. President, out of the gene pool!' But there's a more pressing reason for my call, a special request of you."

"Request away, sir!" I sounded a little punch-drunk.

"I would like to extend an invitation to the inaugural balls, as my personal guest. As you know, I am unmarried and have no second lady to attend with me."

"You want me to go to the inaugural balls as your date?" I squeaked, looking at Genie, whose green eyes grew enormous. Owen grinned.

O'Neill laughed. "I suppose that's one way to put it. But I should warn you, it entails a lot of social interaction at several balls and of course will result in media scrutiny. Not that I want to talk you out of it. I'm quite confident you are the perfect woman to pull this off. You've already made me look better than I deserve once." His tone indicated he was grinning broadly.

"Yes, of course! I will be honored to attend with you."

"The honor is all mine," he said. "Someone in charge of protocol will be in touch on logistics, and I will see you in Washington soon! Thank you, Rowan Layne."

The call disconnected, and I sat there, stunned.

Genie said, "That settles it. Your ultimate superpower is you're a man-magnet! More powerful than any Red Orbiter. More enticing than any Labyrinthian, including Owen here. Though he might be a close second."

Owen laughed. I sat, immobilized.

"You okay there, man-magnet?" said Owen.

I looked at him. "Stick a fork in me; I'm done. Any benefit I might have received from that massage is as obliterated as the planet humans once came from—I'm that gaping hole between Mars and Jupiter." I turned to Genie. "And Congressman O'Neill is gay. Everybody in Nevada knows it—he just hasn't officially come out like he did to announce he was nearly 100 percent Lacertan from Venus. But he is gorgeous. And when did I get old enough to be in the same age bracket as the vice president of the United States?"

"Think of it this way," said Genie. "You were likely already invited to the ball, so now you don't have to decide from among all your men who your date will be!"

I glowered at Genie, mortified that she'd said that in front of Owen.

"You look like you need water!" she said in a rush. "She should drink lots of water after a massage!" she told Owen.

"She needs to eat something too," he said, taking my arm to lead me to his kitchen.

"I'm not sure I'm up to eating," I said.

"Don't make me hand-feed you like I did last night," said Owen, causing Genie's eyes to bulge. But they narrowed again when Rowdy breezed in the door.

"Rowan Layne not up to eating? Impossible!" Rowdy said. "Let's get pizza. I'm starved."

My phone rang. Win calling. "It's all scheduled, sweet pea," he said when I answered. "You'll fly from the moonship three days beforehand to give you time to sleep and readjust to Earth. You'll stay in my townhouse with Maggie and Tim, and you can bring the critters."

"But that means I have less than two weeks left on the moon!" I wailed.

"You can come back anytime you want, Rowan," said Owen once I'd disconnected with Win.

"Can I have my same furniture? I wish I had room for that chaise at home."

"I can keep the chaise for you at my place. But this is perhaps not the time to be overly concerned about furniture?"

Genie said, "Exactly! We have to figure out where you're going to get a ballgown."

"You sound like Mom," I said. "But maybe when she hears this news, she'll forgive me about the shoes!" My pitch bordered on histrionic.

"Does everybody like mushrooms?" Rowdy called out while ordering pizzas.

"Why are you getting pizza when I'm having a crisis?" I screeched.

"I thought you loved pizza." Rowdy sounded pitiful, but I knew it was only an act and prepared to yell again, but Owen cut me off.

"I'm arranging another meet with Byrin tomorrow so she can help calm you down. And you definitely need to eat. Your blood sugar is obviously low."

"You are not the boss of me, Owen the Marine!"

"Do you want *me* to calm your ass down? Because the two of us can head back into my office." Owen's tone and the look in his eyes made me hold my breath.

"Breathe, Rowan," said Genie, giggling. "You're turning as purple as your toenails."

I slumped onto Owen's purple couch. "Well, at least I'm not having a delayed reaction to this news."

"That's for sure. You're gushing forth like a geyser," said Rowdy. "Pizza arrives in fifteen."

"I guess I could just wear my convention dress again." I sighed. "I have it here, and it's accessorized."

"No way! It's already been seen on TV, and we need a formal gown," said Genie.

"Oh crap, I'm going to be on TV again!" I wailed.

"Am I going to have to pay for this ballgown too?" said Rowdy.

"Stuff it, Rowdy!" yelled Genie, a little louder than seemed called for.

"Am I going to have to calm *you* down, Fireball?" said Rowdy. He turned to Owen. "Can we borrow your office?"

"Don't you dare touch me!" said Genie. "How many bimbos did you boink on Mars?"

"Yep, here we go!" Rowdy rushed Genie, tossed her over his shoulder, swatted her butt quite loudly, and headed for Owen's office.

I dared peek at Owen. "I told you not to be so worried and embarrassed," he said.

And if I thought I wouldn't be able to hear what was going on because Owen's office was a secure room, I was wrong. My eyes grew wide as I swallowed convulsively.

"I think I will take some water," I said to Owen. "I thought that room was soundproof or something."

He chuckled. "It is, for normal ears and equipment trying to listen in. I suppose you can hear them?"

I nodded, my face heating along with the rest of me.

"Care to give me a blow-by-blow of what's going down?" he grinned.

"I brought beer!" said Red, joining us in Owen's living room. "Congratulations, Rowan."

"News travels fast on the moonship," I responded. "But thanks. Can I maybe get a glass of wine?" I asked Owen.

"Not until you get some food in your stomach."

"You're being autocratic again. He's so bossy," I grumped to Red.

"You have no idea," said Owen, popping an olive in my mouth, commanding, "Chew."

It was a very tasty olive, so I did, despite Red saying to Owen, "Well done, lad."

"Chow time!" said George, sailing in with Mazy, each holding pizza boxes as Rowdy and Genie emerged from Owen's office and Maggie and Tim also arrived, with wine.

"Did you come up with the topping combinations, Mazy?" I asked as we devoured the pizzas. "They're yummy. We sure could use your skills on Earth."

"I am hoping to relocate when I graduate." Mazy smiled at George adoringly with her tip-tilted bedazzling eyes, so my guess was she'd move to Washington State or nearby. I was pleased as punch for my friend.

"I'm in the same predicament you are, Rowan," said Maggie. "Tim and I are also attending the inaugural festivities, and I don't own a ballgown."

"You never went to a Marine Corps Birthday Ball?" I said as she shook her head. "You were missing out. That was one of the best things about Marine Corps life."

"Maybe we should leave earlier and hire you a designer in Vegas," said Genie. "And yes, Rowdy darling, you will pay for it."

Before Rowdy could respond, Mazy said, "I have a cousin here on the moonship who is an aspiring fashion designer! Both Maggie and Genie wore his dresses to the New Year's party."

Chapter 54

When Byrin said my sleep would be peaceful, she couldn't have factored in effects of that phone call from the next vice president. Hence, I had a nightmare, but I did not wake screaming—or I presumed I didn't because no one came crashing in at three a.m.

Details were murky, but a car blew up. I wasn't in it, because in my dream I saw it, but I didn't *hear* it happen, which was strange. I was able to talk myself down, to quell adrenaline and panic as I deep-breathed to find my center. This, despite Bodie hogging the center of the bed and Morris sticking his butt in my face.

Three hours later, I awoke again, seminaturally because Morris wanted breakfast. The critters and I were not alone in bed.

Roger Rogers was sprawled next to me in nothing but those clinging red boxer briefs I remembered too well, his Superman *S* shield tattoo on full display. Good thing this was a big bed, but his six-foot-seven frame meant his feet hung over the edge.

As I stared at the ridges of a washboard stomach, his mercurial eyes opened. I shifted my gaze to them, and they quickly turned from hazel to bright green.

"Just flew in from Mars? It took you longer than Rowdy in a spaceship. You must be slacking in your old age," I snarked.

"I'll show you old age." I was flipped underneath Roger in the blink of an eye. Superman stuff. Including words spoken inside my head.

He took his time staring into my eyes before kissing me.

"I had some extra business to attend to," he said aloud, letting me come up for air. "And now I'm here to attend to you, beautiful."

"Okay, but I may need an oxygen tank—and coffee. And a transfusion of my wits."

Roger chuckled, and my body quivered, pressed underneath his. "I think your critters are hungry, because one of them is gnawing on my foot."

"Morris!" I hissed. "Do not eat Superman!"

As I got coffee, I noticed the machine didn't make that sound like car tires squealing. I wish mine at home didn't. I gave Roger his in my new Jupiter mug with its red orb swirl, and I opted for the Mars mug, also red. Like the boxer briefs and tattoo, which remained the only things on Roger's overwhelmingly large and beautifully formed body.

I sipped mango-vanilla coffee—tasty—and contemplated the supremely yummy Red Orbiter in my kitchen.

"Okay, I'm just going to come out with it like Lois Lane. Is another one of your superpowers that you can hear from greater distances than other Red Orbiters? Like from Earth to the moon and from the moon to Mars?"

"We've discussed this before, how I have more magnetism than most of my kind." He shot me that cheeky grin, and I suddenly needed to sit down at my dining table.

"Yes, but that was about how you can fly through the air willy-nilly while others need magnetic energy from orbs to ascend and descend."

"Willy-nilly?" said Roger, inside my head. "Like a bird or a plane? Faster than a speeding bullet?"

"Stop mind melding with me! It's disorienting enough that you appeared near-naked, sprawled in my bed. Are you going to put some clothes on?"

"Eventually. Are you going to get yourself riled up again? Claiming Red Orbiter males are keeping things from you?" He ran a hand through towheaded hair. "I never said I couldn't hear you while you were on the moonship, by the way. You simply assumed I couldn't."

"You're still exasperating. Even in outer space."

"As are you, beautiful. Never doubt it."

"I've got so much to talk with you about." I sighed. "I wish we could stay here all day and never get dressed. But, speaking of dress, I have a consultation with a fashion designer in a few hours. Then another much-needed meet with Byrin. And I have to call my family. Plus I'm supposed to meet the Lacertan leaders, but maybe that's tomorrow. And when am I ever going to find time to work on my treaty presentation and write the flipping Red Orbiter book?"

"Breathe, beautiful. We've got time. Finish your coffee. Then I know *I* need a shower. Want to do it together?"

I didn't bother being squeamish about getting naked in the shower with him. Roger knew my body didn't look thirtysomething. He didn't care, so why should I? That's what I kept telling myself.

Afterward, as we dressed and headed with Bodie to the park, I thought how Owen would want to know what showering with Superman was like. Restrained, compared to previous experiences with Roger, but also rejuvenating, and mind- and body-consuming as always.

"Want to have biscuits and gravy, Texas style?" said fellow Longhorn Roger, though he graduated in 1915. "They've perfected a white, peppery gravy sans sausage that's pretty tasty."

I was finally having a meal at a different café near the pet park. "So, this news about you possibly retiring from bodyguarding. Have you too gone down the Rowdy rabbit hole, suddenly hankering for offspring? Because I've got tell you, watching him try to reel in a wife on the moonship has been unsettling. Poor Genie."

"Poor Genie?" said Roger. "That woman needs someone like Rowdy to—"

"Don't you dare say 'to take her in hand'!"

"No, beautiful. To match her spirit. But I'd like to take you in hand for interrupting me."

"That's another thing I want to talk with you about! Because of you and Rowdy snooping, everyone seems to know the details of my sex life like they're part of my résumé!"

"I thought Owen did a great job of explaining why you should not be so hung up about this. I wish you had listened."

"You listened to our private conversation?" I slammed my palm against the table.

"I believe that might have something to do with you saying, 'because of Roger and Rowdy digging up every little salacious detail about me.' You know by now that if I hear my name, I will listen in—if only to make sure you aren't calling out for help. Or anything else you might need."

"Is that some sort of sexual-innuendo jab? Making fun of the little woman?" I wanted it to sound like a taunting sneer, but it was wimpy, damn it.

"Beautiful, your sexual fantasy may be too much of a challenge for some men, but I have no problem with it. And though my name is Domitian, I'm no poser dom. I'm well aware it's about your desires and pleasure, not someone else's idea of dominance. Does that answer any questions or concerns you may have buzzing around in that formidable brain of yours?"

I nodded, gobsmacked.

"Good. Because I still need to answer your previous question. No, I am not wanting kids. But I am considering retiring from this security gig I've been doing for so long. Perhaps finally aging past thirty-three. Settling down with someone."

The implications were staggering.

"Is this about your parents moving into that other realm we haven't yet discussed? And how can you just stop being Superman?"

"After so many years, I'm tired of that too."

I didn't know what to say. As it turned out, I didn't get to say anything. Roger's phone went off with an alarming, high-frequency sound, clearly indicating an emergency. He reached for it, saying, "Speak," in a tone fit for an alien named Domitian.

His attention soon swiveled back to me, piercing me with those now-gold eyes.

"I have to leave you, beautiful. There's been an attempt to kill the senator."

"Please tell me Cassandra's okay." I caught my breath, my stomach plunging.

"Of course. They planted a bomb on her car, and luckily it detonated in her driveway with only she and her Red Orbiter driver inside."

There was no time for Roger to answer my questions about how they survived a fiery explosion, because while I knew *he* could catch bombs in midair and Red Orbiters could stop bullets, I didn't know they could be blown up by bombs and walk away. Definitely not information they'd want revealed in a book.

One thing I did know: My nightmare of a car blowing up last night had turned out to be knowledge bearing like Byrin said. Also, would the psychopathic violence instigated by this president and his enablers never cease?

Chapter 55

After Roger zipped away for Earth, I took Bodie back to the suite and hopped aboard a transpod to meet Maggie at Mazy's designer cousin's place, wondering if she'd already heard news of the attack on Senator Rojas-Ortiz.

I had my answer when Genie was also there, waiting for me on the commerce deck.

"I'm getting measured for a ballgown too. The inaugural will now include Red Orbiter security specialists," said Genie.

"So you know," I said, not wanting to pry them for information.

"Yes," said Maggie, grimly. "No details yet on who was responsible, but it was likely those wannabe militia dudes doing the president's bidding. He does not want Cassandra to be attorney general. He knows she'll prosecute him on day one—him and all his minions."

"I used to think I'd need Kevlar living in Yearntown while writing my column. Now I need it for DC."

"Rowan, you know we've got your back. Rowdy and Roger and I will all be there, along with the Secret Service. Let's not let the bad guys ruin our dress consultation. We're going to look fabulous!" said Genie, steering me in the direction of the shop.

"Okay, but about this ballgown—I don't want anything that will land me on any magazine's worst-dressed list. Mom will never forgive me."

"I hear you!" said Genie.

"And ideally it should be something I can wear with my black-and-teal shoes and blue-diamond earrings. I'm thinking a darker blue like Maggie's dress on New Year's. But floor length, with long sleeves and maybe a deeper neckline."

Mazy greeted us at the door with her cousin. "Welcome, I'm Mazon, and I am thrilled to be working with you today!" He said his name like it rhymed with *raisin*.

Mazon was slight of build, with black hair shaved on one side, the other flowing to his shoulder. One eyebrow was pierced multiple times with graduated spheres in various gems. It looked like a solar system.

Genie said, "Kickass piercings!"

"They're not my only piercings!" Mazon gushed. They were his only *visible* piercings. I looked at Maggie, who somehow maintained a straight face.

"So, do you anticipate a problem being able to finish three gowns in such short a time, now that I need one too?" asked Genie.

Mazon fluttered his hands. "We will work with fabrics and textiles I already have in supply, and I have assistants for the sewing. I am committed to outfitting all of you in the utmost style!"

"Do you have any more of that dark-blue fabric Maggie's dress was made from? The one she bought for our party?" I asked.

"I do," said Mazon, beaming. "Did you know I made the tuxedos your gentlemen friends rented too? But they were not my designs. I can copy almost anything to perfection, but my true passion is creating one-of-a-kind looks. What I intend to do for you!"

I went first, the guinea pig, giving him details about my shoes and what I wanted. Mazon made notes on a device like mine, and Mazy helped him get my measurements, which was when I realized I'd been eating too well on the moonship and wearing too many flowing Labyrinthian tunics. Mazon brought out a bolt of the dark-blue fabric, and I was relieved there was lots of it.

"This is my second-favorite color in the Crayola box of many crayons," I murmured as I ran my hand across the silky textile. "It's called midnight blue."

"That's it!" said Mazon, spinning around. "We are going with a Cinderella-at-midnight ballgown theme. I am inspired!" He threw his hands up in the air and struck a pose.

Maggie went next, and Mazon selected the darkest of green fabric. "To accentuate your eyes," he said. "You will be like the sparkling end of the spectrum on a watermelon tourmaline crystal!"

"I have one of those!" I said.

As Maggie was measured, Mazon said, "You have the body of a champion athlete. We will accentuate these marvelous shoulders and long legs!"

When it came time for Genie, she kicked out her hip. "I'm not bad, I'm just drawn that way!"

"Jessica Rabbit! Yes!" squealed Mazon. Apparently every alien in the galaxy watched American movies to learn English.

Genie said, "I probably need something simple and in black," and Mazon's face fell. He had been headed for red flashy fabric.

Genie rushed to placate. "But we could do a nice, high slit in the leg, maybe? In case I need to run and tackle someone? I also need straps that will hold so my boobs won't pop out."

"I can work with that," said Mazon, eyes wide. I watched him sketch, and it looked like Genie might end up with two high slits, one for each leg. And straps that resembled a maze running down over her eye-popping bodice. "A true Bond girl." He sighed, wistful.

Genie's measurements were flat out unfair. As Mazon worked with her, I had a chance to chat with Mazy.

"I've never seen my friend George so smitten, and not just with your cooking skills."

"But he does run on physics and food, doesn't he?" she grinned.

"That he does. And he's always been attracted to the exotic and beautiful."

"Thank you. He is a kind and fascinating man. I hope we will be able to continue our courtship on Earth."

"I know George hopes that too. Speaking of Earth, I want to write about my experiences here to take home and share, and I would so love to be able to interview you about the culinary school and food preparation techniques. My time is now running shorter than expected, but do you think you could carve out a few hours for us to chat?"

"It will be my pleasure. I will prepare refreshments for us. New things for you to try!"

"Thank you. But don't hold it against me if I'm not as adventurous as George when it comes to eating."

"No one is, dear," said Mazy, her eyes full of mirth.

As we left the shop after thanking Mazon and Mazy profusely, Genie told us Rowdy was paying triple to have our gowns completed on time. His idea.

"He also said O.W. is flying that hairstylist to the stars from LA to DC so he can do your hair and makeup again, Rowan," said Genie.

"So you're speaking to Rowdy?"

Genie scowled. "For now. But I haven't forgiven him for inviting all of those women to the party."

I stopped and looked at her. "You slept with him last night, didn't you?"

"You slept with Roger!" she retorted, stomping her foot and making her enormous boobs bounce, which caused several men on the commerce deck to walk into storefront walls.

"No, I didn't. I awoke in the morning, and there he was. And now I have to go meet with Byrin to fix everything that got undone in the last twenty-four hours." I was proud of myself for keeping a neutral expression.

"I know my brother all too well, Rowan," drawled Maggie. "So I know for sure he did some fixing of his own for you this morning."

"Busted!" said Genie. I heard her hooting even after I'd boarded a transpod.

Chapter 56

As I emerged on the upper deck, I saw a reddish-tawny wolf entering a transpod.

"Did I just see Owen's wolf?" I asked Byrin in her front yard.

"Yes, she was visiting Wily and Sky."

"Does she not live with Owen? Because I didn't see a wolf at his condo."

"She does, but Aries roams freely all over the ship. That's why she's learned how to board transpods to get from one deck to another. Wily and Sky also roam, visiting the park when they choose to be sociable."

"Aries? Owen's wolf is named Aries?"

"Uncanny, is it not?" Byrin's violet eyes danced.

Before I got in the hammock, I filled her in on my last twenty-four hours, including the nightmare that had come true, though it didn't happen to me.

"It is good you were able to work through it calmly. Each time, you will progress."

Afterward, when I was feeling downright sublime, Byrin said, "Let us be sociable now. Please come inside for tea and scones."

"Rose's lime marmalade!" I exclaimed as we sat in a cozy little nook. "I couldn't get enough of this while I was in Great Britain. But I should go easy on the clotted cream. I've gained weight on the moonship."

"Sometimes weight is gained with knowledge," said Byrin. "But it is worth it, is it not? What would life be if we did not indulge and imbibe in things that bring us pleasure? There is a time for restraint, just as there is a time to fully embrace what life has to offer."

"I don't know what I'm going to do without you." I sighed. "I indulge in paper crafting, often to calm my spirits, and I have a rubber stamp that says, 'Have the courage to be gentle with yourself.' I don't think I fully understood what it meant until meeting you."

"We are kindred spirits in many ways, Rowan Layne. Perhaps now is a good time to reveal more about me, and why I choose to be called Byrin."

"I'm so glad you don't go by Lab! Because on Earth that's how we refer to Labrador retrievers, and it wouldn't seem right. Not that dogs aren't better creatures than many humans, but still… I'm babbling again. Sorry!"

Byrin smiled. "Babbling, as you call it, is delightful. I learn much from it about you."

"Are you sure that's a good thing?" I quipped.

"What you don't yet know about me is my given name, which was Aphrodite."

"That's a mouthful."

She smiled. "There was an ancient alien named Aphrodite, which Greeks deemed a goddess. The goddess of sexual love and beauty, because she was beautiful and possessed with an uncontrollable desire. The Romans associated Aphrodite with Venus, which they got wrong. She was of Mars, a Labyrinthian."

"Wow. Tell me more about this uncontrollable desire."

"Aphrodite's story was gruesome. Supposedly she was born from white foam produced by severed genitals of Uranus after his son Cronus threw them into the sea. Aphrodite was then married off by Zeus to an ugly, deformed man. But she nonetheless took many lovers, both gods and humans," said Byrin, smiling. "The only part the Greeks got right was her many lovers, and their diversity. In gender and species."

"You are like the Aphrodite you're named for?" I said, fascinated.

"Yes, and it would appear that you and I have much in common as well."

"The many lovers part? And species—now."

"You and I imbibe for pleasure. But even when we misstep in our journey, when an encounter does not bring pleasure but instead bears a heavy burden, the daunting weight of trauma, we may learn from it. We gain knowledge in our understanding of experiences, both pleasurable and painful. From that we grow, and heal. As we come to understand why we were drawn to an encounter and what we need to glean from it, we can better recognize the time for restraint, yet still fully engage in pleasurable pursuits, wiser than before."

"You've been there too," I whispered. "Down that dark path."

"Yes, on one of my travels. I met someone who turned out to be not what they seemed. I thought my intuition had failed me. But we cannot always see what another entity is intent on hiding. We can find ourselves winding through a maze of which there is no exit, no escape, and no path to truth or serenity."

"I spent three years with someone who used everything I said and everything I was as a weapon against me. Twisting my persona for his own ends, including my legal background. He held a perpetual grudge and could never accept when I chose to make my own path, not the one he devised for me as part of his imagined world. Somehow as a result, I feel incapable of having friends, of trusting in others enough to be a friend."

"Are you beginning to realize your projections of his behavior and mindset onto your psyche? That perhaps this man is the one who cannot have friends, cannot be a friend? That you are the kind and loving person you always were? You just need to trust in yourself. And to remember that you, too, are worthy of friendship—and love."

I looked into the eyes of Wily, sitting next to me, feeling the love and gratitude he had for Byrin, because I felt it too. And I swear the coyote smiled back at me.

"I have a brother who recently went through something similar to you, Rowan. His given name unfortunately sounds like rheumatoid in English, so he goes by Rinth. He's about your age, an environmental scientist working mining issues on Mars, so you have that in common as well."

"I'm no scientist. Though the environmental part is intriguing." I took a bite of scone and a sip of tea. "But is this a bit of matchmaking going on? Another of Aphrodite Byrin's special gifts?" I teased.

"Another possibility in the pursuit of pleasure." She winked, and I almost spit my tea.

“My sister would freak. She already has enough trouble keeping track of my romantic interests.”

Chapter 57

As I departed Byrin's cottage, Owen was waiting among the wildflowers with the wolf.

"I can't believe she's named Aries," I said.

"Mars is the Roman god of war. Aries, or Ares, is the Greek god of war. Once a Marine, always a Marine." He smiled. "Plus, I had Byrin ask her to see if she minded the name. She didn't."

"Tell me about her. She's not a gray wolf, is she?"

"Aries is a red wolf," he said, rubbing her behind the ears. "A species originating on Sirius but commonly found in the southeastern US. Morphologically, the red wolf is between a coyote and a gray wolf."

"So she's a genetic hybrid, like humans?" Aries's eyes watched me as I spoke.

"Yes, very astute of you to make that comparison, man-magnet," Owen grinned.

"Are you going to keep calling me that?"

"I haven't decided. At least until I come up with another nickname. Fireball is taken."

"I hope your presence here doesn't mean you added something to today's schedule because I'm pooped. I want to plop onto my chaise and veg out."

"And so you shall," he said. "I've arranged for you and Red to meet with the Lacertan leaders tomorrow afternoon, because Mazon wants to see you in the morning for approval of his final designs before sewing begins."

"Okay, but can I just say Mazon makes you look bigtime butch, baby!" I skipped away from Owen's reach.

"Cowardly retreat," he said, coming at me slowly, like stalking prey. "Do I need to have food delivered to your suite?"

"No! I still have leftover crab cakes you sent me home with. And I've gained enough inches on the moonship already! I should stop eating altogether, like a Luna moth. They don't have mouths. And what is it with this compelling need to feed me?"

"I like fleshy women. And maybe my nickname for you should be Rowan the Mouthy," he said, walking away from me.

"Look who's retreating now!"

Owen stopped and turned. I considered a mad dash for a transpod. "I just wanted to even the score!" I yelped.

Those purple eyes of his narrowed. "How's it feel to want?"

I got in the transpod, not believing he'd lobbed a classic Marine Corps expression at me before I could use it on him. Damn.

Back in my suite, it was time to let my family know my inaugural news. I called my sister first. Yes, I was being cowardly.

"New development."

"Not another new guy?" said G.

"In a manner of speaking."

I told her about being the new vice president's date, finishing up with the discovery of my new measurements. "I was trying to think of a silver lining and thought maybe weight gain would deter more men. But then Owen pops out and says he likes *fleshy* women! Have you ever heard such a thing? Maddening. And don't you dare ask me which one Owen is again."

"The Marine. From Mars. Physicist brainiac. Is he also handsome and a nice guy?"

"I used to think so, but he's been holding out on me. Those initial quiet types can be tricky. And are you getting at something with your descriptive litany?"

"Owen is your romantic archetype. Definitely so since you mentioned he was quiet."

"I don't want to talk about this right now. I have to call Mom and email Dad, and Mom is probably still mad at me about the shoe store."

"Tell her about your ballgown design. Although maybe not about the piercings of—what was the designer's name—Mason?"

I opted for the Dad email first, telling him all the news he'd enjoy, including the technical stuff I'd learned about the moon as well as Bodie's play pals in the park. Next up, Mom.

"Hello, dear Doodles!" she answered airily, so perhaps I'd been bestowed with the gift of a memory lapse.

I told her my news, playing up the part about Warren O'Neill being a Democrat before switching to the Omni party, in case she'd forgotten, and ending with my dress plans but most definitely leaving out my weight gain—a crime in her universe.

We had a brief pause in the conversation while Mom had to fuss at Dad about something being prepared in the kitchen. "I told you I need *crunch*!" she said, sounding pissy. I stayed out of it, having had too many years to learn to do so.

When Mom deigned to return to me on the phone up here on the moonship, she said, "I want to speak with this *raisin* designer. Is he also a chef? Because I don't want anything tacky for your special ballgown. We don't want you appearing trashy like that awful wife of the president! And that daughter-in-law looks like a cheap hooker!"

While I recovered from that conversation, Rauc called before I could call him.

"Just checking in on you to make sure you're holding up, Copper. I don't want you to worry about the attack on Rojas-Ortiz. We're working the problem. She had plans to call you but asked me to tell you everything will be okay."

"I'm just relieved she's okay. And you tell her that I'm no litigator, but if she wants help drafting those indictments once she's AG, I'm her gal. I'd devote the rest of my life to this prosecutorial process."

Rauc chuckled. "I'm sure you would. But right now, let's focus on your Congressional address. Because you're going to be in Washington for the inaugural, it's been moved up from the spring so you don't have to make two trips."

Chapter 58

As Genie and Maggie and I met on the commerce deck, I said, "I'd just like to have one piece of news coming at me that doesn't completely erase all the work Byrin is doing. How am I supposed to be ready to present to Congress in a few weeks?"

"Please!" said Genie. "You've probably already drafted the whole thing in your head."

"Yes, and recited it in my subconscious all freaking night long," I huffed.

"At least you don't have to leave tomorrow," said Maggie. "I thought Mazon was going to have a stroke when I told him. I'm kind of afraid to go in there now." A former Marine fighter pilot in fear of a diminutive dress designer with multiple piercings. Crack me up.

But Mazon was taking it in stride. While Genie and I reviewed our dress sketches, he draped shimmery green fabric on Maggie's tall frame, fussing about with three assistants. "We will have this completed so your friends can bring your gown with them to Washington for you. It will be the bomb!"

As I looked at screenshots, I was relieved that my Cinderella design was not some Disney-devised puff of a dress but instead had elegant lines. The drama came with a second sketch. "Is this a *cape*?"

"Yes!" said Mazon, pulling pins from his mouth. "You said it would be cold in Washington in late January, so I thought I would design a cloak to match your ball gown. Did you see the jeweled clasp at the throat?"

I looked closer at the sketch on the screen. "Is that a pumpkin?"

"Yes! Like Cinderella's golden carriage! It will have pumpkin-colored gems."

"Citrine?" I assumed an inexpensive quartz.

Mazon grinned. "Burnt-orange diamonds from Mars. I asked Mr. Raucous Wilde, and he said you love that color, so while he could not get you glass slippers to go with your dress, this was what I should make for you. He said Luna Moth Woman needs a cape."

"You spoke to Rauc?"

"Yes, he called me to say not to worry about the cost, and to tell me what he wanted for you once I told him the theme. He has the most amazing voice," said Mazon.

"Don't I know it," I said, giddy to the tips of my toes.

Genie shouted into the ether, "Hey, Rowdy, I want diamonds on my dress too!"

Whatever he replied in her ear, I didn't hear, but Maggie did and grinned broadly. Genie was not grinning. Genie was fuming.

Once we left the shop, I said, "Maggie, will you tell me what Rowdy said to Genie since she's being a poop and won't say?"

"Okay, fine!" said Genie, stomping her foot, making a guy nearby trip and land flat on his face. "Rowdy said he'd give me diamonds, all right. A six-carat red-diamond ring for my finger if I'd marry him and have his babies. He already picked it out!"

"I'm telling you, Genie." I shook my head. "Time to try a dog."

We all went in different directions from there. I got Bodie and headed for the park, ordering a salade Niçoise with OW olives at the European café and making notes about the treaty on my scratch pad screen. But that gave me fits, so I called Rauc.

"Thank you for the burnt-orange diamond pumpkin, my most handsomest, nicest alien in the galaxy."

"You sound pleased. I'm glad. I didn't want you to think I was horning in on your dress design," he said. "Get it? *Horn* in, as in Hook 'em Horns? That's why you love burnt orange."

"That I do!" I grinned to beat the Longhorn band. "You remember everything."

"Part of what we Red Orbiter observers are known for. And I've got some good news."

I gripped the phone in my hand. "Are you sure?"

"Yes, if you like the idea of me flying you from the moon to DC. Oz will hold down the fort here in Vegas because I was slated to attend the inauguration in my official capacity."

"That is spectacularly good news! But 'hold down the fort'? Have you been watching John Wayne movies when you should be doing big, bad Red Orbiter business?"

"Only that one we like, *McLintock!* You're my Maureen O'Hara."

"I'm turning into your queen of diamonds with all the fancy rocks you're giving me."

"No, you'll always be my queen of hearts, my shooting star, and my Copper. And don't think that high-neck design of your cape will protect you from me, even though you'll be another man's date for the ball."

Chapter 59

Our afternoon meeting with Lacertan leaders was in Owen's condo office. I brought Bodie as directed so he could socialize with Aries the wolf. Was my dog going to become as conflicted as I was, with multiple entanglements of different species?

Red was there when I arrived, so we had time to chat before the Lacertans showed.

"Did you hear that my presentation to Congress has been bumped up to right after the inauguration? That better not happen with the Britain part of this gig."

"No, lass, our general elections don't take place until May, so no need to fash yourself. It will not be until after we have new leadership as well."

"Okay, but I'm doing nothing for the next three days but focusing on this treaty and writing. And I'm only going to eat vegetables!"

"Then have dinner with me tonight. Before you self-isolate and pine away. I found a Middle Eastern restaurant onboard, and word has it you had a favorite Lebanese eatery in Virginia as well as a penchant for pomegranates."

"Win told you." I squinted my eyes at him. "He's the only one who could learn that. You spies are sneaky. But okay, if you ply me with pomegranates, I'll acquiesce."

When the Lacertans arrived, I was taken aback because they looked so much like Warren O'Neill, it was uncanny. The light-green-ringed eyes, yes, but also the golden-brown skin. Yet it was their proud bearing and charisma that ultimately made me think of our next vice president. And their self-deprecating graciousness.

They offered profuse apologies for the travesty of Tribble, and I couldn't fathom how such esthetically appealing, dignified entities were the same species, much less from the same galaxy as their toady compatriot. As a result, it took more time than expected to obtain what I sought, which was their concerns on how my nation was disrespecting their homeland—or home ship, as it was.

They were most impressed with Warren O'Neill after meeting him.

"There is hope now, for your nation, for Earth, and for us on the moonship and the species we represent," said the female Lacertan leader. "Hope that springs from the election of new leaders who embrace diversity and eschew hate. There is hope that your people have chosen such leaders out of the ashes of destruction and despair of the last four years.

"The challenge now will be to ensure the new leadership in your Congress will also embrace change, will reflect this change in their decisions for the betterment of all who stand to be affected by them. They must listen, and understand. This is crucial."

Her husband and partner in leading Lacertans spoke next. "We are not so much concerned now about past violations of this treaty as we are about your nations' ongoing and future actions and views." He nodded to both Red and me. "You will be facilitators on whatever changes come forth, and on the attitude they reflect about space exploration."

When the female leader quoted Mahatma Gandhi, "For me, every ruler is alien that defies public opinion," I reached the center of my maze on how to devise a message for Congress.

I realized we the people had spoken, and we were comprised of otherworldly DNA like every other being on Earth. The outgoing president denied and decried this, vilifying aliens as he alienated himself from those he was tasked to serve. The traitor became the very thing he reviled. An alien. An outsider. A danger and a threat to annihilate democracy and all human decency.

Those who supported his bigotry and hate, who cheered his disdain for diversity and diplomacy, from local governments to Congressional seats, were now in contravention of overwhelming public opinion reflected in victory for candidates who represented diversity and did not deny DNA residing in us all.

I told the Lacertan leaders that they, and the wisdom of their words, inspired me. I told them how I would share their words with my nation's leaders, in hopes that they, too, would be inspired and no longer alienate themselves from those they served, and those in space who counted on them to pursue peaceful purpose for the betterment of all species.

Once they left, after extending an offer for me to revisit the moonship as their personal guest, Owen said, “I’m so proud of you. You have been afforded the highest honor possible through that invitation, and you were wonderful. You listened with sensitivity and integrity. What it means to be a true diplomat.”

“Thank you,” I said, relieved because I hadn’t done much talking. “But when do we meet with the moonship leader?”

“You already have. You’re looking at him.” Owen grinned.

“But I thought that—”

“You thought there’d be a supreme leader for the entire ship? Not really. We’re not a nation state like on Earth, or a planet. And we’re pretty informal. I’m like an appointed mayor, someone chosen because I’m willing to take on the role of looking after every resident’s interests. When I’m ready to move on, someone else will step in.”

“But what about Red Orbiters? Didn’t they build the moonship when the real moon was destroyed?”

“Yes, they did, and when Mars ran into problems, Labyrinthians were able to reside here and currently make up the majority of the population. It’s like a city. Species can visit or come to live. Some come to attend school and then move on. Red Orbiters still cover mechanics of ensuring the ship runs smoothly, including its commerce and education opportunities. Earth’s Red Orbiter’s have a say in what goes on here and who fills the role I’m in now. Sometimes it’s a Red Orbiter.”

“What compels Lacertans to choose leaders?”

Owen smiled. “Lacertans are from the planet you know as Venus, also not fully habitable like Mars. This ship currently has a greater concentration of Lacertans than any planet in the solar system, so when the president fired a missile at it, he could have taken out a large portion of their existing species. This was an act of war for them, just as it was for Labyrinthians. But there is something else, in their DNA. Lacerta rotates in the opposite direction of most other planets. Lacertans like to do things their own way, at their own speed. It's my role to make sure that is respected. You helped me do that today."

Chapter 60

"Would you like to join us for dinner?" Red asked Owen before we left his office.

"I can't. A cousin working on Mars is here to give me a mining report so we can determine damages we'll seek against the three banned mining outfits—as well as the US and Russian governments."

"Russians are involved?" I said.

"One of the three companies is operated by Russians officials. Some of the president's financial buddies." Owen smirked.

"Were those armed idiots actually working for Russians and didn't know it?"

"Along with someone else you know," said Owen.

"Oh the irony," I said, shaking my head. "So these damages you're seeking are pursuant to the terms of the treaty, where nation-states are responsible for their actions in space, along with nongovernment-entity actions?"

"You got it. We're dealing with environmental degradation issues in addition to criminal intent to harm those on the moonship."

"I have experience in seeking environmental damages from my work with a tribe in northern Nevada. I'm happy to help if needed," I said.

"I was counting on it, Counselor." Owen smiled.

As Red and I sat down to order dinner, he said, "Tell me what this sudden issue you have with not eating is about, because I know you cannot have lost your enthusiasm for food."

I sighed, contemplating a dish with a mint, cucumber, and yogurt sauce. "I've gained weight on the moonship. Somewhat due to the park and not walking Bodie every day. I'm off my routine."

"You will be back on it soon enough. Enjoy the rest of your time here. I received notice earlier to a brunch sendoff for Maggie tomorrow. I know you're not missing that."

"Damn, I forgot about that. But my plans have changed anyway. After that meeting, I won't need to hole up for days to figure out what I'm writing for Congress."

"Finding your center, are ye now, lass? And we hearty Scots tend to appreciate a woman with a little meat on her bones. So we're ordering both hummus with pine nuts and the baba ghanoush for starters."

"Oh good, because this gal can never get enough roasted eggplant. Or pine nuts."

"Speaking of food," Red said as we used triangles of pita bread to scoop our savory dishes, "I was going to suggest you take a basics class with me at the culinary school that's designed for visitors. But now there is no time."

"You obviously haven't heard what a hazard I am around sharp knives."

"By hazard, you mean to yourself and not men in your immediate vicinity?" said Red.

I smirked in response. "It's also that I find most recipes have way too many steps, with weird stuff like clarifying butter. What is that about? Why does food have to be clarified, like it's a statement that needs an explanation?"

Red roared with laughter. "I don't know about clarifying butter, but one of the basics you'd learn from this class is how to properly handle a knife for chopping those vegetables you claimed were all you'd eat the next few days."

"Okay, maybe I could learn that, but I won't chop onions, and my sister would be envious. Sous chef is her dream job. Me, I prefer ordering and eating."

"Well, you're off the hook this moon trip, It's not offered again until after we've left. But I'm thinking of returning after the inauguration for a few weeks."

"Really? But you need to calendar a special event for early March. My sister and mom are throwing a baby shower for Bruce and Ophelia, and I know you were bummed you had to miss their wedding due to Congressional hearings. Genie told me you went to school with Bruce and your families were close."

"Aye, Bruce and I are the best of mates. And I will plan to be there. Interesting that I'll get to meet the family of Rowan Layne as well. Did you obtain your Scots good looks from your mum or dad, lass?"

"Most of my Scottish heritage comes from Mom's side, but also from Dad's mom. But my father's patriarchal line came straight from London to Texas. Please don't hold that against him." I winced, and Red laughed. "Dad was in the Navy at the tail end of the Korean War, and he likes to reminisce, so he might talk your ear off, though he's pretty much deaf in both ears and likely won't hear a word you say. It's cool that he navigated by the stars."

"Aye, that it is. Did they put enough pomegranate seeds on your meal?"

"Yes. You and I are fruit kindred spirits, what with your love of mangoes and limes as well. Hey! Speaking of England, have you seen Byrin's thatched-roof cottage on the upper deck? We had Rose's lime marmalade with scones the last time I was there!"

"Aye, it is charming. And it looks like Scotland too, lass. As for the marmalade, it's a staple in my home. Why do you think my pup is named Rosie?"

"Seriously? That's a hoot. So what will you name your Scottish fold kitty?"

"If it's a boy, Charlie, for the bonny prince. And it's she's a lass, Rowan might do."

"Wow. I've never had someone's critter named after me." I savored a bite of eggplant and tomato stew. "This food is amazing."

"Have you told your mum and dad what you'll be doing in Britain with me?"

"Not yet, but my sister, Gwynne, knows. She and her husband, Phil, and my dad are big-time into golf."

"Are they now? Perhaps they can accompany you on your trip."

"Okay, but you're not going to expect me to golf, are you? Because I'll have enough of a challenge accompanying you when you address Parliament."

Red put down his fork. "I have a distinct feeling you're missing something in translation, lass. Dinna you ken that both houses of

British Parliament have traditionally only been addressed by heads of other nation-states? What you and I will be doing together on behalf of the residents of the moonship is unprecedented."

Chapter 61

I made a beeline for Byrin's the next day after the brunch for Maggie, and when I emerged from the hammock, an unknown man walked toward me through the wildflowers. Where was Byrin? Was I still in my maze searching for center? Was I dreaming?

Or was this another nightmare?

The man moved, purposeful, as if he knew me. He looked lean and hard and unsmiling. Dark clothing, short black hair with silver streaks, and the deepest of tans, like he hailed from the shores of a Mediterranean island. As he slowly grew closer, his eyes made me think of a field of Texas bluebonnets. He raised his arm, and my mind said, "Gun!"

I came back to consciousness hearing a yipping coyote and looking into calming blue eyes.

"I fainted again!" I gasped. "I never do, but now on the moonship I'm just a constant damsel in distress. That actually wasn't a gun in your hand was it? It was just your hand."

The man stood me upright by my shoulders. "I'm Rinth. No gun." He spoke softly, as if concerned I'd pass out again at the sound of his voice.

"I suppose you wouldn't need one. You feel so hard and strong and—did I just say that out loud?" I gripped his shoulders. "I think I need to sit down."

"Do you want to lie down in the hammock again?" he asked, his voice an erotic dream.

"No! I'm not sure I'm not still wandering in my labyrinth. Where is Byrin?"

"I'm right here, Rowan. I went to put the kettle on for tea. Did you meet my brother?"

"More like collapsed in his arms," I said, panting from an adrenaline surge. "I saw him walking toward me and thought maybe I was having another bad dream."

Rinth chuckled. "If I had a nickel for every time I've been called a bad dream."

Byrin gaped from me to her brother, looking so confused, it was comical.

"Maybe we should get some of that tea in Rowan," said Rinth.

We were seated in Byrin's parlor when I realized his dark clothes were denim jeans, well-worn, with a faded black t-shirt. Everything about him looked weathered but strong.

"So your sister told me you're an environmental scientist on Mars?" I asked because Rinth was sitting tight-lipped, making his cheekbones even more defined.

"And a mining engineer," he said.

"Oh no," I said.

"Another bad dream?" Rinth finally grinned, and what a grin it was.

"No! Sorry! I don't know where my mind is."

"I bet I do." Byrin smiled. "Forgive me. I wanted you two to meet. But I didn't mean for Rinth to startle you. He knew who you were because I told him about you."

Fifteen minutes later I boarded a transpod and called out, "Genie! Emergency girls' night needed!"

"I know the perfect place," her plucky voice popped into my ear. "Meet me on the commerce deck near the salon in an hour."

I went back to my suite to change clothes because I looked a total rumpled mess in the jeans and cotton shirt I'd worn for the hammock. Add one more mortifying detail to my day. And another centering session that bit the dust.

My azure-blue tunic and new sandals would make me feel better, with my labyrinth earrings. Fresh eye makeup and some lipstick for good measure.

Genie was waiting for me. "You look great, but your eyes are kind of squirrely," she said. "Did you get a call from the president-elect asking you to be press secretary?"

"Yikes! No. Bite your tongue!"

"See? Your life isn't so bad." She smirked as we walked into the bar she'd selected.

"This looks like a miniversion of a Vegas casino. Without the smoke and noise."

"It gets noisy when somebody wins something—which has to do with why I chose it. Rowdy can't bother us here. He's banned from the place for being too lucky. He made residents mad by winning all the cool travel packages."

"Yes, but Rowdy can still *hear* you," Rowdy's voice slipped in my ear, and I jumped, but Genie didn't notice. "Rowan, do make sure my woman doesn't end up in some wanker's bed tonight. Because I will hold you accountable. I watch lots of John Wayne movies."

"Does this place have cheesy lounge lizard singers too?" I asked Genie in a rush. Rowdy didn't sound like he was kidding. Serious Rowdy was terrifying.

Genie said, "No, but there's a place with exotic dancers we could go to later. They have an amateur hour where anyone can hop up on stage and swirl around the pole."

Oh, dear heavens, could this get any worse?

"You're making that up!" I tried for jocularity as we sat at a small bar with six stools.

"No, I'm not. I suggested to Maggie the three of us go, and she balked, big-time. She's officially taken by Tim. But you and I could give it a whirl."

Yes, things could always get worse. The universe was not happy with me.

"Aren't you and I kind of taken?"

Genie snorted. "More like you've taken men. What's it up to now, with Owen?"

"Genie!" I hissed as a robotic thing brought our drinks, which still creeped me out. "Maybe Rauc is mine, but Roger and Win and Red and Owen are not! Most of them were taken by their work long before I came along. Damn." I sighed. "All of those names sound overwhelming. I'm going to need a lot of drinks."

I wanted to yell at Rowdy that he'd better get out of my ear, but I couldn't because Genie would hear me.

Genie said, "You've earned it. The drinks and the men. Cheers!"

Bourbon on the rocks for me, and it went down smooth and strong. I was hoping the taste of home might ground me.

"Are you going to tell me what triggered the emergency?" Genie asked.

Upon hearing the word *trigger*, I flashed back to thinking Rinth had a gun and giggled. It was funny, when I thought about it.

No, it wasn't. It was mortifying.

"Let me knock down another one of these, and maybe I'll be ready to tell you. Although after what we were just talking about, maybe not."

"Oh, you're going to tell me, girlfriend," said Genie.

It took three bourbons and a bowl of guacamole with chips, but I spilled it all.

"You're overreacting," she said. "He sounds harmless. A perfectly nice guy who won't hold it against you that you accused him of being a killer and collapsed at his feet."

"Easy for you to say," I said, sucking back bourbon. "You weren't sipping tea in Byrin's parlor, babbling small talk about the most mundane details of your life just to fill the uncomfortable silence. You have no idea how awkward it was!"

"Yes, it was awkward. Please allow me to apologize. My sister likes to meddle in my life. But I swear I didn't find the details of your life to be mundane. And I did not at all mind you collapsing in my arms."

Rinth was standing not three inches away from us. He held out his hand to Genie. "Hi. I'm Rinth, and I promise I don't have a gun. I thought humans like to shake hands. Go figure." He shrugged conspiratorially.

I promptly fell off my barstool—and into Rinth's arms.

Chapter 62

Genie and I went immediately to the restroom, where I thought I might just stay for the rest of my time on the moonship.

"That man said more words out there than he did the entire time at Byrin's."

Genie said, "No wonder you were flipped out. Rinth looks like he stepped out of one of your movie Westerns. Except he's the cowboy, the Indian, the bad guy, and the rescuing hero all rolled up into one fine-looking—"

"Genie!" I screeched. "You have *got* to stop talking about other men. *You-know-who* is listening—*and* in my ear—and he is one intimidating *hombre* when he wants to be!"

"Rowdy Wilde!" yelled Genie. "You leave Rowan alone!"

I heard Rowdy's voice again, but outside the restroom this time. "No, I am not going to gamble!" He burst in like a thundercloud.

"Woman!" he said to Genie. "We need to talk about this issue of whether you're taken or not. And when we're through, there's not going to be any doubt. Let's go."

Genie, hands on hips, said, "Rowdy, this is the women's restroom, and you're being ridiculous." I was impressed with her even tone. I myself dove into a stall and locked the door.

"It's unisex, and you've got two seconds to decide if you want to walk out of here or be carried out. One," said Rowdy.

I had to pee badly but couldn't.

"Rowan?" said Genie. "I am going to go with this crazy man so he doesn't make more of a scene. But I will be back, okay?"

I squeaked, "Okay."

When I emerged from the restroom, Rinth was still at the bar.

"A day that will live in infamy," I said, walking up to him. "Except for meeting you. But not the thinking you had a gun part."

Rinth smiled. "Have one drink with me before I have to return to Mars?"

"Okay, but if I fall off this barstool, just let me land in a heap on the floor. It'll be much more dignified."

"You're funny," he said. "I don't get much of that on Mars, being around miners and scientists."

"Do you like living there?"

"Not really, because right now the conditions are pretty stark. But it's important work to help restore my planet of origin. And I needed to get away for a while, clear my head and ponder my next move in life."

"I can relate to that. Byrin said you'd been through something like what I dealt with. I wouldn't wish that on anyone." I sighed.

"My sister likes to talk about me." Rinth smiled wryly.

"Try being around Red Orbiters! I pretty much have no secrets left in life."

Rinth squinted, little crinkles at the corners of his eyes adding to his allure. "I suppose that could be somewhat liberating."

I took a sip of my drink, absorbing his words. "You know, I never thought about it like that. But it could be, once I get used to it."

"Would you like to tell me a secret, something none of the other men in your life know?"

I was nearly startled off my barstool again. I'd forgotten to heed that Rinth was Labyrinthian and therefore likely intuitive.

I looked into his bluebonnet eyes, knowing he was ordinarily tucked away on Mars, doing some healing of his own.

"I'm not sure I want to write this book everyone is expecting. It wasn't really my idea, and now I can't wrap my mind around how to make it something I'm comfortable with, rather than what it's supposed to be. Or maybe it's just that I don't understand what they want of me, or why." I sighed. "But I don't want to seem ungrateful for the opportunity."

Chapter 63

Feeling guilty over my confession to Rinth about the Red Orbiter book, I had Owen arrange a private tour of the flight school. Something to write about. It was located near the hangar where our spacecraft had docked, part of the ship I had not yet returned to. I wasn't anxious to see bullet-ridden walls.

No bullet holes at the school, though it was full of Red Orbiters roaming about, seemingly all talking. I did some deep breathing and got a little practice on weaving through my labyrinth and reaching my center. That is, until I was approached by an attractive couple who looked to be about G and Phil's age while I was waiting to gain admittance to a flight simulator. As they drew closer, I recognized their all-too-familiar facial features.

"Rowan Layne, what a nice surprise," the woman stepped forward and grasped my hand. "We're Romulus's parents. We're so sorry we didn't get to formally meet at Ophelia's wedding."

My mind did a backflip, trying to fathom why Rauc or Rowdy didn't manage to mention their folks were on the moonship.

The man said, "We heard Ferus was up here for a spell and thought we'd pop in to say hi." The way he spoke indicated he, too, had learned English via movies.

I refrained from asking whether they'd heard that Rowdy was also attempting to provide them with grandchildren in addition to Ophelia's pending triplets. Mostly because I was pretty sure they were really here to check me out. How convenient they'd cornered me while I was all alone. Plus, why did they have to look so damned young?

"It's very nice to meet you," I said, too quickly. "I came to tour the flight school to help me out with writing the book!" My pitch sounded like a strangled chicken.

Momma Wilde smiled. "We're so pleased about the book. Rom has great things to say about you. Uncle Oz too!"

"Rowan Layne, your simulator is ready!" boomed a voice over the intercom. I had no idea what my face looked like, but it felt all squishy.

"Enjoy your tour," said Daddy Wilde, smiling. "I used to teach here, and this is where Romulus trained. We have to head out ourselves now too."

"Yes, but we will see you at Ophelia's baby shower!" said the woman, waving as they walked away.

I could see them speaking to each other and craned my ears to listen, realizing it was the first time I'd attempted to use my skills to spy—very disconcerting. I abruptly stopped.

The flight simulator was a great diversion, despite the twentysomething Red Orbiter who helped me get situated after gushingly asking if I was the lady who was writing a book about them on Earth. At least he was also pleased with the prospect.

For twenty minutes I mostly sat in front of a screen, which was similar to a simulator I'd once tried at the test pilot facility in Maryland's Naval Air Station Patuxent River, where I got vertigo from experiencing what it'd be like to swoop over the Chocolate Mountains in California. Today's view was different, hurtling through space, dodging any number of floating and flying objects. I surprisingly didn't get nauseated, but I was kind of staggering as I left the simulator.

I was led to a lounging area where I could sit and wait for Owen, who was supposed to take me to lunch, then to tour the composting facility on the top deck. After ten minutes, no Owen. So I took a stroll down a long hallway, pausing before a door where I heard voices speaking in low, serious tones. Instead of feeling like I was eavesdropping, I decided to walk through the unmarked red door.

All hell broke loose—or so it seemed from an audible standpoint.

About a dozen red-uniformed individuals surged forth to surround me, all demanding to know why I'd entered a restricted area unannounced. Which might not have been so bad if not for the excruciating siren—like when Tribble brought the armed idiots onboard. And I was adjacent to a blaring speaker.

Tears filled my eyes as my knees crumpled from pain piercing my eardrums, exploding into my brain. I slipped down to the cold, hard floor, hands over my ears, with no hope of finding my center.

Then Owen was crouching down to me and also Rowdy and Genie, and I realized the sirens had stopped, but not soon enough to keep from shouting when I spoke.

"The door wasn't marked restricted! How was I supposed to know?" I screeched to Owen before turning to Rowdy and thumping him in the chest. "And why didn't you or your brother tell me your parents were here?"

"We didn't know," said Rowdy, looking horrified, which normally would have been comical. "And the door's red, which means it's a secure area, but you didn't know."

"It's okay, Rowan," said Owen. I realized I was shaking as he pulled me up. "This is the main control room, and security's been on high alert since this was revealed as a spaceship, not to mention our most recent attack. Threats of sabotage are a constant concern."

"Yeah, it's kind of important we maintain the same orbit as the moon so humans don't freak out and think the world is ending, given how many refuse to accept scientific or historical fact," snarked Rowdy. "Or acknowledge consequences of their own actions."

I whirled on him. "I'm not one of those humans. So lay out the facts, because once again, I'm quite certain there's more you're not telling me."

Owen looked pained while Rowdy continued to stare me down. "You sure you want to know?" he said. "Because it's not likely this will be part of the book."

"Screw the book, Rowdy. Tell me the truth about this spaceship, because from what I've seen, there's no way it was created thousands of years ago."

Owen jumped in. "The moon wasn't destroyed by nuclear war among feuding aliens like Oz said on TV, though it's true Red Orbiters built this ship to replace it. Remember the US Strategic Defense Initiative set up in 1984 by DoD, cutely dubbed Star Wars?"

"I don't like where this is headed." My stomach plunged like I was in the flight simulator.

"SDI was supposed to oversee development of advanced weapons, including lasers and space-based missile systems," continued Owen, purple eyes intently focused on me as he grasped my shoulders. "Instead, they managed to accidently destroy Earth's only moon. In 1991."

"They blew up the moon while I was in law school?" I yelped. "We really are the dangerous idiots we make aliens out to be!"

Chapter 64

"This wasn't how we planned for you to learn about the moon," said Owen as we gathered in his office with the addition of Red, George, and Tim.

"So you did intend to let us know?" I glared at Rowdy, and he glared back while Genie looked crestfallen.

"If you want to blame someone for keeping it from you, the fault's mine," said Owen. "I needed you to focus on the treaty presentation irrespective of the truth about the moon's demise. It's critical to address present day, not past transgressions that very few know about."

"Who does know?" I struggled to use a civil tone.

"Not Congress, not intel agencies, and definitely not the present administration. It became the greatest government cover-up to date. NASA personnel worked with a handful of top DoD officials to consult with Red Orbiters on how to prevent absolute panic on Earth."

"I suppose it would do no good to tell anyone right now, especially Congress, what with too many in total denial about any truth. They'd just claim aliens made it up to make America look bad," said Tim, looking grim. "Not to mention the fallout within the defense missile community if this news gets out."

"Aye, as well as national security and US foreign relations," said Red.

"Please tell me no one was on the moon when it happened," I said to Owen.

"No, Earth's moon hadn't been inhabited in centuries. Mostly due to pesky humans constantly coming along and planting flags." Owen grinned, and I tried to.

***

One week later I had survived a dress fitting with Mazon, two meetings with our treaty group, and two more sessions with Byrin, but I had to confess I'd done very little additional touring. I was now headed out to chat with Mazy about moonship food with a plan in mind for an upbeat writing project. No, it wasn't the Red Orbiter book. But yes, I'd drafted my statement to Congress. And no, it couldn't include the moon revelation, which still rankled, because the thought kept niggling that Rauc or Oz could easily have told me long before I ever set foot here.

At least at the last treaty meeting, the Lacertan leaders had given me a standing ovation when I did a test run, reading my presentation aloud. I probably wouldn't get that in Congress.

Mazy was in her chef's uniform and had a table spread with food. Luckily, George was there so he'd eat whatever I balked at. She'd asked for a list beforehand of "flavors my palate did not prefer." A nice euphemism for *yuck*.

On my list were goat cheese, horseradish, brussels sprouts, and the most evil green food in the galaxy: wasabi. She said there'd be no meat, so we needn't worry about my aversion to lamb, turkey bacon, and duck, especially pate, or the reality that I pretty much only ate fish and seafood these days—preferably cooked.

Mazy began her presentation. "We focus on flavor, with no chemical additives, of course. If you think about it, many meat dishes on Earth aren't primarily about meat, but are about how it is prepared. In sauces, for example. Or spices adding flavor in the cooking process, such as barbeque. We are working to re-create popular dishes, preserving their flavor without meat."

"Does that include seafood?" I asked.

"Yes. The Cajun shrimp dish you had on Tim's birthday was not shellfish as you know it. We cultivated a hybrid vegetable using cauliflower, bean curd, and additional ingredients to create something with a similar texture to shrimp, using spices to simulate its flavor."

"It was tasty! It's funny, I used to detest tofu, but now I can't stomach meat. And was it the moonship that came up with the newfangled cauliflower pizza crust?"

"Yes." Mazy smiled. "But I hear that crust they've been making on Earth has terrible texture. Way too—what is the word? *Mooshy?* The problem is chemical additives."

"Makes sense. But please tell me the scones I ate weren't made with cauliflower."

"No, the British might fire a missile at us like your president if we did that," she said, straight-faced. My stomach lurched.

"She's kidding!" George said. "Mazy has one twisted sense of humor."

"Okay, but hopefully not with food. You won't try to slip wasabi into anything, will you?"

Mazy laughed. "Let us go back to the meat issue for a moment, because you said this is for your writing, and I know Americans get all up in arms about their beef."

"I wish that was a joke, but it's all too true," I said.

"We are not so much intending to offer fake meat, like your veggie burgers." She wrinkled her nose. "We are creating alternatives focusing on flavors and textures the palate is used to. Throughout history, cooking has been more about varying ways to prepare meat and other foods, and often included sauces and stews to camouflage substandard meat."

"Like beef stroganoff," said George, "which really isn't about the meat at all."

"What about cheese?" I asked. "Because your fondue is amazing."

"Plant-based, often with minerals from other planets. Much of what we use comes from Cultura, which you know as Saturn. Named for its predominance of vegetables, fruits, and herbs."

"I have DNA from there, 11 percent. My sister has more, which she's thrilled about because she's so into cooking. But I have a question," I said.

"I warned you," George said to Mazy, and I made a face at him.

"I could swear those crab cakes you made were actual lump crab meat."

“They were,” said Mazy. “We often obtain things like blue crab to study so we might learn how to provide an alternative when it is no longer available.”

“You’re talking about decimating species by heedless consumption, aren’t you? And habitat degradation.” I sighed. “How is it we haven’t yet managed to blow up our own planet?”

Chapter 65

"I want to call it *Moonliving*, kind of a play on the word *moonlighting*," I told George and Owen sitting in his office. "And I want it to be a blog about the moonship."

Owen said, "I loved that *Moonlighting* TV show."

"Me too." I smiled.

"Okay, cool name and idea," said George. "How does it relate to OUTWARD?"

"I was thinking about what you said, about OUTWARD's mission, how it includes outreach. First I considered another newspaper column, but everything is online now anyway, and I don't want it to be under the control of a media conglomerate. That's why I'd like to do this blog through you guys. I would like your backing for promotion and production, as well as oversight for content accuracy, given the subject matter."

"Tell us more about your planned content," said Owen.

"The idea is to inform those on Earth about life in the moonship. To educate but also to entertain. I'll start with my personal observations and experiences, but I can also interview various experts. I've already met with Mazy about the culinary school. But I can talk to technical folks about the sewage system, the composting process, and the cleaning system, not to mention how it's powered by solar wind. There's the agriculture and restaurants and night clubs. And how they like to celebrate Halloween, plus the pet park and pods. So many things Americans or others might find fascinating, and can learn from!"

Owen said, "Okay, Rowan. Do you—"

"Wait! There's more! I can talk to folks on Earth like the governor's wife who lived here, interview her about her experiences and the cultural aspects of moonship life. And I can cover Mars too, because of Labyrinthian ties. And Lacertans! This also means I could return periodically, because I'd really like to continue meeting with Byrin. And also the best part. I want Owen to be my editor. For fact-checking and as a sounding board." I turned to him. "You said you read a lot! And remember when we met, you said you liked how I turn a phrase?"

George said, "Rowan, please take a breath. This is not a hard sell. We've always wanted you to work for OUTWARD but realized it needed to be in your own way. We've been waiting for you to find something you'd like to do with us since you created our initial promotional materials. I think this is a great idea!"

"So do I." Owen grinned. "Although I'm not sure how great an editor I'll be. You're the ultimate wordsmith. But I don't mind the idea of helping you out with those subjects you might wrangle with, or have endless questions about. This could be fun."

"Oh I'm so relieved! I've been wondering what I had to offer OUTWARD, but you know I'm no scientist or engineer. And I've always wanted to try a blog. And though I don't mind being a research guinea pig with my hairless cochlea, I doubt I'll ever be comfortable using my abilities in a clandestine capacity for the auditory division like Tim."

"Win's not going to be happy, but he really shouldn't be surprised," said Owen.

"We'll set it up with Bruce when we return, but you know what his first question will be. Along with Rauc and Oz," said George.

"The Red Orbiter book." I sighed. "I'll still write it if that's what they want. It's why I've taken so many notes here. Though there's an awful lot that can't go in it." I looked at Owen.

"All right, folks, I'm heading out," said George, slapping his thighs and standing. "Mazy and I are trying to fit in as much time as possible together in these last few days. I can't believe it's almost over. But we'll both be back, right Rowan?"

"That's my plan!" I blew him a kiss as he left Owen's office. Now I was alone with those purple eyes, and they were looking at me in an assessing manner.

"You're still peeved at me for withholding the moonship bombshell. Let me try to make it up to you. You said you wanted to include Mars in this blog, but you haven't been there. Care to take a little trip—just a touchdown, really—to look around? That way you'll have seen firsthand what you write about."

"We could do that?"

"There and back in less than twenty-four hours. And I can tell what you're worried about. He isn't there; he's already on Earth, banned from Mars along with everyone he worked with and for. And if it would erase your pain, we'd have banned him from the entire universe if we could." Owen smiled, coaxing me to smile.

"Luna Moth Woman wouldn't pass up such an opportunity, so neither will I! I'll ask Genie and Rowdy to take care of the critters."

"Good. Let's leave tonight."

Chapter 66

It was my first time in a flying saucer for any length of time. The layout was similar to an orb, with the biggest difference being a control center in a bubble at the top, with a clear roof. It made for a pretty spectacular astronomy lesson along the way.

I said to Owen, "I know you didn't learn to pilot this thing in the Marine Corps."

"No, at the moonship flight school. I didn't fly for the Corps."

"What did you do, in recon?"

"Other things." He grinned.

"Interrogation, right?"

"Isn't that your specialty?" he quipped.

"Fine. Stubborn man. Tell me about how this is going to work. I know I can't just walk around on Mars, right?"

"You'll wear a suit with a helmet, not unlike what Earth's astronauts wear, when we're out in the atmosphere. And I have a small biosphere, like a tent but larger, that I use when I visit. It's got all the basic amenities and is sort of like this control room."

"Shaped like an igloo?"

"Yes." He grinned. "But not made of ice. The entire exterior is like one-way tinted glass. No one can see in, but we can see out while we're inside."

"Fascinating," I said. "So this spacesuit, do I have to worry about it fitting me?"

"No, because I got your measurements from Mazon in order to bring what you'll need."

"I might expire from mortification right here in this flying saucer."

"Fleshy women. Remember?"

"Yes, I remember! And what does that even mean?" I muttered.

"We'll travel over a bit of rocky terrain in a vehicle much like a Jeep."

"Can I bring back a rock?" I was getting excited.

"Perhaps," said Owen, cryptically. "But it might not be what you think."

"I was hoping for a red rock that looks like Valley of Fire. Whoa! What just flew by?"

"A chunk of rock. What's called a meteorite when it lands on Earth. And no, you can't have one." He grinned.

"It's like a crazed version of dodgeball. What happens if one hits us?"

"Potential damage to the spacecraft. That's why I tend to fly around them."

"Maybe I should stop asking questions and let you pay attention to flying."

I tried to stay quiet, I really did.

"How is it we can get there so quickly? Isn't it much farther to Mars than to Earth?"

"Yes, but we're in a smaller craft traveling at much faster speed than you were in the Red Orbiter craft. When we get there, you'll need to spend some time off your feet to adjust. You might feel lightheaded for a while."

As we landed, I felt us come down on a surface, but it was dark, and I think I'd been napping. Some copilot I was. And flying saucers really do open like they do in the movies, but this one had a tunnel tube extended from the exit into an entrance of Owen's biosphere. So I didn't have to don my spacesuit just yet, which was good because all I wanted to do was get horizontal.

The first thing I noticed inside the biosphere was a nice big bed. I sprawled onto it before realizing how suggestive that might be.

Owen approached me with a cylindrical flask. "Drink this, it's mostly water but also electrolytes and other minerals to replenish you."

It tasted a little citrusy, which was fine by me.

"I'm really on Mars, with a Martian!" I erupted into a fit of giggles. It was like adjusting to high altitudes in Earth's mountains. "I know I'm not supposed to call you that! But did you ever see that show *My Favorite Martian*? Are antennae going to come out of your head now?" I was positively giddy. "Is that the show with the talking horse too?"

"Rowan, do you want help undressing? The reason we flew at night is to give you time to rest before we look around in the morning."

I stared up at him as he removed his flight jumpsuit. "Are you going to get naked? There's only one bed."

"Yes, there is. But I can sleep in the saucer if you're worried about it." He was down to a pair of boxer briefs, and I caught my breath. Owen had a tattoo too.

When I said the words *tattoo too* in my head, it made me erupt into giggles again.

"You know," he said, sitting down on the bed. "Some men might be concerned about a woman chuckling when they remove their clothes."

"Your tattoo. On your chest. It's a labyrinth. Do I get to find the center?"

Chapter 67

When I awoke, it was almost as if I was lying in the middle of Valley of Fire with vivid jagged-rock terrain surrounding the biosphere. But it was Owen the Marine surrounding me, his body entwined with mine on Mars.

It was dawn, but hours before, I'd reached for him—and he'd obliged. Removing my clothing, eradicating emotional wounds. Many times over, until I was more lightheaded than when we began.

He stirred now, rolling onto his back with me in his arms so that I straddled him, gazing down at those purple eyes above a labyrinth tattoo. He pushed my hair from my face and smiled.

"Good morning. Time to pay for those Martian-antenna smartass cracks."

Later, all decked out in my spacesuit like John Glenn, we hopped into the Mars version of an ATV. After I made him stop about fifty times for rocks that caught my eye, Owen warned like a parent, "Don't make me pull this car over again," and I had a new fit of giggles.

Eventually the barren terrain made me grow somber. "There's such a scarcity of plant life—or any life," I said, feeling sad. Was Earth headed for the same environmental devastation?

"We're working on revitalization. There's areas of deforestation with restricted access to give life a chance to flourish without people or vehicles eroding the soil."

"Are we going to the mines?" I asked, wondering if we might see Rinth but not wanting to say it aloud and have Owen hear between the lines about my interest in his cousin.

"Not this trip. It's an even rougher area, and there's really not much to see aboveground. I've brought you to the most scenic part near my biosphere. Someday we'll come for a longer time and you can see more, including the rocky coastal area of otter fame."

"Yes! Martian otters! I've loved what I've seen so far, and I so appreciate your bringing me. Although parts of it I really shouldn't blog about." I snickered. "Why can't I stop laughing?"

"It's the atmosphere. Unless it's commentary on my manly abilities," Owen drawled, driving us back toward his biosphere, still connected with the saucer.

Once back inside and out of my cumbersome spacesuit with its fishbowl helmet, Owen handed me a small jewelry box. "A token of appreciation from me, on behalf of residents of the moonship."

"But you've given me so much already!" I waggled my eyes at the bed. "And I have all of these cool red rocks—"

"I ought to give you another red ass," he said. "And I will if you don't open that box."

I opened the box. A red diamond ring set in gold. Brilliantly faceted, the color of pomegranate seeds. Thankfully not as huge as Octavius Wynne's, but it had to be three carats.

"Scarlet and gold, the Corps colors. My, my Marine. I know you're not proposing marriage simply because we had sex," I teased.

He pulled me into his arms. "That was way beyond sex. We're alike, you and I. Each of us searching but not wanting to settle down. The ring can remind you of our time together, remind you to come back and see me, here among the stars."

Chapter 68

"Did we get all my artwork and mugs loaded? I have my quilt with me. Has Mazon come with our dresses yet?" I looked around frantically in the spaceship hangar.

"I'm here!" Mazon glided in with two long wardrobe bags, trailed by an assistant carrying two more. "Your cape has its own bag, Rowan!"

"Aren't you a dear!" I said. "Have you given more thought to what you want us to say when asked by the media who did our dresses?"

"I'm going with your suggestion. Mazon in the Moon!" he gushed.

"I've brought food for your voyage!" said Mazy, trailed by assistants carrying large containers.

George said, "Great! What's everyone else going to eat?"

Rowdy called out from inside the spaceship, "Rowan, why do you have more suitcases than you brought up here?"

Genie yelled, "Rauc, your brother's picking on Rowan!"

Red approached carrying luggage with Rosie on a leash. "I've got extra baggage too, Rowdy!" said Red, winking at me. "Cookware."

Tim walked into the hangar, also with luggage and Astro in her kitty carrier.

Rowdy popped his head out of the spaceship. "Are you the extra baggage, Red? Because I don't recall you being on the trip up here. And damn if we don't appear to have more animals than people."

"Be glad I didn't bring my bagpipes," Red snarked.

"Well, it's a good thing Maggie already left, or we might be too heavy to launch, what with all the extra shoes and dresses we're hauling," said Rowdy.

Owen approached and pulled me aside. "Byrin said to give you this, and I'm supposed to tell you to only use it for tea, not coffee!"

I unwrapped cloth around a handcrafted mug with a colorful depiction of the moon and stars. Elegantly scribed was, *Shoot for the moon. If you miss you'll land among the stars.* One of my favorite expressions, and somehow Byrin knew.

I started to cry, and Owen pulled me into his arms.

"I began this voyage crying so I guess this is coming full circle?" I tried to laugh.

"We will see you before you know it. Thank you for your time here." Owen kissed me once, lightly, and backed away. I could feel those violet eyes following me as I turned to head for the spaceship.

Rauc stepped out onto the ramp. "Okay, crew, let's get our launch on."

Rauc and Rowdy were our pilot and copilot, like old times in their orb days. I stepped into the control room as everyone got settled. All four critters had made a mad dash for the lounge, commandeering the couches quite noisily.

"Can I stay in here with you for the launch?"

Rauc pulled me into his lap. "I promise you there will be no bombs or anything else coming for us. And Roger is on high-alert standby, regardless."

"Okay, but we're not really going to be too heavy to lift off, are we?" I asked.

"Rowdy, you need to zip it for the entire flight," said Rauc, glaring at his brother. "Maybe Genie should have copiloted."

"She won't fly with you ever since Rowan had a meltdown on the Planet Wynne escalator when she saw you with her." Rowdy smirked. "She still has nightmares about it."

"Rowdy Wilde!" said Genie, bouncing into the control room. "You are so full of it!"

"Full of love for you, Fireball. Come here and I'll show you," Rowdy beckoned.

"How are we ever going to make it to DC in one piece?" I said to Rauc.

After launch, I got woozy and was afraid I'd topple over, not having slept much my last couple of nights on the moonship. I went to my room and crawled into bed, telling Genie to wake me if I didn't rise before our Chesapeake Bay landing.

I awoke hungry several hours later with Bodie pressed against my feet and Morris at my head, Rosie and Astro pressed to my sides. I semi-staggered to the lounge area, where George and Tim and Red were gathered and luckily hadn't eaten all the food.

"Mazy said to tell you she prepared a special plate just for you," said George, clearing a space at the table and setting down a dish from which I recoiled. It looked like sushi and a big gross glob of wasabi.

"Got ya!" hooted George, snapping a photo of the look of horror on my face. "It's guacamole and fish tacos! Mazy is going to love this!"

Recovering from that jarring episode, I headed for the control room, bearing food. "Anybody hungry?"

Rauc said, "Sure, Copper, come sit with me." He pulled me into his lap as I stared at the big screen, seeing Earth in the distance. A mesmerizing sight.

Rowdy said, "Cool, pizza!" and bit into a slice.

"When we land in Chesapeake Bay, will that bother the blue crab?" I asked.

"It wouldn't"—Rauc's lips twitched—"but we're now landing in the Appalachian Mountains of West Virginia."

"Why?" My stomach roiled. "Was there a security issue in Maryland?"

"Always a possibility, but the change was made because your pals the Greens would like to meet with you when we land. They chose the remote location, which will be less predictable for a Red Orbiter craft landing. Win will also be there when we arrive."

"Okay, wow. I wasn't looking forward to getting queasy on the boat ride to reach land, but do you know what the Greens want to discuss?"

Rowdy interjected, "You're worried about getting queasy in a boat on a bay when you've been flying all the way from the moon?"

"My motion sickness is at its worst on water," I said, giving him my best stink eye.

Rauc said, "Rowdy, why don't you get more pizza?"

He left without a fuss, probably due to hunger, leaving Rauc and me alone.

"It has to do with the bombing attempt on Senator Rojas-Ortiz," said Rauc.

"And what is the status of that investigation? How are you getting around the fact that she wasn't killed?"

"The official statement is that no one was in the vehicle when the bomb went off."

"But won't those who planted the bomb likely know differently?"

"That's why Greens are involved. If the perps know, they won't remember it correctly."

"What happened?" I squeaked.

"Yesterday, Greens abducted two men and one woman involved in the attempt to kill Cassandra. You should know there was also a failed attempt to bomb the home of Warren O'Neill several days ago. Greens want to consult with you about potential next moves."

"What the hell? They attacked the vice president-elect's home too? And why do Greens want to talk to me?"

"The three individuals they abducted are your neighbors. They live on the street behind your house."

Chapter 69

Win enveloped me in a tight hug as I disembarked from the spacecraft on Spruce Mountain, where it was quite cold and snowy, the air pummeling my lungs as I inhaled the atmosphere of Earth once again.

"If I get sleepy and look like I'm going to do a face-plant, please catch me," I said to Win as we entered a nearby craft shaped like a Tic Tac, where Greens awaited in a room containing nothing but walls of electronics with flashing lights and beeping noises.

I felt the now-familiar drifting of wispy clouds through my cerebral cortex. "Welcome. Rowan. Cold. Hands. How. Is. Bodie." One of several three-foot-tall creatures took my hand in their three-fingered hand, speaking telepathically in a mechanical, yet pleasant, tone. Two others gently grasped my arms, as if checking to see if I was okay.

"So nice to see you again. It is a bit chilly up here, but that just makes it more remote for our purposes! Bodie is fine. He made lots of new friends on the moonship. It was quite an adventure! I hear you've had an adventure of your own while I was gone. Did you catch someone while watching my neighborhood?"

"Loud. Noises. Scare. Bodie. Big. Trucks."

"So it's the neighbors that have been setting off firecrackers. Figures," I said. "Were they still driving down the street, revving their engines, trying to intimidate? How stupid do they have to be to think their HUMANS FIRST! flags and stickers will somehow make others support their idiocy? They look and sound ridiculous. A last gasp of denial that life has changed on Earth. Aliens are here, and we are them whether they like it or not."

Greens nodded, their eyes not blinking. "Same. Truck. Bombs."

I sighed, yawning. "I guess it isn't surprising that folks this stupid would use the same loud, easily identifiable vehicles to commit crimes. But it is scary. Are they part of a larger group, used for criminal purposes because they are that stupid?"

Win said, "Yes. Groups similar to those in Yearntown. Stockpiling guns and harboring hate. Also with too many public officials involved, including some police."

The Green still holding my hand said, "We. Have. Them. You. Want. To. Speak?"

"Do I want to speak with them? I've thought many times about what I'd like to say to people that selfish and mean, only to realize it could put me in danger by identifying myself, given the police do nothing to stop their reckless activity. But talking to them would be futile. Reasoning or appealing to basic human decency doesn't work when people are too dedicated to their hate, too willing to embrace ignorance, to be gloatingly proud of all they refuse to understand or accept."

"We. Stop," said the Green, pointing to an oversized, ovular head.

"Have at it. Do your mind-manipulation thing to stop this madness. You know best what will work in this instance. But one request, if I may? Could you confiscate all their firecrackers?"

***

"I thought Greens were going to have a coronary when you collapsed in my arms, right after requesting they search and destroy all cherry bombs," said Win. "They thought something bad had happened to you. I was doing some fast talking!"

I sat up in Win's guest bed laughing. "How long did I sleep?"

Win looked at his watch. "About thirty hours. You missed the two vans bringing everyone down the mountain to Virginia. Except for George. Rauc flew him back to OUTWARD headquarters. He said he preferred Washington State to DC these days."

"I don't blame him. Where is everyone else?"

"Rauc's back, and Greens are keeping an eye on the spacecraft in West Virginia. Octavius Wynne rented a block of rooms at the Hay-Adams for the Red Orbiter security contingent and Red, because I didn't have room for him here at the townhouse. Maggie and Tim have the main bedroom because they're going to be living here, and I've got the other guest room. I thought about putting you in my bed but didn't want to cause an awkward uproar." Win grinned, and I felt it in places I shouldn't but always did with this man.

"Where are the critters?" I looked around for Bodie and Morris.

"We've got Astro here as well as Rosie while Red is at the hotel, so the four varmints have existed in two modes. Rambunctious or exhausted slumber."

I giggled. "So I have until tomorrow afternoon before I get painted and primped and ready to be a belle at the balls?"

"Unless you want to attend the inaugural ceremony, but we would prefer you didn't. No one knows what the fading-fast idiot will do, or whether he'll even be there. More problematic is what his cult members might do to avenge his nonexistent honor."

"Sounds ominous. What else did I miss while snoozing?"

"The day you returned to Earth, the president claimed he'd been abducted by aliens, little green men specifically, so he would not be able to attend the inaugural ceremony," said Win.

Chapter 70

"Was the moron-in-chief abducted? And, if so, how was he able to announce it?"

"Hell no," scoffed Win. "He thinks if he disappears, it'll prevent indictment. He's trying to find a way to leave the country. As for the announcement, the vice president held a press conference on the White House lawn yesterday afternoon decrying the green alien abduction."

"So that's twice the devious duo cluelessly mentioned Greens. Not good."

"Which is why the press conference was inexplicably attacked by dust devils, causing the vice to be rushed away to a 'secure location.' Except Greens snatched him and two Secret Service agents en route. The agents received erased memories of the abduction. Vice got an attitude adjustment and will not be making any more statements to the media about green aliens. Ever. He'll be lucky if he remembers he was vice president."

I snickered. "So what about the president's alleged abduction?"

Win snorted. "He lasted all of eight hours in the White House bunker before he began tweeting, claiming he was doing it secretly from an alien spaceship. No one but his rabid cult members bought it. They're roaming around in pickups, guns at the ready, thinking they'll happen upon a flying saucer with the president in it."

"I can just imagine what the Twitter universe had to say," I said, hearing my stomach rumble with hunger.

"I screen-saved some choice tweets, just for you, sweet pea," said Win, sitting down on the edge of the bed and showing me his phone.

My favorites were:

"Are the aliens down in purgatory with you, bunker rat?"

"Did the little green men eat his homework, too?"

"When we told you to leave the gene pool, we didn't necessarily mean the planet. But have at it. Adios!"

My stomach rumbled again. "I'm starved," I said, climbing out of bed.

"Has anything happened with the neighbors that Greens abducted?" I asked, sitting in Win's townhouse kitchen drinking gallons of coffee and eating anything palatable I could find.

Win smiled. "Greens deposited them yesterday at the Las Vegas FBI office, where they made a full confession regarding the bombings, naming or identifying anyone else involved. The list is quite extensive and includes Armed Evangelicals from Pahrump and various HUMANS FIRST! groups throughout Nevada. They also made statements to North Las Vegas police regarding their intimidation tactics these past few months."

"How do we know anything will actually happen, given this is the current attorney general's FBI we're talking about, and certain police haven't exactly been proactive?"

"It helps to have extensive footage of their confessions provided to the media," said Maggie, walking in with Tim. "It's insane out there. Mass arrests of armed idiots losing what's left of their minds, raging in the streets."

"So they'll finally recognize and arrest the actual perpetrators of terrorism?" I snarked.

Maggie sat across from me, smiling deviously. "Red Orbiters don't just observe. We record. Operation Three Strikes has begun."

"I'll drink to that!" I said, sipping coffee.

"The ball is being hit out of the park as we speak," said Tim, grinning.

I looked at Win for confirmation. "I think the Red Orbiter in the room deserves to impart this news." Win smiled at Maggie.

Maggie said, "Today, so as not to draw attention from tomorrow's inauguration, the North American Red Orbiter organization has released every single taped conversation or event involving criminal activity by the president and his extended coterie of corruption. More than four years' worth of damning evidence."

"How many are going down?" I asked, holding my breath.

Win said, "The evidence implicates the president, his wife, his son and running mate daughter-in-law, his brother, the vice president, the attorney general, of course, but also the postmaster and a majority of his remaining cabinet members. It also includes the senate majority leader, twenty Republican senators, plus their colluding colleagues in the House."

"So what happens next?" I was afraid to hope.

"Numerous indictments in coming days. But most importantly, tomorrow those Marine guards who stand outside the White House doors will now be physically removing the president from the premises should he follow through on his threat to refuse to leave."

"Which is why," said Raucous Wilde, walking into the kitchen, "we really need you to lie low today, Copper. Because there are unfortunately a contingent of unidentified secret police still attempting to do the president's Banana Republic bidding."

Chapter 71

"I'm ready to chop off a few inches. Maybe layering around my face," I said to the hairstylist O.W. sent along with a makeup artist for Maggie and me.

When Rowdy and Genie arrived with our limo, Rowdy looked at me in my pumpkin-clasp cape and said, "Your carriage awaits, Cinderella! Wicked new haircut!"

As we navigated inevitable clogged traffic headed into DC on I-66 in Arlington, Maggie said, "This is by far the worst place I've ever driven."

"A major reason I left," I said, just before an unmarked van careened along our left side on a narrow shoulder, attempting to force us across to the right shoulder.

I said in a panic, "That van looks all too familiar!" as Maggie said, "Roger that," apparently replying to a voice in her ear.

"We've got this," said Genie, turning to me from the front seat.

"Okay, but I can't believe this is happening a block away from my high school!"

Rowdy pulled onto the shoulder, stopping abruptly, the van's tires squealing as it swerved in front of us and also stopped. "Wait for it," he said.

Six desert-camouflaged, heavily armed henchmen exited the van, nothing but the word *Police* on their uniform.

"Not again," I yelped.

"Now!" said Maggie.

Rowdy, Genie, and Maggie exited our limo in a flash and rushed the astonished thugs, the gals taking them down three each, all before they could fire their weapons. Said rifles were handed off to Rowdy, who placed them in the limo trunk after helping hog-tie the fallen lying on the side of the road. Genie and Maggie had not a hair out of place or a wrinkle in their elegant gowns. Surprising, given the goon gunmen hadn't let women assailants stop them from fighting back, to no avail. Without weapons, their thick arms and legs flailed impotently when confronted with superior wits and speed. Not to mention spiked heels.

I taunted, leaning from the limo window, "Did that hurt? It looked seriously painful."

Folks crawling by in clogged traffic honked and cheered. But the best part was when the van's driver thought to make a getaway by heading for the nearest exit from the shoulder. Whereupon Roger, aka Superman, in an all-black tuxedo swooped down and lifted the van, carrying it off with its driver. It was dark and happened so fast, folks likely were focused on the stranded secret police as we left them behind to fend for themselves, without guns or transport.

Roger drawled in my ear, "I've taken the van driver to a place where he might reflect on the error of his ways."

I erupted into nervous giggles. "You put the van in the reflecting pool?"

"Better than the tidal basin, don't you think, beautiful? And he won't be there long. Park Police have arrived. Footage of attack now being provided to all media outlets."

From there, it got tricky, because we did not want to pull through the White House gates with a trunk full of semiautomatic weapons, so we parked at the Hay-Adams, and Rowdy and Genie escorted me through Lafayette Square to the famed gates.

In the next hour, I met our first female president and the first gentleman and was back inside another limo with Warren O'Neill and the Secret Service, headed for the first ball. My responses to media questions were: "The vice president and I met when I moved to North Las Vegas and became his congressional constituent," "No, we did not attend the University of Texas together. I was there for an undergraduate journalism degree. The vice president later obtained a master's degree from the LBJ School of Public Affairs," and finally, "My dress was designed by Mazon in the Moon. Contact Octavius Wynne in Las Vegas for more information."

Vice President O'Neill repeatedly thanked me, revealing how he'd planned to come out as gay after he'd announced his DNA results and switched to the Omni Party, but then he was selected as the VP candidate. Now the decision to reveal, and the timing, weren't entirely his.

"But do you have a special someone who is missing out on all of this?" I asked.

O'Neill grinned. "If I did, I might have insisted on having them accompany me."

"Okay," I said. "What do we do about the fact that we've never danced together, and I don't have much training in whatever those formal dances are supposed to be?"

"I've got it taken care of," he said, light-green eyes glowing.

Maybe I was born to do a Texas two-step with a fellow Longhorn and brand-new, otherworldly vice president of the United States—to Willie Nelson singing "Living in the Promised Land," eight miles from my childhood home. And then there was our freestyle dance to a tune from our era, "Shining Star" by Earth, Wind & Fire.

It was at the third ball of the evening where the HUMANS FIRST! lackwits made their move to avenge the disgraced president. The problem was, this was the ball attended by my friends, and when I went to the restroom, I did not do so alone. Maybe it was Genie's hourglass figure in a seriously sexy dress that made them underestimate my Red Orbiter pal.

And though they had the presence of mind to cover their faces for this cult caper, the cheap kids' Halloween masks were pathetically hilarious. There must have been a sale on Disney characters from *Frozen* at their local dollar store.

The two women who attempted to accost me in the restroom were Elsa and Anna, while the three men sported Olaf, Kristoff, and Sven masks—in stark contrast to the vicious anti-alien obscenities all five spewed in psychotic rage while brandishing guns.

Genie took down the screaming women on the restroom floor, their pistol-wielding hands crushed by her stilettos. As she stood over the hog-tied figures, slapping duct tape over their mouths, I bent down to yank off their masks.

"These were all y'all could afford? Did you deplete your finances on firecrackers or bullets? You know, ladies, you really need to just *let it go*."

Rowdy, Win, and Red, having easily outmaneuvered the three armed men, joined in a rousing rendition of "Do You Want to Build a Snowman?" as Secret Service hauled the men away. It got hearty applause from all who witnessed the event.

Rauc was there in seconds and had me in his arms. "Are you okay, Copper? Because you're rocking that sultry new hairstyle."

"You know? I really am good," I said, grinning. "Do you think the vice president would mind if you and I did a little two-stepping too?"

Chapter 72

"Doodles, what are you wearing to Congress??? How is weather in Washington??? Cloudy here, maybe snow!!! Ugh. (cloud, dress, shoe, heart, thumbs-up emoji)"

I replied to Mom, "I had Mazon the dress designer make a taupe pantsuit for me! Possible snow here too. I'm wearing the red boots you got me last year!!! Heading out soon!!! Love to you and Dad! (kissy face emoji)"

Mom texted, "You tell Congress it had better shape up and get with it!!! Tell them you are Doodles and they'd better watch out!!! (shooting star, applauding hands, heart emoji)"

I'd already donned my new suit, which was in the second wardrobe bag Mazon had brought to our spaceship launch. I had it preapproved by Owen-the-moonship-mayor, as it was made with the fabric of the uniform worn by diplomats and leaders. Mazon created a design for my mature figure that was professional yet flattering, and it came complete with the official red moon patch and red buttons Mazon promised would not be diamonds.

My sister called to wish me good luck. "Mom texted everyone in the universe bragging that you two-stepped with the vice president to Willie, so that's going to be hard to top. But at least you're wearing taupe, her second favorite color."

"I thought it would be a nice tribute to the moonship," I said, slipping on the red diamond ring from Owen and my labyrinth earrings.

"Are you nervous?"

"Strangely, no. It's like coming home, because this area was home for many years. And as long as we have no unexpected attacks—oh my gosh, I am now officially nervous! Owen the Marine just walked in."

"I didn't intend to make you nervous," said Owen as I got off the phone with G. "I'm here to support, plus I didn't want to miss out on seeing you in that suit. Great haircut, babe."

"Thanks, but are you really going to be there for my address?" My heart thumped.

"Seated by your side, with Red. I'll assist with questions regarding the moonship's position on misuse of military might by Space Force."

"This just gets better and better," I said, hugging him.

Red popped his head in. "Our chariot awaits, lass. And you're upstaging me with that fine suit." He wasn't in full kilt regalia, much to my disappointment.

Rauc, Win, Owen, Red, Tim, Maggie, and I rode to Capitol Hill with our security team of Rowdy and Genie, with Roger waiting at the other end in Senator Cassandra Rojas-Ortiz's office. One week after the inauguration, she was in transition, awaiting Senate confirmation of her appointment to attorney general.

"How are you holding up, Rowan? Ready to take on the lions?" The senator grasped my hands, her signature red lips smiling broadly.

"I'm great, given no one tried to run us off the road! But could you ask all the Red Orbiters working behind the scenes to tone it down and maybe not talk all at once?" I teased.

"Is it still stressful for you, hearing our voices?" Rojas-Ortiz asked.

I laughed. "Surprisingly, it's comforting to know they're here."

The senator grinned back at me. "Aliens abound!"

Olivia Warnock, my law professor's daughter and the cofounder of the Other Worldly Coalition stopped by in her official capacity as a newly elected senator from Maryland. "I want to thank you, Rowan, on behalf of the coalition."

I also finally met Olivia's Red Orbiter physicist husband, Dr. Ogden West, or Oggie, as his best buddy Roger knew him from UT. "This Red Orbiter and fellow Longhorn thanks you as well, Ms. Layne. Roger speaks very highly of you, and we are all looking forward to the book."

Even in the hallowed halls of Washington, I couldn't escape the pressure of writing the be-all, end-all Red Orbiter book.

Oddly enough, the weird thing about presenting to Congress was sitting in front of a microphone. Part of me wanted—needed—to pace the floor like I was addressing a jury or a group of students.

I began, "In the last century, John F. Kennedy said, 'Many years ago the great British explorer George Mallory, who was to die on Mount Everest, was asked why did he want to climb it? He said, "Because it is there." Well, space is there, and we're going to climb it, and the moon and planets are there, and new hopes for knowledge and peace are there.'" I paused for breath, and effect.

"*Knowledge and peace.* I am here to tell you that in this century, we as a species, as a nation, have lost sight of both, here on Earth and in our quests to space. Perhaps it's because too many of us were weaned on movies and television depicting those who come from afar as threatening, dangerous. Alien entities to be feared, and reviled. And if you're among those looking in terror to the skies for that evil overlord out to destroy America and all of Earth, look no further than what we've endured here on the ground the last four years. Sowing the same seeds of hate that were planted deep in our soil centuries ago."

I didn't actually pause again, but I was nevertheless interrupted.

"Why are you here to tell us anything? Aren't you just the vice president's girlfriend or some Red Orbiter sidekick? Do you pal around with little green men too?" raged a congressman, lunging to his feet and flapping his arms, showing huge sweat stains in his shirt because this was the guy who refused to wear a suit jacket. But he never passed up an opportunity to grandstand or bluster. This despite being embroiled in a scandal with high school girls in a locker room—while he was coach. The only reason he got reelected was his district was so laughably carved up to prevent a progressive candidate from winning, it looked like the meandering path of a river.

I stared at him with disdain, waiting a few seconds before responding. "I believe I was speaking. Do you have a problem with a woman speaking truth to power?"

The congressman turned even redder with rage, sweating through his dirty-blond stringy hair and screaming into his microphone, "What qualifies you to speak?"

"The same thing that qualifies me to vote. I am a citizen of this nation. What qualifies you to rudely disrupt my address to this governing body?"

Red leaned into his microphone. "Is the horse's ass from an obscenely gerrymandered district also going to accuse me of being the vice president's boyfriend? Because I demand equal time for his bigoted buffoonery."

Chapter 73

After the congressmen got the gavel banged on him and was told to stand down—three times—I proceeded.

"I planned to speak today solely of the Outer Space Treaty of 1967 and how our nation and others got it so very wrong. But it's worse than that, and we've done this before, going back to our premise that we Pilgrims were first in time to this land we now call home. We proclaimed it our Manifest Destiny to plunder, to ignore existing identities and culture—and to annihilate them when they objected by defending themselves with the very violence perpetrated on them.

"The treaty grandly proclaims exploration and use of outer space shall be carried out for the benefit and in the interests of all countries, and shall be the province of all mankind. But the signatories failed to account for the possibility—now reality—of other life forms, other entities in space. Not countries, not *mankind*. Not subject to the whims and edicts of *humankind*.

"The treaty blithely assumes free access to all areas of celestial bodies for scientific investigation in outer space without considering it may not be a human privilege or right to do so using any methods we choose. We've already ordained ourselves superior to heedlessly consume our own planet's flora, fauna, and resources as if they were limitless, as if without consequence to every living being. And when we learned they were not, we looked to space to feed our all-consuming need to dominate and destroy. We are the menace we have made aliens out to be." I glared at the gerrymandered jerk, still wriggling with sweaty rage.

"Ironically, this treaty was formed during the three-year run of the *Star Trek* original series in the late sixties. We created it as if we were the Federation intent on following a prime directive prohibiting interference with internal and natural development of alien civilizations. But do you know why *Star Trek* was canceled? It appealed to a comparatively literate group of folks, hence low ratings. The general public wanted Darth Vader, and they got it, not only in the Star Wars franchise, but in their president, more than half a century later. And America's lack of literacy has only gotten worse as we have increasingly projected aliens to be the power-mongering monsters."

The congressman slapped his hands on the table in front of him and prepared to rise to his feet. Curiously, he was slammed backward against his chair by an unseen force, as if hit by a dust devil, causing him to land in an ignominious heap on the floor, tie askew. His mouth gaped open silently, crazed eyes going wide as if listening.

Fluffy clouds filled my mind along with the words, "Rowan. Please. Continue." So I did.

"Our last president was a maniacal marauder who attacked others without provocation simply because they did not exist to serve him, to be something he could profit from or demean. Citizens who were following a path provided by providence and our Founding Fathers. He and those who embraced his hate decry the existence of aliens because they paint them in their own image, creatures with all of their faults and insidious intentions, possessing none of the gifts of humanity: love, compassion, understanding. A quest for knowledge with peaceful purpose. As Thomas Jefferson wrote to John Adams, 'Bigotry is the disease of ignorance, of morbid minds; enthusiasm of the free and buoyant. Education and free discussion are the antidotes to both.'

"Here in the US we have created a so-called Space Force as if we're a benevolent Starfleet boldly embracing outer space. Except it turns out, it isn't some destination no one has ever gone to before. And we have the message of the last secretary of the Air Force that we're not merely seeking out new life—we're seeking to *dominate* it. For what? To keep us safe from those on whom we project our own nefarious, destructive intent?

"We seem to have forgotten the difference between shooting for the moon—and shooting a missile directly at it and its people. Benjamin Franklin said, 'Those who would give up essential Liberty, to obtain a little temporary Safety, deserve neither Liberty nor Safety.' We can no longer claim that abuses of power triggered by fearmongering within our Space Force, or our Department of Homeland Security, keep us safe or preserve liberty.

"I encourage all of you today, as leaders in your states among these United States, to reject past alienation of 'we the people,' and stop rejecting that which we hold as truth. Seek an invitation to visit the moonship as I did. There you will find leaders of integrity who will remind you, as Mahatma Gandhi said, that 'every ruler is alien that defies public opinion.' Do not alienate yourselves from those you are tasked to serve in Congress. Do not alienate from your oath to uphold the Constitution.

"Neil Armstrong said, 'It suddenly struck me that that tiny pea, pretty and blue, was the Earth. I put up my thumb and shut one eye, and my thumb blotted out the planet Earth. I didn't feel like a giant. I felt very, very small.' If you choose to explore space, it will take courage and humility to walk in the footsteps of Astronaut Armstrong.

"Benjamin Franklin, signatory to that Constitution all of you took an oath to uphold, said, 'There are three things extremely hard: steel, a diamond, and to know one's self.' This takes courage and humility as well. To recognize that we are all very small in outer space, yet can do great things if we don't lose sight of our humanity, of human decency. We are not gods. We are not supreme rulers of the universe. But like Benjamin Franklin, we all have alien within us."

Chapter 74

While I was in Virginia the week between the inaugural balls and addressing Congress, Win took me on a tour of Origins, the DNA testing company that set precedent by declaring it would not only determine individual percentages of extraterrestrial DNA, but it could also reveal planetary origins due to methods devised by international scientists and based on declassified government data. This after the beleaguered WhoAreYou.com got nailed for hiding alien DNA results from millions of customers.

It was an Origins spit test that I and my family had used to discover our alien DNA, and I later learned Win was a founder of the company. While on the tour, I peppered him with questions about maintaining ethical standards, given the appalling lack of candor and credibility of Origins' competitor, embroiled in two class-action lawsuits from more than five hundred Indian tribes for falsely telling customers their alien DNA was Native American.

I also used that time to ease into Win's ear my reticence in doing surveillance with my hairless cochlea for OUTWARD's new acoustic facility in Las Vegas, which is where I was headed now. It turned out to be ten miles north of my house in an expanding industrial area where freeway was still under construction. This caused more consternation, though I knew better than to think the location was chosen for its proximity to my residence.

Win walked toward me in the vast empty parking lot as I parked. His stealthy stride addled my nerves even as he stirred my hormones.

"Why the huge lot?" I asked, getting out of my car.

Win draped the arm with the bullet in his bicep around me, pointing to a section of the parking lot. "That will be a landing area for orbs and the smaller version of the new Red Orbiter spacecraft. I'm also going to cordon off an area to teach Tim evasive driving, so he'll have skills like he just came off the farm."

"You're teaching Tim all the finer points of spy craft?"

"Yes, and your shoulders are way too tense. How long's it been, sweet pea?" He ran one of his ambidextrous hands down my spine. "You're clenched up tight."

The man was walking sex on a stick. "I know what you're asking, and I'm not going to answer no matter how many times you ask," I said as we entered the large nondescript building. "Where are you staying? Still in the RV at Valley of Fire?"

"No, though I still have the RV. I'm staying at Tim and Maggie's new house in that planned community out this way, Skye Canyon. They closed on the house in November, and of course are now living in my townhouse in Virginia while Maggie's in Congress. During times they're back here, I can stay in the RV or a suite at Planet Wynne to give them privacy."

"So are you going to get a place of your own at some point?" What I didn't say was how glad I was his residence wasn't in this building. Me being near Win in the close proximity of a bed was trouble.

"I haven't decided where or what yet," he said.

"That's why I'm in a rental house." I sighed.

We entered a sparce office area that at least had upholstered chairs.

"Okay, sweet pea. Sit. Spill. All that tension you've been holding in," said Win, indicating one of the chairs. "No more small talk."

"Bossy as ever," I griped, but I did sit. "It's about participating in activities at this facility. I don't really want to learn how to do things like interpret Greens' electronic code. I may have extraordinary auditory abilities, but I don't have your gift for languages, or a desire to learn in order to listen in."

"It's okay, Rowan," Win said, crouching next to my chair, his smile making his steely-blue eyes less intimidating. "This is not a surprise, and I understand."

I exhaled loudly and swatted him on the arm. "Why didn't you tell me this back in Virginia?"

Win slid into the chair opposite me. "I was waiting for you to fully formulate and articulate your thoughts. In the interest of avoiding accusations that I was telling you what you should think or how you should feel."

"Yes, but you could have told me how *you* feel."

"That's irrelevant. My interest is in helping you understand your abilities. You can use whatever knowledge you might gain from this facility in any way you choose."

I sighed. "At this point I'd rather learn why it is I can hear Greens speaking telepathically to me than translate what they're saying to each other."

"I don't think anything we could do here will give you better answers about Greens than the DNA test we did through Origins." Win smiled, reaching out to tweak my knee. "Most of us envy your ability to receive their communication, not to mention the astounding and wonderful fact that they choose to speak to you. But why don't you let me give you the grand tour of what we've set up so far, and then I want to chat about something involving Origins."

As we walked through various areas with lots of complicated-looking electronic equipment and wires, Win said, "I know this probably looks like a bunch of clinical, technical stuff to you, but here's something you might find interesting. Each person's voice has a unique tone all its own. Carrying signature traits and idiosyncrasies, no two voices are alike."

"Like fingerprints?" I said.

"Exactly. And every time we use our voices, we send our energetic imprint out into the universe and to others around us."

"Now you sound like Byrin." I grinned.

"Thank you." He tweaked me on the nose. "Do you realize you may be the only person on Earth who gave herself tinnitus to avoid receiving the energetic imprint of others?"

"It's a hell of a voluntary affliction, for sure." I reached out to tweak his nose, but he had my wrist before my hand got close. Luckily, he kissed my palm and relinquished his hold.

"There is more than one way to listen, sweet pea. It doesn't have to be about spying or counterintelligence. Your relationship with Greens is a prime example, considering their willingness to share their energetic imprint with you. Listening, or the ability to do so, can also be about friendship, and alliances."

Chapter 75

"So what's this about Origins you wanted to discuss?" I asked Win once we returned to his private office.

"First, let's talk about all the buzz surrounding you after your address to Congress."

"Do we have to?" I winced.

"The world apparently can't get enough of Rowan Layne asking Congressman Jerkwad if he had a problem with women speaking truth to power. Do you realize how many folks want you to run for Congress? And not just your average citizens on Twitter."

"Yes, I know," I said, pacing around his office.

"How do you feel about that? Have you given it any thought?"

I whirled to face him. "I've been down this road before. Not just after speaking at the Omni convention, but as an environmental consultant for a tribe, where I learned to be wary of people who are all-in for me sticking my neck out to solve their issues—without any effort, support, or loyalty on their end."

"Sounds harsh," said Win, sitting, so I sat too.

"Really? I think I'm being diplomatic here. Democracy requires effort, including people giving more rational thought to whom they vote for at a local and state level. Too many often won't lift a finger to help themselves or anyone else when the going gets tough because their elected official can't wave a magic wand on their behalf. Plus, it's okay to send my life into turmoil so long as no one else is inconvenienced?" I could feel my blood pressure rise and took a deep breath.

"Are you sure you're talking about running for office, or is this some other issue?"

"I don't know." I sighed, suddenly feeling tired. "But you know they'd rip my past to shreds, including that I'm way old enough to have had a past. Why put anyone through that? I've chosen to be an activist by *writing*. And even in that endeavor, I must remain vigilant to keep others from attempting to mold me into something I'm not in order to meet their needs."

Win uttered a low whistle.

"What?"

"I'm not sure this is great timing, but what the hell? Origins' first annual report." He tossed me a slick pamphlet with a colorful strand of DNA on the cover. I flipped to the first page and a photo of Win—and Red MacLeod. "Red founded the company with me, and we have a facility in Edinburgh as well as Virginia. We are now the most popular and trusted DNA testing operation in North America and Europe, and we're currently looking to site an additional facility in Canada. Origins is an international corporation."

"This is exciting. How do you both find the time?" I marveled.

"One way is hiring others to manage the facilities, but we remain at the helm of the company as its founders. Which means it's our job to nominate individuals to be elected to the board of directors by our shareholders. Red and I want to nominate you."

"*What?*"

"We want you to help keep the company honest about how it handles individual DNA data." Win smiled. "I know it's a subject of great concern for you."

"Because of folks like the ex-president and his cronies trying to weaponize this information?"

"Exactly. You're ideal for this role, Rowan. Its three primary legal duties are duty of care, duty of loyalty, and duty of obedience. Red and I have full confidence in your ability to fulfill the first two duties, although we're not so sure about the obedience part."

"Perceptive of you," I snarked. "This isn't a full-time job, or really a job at all, right?"

"No. As you probably know, it would be a conflict of interest to have employees serve as board members. They're considered a governing body that meets regularly to oversee how a corporation carries out its mission. Members are typically outside experts in various subjects, which in your case is legal ethics. Compensation varies, but we're offering stock options and reimbursement for all travel expenses, though many meetings are done remotely."

"I get the legal ethics part, but seriously, why me?"

Win handed me a printout titled, "Essential qualities of a board of directors member."

I read:

- Able to lead and influence
- Straightforward and impartial
- Knowledgeable and insatiable learner
- Values discretion and confidentiality

"It was that *insatiable* word that immediately made me think of you," said Win.

"Is that sexual innuendo?" I squinted at him. "Because I'm pretty sure you're not supposed to harass your board members."

"Not unless you want it to be, sweet pea," drawled Win. "But I was referring to your appetite for asking questions. And was that a snarky acceptance?"

***

"I think Morris is mad at me," I told my sister over the phone. "He didn't cover his poop in his litter box this morning, which my nose detected the minute I woke. He is either missing that fancy pet pod or his gal, Astro. And Bodie's been pining too, dragging his butt on walks like they are just too boring and constricting after the moonship pet park. I told him he would see Rosie again in a few months, and speaking of that, Scotland keeps cropping up."

I told G about my meet with Win and the Origins board of directors, which would take me to Edinburgh, where I would already be headed after the UK May election.

"You finally told Win you don't want to learn to listen at the acoustics facility and you ended up with another offer? You go, girl!"

"As long as it doesn't take away too much writing time. I've still got the flipping book, and now I'm doing the *Moonliving* blog too."

"You really should talk to Rauc about your concerns about this book. Clarify things."

"I know." I paced my kitchen with a cup of coffee. "But he's been suspiciously not reaching out to me since we got back. I don't know if it's because he's busy with Red Orbiter business or he knows about my book ambivalence. Maybe he doesn't want to see me anymore."

"You've only been back a few days. He's probably giving you a chance to settle in."

"It just keeps bugging me. Something Rauc said about how it wouldn't be a tell-all like people think. But isn't that what folks want? I know it was important to cover Red Orbiter observations about humans, but couldn't it also include my observations about them?"

"I think you have your answer. Ask yourself what you want out of this book, given you're the one who's writing it," said G.

Chapter 76

Genie popped into my ear as soon as I got off the phone with G. "Can we have lunch today? Isn't that a thing girls do, like girls' night? Girls' lunch?" I had never heard her so frantic.

"Sure, we can do lunch. What's wrong?"

"Nothing's wrong! Why would you say something's wrong?"

Something was definitely up. I hope she hadn't heard my lamentations about the book.

I parked via valet at Planet Wynne and made my way to the Oregano Wortnik café, where Genie was seated at a table outside the restaurant.

"I have perfected my dog cookie recipe!" she trilled. "I added beet juice for color, and now they're red orbs!"

"So you're staying in a suite here at Planet Wynne?" I fished for a clue.

"It's convenient until I figure out what I'm going to do, and I have access to a huge kitchen for baking."

"Is that what we're here to discuss?"

"Oh," she said airily, picking up a menu, "I thought it would be a good chance for you to practice finding your center in public to deal with all the voices. Especially since you didn't get to at our last girls' night on the moonship because it was ruined by *you know who*."

Now we were getting somewhere. "Okay. Should we order, or should I give it a try now?"

"I already ordered that pizza we like, so go for it, girlfriend." Her tone was high-strung, not exactly putting me in a relaxed state.

I leaned back in my chair and closed my eyes, focusing inward, pushing past the multitude of voices around me to make my way to my center…

"I'm pregnant!" Genie blurted.

I opened one eye, my mind spiraling backward to depart my maze.

"And that's not all! It's sextuplets!"

I opened my other eye. "That means six, right? I…I have no words."

"But you have to have words! This is not the time for Rowan Layne not to have words! I need words! I need you tell me it's going to be okay!" Genie slammed balled fists on the table.

"I knew Red Orbiters were prone to multiple births, but six seems a bit excessive. Then again, it's Rowdy involved, so—"

"Don't say his name!" she screeched, making even more people look our way.

I leaned in and whispered, "He doesn't know?"

"No! And whispering doesn't keep him from hearing us!"

"Genie let's try to be calm about this. When did you find out?"

"Right before I asked you to lunch!" Her pitch remained histrionic. "Apparently it happened in Owen's office after we learned about you being the VP's date. And what am I going to do with six kids when I don't even know if I want to be in a relationship? You have to help me with this, Rowan!"

I was stunned. This meant I actually *heard* Genie get pregnant when she was in that office with Rowdy, who hauled her in there. "I'm not sure I'm the best person for this. Maybe we should talk with Ophelia. Are you worried about carrying that many babies full-term?"

"Why would I be worried about that? I just have to pass the eggs in five months." She shrugged. "The important part is keeping them safe for two months until they hatch."

I spit the water I'd been attempting to drink all over Genie and the table, knocking over my glass to add even more of a splash.

"And then the first year is a little hectic, but it's dealing with *you know who* I'm worried about," Genie rambled on, unaware.

I tried to right my glass but failed. "What? Eggs? *What?*"

"You didn't know? Rauc and Rowdy haven't told you anything, have they? How are you supposed to write that book—oh crap! I said his name." Genie screwed up her face, looking like an anguished fairy.

"My sentiments exactly on the book. And no wonder you guys are into multiple births if you don't have to carry and push out actual babies after nine months. This is amazing. I might have had kids if I could do it the Red Orbiter way."

Genie's green eyes popped. "You're kidding, right? You're my single, childless role model. What am I supposed to do now?"

"Well, it's true I'm not ready to settle down, even at my age. Is it because the two times I attempted living with someone after marriage, both men turned out to be poser pathological liars and one was a total psychopath? Or maybe I'm just not cut out for monogamy," I pondered.

"*Hello!* We're talking about me and my six babies with the craziest Red Orbiter in the solar system here!"

"Crazy *for you*. That man is seriously in love with you, Genie."

"Yes, I am. And you're going to marry me, Fireball. There's a chapel around the corner," said Rowdy, appearing at our table, looking surprisingly calm and inordinately happy.

"Rowdy Wilde! I am not ready to get married! Can't we at least wait until I pass the eggs?!" screeched Genie as a server set our pizza on the table and hastened away.

Rowdy sat down, picked up a slice of pizza, and took a bite, smiling.

I was smiling too until Roger also appeared. "Okay, I know for sure neither one of us said your name." I looked way up at him. "I, for one, was exceedingly careful."

"I'm sure you were, beautiful." He leaned down and took my arm, lifting me from my chair. "We're going to leave these two to their happy news, and you and I are going to have a talk. You've been actively avoiding me. And did you use valet parking, or do I need to address that again too?"

Chapter 77

"Rein it in, Domitian," I said as we entered Roger's hotel suite. "I'm still reeling over that egg-birthing news. And gee, wouldn't it have been nice to have a clue before now? Were y'all going to wait until I wondered why Ophelia didn't look eight months pregnant? I bet my sister and mom already knew about this and just assumed I knew too. *But nooo!* Not the person y'all tasked with writing the whopping Red Orbiter book!"

"Are you quite finished?" drawled Roger, towering over me with those green-glow eyes. "The book isn't supposed to be about Red Orbiter physiology. You know that."

"What if I want it to be about my observations of Red Orbiters? And another thing!" I thumped him in his chest where the red *S* shield tattoo was hidden underneath his clothes. "I don't want to be the reason Superman goes out of commission!" I paced around his suite. "Are you sure this isn't all because I present some sort of novel challenge for you?"

"What if it is?" He ran a hand through spiky blond hair. "We're attracted to others for many reasons. Drawn to them because of something in them, or something in us that responds to them. At least with us, we know it isn't solely physical attraction. It's deeper. DNA deep."

Roger yanked me into his arms, and it was as if my body melded to his. Fused, forged with fire that transcended physical desire.

Hours later, he got up to bring me water, and as he walked back to bed, I gasped. "Oh my gosh. You have no navel. Of course! Because there's no umbilical cord to—"

"I told you the human eye wasn't all that observant," drawled Roger.

"When we're together, I haven't exactly been focused on your navel, or lack thereof!"

"You wild woman, you." He knelt on the bed, his massive torso looming over me.

"I meant I was focused on the Superman tattoo!"

"Sure you were, beautiful."

An hour later, I said I needed to go home to feed my critters.

"Why don't I come with you?" said Roger. "I want to fill you in about Red Orbiter childhoods to stave off another hissy fit. Then we can get dinner before we fly tonight. Because we *are* going to fly again, beautiful. All night long."

I had hot flashes as I watched Roger's hands on my steering wheel. He drove because I felt ridiculous at the thought of my squiring Superman about town in my SUV, and this way we didn't have to worry about getting my car back home in the morning.

"Are you going to at least keep the red Ferrari even if you retire?" I asked.

"Probably. It's custom-made for my frame."

"How so?"

"Didn't you notice it doesn't have a backseat, just like I don't have a navel?"

I sat there, feeling sheepishly like a very nonobservant human until Roger cheered me up by running his hand across the back of my neck. Good thing I wasn't the one driving as I spontaneously orgasmed speeding along on I-15.

Bodie hadn't left any protest piles, and the critters both enjoyed crawling all over Roger. We got a bite to eat at a nearby Thai place I'd been wanting to try. Ginormous Superman took up a third of the seating space, and one couple mistook him for an action-movie star and asked for his autograph.

"Maybe you should show them the tattoo," I whispered.

"You'll pay for that later, beautiful." Roger's eyes glowed unnaturally green as his sculpted lips tilted into a grin despite his attempt to look menacing.

"So tell me about your childhood," I said.

"Not my childhood. It's the Red Orbiter childhood growth timeline I wanted to impart, so you don't freak out when Ophelia and Bruce's triplets turn five in one year."

I stopped eating my pad Thai.

"Red Orbiter babies progress through childhood faster than humans. Not as fast as dog years, but the equivalent of five human years of aging occurs in the first year of life. Then we age five years for three consecutive years, until we're twenty. We're only kids for four years in the human timeline. After that we progress pretty much at the same rate you do, until we decide to stall, but it has to be after those first four years, once we reach the human age of twenty."

"Well, no wonder Red Orbiter parents look so young! If kids grow up that fast, they end up being only four years younger than those who birthed them. That must be weird," I murmured.

"What are you talking about?" said Roger, looking at me like I was whacked.

"I met Rauc and Rowdy's folks on the moonship and was surprised they look barely sixty. Anyway"—I squared my shoulders—"your childhoods are very short, and you don't get to choose to stay in it. Maybe that's a good thing. Less time to get screwed up by adults. Not necessarily by parents, but by the world of judgment and expectations heaped on little humans. But it's kind of sad too."

"It really isn't for us; it's our reality. Humans often say childhood goes by in a blur in many ways." Roger shrugged. "It's the later years presenting most challenges."

"So maybe this stalling at a certain age and living for extended periods of time isn't all it's cracked up to be?"

Roger smiled. "Probably not, after a certain point. But as I've recently discovered, we have no way of knowing beforehand when we'll wake up one day and say, *I don't want to do this anymore*—or what might drive us toward that realization." He looked at me intently. "For my sister, Maggie, it was falling in love with Tim that made her decide to stop stalling and grow old with the one she's chosen."

"Well, whatever you decide to do in terms of retiring from personal security, I still feel better having you around. And I am a better person for knowing you, and your special gifts."

Later, as Roger lifted me in his arms and ascended into the sky, he said, "It's February and too cold in most places I'd like to take you to hear the voices of the ancient ones again. So tonight we'll return to a place you once knew well, where whales pass through this time of year."

Point Loma, San Diego. Except I wasn't addressing environmental impacts of homeporting nuclear aircraft carriers at a nearby naval base. I was on the shore making love with Superman, who told me quite clearly inside my head, but not out loud, that he loved me. The whales made encouraging sounds of approval.

Chapter 78

I fretted three more days over contacting Rauc about the book, and each hour brought more dread when he hadn't reached out to me.

Sipping Hawaiian hazelnut coffee that tasted like coconut macaroons and made me think I should go to Hawaii instead of Scotland, I looked at my Valley of Fire mug, hoping it would somehow send a signal to the universe that I needed to hear from him.

"Good morning, Copper," said Rauc in my ear as I silently sent up thanks. "I've waited long enough to hear from you, so I'm popping in without warning. Actually I do have a warning. Don't do this to us again."

I winced and set down my coffee mug. "I know, I'm sorry. I've been a bit down lately."

"You're entitled to feel let down. You did more in the month of January than many people do their entire lives. But now we're going to get cracking in February. And this is not a request. I'm putting on the big bad Red Orbiter leader hat and calling an official meeting at headquarters. Except it will only be you and me, and it will last for three days."

"Sounds ominous."

"That's snark, right? You might want to rethink that. At this meeting we will discuss every question you've ever had about my species, and I will endeavor to answer and to anticipate potential questions. Oz will be on standby, because some things were to be revealed through an interview with him, if you recall. Also Valentine's Day will occur during this time, and I will definitely be giving you something red, and we *will* talk about the book."

I held my breath.

"And whatever the outcome, we will be okay, Copper. Report to the Planet Wynne flight deck in three hours with critters. Your red orb transport awaits."

***

"Genie said the tricky part is keeping the eggs safe for two months after she passes them and before they hatch. Is this when Red Orbiters are most vulnerable?" I asked, relaxing in bed, after making up for lost time. Rauc now had residential quarters at the Valley of Fire complex, with a brand-new pet pod installed this week.

"It's really the only time we're vulnerable. Because it is the only time we can be destroyed, as in killed. This information cannot under any circumstances be shared."

"Okay, I understand. So the other sort-of-death part. Going into another realm like Roger and Maggie's parents did recently?"

"It is a form of rebirth. We come back as another Red Orbiter. We choose when, but not who we reemerge as or where. And we never know what special gifts the next life will bring. We also partially remember past lives, in glimpses, often through people who may seem familiar. Reemerged Red Orbiters frequently become honorary family members to those they feel a connection with from previous life, likely through ancestry."

"Are you one of those who have had multiple lives?"

"No, Copper," Rauc said, pulling me close, his arms wrapped around me. "I can see why you might think that, given one critical factor is we can only procreate in our first life. In all subsequent lives, we may only exist in another capacity."

"Wow. So shouldn't you want kids in this life?" I rose up above him, looking down into sweet teal eyes. "You aren't giving up having children to be with me, are you?"

"We've had this discussion before. You and I are similar, in that we never had a burning desire to procreate. It's not our special gift in life, not our legacy. I haven't changed my mind."

"Okay, good. Watching Rowdy find a mate on the moonship was pretty funny, but scary."

Rauc chuckled. "It seems my brother has now made up for lost time."

"So, can you stall your age in any of your lives?"

"Yes, because the reason for stalling is not always procreation. And obviously, not all choose to procreate, just like humans. Our numbers never really decrease due to reemerged lives. Plus, enough of us are newly created to perpetuate our species, especially through multiple births. Did you see how I just answered a question you hadn't asked?" Rauc grinned.

"Yes." I laughed. "And Rowdy and Genie are certainly doing their part! Not to mention your sister with three on the way." I paused. "Shouldn't Roger have kids to pass on the Superman gene?"

Rauc smacked my butt.

"What?" I yelped. Maybe I shouldn't have said Roger's name, especially given he might hear me.

"That was just for good measure. To answer your question, Roger's gifts don't work that way. They occur randomly, like human genius. He is not more likely than any of us to produce a mini-version of himself. The unknown for us, once again, is not knowing where we will reemerge possessing varying special gifts."

"This is a lot to take in," I said, wondering if any of it could be revealed in the book.

"Yes, it is, which is perhaps why you weren't told everything all at once, in the very beginning, do you think?" Rauc swatted my butt again. "Maybe you needed time to get to know us first?"

I flushed, then frowned. "You getting a little heavy-handed, Red Orbiter?"

"You have time for one more question tonight before I get even more so." He grinned, making my heart and the rest of me flutter.

"Have I already met someone who has had multiple lives?"

"Yes, Uncle Oz. Who is not, for that reason, my biological uncle. Ophelia told you he's our mother's brother as part of the Red Orbiter image that we are not so different from humans, with families and children. Also Rose Bergin. And Octavius is not actually Cassandra's uncle. Not only has he been around for quite a while in this life—it's also not his first."

"Wait!" I sat up in bed. "When Oz was on *60 Minutes*, he said two Red Orbiter pilots crashed to their death in Virginia City's Great Fire of 1875. Except you can't die. And was this part of a past life he was talking about?"

“No, dear, it was my current life,” boomed Oz in my ear, out of the ether. “I was one of the pilots and in fact landed to help put out that fire. I’m about three hundred years old in this life, and on my fifth or sixth life. It’s hard to keep track now.”

Chapter 79

"I said on TV that Red Orbiters died in the Virginia City fire because many humans would be terrified and threatened by the knowledge we can't be killed after we hatch," said Oz, walking with me and Rauc among Valley of Fire petroglyphs no one knew existed.

"But if humans already believe you *can* be killed, why can't I reveal how you procreate differently than we do, emphasizing similarities?" I paused near a spiral-shaped petroglyph. "People won't know or assume your only vulnerability is your unhatched eggs."

"Exactly," said Maggie, slipping into my ear and apparently Oz's and Rauc's. "I agree with Rowan. There are many things she can help us realize we don't need to leave out of the book, things that can be presented in a proactive way. If we'll listen. That's what we're supposed to be good at, right, guys?"

"Senator Rogers, you are a woman after my own heart," I said, bursting with this news of her alliance.

"Please, it's Maggie, especially when I'm in your ear. I was going to surprise you with an official phone call, but then I thought, why not make use of our special gifts to give you an update on recent congressional activity? Based on what you and Red had to say, it is being recommended that Space Force be reorganized, not as part of the Air Force or DoD. Possible replacements are a Department of Space Outreach. Another suggestion is that Homeland Security be disbanded, because we already have a defense department, an NSA, and the CIA."

"Wow, that's great news. Is anything happening with the Other Worldly Amendment tanked by Republicans?"

"It's revamped for another go at recognition of human hybrids and aliens as people under the Constitution, now that we have the necessary votes in the Senate," said Maggie.

"You'd think it wouldn't be so difficult for certain members of Congress to realize this includes all of them."

"Speaking of that"—Maggie chuckled—"your best buddy the gerrymandered congressman has been mumbling like a zombie, claiming he was abducted and probed by little green men. Everyone says it's a ploy for political sympathy, given the scandal centered around him grows worse. They also think he might have completely lost his mind."

"Too bad Greens probably can't make him lose his misogyny. There's too much of it in Congress," I muttered.

"Yes, but change comes regardless of how diligently the tired old guard fights against it," said Maggie. "It's no different than the military. A last raging gasp of futility against the inevitable."

"The irony strikes deep," I said, gazing at a petroglyph that was clearly an alien depiction. "Here we are trying to deal with our partial alien identities, and with extraterrestrials among us on Earth, and our world in so many ways still has not embraced women in the workplace, in power, or as equal beings among men."

***

Rauc and I were having a romantic Valentine's dinner cooked up by Rose Bergin at Galaxy Table in Planet Wynne. The same private table behind a screen where Tim Rider once revealed to me he wanted to be a whistleblower at Homeland Security.

I held up a bite of tart made with pomegranates and berries. "Is this the something red you said you'd gift me with today?" I pursed my lips provocatively.

"No, Copper, that'll happen in bed tonight. Perhaps in retaliation for that red diamond ring on your finger." Rauc's eyes gleamed wickedly.

"You should know that was in appreciation for my work on behalf of the moonship."

"I am aware, my lady. And here is my token of appreciation, and love." He handed me an oblong red box. "For my queen of hearts."

I opened it to a glistening bracelet, a strand of heart-shaped red diamonds linked together.

"I am overwhelmingly touched," I said, tears in my eyes, "and concerned I will soon be worth my increased weight in diamonds. Is this from Rowdy's gambling winnings?"

Rauc grinned. "It is a well-kept Red Orbiter secret that I am lucky as well. At cards. My specialty is poker. I believe I won the goods for that on a royal flush, like your face flushes so prettily, along with that rosy red be—"

"I get it!" I said, popping the remainder of my tart in his mouth.

Later, I sat up in bed. "I forgot to ask, where is O.W.'s new winery?"

Rauc said, "One of these days, I hope to wear you out enough, you won't have energy for questions in bed. But the winery—called O.W. Winery, of course—is in Oregon. It's also where the baby shower is now being held, due to such a large crowd of Red Orbiters coming in for it."

"How did I not know this?"

"Don't start with me, Copper."

I swatted his shoulder. "I meant from my sister. The shower is in two weeks. Are you taking us in your orb?"

"No, the larger new craft with the pet pod. And though I plan to have one installed in my orb, we're gradually phasing out orbs. I'll keep mine for old time's sake, and they'll still be used by some observers for short trips. The newer crafts have better aerodynamics and stealth."

"But you're Red Orbiters. How can you get rid of orbs?" I shifted, poking him with my knee.

He sat up as well, but only to push me back down and lean over me, teal eyes hinting at mischief. "That's not why we're called Red Orbiters."

"What?" I tried to sit up, but Rauc's hand splayed on my chest.

"We're actually named for the eggs we hatch from when we're born. They're red orbs."

"Oh, that is so going in the book," I said.

Chapter 80

I heard Mom from across the large, high-beamed O.W. Winery room. "She laid eggs. Just like a hen. Except they're round, and red. And the babies will hatch next month. I think it's so smart. So with it! A much better way to give birth, especially with triplets! Doodles kicked like a *dadgummed* football player so much, we thought she was a boy."

"Who's Doodles?" asked whomever she was talking to as I cringed.

"Word of advice," I said to Maggie and Genie, sipping wine at a most festive baby shower, even if the winery tasting room wasn't fully completed. "If Red Orbiters truly have things they want kept secret, don't tell my mom."

"Don't tell me what, Doodles?" said Mom, approaching.

"Rowan was just saying not to tell you the surprise yet, Mrs. Layne," said Maggie. I looked at her like she'd grown horns. "But I think we should go ahead and tell her."

"Please call me Audrey, Senator Rogers. It is truly an honor to have you here at our shower!" Mom grasped Maggie's hand. "And what surprise are you referring to?"

"The surprise is what I brought with me, from the moonship," said Owen, strolling up with a big grin, introducing himself. "Owen Marsden, ma'am. I'm a friend of your daughter's. She said you had trouble finding shoes in your size. But we found you three pairs in 7AAA narrow black flats for you to try. I can return what doesn't work, and we can keep trying."

"You are a total love!" Mom lunged at Owen, taking his face in her hands. I looked at Genie, who winked at me.

After more flirtation in which she neatly managed to slip in how she was more *matooer* than she looked, Mom said, "Doodles! I almost forgot!" She reached into the pocket of her snazzy black jacket with large red polka dots. "In the magazine where I tore your horoscope out, there were two more lucky numbers, and I found them the other day." She handed me the tiny scrap. "And do you like my new outfit? It's red orbs!"

"That is a darling jacket!" said Genie as I read the numbers, seventeen and fourteen.

Mom sailed off to reveal my childhood nickname to the rest of the Red Orbiter population, but not before advising us, "Remember, gals, no frown wrinkles!" as I showed the paper to Genie and Maggie, with Owen looking on.

"Does anything come to mind?" said Maggie. "I don't think it's space mileage."

"I know what it is," I said. "Seventeen is my total percentage of human DNA, of which 14 is from Scotland. It sure looks like the universe thinks I'm supposed to travel there this year."

"Oh good," said Genie. "I was afraid one of the numbers represented the compilation of men you've amassed since going to the moonship."

"Now you sound as snarky as Rowdy," I said. "Is my previous recommendation that you get a dog together not sounding so bad these days?"

"Am I going to have to throw water on you two?" said Owen, laughing.

"Did I hear my name?" said Rowdy, sauntering into our little group, putting his arm around Genie, who stuck her tongue out at me before giggling. "I know you've been concerned about my potential prowess, Rowan, but is fertilizing six of Jessica Rabbit's eggs manly enough for you?"

"Rowdy Wilde, what on earth are you going to do if you end up with six girls who look just like Genie with your devious mind?" I said, blowing him six kisses.

"I know what the numbers mean for me!" said Maggie. "Combined, 1714 is my assigned number as a newly sworn freshman senator! But it means I got a really sucky office," she grumped.

I explained to Owen, "We're both Aries, so we have the same horoscope."

"I'm Aries too," he said, his purple eyes full of secret smiles. "One of the many things we have in common, and the reason for my wolf companion's name. We have the same birthday, Rowan. The day the now-indicted degenerate fired a missile at my moonship."

"You've been holding out on me!" I said, finding myself alone with Owen in the crowded room. "I'm so glad you made the trip for this. And those shoes for Mom! You are gunning for sainthood. I miss you. And Byrin."

"She tasked me to give you a special message after she read a copy of your speech to Congress. She deemed it to be a true work of art, like a beautiful quilt, full of all the ideals and qualities that make you so special."

"You Labyrinthians sure are charmers, and good for my ego," I said, hugging him. "How have things been going up there? What happened to Tribble?"

"He has, sadly but deservedly, been banned from the moonship for life. It would not have been such a severe penalty had he not fired a loaded gun at me and others. Ultimately, the decision was made by the Lacertan leaders, who also send greetings. And Tribble is now on his way to Uranus, the only planet in the solar system that would take him."

"There's a joke in there, I think. But I have something else to ask."

Owen moved in close, those purple eyes penetrating mine. "What is it? About Roger?"

"Sort of. He said he was late getting back to the moonship because of last-minute business on Mars. I haven't asked him about it."

"I'm sure he didn't say why so as not to burden you. He waited until he could catch Lucas semi-sober to tell him it would not be in his best interest to attempt to ever contact or approach you back on Earth. Roger showed Herculean restraint. But Rowan, we would have told you if we thought you'd have problems with him."

"Oh gosh. I appreciate that, but let's talk about something more pleasant." I floundered for a topic. "You have a belly button, don't you?"

"Yes. Labyrinthians don't lay eggs like Red Orbiters." He grinned. "But we all go about the process of impregnation the same way. I wouldn't mind making babies with you."

My heart pounded. "Please tell me that's not possible. That you Martians can't somehow magically impregnate me at my age."

Owen laughed, a deep belly roar. "No. But did you just call me a Martian again?"

"And why haven't you asked me the same question, beautiful?" said Roger, slipping smoothly into my ear despite being somewhere in the room.

Chapter 81

"Hey, you two!" said George, approaching Owen and me with soon-to-be-daddy-of-three Bruce Robertson, along with Red and Win. "You're going to want to hear what Phil has been looking into for OUTWARD." My brother-in-law was also a recent recruit, for investment opportunities.

And I was going to choke Roger. Bad enough that Owen had me flustered at a flipping baby shower. Here I was doing pretty well at centering, not letting all the voices get to me. Then again, it was so loud when Red played the bagpipes, I couldn't hear my own ringing ears.

Phil said, "I've been looking at the aging process, having recently turned sixty-five. Over the years, various scientists have looked at time travel, where humans go back to a specific age or point in time before they existed. But these studies haven't been about preventing aging."

"So what are you looking for?" I asked. "Because there's already a method wherein humans stay the same age over time. Soap operas and books." I grinned.

"Good one," said Phil. "I've looked at scientists who may have inadvertently worked on or developed a potential method for humans that resembles this stalling Red Orbiters can do, to stay at one specific age. So far, those who've come closest are working with electromagnetism."

George explained to me, "It involves interaction of electric currents or fields and magnetic fields. It's a branch of physics involving the study of electromagnetic force."

"Of course," I said. "Red Orbiters and magnets go hand and hand. But this isn't like electroshock therapy, is it? And I get the electric current part, like lightning? Where do magnets come in?"

Phil said, "An electromagnet runs on electricity. It's a temporary magnet generating a magnetic field only when electric current is flowing. Unlike a permanent magnet, the strength of an electromagnet can easily be changed by changing the amount of electric current flowing through it. Poles of an electromagnet can even be *reversed* by reversing the flow of electricity."

"Like reverse engineering but reversing the flow of time instead? Are you seeing how Red Orbiters do it with their bodies, their magnetism, in order to determine how humans might also stall their age?"

"I'm looking for scientists of Earth who may have already discovered, without knowing it, a method to stall time using enhanced electromagnetism," said Phil.

"Great. I'm pushing sixty, and now you might find a way for humans to stay young?"

"How do you think I feel?" said Phil. "I'd like to at least be able to stall at an age when I still had hair."

I giggled. "This is funny, Phil, given your wristwatch collection. Time is sort of your thing. Which makes sense, what with your predominant Saturn DNA. You know, the god of time?"

Bruce said, chuckling, "You know they were aliens and not gods, right?"

"Hey!" I sloshed my wine. "Could that be it? Could human hybrids having Saturn DNA be part of the answer as to who might ultimately have the ability to do this?"

"That would be great news for your sister and me," said Phil.

"Or maybe it has to do with humans who have more electricity running through them somehow. More electromagnetism?" I said.

"Maybe you better study your sister-in-law, Phil," quipped Win, eyeing me. "Word has it, a Navy captain banned Rowan from his office because he believed she had the power to blow up hard drives just from walking into the room angry."

"Aye," said Red. "It's those fiery lasses one must take care around."

Chapter 82

"Do you realize Dad now golfs with aliens from the planet with a moon where golf originated?" I said to G, watching Dad talking animatedly to Genie and Bruce's parents, his new golf buddies. "This shower turned out wonderfully, considering the guest list skyrocketed. You and Mom outdid yourselves. And I hear you're the one who can tell me all about plans for this fabulous winery."

"Thanks! It's been so fun. And for once I know more than the go-to gal for all things Red Orbiter! I'm excited about it being so close to home. O.W. asked me to be involved in décor and design of several private tasting rooms. I get to select art, furniture, even wineglasses. And I can't wait for the restaurants!"

"Are you doing the sous chef thing too?"

"Maybe just for fun. O.W. is going all out, Vegas style, with a culinary compound of epic proportions. One signature high-end restaurant called Galaxy Vine that Rose Bergin will oversee, and two cafés, one called Red, the other White. How cool is that? And George's friend Mazy who you met on the moon is coming down to be head chef for the cafés. O.W. also has plans to expand with a winery in Washington."

"So it truly will be O.W. Winery, with locations in both Oregon and Washington," I quipped. "But that's thrilling news about Mazy. You'll love her wicked sense of humor."

At one end of the room, lovely and willowy marine biologist Ophelia stepped up to a microphone with signature Red Orbiter red hair and green eyes. "If I could take a moment of your time to say a few words and to thank everyone for being here at this special occasion for Bruce and me," she in her melodious voice. "First, we owe much gratitude and appreciation to Gwynne and Audrey for putting this soiree together so splendidly, and graciously, given so many of our friends decided to travel from, well, all over the galaxy. I did not receive the party-planning gene, but you two ladies clearly did."

Everyone applauded my sister and mom, who were both beaming.

"So," Ophelia continued, "Bruce and I and our extended family, which now includes your family, we thank you. We cannot say it enough, but I will return to this topic of family in a moment. First, it is customary for us to announce names we have chosen for our offspring, which will be Ferus and Roman, in honor of my brothers and their given names, and our daughter will be Janus, for a distant ancestor of Bruce's."

There were many cheers, but Rowdy aka Ferus cheered loudest.

"Okay, pipe down, bro," said Ophelia to laughter. "It is also customary for Red Orbiters to have honorary relatives to participate in guiding our offspring as they progress through this life. Bruce and I have that in uncles Oz and O.W. And now our children will also have uncles Red, George, Owen, Win, Tim, and Roger. We have also asked Audrey and Gene Layne to be honorary grandparents, and Gwynne and Phil Hanson to be aunt and uncle."

My sister whispered to me, "I'm going to be Auntie Gigi!"

"Bruce and I haven't had a chance to ask you in person yet because you've been kind of busy this year so far," said Ophelia, "but Rowan Layne, how do you feel about being an aunt?"

Chapter 83

"How do you feel about those names? I'm surprised they didn't name the girl after Genie. And how did they know the genders?" I ask Rauc as we traveled back to Las Vegas. Eventually I might learn to fly one of these things if I sat in his lap at the controls enough.

"Genie said not to. She can't stand her name, Eugenia, remember? And I told my sister not to saddle a kid with Romulus, so she went with Roman. At least Ferus sounds like the popular name Ferris, and Janus is much like Janis. As for gender, if an egg is dark red, it's male. If the color is lighter, almost pink, it's female."

"Uncanny," I shifted about on his lap. "I never asked you the name of the planet humans came to Earth from, the one that used to be in the gap between Mars and Jupiter?"

Rauc's lips twitched. "Humanus."

"Great." I snorted. "Even our planet of origin was sexist. It just had to have *man* in there. Why couldn't it have been called Womanus?"

"Still making me laugh, Copper. So how'd you do? At the shower. Not letting all those Red Orbiter voices get to you. Are you feeling good about the tools you have to help you?"

"Yes, I'm feeling very hopeful and happy. But can I just say, who knew, after all those elementary school years of getting dissed on report cards for not *listening attentively*, that I'd now be avoiding doing so? Instead I can be selective in what I choose to garner my attention, my focus."

"Speaking of focus. Have you come to any decisions about the book? How do you feel about proceeding down that maze?" Rauc looked nervous, and I didn't like seeing him so.

"Do you know how sorry I am for subjecting you to my doubts? I've never wanted to seem ungrateful for this unprecedented opportunity." I hugged his neck.

"Expecting you to write a book about how we see humans so soon after learning of your own abilities put a heavy burden on you.

You've needed time to process, to find your own path. To decide what you want to do, and who to do it with. Plus, there is so much more to learn along the way."

"For the book, people want to know what you do and how you're different, but also need to know the many ways we're alike. That makes it less frightening and easier to understand." I smiled and kissed him. "Not that you're at all frightening to me. But you've been observing us so long, you might have taken on some of our quirks. And that's okay. It's only human." I grinned.

"I'm not frightened by you either, Copper, but Rowdy might be." He chuckled. "When I first decided a book would be written by you, I did so in an official capacity, knowing I was next in line to lead Red Orbiters of North America. I knew what I wanted and went for it, but at the time I might not have fully thought it through. I was so enthralled with you."

"I was just as swept up by you, too, you big bad Red Orbiter."

"I have to fly us home, Copper, and you're making it difficult to concentrate squirming on my lap. What I want to say is, I thought I knew what the book would be and its purpose, but you've made me realize that not's entirely so. But the things I was correct about were the timing and the author. You. It's time to get our story out there, but it doesn't have to be tomorrow."

"Thank you," I said, my arms around his neck, trying not to squirm too much. "You are still and always will be the nicest, handsomest alien in my universe."

"Sexiest would be good too. And smartest. But there's one thing I want to tell you while it's on my mind. It can't be in the book, but you should know I told the new president and VP about our ability to block bullets and bombs. It will now become another government secret."

"You'll be like Greens? And the moon? Another cover-up?"

"Yes. And like Greens, this is useful for our security. The government will deny what our bodies can do while promoting wild ideas that we have some sort of defense device, some magic weaponry."

"Because Americans only understand weapons to be used against them? As opposed to recognizing that others might be engaging in self-defense of us and our weapons." I sighed. "Just as people would never accept Greens were here first, the original Earthlings."

"Cheer up, Copper. It's not all bad. Why don't you give some thought to where you'd like me to take you for your upcoming birthday? We could go back to Monterey Bay, and you can cavort with alien otters." Rauc jiggled me on his lap.

"I'm not so sure we should do that." I pouted. "The time before last, you disappeared for months as soon as we returned."

"Well, this time, you'll be the one leaving for Scotland soon after. And I'm okay with that. More wondrous knowledge awaits Luna Moth Woman and her mighty pen."

Later, back at home with my critters vying for attention, I thought about my many experiences with Rauc and Rowdy, Roger, Genie, Maggie, Bruce, and Ophelia. Not to mention Cassandra Rojas-Ortiz, Rose Bergin, Octavius Wynne, and ancient Uncle Oz. And I realized I'd been writing this book in my own way, as I met each one of them.

I'd made speeches promoting them—indeed, I'd written about them well before we met. I'd made love to them, argued with them, eaten their food, traveled to the moon in their spacecraft, and learned of their special gifts. I attended their weddings and baby showers, born witness to how they procreate. Different from us in many ways, but not so different in others. Alien origins and languages, yes, but the language of love was universal.

I had learned much from Red Orbiters and other aliens. It hadn't been necessary to go flying around in an orb with Rauc and Rowdy, observing how they observe us. I'd been doing it all along, and not by merely listening in.

Sharing this knowledge through the written word was second nature.

I hadn't been able to bring my scratch pad home from the moonship because it wouldn't operate properly here on Earth. I told George and Owen that OUTWARD better get right on that. But for the time being, I had my notes preserved on a flash drive I could use on my laptop here at home. Not to mention page upon page of notes in myriad ink shades copiously saved over many months.

I sat down at my desk, staring up at Byrin's solar system quilt. At long last, I began to write.

Milton Keynes UK
Ingram Content Group UK Ltd.
UKHW010745030424
440506UK00014B/2091

9 781647 192167